Love Always Hopes

Written by

Cecelia Hopkins-Drewer

ISBN: 978-0-6481160-7-3 (6x9 paperback)
Published by CGH Literacy Institute
Adelaide, South Australia, 2019

ISBN: 978-0-6481160-7-3 (6x9 paperback)

Cover Photograph by Allan Schultz

Fictional disclaimer:

All characters and events in this work are fictional, and while an effort has been made to recreate the era of the 1980s and incorporate selected aspects of history which are general knowledge; the story was written for entertainment purposes. The characters have no existence outside the imagination of the author and any similarity to persons or events outside the text is the result of coincidence.

CONTENTS

PROLOGUE:

Allegra and her young children, Ellie and Terry, had been exploring the past with the aid of an old diary Allegra's mother had kept from 1984. At first the process had been mere rainy day fun, but then it got serious, and Allegra had sought out Aunt Kathy's diary to see how the story continued in 1985.

Reading through Aunt Kathy's diary, they had been surprised to discover Grandma had a serious boyfriend, two years before she married Grandpa. Allegra's mother had never mentioned this boyfriend; but now that Allegra thought about it, she had received regular gifts from his parents. They were a kindly couple, whom she had always referred to as "Grandmamma and Grandpop Parker".

Allegra had been brought up to call her parents' closest university cronies, "Aunt" and "Uncle" although they were not related, and she had assumed there was a similar reason why she seemed to have five sets of grandparents. Most other people had four sets of grandparents - although with modern blended families, the assumptions regarding nuclear families were changing! Now, however, she knew the real, and very tragic reason behind the relationship.

Ellie and Terry in their childish innocence, continued to clamour to hear more from the diaries. Allegra had therefore been forced to appeal to 'Aunt Cara', who had been the only one of her mothers' peers to keep a diary in the year of 1986. Aunt Cara, who was a great roustabout, even in her middle years, apologised for the messy writing and frequent crossing out, but admitted she still had her old diary.

Allegra thanked Aunt Cara and sought out a quiet place in which to peruse the text. Given the shocks contained in the previous volume, she though it would be wise to preview the narrative, before sharing it with her children. She began to read:

"Are you still going out with that black boy?" my Mama said after the mail arrived that day carrying a letter from Kaleb.

"Please don't call him black Mam," I begged. "It sounds so racist!"

"I know he is an intelligent, well-educated young man, who is a lovely Christian and aims to be a minster," Mama replied. "My concern is more that he is American. What if you two get married and he takes you back to America to live permanently? Have you thought about that, Cara O'Brien?"

"I would miss you, I know," I said. "But you don't need to worry — we have no plans to get married or anything at this stage."

Indeed, according to Kaleb's latest letter, his attendance at Silver Springs University this year was somewhat in doubt. With the American academic year and the Australian academic year being different, his exchange scholarship was not being renewed until August, which would be way too late for a March start in Australia. Kaleb was looking into attending his parent educational institution until the following academic year, so that he would not fall behind.

I also had a letter from Dylan Perett, my long-time friend and former suitor. Dylan had sworn off dating due to being unfairly treated by his first real girl-friend Annie. It was a phenomena Australians referred to as 'once burnt, twice shy'! Dylan also wrote that he had worked long hours over the holidays, even getting over-time at Christmas and New Year's.

I was bound to secrecy regarding the name of his employer. Silver Spring's University was a private educational institution and due to the strong teetotal influence of the Reform Church administration, Dylan could be expelled for working for a winery in the Hunter Valley, despite grape growing being a respectable form of agriculture.

However, the outcome of Dylan's recent work was that he had earned enough money to buy a car, as well as pay his fees. He had bought a Suzuki LJ50 hardtop and was planning to drive it up to the university that year. This sounded great, as like me, most of the Biology class loved camping and hiking.

My friends all say it is my turn to keep a diary of our group's activities this year. Kathy is too busy canoodling with her ministerial student boy-friend, Andrew; Stephanie is grieving her recent loss and Phoebe is planning her wedding to Hank. So with Kaleb away in the United States and Dylan no longer asking me out, I am the nearest our group has to someone single and fancy free, which apparently is a pre-requisite for diary keeping. Here goes guys...

CHAPTER ONE: PICKING UP THREADS

Cara and her little sister Bede arrived at Northcoast station and looked around for the small bus which would take them out to Silver Springs University. The trip from Geelong had been uneventful, if a little boring. They had said farewell to their parents at Geelong, caught the train into Melbourne, changed to an aeroplane heading towards Brisbane, and then hopped across onto the train travelling to Northcoast.

It was a warm, wet day as befitted the tropical climate of South Eastern Queensland. The semester commenced at the beginning of the last week in February, and both girls were keen to return to their studies. Cara and Bede were very different in personality, and although Bede had been at Silver Springs the year before, the only activity they had really shared was Aerobics.

Cara, whose name meant 'dear', had always been a hoyden, and loved any form of sport. Almost as many of her friends were male as female. She was studying Biological Science with a minor in Chemistry. Cara habitually wore jeans, or sometimes a denim skirt with a stretchy top and sensible shoes. She belonged to the campus Adventure Club which organized camping, hiking and boating trips.

Despite being named after Saint Bede, who was male, the younger sister Bede was a girly-girl, and on top of that, she was inclined to be a bit sassy. Bede was studying Home Economics and loved fashion. Most of her friends were girls and she preferred curling up with a romance novel to trapesing through the countryside in search of adventure.

Cara espied the university bus in the distance and began to wave. As the minibus drew closer, the girls could see it was being driven by their friend Luke. Luke had been the university driver since his first year, being one of the students who was more advanced in the life-skills department, and already had his full license. Being a Theology student, he also needed the money, even if the demanding hours cut into his study time.

The minibus drew up alongside Northcoast station, and Luke jumped out to help Cara and Bede with their luggage. "Hello girls – were you two the only ones on the train from Brisbane?" he asked.

"I think so," Cara said. "I didn't see anyone else."

Luke checked his watch. "If you girls don't mind waiting for a moment, there is a train due from North Queensland. David called ahead to say that he and Debbie would be on it."

"Cool," Cara said. "It will be great to see them."

"If we've got at least ten minutes, I will run and look at the fabric store," Bede said.

"Sure," Luke said. "You'll have plenty of time while I load their bags onto the bus."

"Thanks," Bede said. She blew Luke a kiss and disappeared across the street.

"How were your holidays?" Cara asked Luke.

"Pretty good," Luke said. "Christmas and New Year were quiet, but I've been back for a while couriering anything that needed moving around here."

A train appeared from the north and slowed as it approached Northcoast station. A few minutes later, it pulled to a halt and David and Debbie disembarked, dragging their bags along with them. Luke hurried to relieve Debbie of her biggest bag.

"Hey you two!" Cara cried in excitement.

"Hey yourself," the lively, outgoing David replied.

"Hello Cara," Debbie added more sedately.

"What have you been up to?" Cara inquired.

"Just visiting David's folks for the last week of the holidays," Debbie replied.

"No engagement or anything?" Cara joked.

Debbie shook her head. "No way! We have one bride in the group, Phoebe and that's enough."

Phoebe had been Cara's room-mate the previous year and she was planning an Easter wedding to her mechanic boyfriend Hank. They had met while Hank was completing his commercial Pilot's License through Silver Springs University.

Cara and Debbie were bridesmaids and the rest of the friends were helping make stuff for the wedding, because Hank's money had gone into a small house for the couple. Phoebe's parents were also helping financially, but no one really expected the parents to pay for everything anymore!

Luke finished stowing the luggage in the bus and was just about to drive off, when the bus from Armidale drew into Northcoast station.

"We might as well see who is on this," Luke said, as Bede ran back to the bus puffing in alarm because she thought it was about to take off.

Sure enough, several students disembarked, including Kathy and her boyfriend Andrew. Kathy was from Armidale, and Andrew was from Canberra, but he had been to visit Kathy for Valentine's Day on the way back to university. Cara and Kathy exchanged hugs, while Andrew and David, who were both Theology students, greeted each other warmly.

"It seems like forever," Cara gushed as she greeted Kathy.

"Only Christmas and New Year," Kathy said. "And half of February."

"Has anybody heard from Stephanie?" Debbie inquired.

Stephanie had been Kathy's room-mate the previous year, but Kathy had claimed a single room, which was her right as a potential graduate. Cara and Stephanie had a lot of classes in common and planned to room together this year.

Kathy shook her head. "I haven't heard since she sent a card for Christmas. She said she was alright, but I've been terrified she would decide not to return to Silver Springs this year."

"It is okay," Cara said. "Stephanie wrote to me last week and asked me to keep the room for her."

The friends all drew sighs of relief. Their concern for Stephanie stemmed from the fact that the girl had lost her boyfriend Bradley through a motorcycle accident in November the previous year.

Luke closed the bus door. "We'd better be off now, or I'll not be back in time for the next train from Brisbane. There are quite a few expected on it."

The bus drew up at the girl's dormitory and Luke helped everyone unload their luggage. A warning message was sent through the public address system alerting residents that males were in the dormitory delivering luggage to the rooms, but no one was really concerned at this stage. By the next day, the rules on segregation would come into full force.

Bede went off to her room, while Cara, Debbie and Cathy made their way to the basement. This may sound like a dungeon, but really, as the campus was built into the side of the hill, most rooms had windows, and the back door opened at ground level. The basement offered a degree of privacy which most upstairs rooms did not, and was the secret of the third year students.

The first room in the basement was absolutely huge, and comfortably accommodated three people. This room was being shared by Debbie, Tess and Joelle. The previous year, it looked as though Joelle would be left without a roommate, but on the discovery of the triple room, the problem was solved.

The next room was a single room, which was occupied by Kathy on account of her senior status. Following that was a double room, which would be shared by Cara and Stephanie. Beyond that was another double room, which Danielle and Elisabet had elected to share.

Stephanie had not arrived yet, so Cara's room was empty and boring. She decided she had better things to do than unpack, and wandered down to the gymnasium to see if any of the guys were around. There she found some sporting friends and sunk a few baskets.

The previous year, Cara had played women's basketball, however, the girls' basketball league on campus received a lot less support than the boys. She had decided that if there was a timetable clash with any of her laboratories, she might not compete again, but would concentrate upon Adventure Club activities.

The next day was registration day, which was a big deal for the first years, but a fairly simple matter for third years, as most of their subjects were dictated to them by their previous year's choices. All Cara had to do was fill out her registration form, sign it and pay her fees at Student Services.

Stephanie arrived around eleven o'clock and just managed to get her form in and paid by the deadline. Cara would have been worried, except the letter she had received, indicated her roommate would be catching the last possible plane out of Adelaide. With an early morning flight, she could be in Brisbane by lunch and catch the train on to Northcoast.

Cara and Stephanie were doing almost identical subjects. They both had Plant Biology, Sociology and Group Theory, and Practice Teaching. Both had also selected a house requirement of Agriculture. The only real difference was that Cara had Chemistry, while Stephanie had Drama. The subject line-up would change slightly for second semester, but it was only slightly as Agriculture would be exchanged for Computing.

Their registration business complete, the room-mates had time to hang out together. Cara gave Stephanie a huge hug, which Stephanie returned warmly.

"What did you do over the holidays?" Cara asked curiously. It was difficult to know what to say to someone whose beloved boyfriend had died the previous semester. Asking whether Stephanie had a 'good' holiday seemed kind of wrong, so Cara settled on this compromise.

"I went swimming," Stephanie said. "There is an aquatic centre not too far from my house. I bought a month's membership and went there every day in January. The water was soothing, and it was not one of the things Bradley and I used to do together, so I could float and dream."

"It sounds nice," Cara murmured.

"I did a lot of laps too," Stephanie said. "As if by getting fitter I could become emotionally stronger. And to a certain extent, I was trying to work all the anger and denial out of my system."

"Did it work?" Cara asked cautiously. All of the friends wanted to hear Stephanie say she was all right, but they were also afraid the bereaved girl might start saying she was okay because her friends wanted her to be.

"In some ways," Stephanie said. "How were your holidays?"

"Quiet," Cara said. "We went shopping and to the beach, but you know how Bede and I are not much company for each other?"

"I do," Stephanie laughed. "And yet, I like you both for different reasons."

"Well Bede and you both like to sew," Cara observed. "And you are both romantics."

"Not really," Stephanie frowned.

"Don't try to deny it!" Cara insisted. "I know you think it has been knocked out of you several times, but it hasn't really. I'm sure you still love flowers and kittens, and books with happy endings."

"I have to admit I still do," Stephanie said. "It is finding them realistic that is now the problem."

"It will come back to you," Cara said. "Now I never had much of a soft spot for that sort of thing. Give me my hiking boots, and a boat and a bit of competition to get my teeth into."

"You like birds," Stephanie observed.

"Ah yes I do," Cara agreed. "However, I never heard that described as a romantic thing."

"Perhaps not," Stephanie wasn't looking for an argument. "What about Kaleb – is he coming back?"

"Unfortunately Kaleb doesn't have scholarship money again till August or September," Cara reported. "He will be using it to pay to do his future studies in Australia."

"Weird," Stephanie mused.

"It's the American academic year – all twisty compared to ours," Cara observed. "Now that leaves me a little bit concerned what to do about Dylan."

"Dylan has been great," Stephanie observed. "He wrote to me a couple of times in the holidays."

"Do you think he likes you?" Cara asked curiously.

"No, nothing like that," Stephanie said. "He was just being supportive."

"With Kaleb away, I'm afraid he will be back after me then," Cara said.

"I don't think so," Stephanie said. "The experience with Annie last year has matured him. It sounds as though there will be three of us at least taking a break from the dating scene."

Tuesday classes commenced and Cara had a full morning. Lunchtime she was surprised to see that Damaris, who had been a hospitality student the previous year, was serving the food.

"Hello Damaris," Cara said.

"Oh hello, Cara," Damaris said. "I applied for work here and I got the job!"

"Congratulations," Cara said. "Everyone said you were a great cook."

"Thanks," Damaris said. "And it's handy for Michael, as he has another year here too."

"There is that," Cara said. "But I wouldn't hang around waiting for any guy."

"Oh I'm not waiting," Damaris said airily. "I am working and being paid well."

The line in the cafeteria moved along just then and Cara passed into the dining room. She sat down with Stephanie and Dylan.

"Hello Dylan," Cara said.

"Hi Cara," Dylan returned. "How's things?"

"Great," Cara responded. "Are you looking forward to our Chemistry laboratory this afternoon?"

"Not exactly," Dylan said. "All those reports – the Chemistry Doctor is so strict! Where is Kaleb by the way?"

"His scholarship is on hold until September," Cara said. "He might be back here later."

"How frustrating," Dylan said.

"We knew this could happen," Cara said. "There is nothing we can do but write." She waited for Dylan to say something inappropriate, but he did not. He really had changed since last year.

"When will we see your new car, Dylan?" Stephanie asked.

"Not this afternoon because of Chemistry," Dylan said. "And it's not a car Stephanie dear, it's a light jeep."

"Ooh exciting," Stephanie said.

"What is exciting?" Garry said, approaching the table and putting his tray down beside Dylan.

It was Stephanie's turn to look embarrassed. Garry had been her boyfriend before Bradley, almost two years ago now. He had left Silver Springs University for a semester to take care of his mother who had a cancer scare. Stephanie was pleased to see Garry back, of course, but things were just a little awkward.

"Dylan's new car," Cara on the other hand, was perfectly at ease talking to Garry.

"I'll take you guys out sometime," Dylan promised. "The gang is back together again!"

"It's great to be back," Garry said. "Now for Chemistry. I hope one or two fourth years have signed up, or we will be a sorry little group."

"We might have Zack," Dylan said. "He is a Science major and the subjects run on alternate years don't they? So he will need Biochemistry still."

"I will probably be the only girl," Cara sighed. "It's a bit lonely for a female in the Sciences."

"I would join you if I could," Stephanie said. "But I have too many clashes to fit Chemistry into my timetable."

"Never mind, you will have me," Garry said.

"Thanks Garry," Cara said. "We did miss you last semester."

Kathy and Andrew, Stephanie, Cara and Garry were out in the student car park looking at Dylan's Suzuki jeep Wednesday afternoon.

"It looks just perfect for camping and mountain climbing around

Silver Springs," Cara exclaimed.

"That is just what I thought," Dylan agreed neutrally. He did not immediately offer to take Cara somewhere, like the old Dylan would have done.

"I can see the wander-fever in your eyes, Cara," Kathy commented.

Cara blushed: "I thought maybe some bird watching?" she suggested.

"That sounds all right, except we are doing Plant Biology," Stephanie observed.

"Bird watching is a good idea Cara," Garry said, breaking the impasse. "I bet we will all go sometime."

Andrew was asking Dylan questions about the Suzuki's fuel consumption and other automotive mysteries, when a police car drove past and up to the visitors' car park. Kathy grabbed her boyfriend's arm, filled with horrid memories from the last time the police had come onto campus, which was to tell Stephanie that Bradley had been killed.

"What are the police doing here?" Kathy cried.

Stephanie sighed. "They are investigating Bradley's death I expect," she said.

"I thought that was an accident?" Kathy said.

"I resisted looking for someone to blame," Stephanie explained slowly. "Because I thought that was just the grief talking. But apparently, Hank had checked the bike over Thursday afternoon and it was perfect. The police believe it must have been tampered with sometime between Thursday evening and Friday afternoon when Bradley left."

"Why do they think that?" Dylan inquired.

"They are keeping the details to themselves," Stephanie said. "And I'm not sure what the legal situation is. It is clear the truck killed Bradley - but if the bike had not broken down, he would not have been stranded there."

"Vandalism?" Andrew suggested.

"I think felony tampering or even malicious tampering, if we have such an offense in Australia," Stephanie said. "When I tried to look it up, my sources were American encyclopaedia."

"Aggravated criminal damage perhaps," Garry suggested.

"I don't know," Stephanie murmured. "Maybe. Anyway, they could ask you all, whether you know anything that could help. Or where you were that afternoon or something."

"My memory of that day isn't that good," Cara said. "I think I had a couple of assignments to finish."

"We all had assignments to finish," Dylan said. "Education and Psychology I think. That pretty much rules out all the Education class."

"The Theology students took Psychology too," Andrew observed. "So that would have occupied most of last year's second years."

"I am lucky my family can place me in Wollongong," Garry observed. Stephanie flinched. "Why is that?"

"I'm classed as your ex," Garry said. "I admit I have worried about it."

"We were still friends," Stephanie stammered. "And you and Bradley were still friends too."

"But that is not the way of the world," Garry explained. "I knew that someday questions would be asked as to why Bradley was coming to see me."

"I think he wanted to be sure you were okay with him proposing to me," Stephanie said. "Like I said once, Bradley never lived to propose, so I can't be certain – but he had a momentous air about him. His original suggestion was that I come to Wollongong too, that way we would see you properly as we had only spoken over the phone."

"And to someone who didn't know how our friendship group on campus worked, that would sound like a very odd situation," Garry said. "I've always been very glad that I escorted my mother to her radiotherapy that afternoon and my whereabouts were well documented."

"I can't take any more of this," Stephanie said, turning away. "Please take me back to the dorm Kathy. The rest of you can go out with Dylan if you like."

"Sure Stephanie," Kathy said.

"I'll come with you too," Andrew said. "At least as far as the door."

"Thanks," Stephanie said.

Dylan, Garry and Cara were left standing by the light jeep. They exchanged uncomfortable glances.

"I get the impression she's more upset by what you said, than the Police investigation," Cara remarked to Garry.

"I am sorry," Garry said. "But it is the obvious – the elephant in the room. Everyone always suspects the ex-boyfriend."

"Well what about Stephanie's other ex, Jeffrey Mannington? He was a much more suspicious character than you," Dylan observed. "Can he prove where he was that day?"

"He works in Brisbane," Garry said.

"But can he prove it?" Dylan queried.

"Knowing Jeff, he was a bit of a loner outside of work hours," Garry said. "And Brisbane is less than an hour away. But if he came up to campus, someone is sure to have seen him."

"I guess that's one of the things the police will be looking to find out," Cara said. "Can we go for a drive now?"

"Are you sure it's okay for us to leave campus with the police here?" Dylan inquired anxiously.

Garry shrugged. "There are plenty of students around for the Police to talk to, and we are not going interstate or anything."

"Where to then?" Dylan asked.

"Black Mountain," Cara suggested. "I want to see if there is a real mountain."

"I don't think there is," Garry said.

"There must be!" Cara insisted. "How would it get the name? What about the nearby state forest?"

"Okay," Dylan said. "Let's go."

Biology was a time-consuming and difficult study choice, so over the years, the Biology class had dwindled in numbers, and was as small as the Chemistry class. Cara almost expected Dylan, Stephanie, Garry and herself to form the complete class, but Danielle, a Geography major, had elected to join them. Plant Biology was almost a complete field of its own so the pre-requisites were waived for someone who had several years of a similar science.

Their Biology group had been friendly and relaxed in the past, but today Stephanie and Garry were barely speaking. It was unusual for Stephanie and Garry not to be speaking, because they had always been friends, and Cara had to admit that the only thing that could really warrant such a circumstance was Bradley's death. Hence the two boys worked together and the three girls formed their own study group, a form of ghettoization most unusual for their class.

They began by studying the basic parts, structure and process of a typical plant in the theory lecture in the morning. The afternoon laboratory was full of drawings and observations of plants. It was interesting work and the time flew, making the whole class late up to the cafeteria for tea.

Being the only ones commencing their meals when the others were finishing, the Biology class all sat together. Danielle, who was unaware of the tensions in the group, brought up the latest subject of gossip.

"Have you seen the campus social calendar yet?" Danielle inquired.

"Err no," Cara admitted. "Has it been printed up?"

"I got a glimpse down at Student Services," Danielle said. "There isn't going to be a Reverse Tea this year."

"No Reverse Tea?" Stephanie was puzzled. The Reverse Tea was a 'Sadie Hawkins' style event where the girl's asked the guys out. It was usually used to kick off the university social calendar, because the girls were more out-going than the guys. "What will they do to get people mixing then?"

"I think they are going to have a Masque Dinner instead," Danielle said.

"That sounds rather fun," Cara observed.

"Whatever was the reason for dropping the Reverse Tea?" Stephanie inquired. "Did anyone say?"

"Apparently a lot of guys have complained and they managed to swing the Reform Church management to their point of view," Danielle said.

"What did they complain about?" Cara asked.

"The girls asking the guys," Danielle said. "They said it was immoral and against the natural order of things!"

"What?" Stephanie exclaimed. "The Reverse Tea was the only campus social event that wasn't strongly patriarchal."

"It's true," Garry said. "There is a group of guys in the dorms that have formed a club."

"What do they call themselves?" Cara asked. "The chauvinists' club?"

"No, the 'men's rights' group," Garry replied.

"And do you two belong to this group?" Stephanie inquired.

"No way," Dylan said. "I would be happy for the girls to queue up to ask me out."

"I thought you were off dating?" Cara couldn't stop herself saying. It just somehow slipped out.

"When I'm not off dating," Dylan explained with uncharacteristic patience.

"So which guys are in this group?" Stephanie asked curiously.

"Arthur Mason is the leader, Tony Dantean is a member, and Vincent Wilson is somewhere down their ranks. Damaris' Michael might have been invited. We suspect that he is a secret member, because Damaris would kill him if she found out," Garry said. "I don't think that Zach is one of them, but he was part of the sporting elite on campus last year."

"Amazing there is a gang of snobs on campus again," Cara observed.

"Don't they want girlfriends?" Stephanie inquired.

"They want doormat girlfriends actually," Dylan explained.

"There aren't any of those around here," Cara exclaimed.

"You would be surprised," Danielle said. "I went out with Michael once years ago, and they say he has changed, but I still think Damaris is welcome to him."

"Damaris is no push-over," Stephanie observed. "Michael will be in trouble if she finds out."

"What would she do?" Danielle asked curiously.

"Well if talking to him didn't work, she would stop feeding him delicacies she has cooked," Cara said. "Damaris and Michael have a very simple relationship."

"It might be perceived as somewhat traditional," Stephanie observed, "But trust me, the hands that rule the stove rule the roost as well. At least in their arrangement!"

Friday morning, Cara found an airmail letter from Kaleb in her student post-box. She was pleased and put it aside to read later. After classes finished she went to lunch in the cafeteria, and when she returned, she had the room to herself. It was the perfect moment to open her letter.

Kaleb wrote that he would probably fall slightly behind with the number of units he was able to complete at his American university that year, given that he was out of synch with the other students. He worried this might make Cara lose interest in him, as he was already one class behind her at Silver Springs University.

Cara found her nicest stationary and commenced a reply. She assured Kaleb that she would not change her mind about him, although she admitted the long separation might be more of a threat, than his academic progression. Then she told him about Dylan's new vehicle and the peculiar circumstance of the police coming to campus to investigate Bradley's death. She signed it 'love and kisses', and sealed the envelope up safely.

Cara ran down to the university post office and dropped her letter into the Australia Post box in the hopes that it could still catch that day's mail. Then she went across to the cafeteria to tea, where she caught up with Stephanie. The girl's returned to their room together and began to prettify themselves for vespers.

Cara's family were traditionally Presbyterian, which was roughly the third largest religious group in Ireland, where the O'Brien family originated. Grandmother O'Brien still persisted in considering herself Presbyterian, but Cara's parents had moved with the times and joined the Uniting Church.

It was the Uniting Church that organized the Friday night meeting on campus, affectionately known as 'vespers'. Vespers was usually quite enjoyable, as the Uniting Church were a socially conscious and inclusive group.

Cara was somewhat surprised when her name was called over the public address system: "Cara O'Brien and Stephanie Lowood to the foyer".

"That will be Dylan," Stephanie said. "When we were studying in the library earlier he said he would pick us up for vespers, I hope you don't mind."

"Of course not," Cara said somewhat acerbically, "As long as he thinks he is here for you."

"Sure," Stephanie said. "He is here just as a friend."

When the girls reached the foyer, they saw that Dylan had Garry with him. Cara had a moment's satisfaction, as she saw it was now Stephanie's turn to look mildly embarrassed.

The little group oriented themselves so that Cara was beside Garry, with Stephanie in the middle, and Dylan on the other side of Stephanie. That way each of the girls was beside a boy with whom she had always been platonically friendly.

Upon reaching the women's assembly area, Cara spied Debbie and David. She led her group to join the couple in the pew. Vespers that night included a welcome to campus for the year. The Uniting Church minister who also functioned as one of the Silver Springs University chaplains spoke about the missionary journeys of the apostle Paul and likened their coming year at university to a Christian journey.

The Chaplain also quoted First Corinthians, chapter 9, verse 24: "Do you not know that those who run in a race all run, but one receives the prize? Run in such a way that you may obtain it," and urged the students to strive for academic achievement and spiritual growth.

CHAPTER TWO: WEDDING PLANS

Hank arrived early the next morning to transport Cara, Stephanie, Debbie and Bede across to his house to help Phoebe with the wedding preparations. He was driving his Falcon 500, which had bench seats and could accommodate four passengers. Cara was excited because this would be the first time she saw the house that Hank and Phoebe were in the process of buying.

The first thing the girls did on arrival was greet Phoebe warmly with hugs. They had seen her briefly in classes they had in common during the week, but she lived off campus and was currently completely consumed with wedding planning, setting her apart from the group during the week.

"You look pretty," Cara gushed. "Being engaged must suit you."

"I love Hank, I love the house, I love it all," Phoebe admitted. "Come and have a look around."

The house was brick with an iron roof. It was true that it only had one bedroom, but the lounge was a good size and the kitchen an old-fashioned eat-in room with heaps of space. Phoebe and her mother, who was staying as chaperone until the wedding day, had set up their beds in the enclosed verandah. This was suitable as it was summer, and the breezy summer nights were quite pleasant.

Hank explained he hoped to have proper cladding on the walls of this area before winter came. He also planned to insulate it, thereafter it would become their living area, freeing the current lounge to function as a second bedroom. The yard had plenty of space and was mostly wild, being bush rather than garden. The tumble-down shed at the back was huge and was set to be Hank's pride and joy, once he had replaced the iron and several of the supports.

The tour complete, Phoebe led the way into the kitchen and began to boil the kettle for coffee, tea or herbal tea as her visitors desired. Hank contrived to take Stephanie aside into the lounge room, but as it was adjacent, Cara could overhear their conversation.

"I'm sorry about going to the police," Hank said in a low voice. "But the thing about Bradley's bike kept bothering me."

"Don't worry about it," Stephanie murmured. "The matter is in the hands of the authorities, which is where it belongs. Besides, I'm sure the police would not be investigating unless they had some evidence of their own."

"Even if they find someone, it won't bring Bradley back," Hank muttered.

"But it could help his parents," Stephanie said. "I think my grief will stay the same, but his father feels so guilty for helping Bradley with the money to buy the bike."

"The bike was good," Hank said. "His father doesn't need to worry about that."

"And Bradley was a safe rider," Stephanie said. "Or I would never have ridden with him."

"It could have been just one of those horrible random things," Hank suggested.

"It could have been too," Stephanie said. "That's what I thought – but if the police think otherwise..."

"Phoebe will be wondering where we are," Hank said. "Let's go back into the kitchen."

After tea and coffee, the girls settled down to work on the bridesmaid dresses. Phoebe's favourite colour was purple, so she was having pale lavender bridesmaids. Bede and Stephanie were making the dresses out of lace and working together to make sure that both Debbie and Cara were dressed alike. The bridesmaids would be carrying bunches of lavender in their hands and wearing wreathes of flowers in their hair.

Phoebe's wedding dress was shop-bought as a present from her mother. The bride's dress was securely hidden inside dry-cleaning bags to ensure that Hank did not see it hanging in the tiny house before their big day. It had not been outrageously expensive, but was unashamedly a copy of the one Madonna wore when she had married Sean Penn the previous year.

The bodice was strapless and boned, while the skirt was a froth of tulle. A cluster of tulle decorations was attached to the drop waist, and the dress was ideal for displaying a youthful good figure. Madonna had attached her veil to a black hat, but Phoebe was having a much more feminine tiara.

Bede and Stephanie busied themselves measuring Debbie and Cara. Then the girls laid the material out and cut two copies of the pattern, one in lace and the other in the lining material. The girls carefully separated the cut pieces, storing all the pieces for Debbie's dress in one plastic bag, and the pieces for Cara's dress in another. They would be able to do the sewing in free moments back at the dormitory.

Phoebe's mother was going to do the flowers and decorations for the small rural church Phoebe and Hank had chosen, and Damaris had been booked to do the catering. The cake had been ordered from the bakery in Northcoast, which occasionally produced professionally decorated cakes as well as daily buns and treats.

"It's so exciting," Cara exclaimed, hugging Phoebe. "I can't believe your wedding is only three weeks away!"

"Nor can I," Phoebe exclaimed. "But Mum has been so great, helping me around here!"

"Your Mum is lovely," Stephanie exclaimed. "However, Bede and I need to get back to the sewing machines now."

"I will get Hank to drop you back to the dormitory," Phoebe said.

Sunday, Cara and Stephanie awoke early and attended the Inter-denominational praise service. Despite its early timeslot, the Inter-denominational praise service was the most popular worship service on campus.

The event was inclusive and concentrated upon worshiping the Lord through contemporary youth songs. The message was often delivered by a trainee minister, and Cara felt a minor sadness as she remembered how much Kaleb had looked forward to his debut as a speaker at these services.

The girls sat with Kathy and Andrew. Andrew was always in his element at any type of worship, as he was the most earnest young ministerial student Cara had ever met, while his worldlier girlfriend Kathy was slightly tired eyed because she loved to sleep in on a Sunday morning.

Their friend Joelle often played the organ for worship, and as her boyfriend Tom was alone, he came and sat next to Andrew. The morning's speaker was Larry, and his girlfriend Anita was operating the over-head–projector which displayed the song lyrics on the big screen.

Larry was very progressive and had done some of his practical experience with the Christian Life congregation in Baulkham Hills, a suburb of Sydney. He spoke about the gifts of the spirit, including preaching, teaching and counselling; and prayed that the students would be supported throughout the year in their efforts to develop their talents for the Lord.

After the Inter-denominational praise service concluded, Kathy and Andrew moved on to attend the Reform Church Service. If Kaleb had been on campus, Cara would also have done the Theology girlfriend thing and attended all the services with him. However, Cara did not want to attend the services alone and be reminded that she was missing him.

Stephanie returned to the room to continue sewing the bridesmaids' dresses, so Cara hung out in their room, watching her dress come to shape panel-by-panel under Stephanie's deft fingers. When it was time for the cafeteria to open, she left her roommate to the sewing and went to eat an early lunch.

In the afternoon, Cara decided to commence her student employment and pulled the large mower out of the storage shed. Mowing was an unusual work choice for a girl, but Cara enjoyed being outdoors, and with the ride-on mower and other excellent equipment, tending the lawns that covered the rolling back section of campus was not difficult.

Monday classes continued with Sociology, and theory sessions for Practice Teaching in the morning. Tutorial groups and assignments were also allocated for some of the larger classes. After lunch, Cara and Stephanie commenced Agriculture. This was a house subject and was therefore available to all third year students. However, because it was practical and physical, the unit had attracted a limited enrolment.

Dylan, Danielle and Garry had signed up, so the whole Plant Biology group were there; joking that they would have plants growing out of their ears before the end of the semester. Tess had also joined, because she said it would give her something to do while Luke was busy driving the university car, and Tom had enrolled to would fill the long hours Joelle was busy practicing her music. Elisabet had been a surprise enrolment, because the dainty girl usually stuck to the more artistic subjects.

During the first class they studied a little theory, covering the basic nutrients plants required to grow, ideal season for planting and some of the most popular small market crops. Then they toured the greenhouse. At this stage, gardening looked like great fun, and Cara could not wait until the next week when they might get their hands dirty.

Tuesday Cara had classes in the morning and a Chemistry practical after lunch. The particular third year unit they were enrolled in covered Biochemistry. The first lectures had been introductory, reminding students of their previous studies in Chemistry and explaining the interdisciplinary nature of Biochemistry.

Biochemistry predominantly focused on chemical substances and interactions found in plants and animals. It also utilised insights from Physics and Biology. Essential to this study was the understanding of the processes of photosynthesis, respiration, glycolysis and metabolism.

The students began their laboratory session by testing foods for glucose and starch. One of the simpler tests involved adding iodine solution to food samples, and watching for the red-brown iodine to turn blue or bluish black. This proved that the food contained energy giving glucose.

A slightly more challenging test involved boiling green leaves in water and then dipping in hot ethanol to remove the colour. The leaves were then tested with ethanol to demonstrate they contained starch. Some leaves on the pot plant had been covered up since the previous week. When these leaves were tested, they showed very small amounts of blue, demonstrating that in the absence of light, photosynthesis did not occur and starch levels were reduced.

The rest of the session was spent viewing, modelling and drawing biomolecules. Cara was slightly dizzy by the time the laboratory had finished. She was also worried because she realized that the biomolecules were far too complex for her current understanding. There were also large jumps in the equations that she could not understand, and just had to accept. Altogether, she felt that the topic lacked the neatness and precision of Inorganic Chemistry.

Wednesday after lunch, Cara went across to the library to write up her Chemistry practical report. The lecturer was always very strict, even to expecting every page to be ruled up perfectly, so she always worked with care. She chose one of the large tables in the science section and sat down. It was not too long before she was joined by Zack and Garry.

"Hi," Garry said. "May we join you?"

"Yeah sure," Cara said, pulling her text books closer to make room on the table. "What are you doing?"

"Same as you," Garry said. "Chemistry write-up."

"There was something I wanted to talk to you about actually," Zack said. "But I have been waiting until your room-mate was not around to do so."

"Eh?" Cara was puzzled. "What can't you say in front of Stephanie?"

"It's about the police," Zack said. "They have been back, and they had a talk to me."

"What were they asking?" Cara was curious.

"They were asking whether Bradley had any enemies," Zack said. "And I said none that I knew of – Bradley was a popular guy. He was also a brilliant basketball player. He carried his team almost."

"Yeah, Brads was pretty good," Cara said.

"My team beat his team first semester, but he beat my team second semester," Zack said. "I certainly did not hold that against him!"

"That is the nature of the game," Garry observed. "You win some and lose others, you have to be a good sport about it."

"Of course," Zack said. "Although I do like to win. I expect to do well this semester. Are either of you playing?"

"I have three late afternoons," Cara observed. "So I actually thought I might try a different sport. One I can do more in my own time - like swimming."

"I also have three late afternoons," Garry said. "And my room-mate now has a vehicle, so we were thinking of going out into the mountains a lot more. I don't think I will be competing."

"We wish you all the best of luck Zack," Cara said. "And if you are in the finals, we will definitely come and watch."

"Being an A grade captain, there is no way I would give it up," Zack observed. "But if I were only B grade or C grade, I might think about it. The competition is much less exciting at that level."

"Naturally," Garry observed. "What does this have to do with the police?"

"Well, after they spoke to me, I remembered there was an incident last year," Zack said. "It was one reason young Michael was brought up to A grade and into my team for a while."

"I think I remember something," Cara said.

"Yeah," Zack said. "Tony Dantean had been playing roughly and made too many fouls. It was not sportsman-like play and also cost us some games."

"Hmm," Garry said.

"Well, I asked Bradley to move Tony. Bradley consulted with the rest of the committee, and then moved Tony down to B grade," Zack recounted. "It wasn't Bradley's decision alone, but Tony did appear to hold it against him."

"Did you tell the police this?" Cara asked.

"No," Zack said. "Like I told you, I remembered later. And despite all that – Tony is a sort of friend."

"Being moved from A grade to B grade, when he had been a captain the previous year, if I remember rightly, would have been quite a demotion," Garry mused. "I can see Tony being angry."

"Tony simply isn't an A grade player, he isn't fast enough," Zack said. "He gets rough to try to compensate when he is out of his level."

"Yeah," Cara said.

"I think you should tell the police," Garry observed.

"I dunno when they will be back," Zack said. "And I can't 'dob' Tony in – there's a guy code."

"Whoever damaged Bradley's bike forgot that code," Cara observed. "Even if they didn't mean for Bradley to get killed."

"I know," Zack said.

"Neither of us were on the team or the committee," Garry said. "If we were to tell the police, it would be hearsay. You are an actual witness."

"We don't know there actually is a connection between Tony and the bike," Cara said. "If any of us tell the police, the police still have to find the evidence. If Tony didn't do anything wrong, you wouldn't even be getting him into trouble."

"That is true," Zack said. "I have to think about it."

The three students settled down to completing their Chemistry reports and all other concerns disappeared from their minds. Chemistry reports were serious assignments.

Thursday dawned rainy. Cara watched the sky anxiously, and then she and Stephanie went down to the Plant Biology laboratory bundled up in raincoats and wearing boots. The rest of the class, did the same because they knew the Biology Master would not change his mind about an excursion once it had been planned. Danielle, who was new, had to return to the dormitory and came back wearing a long raincoat.

They all bundled into the Biology Master's range rover and drove out to one of the tropical walks in the Imbil State Forest. Indeed, they were pleasantly surprised that the forest canopy was so thick they could barely feel a light mist once under its cover. The Biology Master looked very smug as the students exclaimed over the difference.

"The coverage is why forest floor vegetation is so unique," the Biology Master explained.

They set off on a long hike with the Biology master pointing out plant structures as they passed. Their lecture had been about different leaf types, and if you thought a leaf was just a leaf and a stem just a stem – you would have been very surprised!

Garry fell into step alongside Cara. "Have you heard from Kaleb?" he asked in a friendly manner.

"Last week I had a letter," Cara said. "I wrote back, but the mail between Australia and the United States can take a while."

"Between places in Australia too," Garry murmured. "I remember when I was writing to Stephanie."

"Yeah," Cara mused. Garry did not have to say anymore. Those days were before Garry's Mother had her brush with breast cancer. "It seems like an age ago – and we were kids then," Cara murmured.

"I know," Garry agreed.

"How is your mother now?" Cara asked.

"They say she will be alright," Garry said. "There is nothing left of the cancer and no reason it should reoccur."

"I am so glad," Cara said. She glanced ahead to where Stephanie was walking with Danielle and Dylan. "Does Stephanie know?"

"Pretty much," Garry said. "We can't talk like we used to, you have seen how things are."

"It will get better over time," Cara mused.

"Like you and Dyls eh?" Garry suggested slyly.

"Dyls is different," Cara said. "He has changed since Annie dumped him, and talks mostly to Stephanie now."

"Give it some time," Garry suggested. "Your friendship should recover."

The Biology Master called them to attention to inspect some leaves. They observed the main parts including, tip, apex, mid-ribs, margin, veins and petiole. Then he plucked leaves from different plants and compared them. The main body of the leaf could be entire, serrate, crenate, lobed or parted, giving each leaf its distinct shape. This shape could also be used to identify the plant species.

Friday Stephanie had Cara's bridesmaid's dress ready for a fitting. The dress had a sweetheart neckline, and semi-fitted bodice ending in a slightly lowered waist, above a gathered skirt. The bodice and skirt were fully lined, but the puff sleeves were made of delicate lace. The dress was ankle length and its simple design made it suitable for wearing to formal events after the wedding.

"I love it," Cara exclaimed, spinning around on the high heels Stephanie had requested she wear, so the seamstress could measure her hem length. "You are so clever Steph!"

"I'm pleased with the way it is hanging," Stephanie muttered, her mouth full of tape measure. Putting dangerous things in their mouths while working appeared to be one of the strange habits of dressmakers.

There was a knock at the door and Bede entered carrying a similar bundle of lavender lace. She was followed by Debbie.

"Now, let's see how the two look together," the younger O'Brien sister exclaimed. "Hurry up, Debbie, get changed."

Debbie shrugged out of her every-day top and into her bridesmaid dress. The bottom hem of her jeans showed below the full skirt. Cara giggled.

"Take the jeans off," Bede ordered, "They will alter the hang." Debbie had also brought her bridesmaid shoes to the fitting. She slipped them on her feet. Although the dresses weren't completely finished, the effect was charming, and Bede and Stephanie fell to congratulating each other on their handiwork.

"Did you ever think what you might have worn if you had married Bradley?" Cara asked.

Stephanie shrugged. "Is there any point talking about it now?"

"I think it's okay," Debbie said. "You can keep your good fantasies even though you want to lose the grief."

"Well I hadn't decided anything for sure," Stephanie said. "Even if Bradley had asked me that weekend – I don't see how we would have afforded marriage for several years. I did have a magazine clipping of a drop-waist dress, made of heavy lace. It was slim-line, with an uneven hemline, a v-front and cathedral sleeves that belled open below the wrists."

"It sounds lovely," Cara exclaimed. "And the bridesmaids?"

"I don't know," Stephanie shrugged. "You and Kathy of course. Something simple, maybe a sash at the back, in a dusky rose colour."

"It sounds different," Debbie said.

"Well, it's just a designer's fantasy," Stephanie said. "And the main thing would have been to have Bradley there."

"Yeah," Cara said.

The girls were quiet for a minute and the tedious process of pinning the hems continued. Then Bede broke the silence. "I say you girls, you will never guess who has asked me to the Masque Dinner?" she said.

"We don't know the guys in your class," Stephanie returned. "So guessing is pretty hard for us."

"He isn't in my class, he is in your class!" Bede returned.

"Hmm that's different," Debbie said. "Ah - Craig is single, and I believe he is nice, if a little quiet.”

"It's not Craig," Bede laughed. "I hardly know him."

"He plays the violin," Stephanie explained. "I think he went out with Joelle in our first year."

"Um, I can't really see you with Dylan or Garry," Cara observed. "Even though both are technically free agents."

"No, not Dylan or Garry," Bede said.

"Please don't say Tony Dantean," Stephanie said sharply. "He has something of a reputation you know."

"No, not Tony," Bede said. "But you are getting closer."

"Um, not Arthur Mason," Cara said.

"Well yes actually," Bede replied.

"And what did you say?" Cara inquired. "I know we don't hang out much, but I don't want anyone hurting my baby sister."

"I said 'yes'," Bede said. "Is there any reason why I should not have?"

"Well they say he is leading a men's liberation group this year," Cara replied. "It sounds quite chauvinistic."

"Why would he ask me out then?" Bede said. "I don't tolerate bigotry."

"But you are a Home Economics major and Arthur might think you are old fashioned," Stephanie suggested.

Bede shrugged: "He is in for a shock then."

"He is indeed," Debbie laughed.

"You are also younger than him, so he might think he can tell you what to do," Cara observed.

"Another thing he will have to get over," Bede said with a grin on her face. "And it is only one dinner you know. We are not going steady or anything."

Bede finished pinning Debbie's hem, and Debbie climbed out of the bridesmaid's dress carefully. Bede folded the material and placed it in her sewing bag to await the final touches. "I'll see you guys later," she said. "Don't take life too seriously."

After the younger O'Brien had left the room, Stephanie began to look thoughtful. "That raises the question, girls – who are we going to the Masque with?" Stephanie said.

"I'm going with David of course," Debbie said instantly, which made both Cara and Stephanie laugh. "I'm surprised to hear you are thinking about it though."

"Well," Stephanie said. "I am on campus, so social events are an issue for me, unless I take my tea down to Bradley's grave, which really wouldn't help me much. Dylan has offered, but I don't know how long I should take advantage of his kindness."

"This is only the first function of the year," Cara said thoughtfully. "I'm sure you can go with Dylan. Later in the year – maybe you will have to draw some boundaries."

"That's about what I thought too," Stephanie said.

"I know it's not the Reverse Tea this year," Cara said, "But I assumed I could ask Garry as a friend – if you don't mind of course."

"Not in the least," Stephanie said. "Go for it."

However, Saturday morning at breakfast when Cara asked Garry to the Masque Dinner, she was surprised to find that he had already asked Danielle to accompany him to the event.

"She is the new girl in the class and I wanted to make her welcome," Garry explained.

"Steph and Dyls, you and I have all been hanging as a group," Cara said somewhat disheartened, "And I just assumed we would continue."

"Oh I'm glad the group is back together again," Garry said. "Don't get me wrong! And I know you are in a spot with Kaleb over in America... but I felt the need to be moving on."

"Okay," Cara said. She felt mildly embarrassed being caught asking a guy who didn't want to take her out. She also felt slightly betrayed, having relied on his friendship.

"What are you doing for the rest of the morning?" Garry asked to change the subject.

"Stephanie and I were planning to go for a swim in the pool," Cara said. "And then sometime today I need to mow the lawns. It's my student employment for this year."

After breakfast Cara connected with Stephanie back in their room. The girls collected their bathers and went down to the pool to take a swim. Cara did a serious number of laps, but Stephanie stopped after a while and floated around relaxing. By the time they were finished it was almost time for lunch. They got changed and went to the cafeteria.

After lunch, Cara spent several hours mowing lawns, while Stephanie planned to start on her Education and Practice Teaching assignments. When Cara returned to the room, she was mildly surprised to find a note from Stephanie explaining that Dylan had taken Stephanie, Danielle and Garry for a drive out to the Ringtail State Forest to look for possums. They planned to stop at a service station which doubled as a snack bar, and would be missing tea on campus.

Cara supposed that the Suzuki only seated four safely, and that if Garry had a new girlfriend, this would be the way of things for now. She had her tea in the cafeteria with Debbie and David, Joelle and Tom. Then in the evening she watched some television in the recreation area with Joelle and Tom.

They were joined by Elisabet and Craig, who claimed they were not a couple, but 'just good friends'. Apparently Craig was encouraging Elisabet to take an interest in Music, and even sit exams in the hopes of qualifying for a Music elective in her final year.

Sunday morning Cara attended the Inter-denominational praise service. Andrew was taking a turn preaching for the Reform Church service, so she accompanied Kathy and Stephanie. It was always remarkable how Kathy's habitually unassuming boyfriend came out of his shell in matters theological and delivered a resounding sermon.

Unlike the other speakers that year, who had incorporated the beginning of the year into their topics somehow, Andrew spoke about the perennial subject of forgiveness and the Christian obligation to forgive those who wrong them in return for God's generosity. This was based upon Mathew chapter 6, verse 12: "And forgive us our debts, as we forgive our debtors."

Sitting at lunch with Andrew and Kathy, Cara listened to Andrew explaining that while his text had been taken from the Lord's Prayer, his inspiration was in part the investigation into Bradley's bike. The police had spoken to him, and seemed to be looking for someone who had held a grudge against Bradley. While Andrew couldn't think who might possibly have disliked Bradley, they would have been far better off forgiving and moving on, instead of allowing it to fester until they sought to cause Bradley inconvenience.

Andrew glanced across at Stephanie somewhat nervously as he explained his reasoning, but she merely nodded. "I had heard the police were pursuing a line somewhat like that," Stephanie confirmed. "I couldn't help them much because everyone that I knew loved Bradley."

"Bradley was popular," Cara murmured.

"There is only one person I can think of who held anything against

Bradley," remarked Phoebe, who was visiting campus with Hank and her mother.

"Oh who was that?" Kathy exclaimed.

"Rob was not very impressed when Bradley took you out on his bike just after your break-up last year Kathy," Phoebe said.

"I hadn't even thought about Rob," Kathy exclaimed.

"Nor had I," Cara said thoughtfully. Having left campus, the young pilot had slipped from everyone's mind.

"But Rob finished his course first semester last year," Kathy objected. "He didn't even return to attend his graduation."

"It is true Rob did not attend his graduation," said Hank, who had also completed his pilot's license the previous year. "But he did fly a light plane in from the Northern Territory a couple of weeks before that."

"I didn't know," Kathy was bemused.

"We didn't say anything," Phoebe said. "You were happy with Andrew by that time."

"The timing could be coincidental," Stephanie said.

"Have you told the police yet Hank?" Kathy inquired.

It was Phoebe who answered. "Yes, Hank told the police, but we really don't think Rob did anything to Bradley's bike."

Hank nodded, "As far as I know, Rob simply made a delivery and flew out again the same day."

"Could he have hung around longer?" Andrew inquired.

"Possibly, but not likely," Hank said. "The flight plans for even light planes have to be logged."

"I agree," Cara said. "A bike ride doesn't seem to be enough motivation. Especially as Bradley was only doing Kathy a good turn after her break-up."

Monday in Agriculture, Cara's class studied the theory of aquaculture and inspected the plant nursery set up in the greenhouse. Several rows of plants were growing with their roots just in water under the lamps. The Agriculture Instructor explained that specific nutrients were infused into the water to allow the plants to achieve full growth and even bear crops.

Then they crossed over to the trays of potting mix standing on another bench. Their task for the day was to plant seeds in the potting mix, and with tender love and care, those seeds would germinate within a few days. By their laboratory the next week, each student should have a healthy tray of seedlings at various stages of maturity, depending on the species.

Tuesday in Chemistry, the students observed anaerobic respiration in yeast and then in germinating seeds. They also looked at a single celled organism under the microscope and attempted to identify the structures in which the essential chemical reactions took place. Garry observed that he felt like he was back in Biology class, and Zack, who did not do Biology with the others, laughed.

The last experiment was much more Physics-like however. The students attempted to denature the protein lysozyme in egg white by adding different concentrations of urea. The products were then analysed under a spectroscope. Cara wasn't very experienced with that sort of thing. The spectroscope was attached to a very basic printer and she could see that the different samples produced different lines.

Cara also knew they were meant to be demonstrating the Gibbs equation somehow. She could manage this equation if someone gave her the numbers to put into it, and she understood that it was describing the energy produced or consumed by making and breaking chemical bonds.

By the end of the laboratory, however, Cara was completely confused and metaphorically tearing her hair out. Zack, who had more experience with that sort of thing, promised to meet her in the library the following day and help her with the write-up.

Chemistry reports were always due within a week of the practical session, so Cara met Zack in the library Wednesday afternoon to work on her write-up. Garry, who was passing through the science section, saw them and stopped to talk.

"Hello Zack," Garry said. "Hello Cara!"

"Hello Garry," Zack said. "Have you started your Chemistry write-up yet?"

"Tomorrow," Garry said. "I have to work in the laboratory this afternoon."

Garry had always been clever in the scientific field and had done a semester of pure science at the University of Wollongong the previous year, so he was employed as a laboratory assistant through the student work program. This meant he maintained the laboratory inventories, serviced equipment and laid out the materials lecturers had requested for particular experiments.

"I expect you won't have any trouble," Cara said. "But Zack is helping me today."

"Good for Zack," Garry observed. He paused as if a thought had just occurred to him. "Zack are you taking anybody to the Masque Dinner Saturday night?"

"I hadn't really thought about it," Zack said. "A lot of my friends have already graduated, including the girls I was friends with!"

"Cara doesn't have a date," Garry informed him. "Dylan is taking Stephanie, and I'm taking Danielle."

"Indeed?" Zack remarked nonchalantly. "How about you and me, Cara O'B?"

"Err - what?" Cara was flustered. "You know I have a boyfriend in America don't you?"

"Sure," Zack replied. "America's pretty far away. I don't think he'll be here in time to take you next weekend."

"All right then," Cara said. She caught the glint in his eye. "As long as there isn't there anyone else you want to ask?"

"Not really," Zack replied. "Between study and training I'm too busy to chat many girls up."

Cara reflected that Zack was really quite nice in his way. He had always floated on the edge of the snobby set, being a year ahead of their group in his studies and a star basketball player. However, she could see that was partly a façade designed to cover up how isolating being a science major could be.

"I would be happy to go with you then," she said. The subject of the Masque Dinner disposed of, Cara and Zack got back to their work on the Chemistry report. Garry continued his way across campus to the laboratory block.

Thursday was raining so hard that even the Biology Master acknowledged they could not go outside in the afternoon. Instead they watched a film about logging and conservation; and when that was finished, the students were sent to the library to research South American rainforest plant species endangered by logging.

The Biology Master did not accompany the class to the library, but placed them on their honour to put in their best effort until the end of the official class time. Under the circumstances, no one felt obliged to stay late and they arrived at the cafeteria at a normal time for tea.

Friday morning Cara had a full quota of classes, and in the afternoon she decided to do her mowing because the following day would be full of preparation and excitement for the Masque Dinner. She spent the afternoon pleasantly puttering around the slopes at the back of campus on the ride-on mower. The morning had been sunny, but some of the lower lying patches were too muddy for the mower, so she was obliged to leave them for another week.

With earmuffs on her ears, a cover-all over her clothes, a hat on her head and goggles on her eyes, Cara knew that very few of the other students recognized her as the girl they knew when she was working. Cara found this mildly amusing, although she wasn't so amused when she discovered someone had dumped a sack of rubbish in the bushes behind the tool shed. Cara picked the bag up and heaved it into the blue metal dumpster bin, grateful that it did not split open. She then cleaned the mower off and parked it safely in the shed, hurrying to wash off for tea and pretty herself up for vespers.

At vespers, Stephanie and Cara chose to sit close to Bede and her upcoming date, Arthur Mason. Cara's wicked young sister was teasing Arthur, looking up at him with huge eyes and asking him what 'men's rights' his informal group was designed to represent.

The unimaginative Arthur had no idea he was being teased and was answering Bede's questions in a perfectly serious fashion, explaining that according to Ephesians chapter 5, verse 23, the husband was the head of wife and leader of the family. "We take the next passage to mean that the husband represents Christ to his wife," Arthur continued.

"Surely that is a heavy responsibility," Bede gushed. "Think of all that Jesus has done for this world."

"You are right," Arthur said. "It is a responsibility as well as a privilege to be a man."

Cara chuckled to herself. Bede appeared to have the men's liberation leader well in hand. Of course, Arthur Mason was only the group leader. He was not necessarily the most extreme group member.

CHAPTER THREE: THE PLOT THICKENS

One of the novelties associated with the Masque Dinner was that the students all had to make a mask to wear. It was a fun idea, so nobody minded, but apparently the idea originated with the men's liberation group whose members had been promoting some talk that make-up on a woman's face 'bore false witness'.

Cara giggled at the thought that the 'men's libbers' were so short sighted they could not see past a little powder and lipstick. A mask, on the other hand, was presumed to convey modesty according to all the traditions that required women to cover themselves!

The girls had all brought craft materials to Stephanie and Cara's room and pooled their resources. All the girls had chosen what was known as 'half-face masks' so they would be able to eat wearing them. They had a cardboard pattern traced from a party mask and were decorating them with coloured paper, paint, stickers and feathers.

Cara was going for the black and white, traditional harlequin look, lightened with a few silver sequins. At the last minute, she accepted Stephanie's offer of a bundle of coloured ribbons, which she stapled to the side, just where the elastic that held the mask in place joined on. The ribbons hung down either side of her face, framing it in a manner the girls agreed was most attractive.

Some of the girls were making their boyfriend's masks so that they matched. Debbie had covered one of the cardboard patterns with a white fabric featuring a delicate floral print, with a small paper flower on one corner. She had made David a corresponding masculine looking dark green mask decorated with leaves.

"David was a little concerned that masks might have some pagan connotations," Debbie remarked. "But then someone said that Carnevale was actually a Christian festival."

Stephanie, who loved the history of festivals, nodded. "That's right," she said. "It was celebrated on Shrove Tuesday, the day before Ash Wednesday and the beginning of Lent."

Kathy, who was an Art major, had been molding her and Andrew's masks out of paper-mache all week. She now had a solid base with the first of orange and red coats of paint applied. The rest of the decorations were going to be sequins and flame shapes cut out of foil.

"Are they crowns?" Debbie asked.

"Err no," Kathy said. "They are Pentecost flames. Andrew's idea of course."

Joelle had covered her mask with white velvet and added two delicate pink tipped ears. She had drawn whiskers on the side and added a pink bow just over one eyebrow. The matching mask for her boyfriend was black, with the whiskers drawn in white fabric paint. Tom's mask sported no ribbon.

"It's sweet," Stephanie said. "Let me guess, you are a cat and tomcat instead of Joelle and Tom?"

"Why yes," Joelle laughed. "A nice little pun on my boyfriend's name."

"And Tess, you and Luke are two of God's flock?" Cara suggested glancing across to where Tess was earnestly sticking balls of cotton-wool onto a pattern.

"Ah, yes," Tess said. "But Luke is the black sheep, she indicated a pile of cotton wool she had attempted to dye a brown colour. "I just hope this all has time to dry before evening."

"The craft glue is very fast drying," Kathy observed.

"Yeah, but some of us have used a lot!" Tess observed.

The masks complete, the girls set them aside to dry and hurried across to the cafeteria for lunch. After lunch some had assignments to do, while others spent the whole afternoon on each other's hair and make-up. It was early evening when Zack and Dylan arrived at reception, and called Cara and Stephanie down to the foyer. The guys had obviously shared their costume ideas because the girls found themselves confronted by a pair of eye-patch wearing pirates.

"You look great," Cara exclaimed. "Although I'm not sure an eye patch really counts as a mask."

"The hats are cool," Stephanie exclaimed.

"I've got a sword too," Dylan said, pulling a plastic cutlass out of his belt. He waved it in the air and backed Stephanie up against the nearest wall. Stephanie laughed despite herself.

"It's a cutlass," she corrected primly. "I like your costume and accessories, but I would prefer we were on our way to the event."

"Aww..." Dylan tucked the plastic cutlass back into his belt. "No more fun then. Let's go across to the cafeteria my lady."

Cara was pleased to see the old Dylan emerge, however briefly, while joking around with Stephanie. This was more like the Dylan she had known, before he had been dumped by Annie.

"I have a light sabre," Zack said looking at Cara hopefully. He had a plastic tube strapped to his side. "I'm a pirate from outer space."

"Fancy that," Cara remarked. "No, don't bother to get it out." She gave Zack a friendly shove in the direction Dylan and Stephanie were travelling. "What are the physics of the light sabre? Is it like a laser beam?"

"No - because a laser beam is continuous, and it's also reflective," Zack explained. "A saber is not continuous."

"So what is the force inside?" Cara inquired.

"Technology that has not been invented," Zack said. "It has to be futuristic to count as science fiction."

"Yeah I see," Cara agreed.

"The concept is partly physical, and partly philosophical, that is what makes it so tricky," Zack continued.

"I know, good guys get blue, bad guys get red," Cara observed somewhat simplistically.

"You have seen *Star Wars* then? What about *Return of the Jedi*?" Zack inquired.

"I've been waiting for the video," Cara said.

"*Return of the Jedi* came out about when university went back," Zack said. "Dylan checked and said it was still on the new release shelf in the Northcoast video store."

"We are going to hire it one weekend," Dylan remarked. "Michael has a VHS player, one of the perks of being a rich kid."

"We will sneak you and Stephanie in to see it," Zack promised.

"Into boy's dorm?" The law-abiding Stephanie sounded scandalized.

"Technically, the men's assembly area is not out of bounds," Dylan said. "We checked. Women are just not invited inside very often."

They had reached the cafeteria now and Dylan led the way through the maze of tables to where they were sitting, which turned out not too far from Bede and Arthur Mason.

The male population of Silver Spring's University, who were sometimes slow to participate in dress-up events had apparently embraced the mask idea with enthusiasm. There were Batman and Superman masks, monkeys and even monsters, showing that the boys had hit the party aisle of the Northcoast stores. A number of boys also sported swim goggles in different stages of adornment.

Normally Garry would have sat with Zack and Dylan, but as he was on a date with Danielle, the group dynamic had changed. They could see him several tables away, seated with Debbie and David, Andrew and Kathy. In fact, the view made Stephanie slightly uncomfortable, so Dylan and she swapped seats to place her back to the couple.

"Garry thought you wouldn't mind," Dylan whispered. "You two being broken up and all."

"I don't exactly," Stephanie returned. "It's just a bit weird looking directly at them."

The food began to arrive, starting with miniature pizza pockets as an entrée, followed by an antipasto board, then eggplant and parmesan pasta bake, finishing with rich lemon and berry cheesecake. Even those students who did not normally like eggplant or zucchini agreed the main course was delicious.

"Damaris has outdone herself this time," Cara exclaimed.

"Yes, the food is fantastic." Stephanie agreed. "I think I detect a slight Italian theme, don't you?"

"Duh!" Dylan said. "It's a Masque Dinner. It should be Venetian."

"Granny O'Brien says they still have Pancake Day back in Ireland," Cara said. "I would like to go someday."

"You are more likely to go to the United States," Zack observed.

"No I'm not," Cara spoke without thinking, making her friends all stare at her.

"But what about Kaleb?" Stephanie exclaimed.

Cara shrugged. "He might decide to stay in Australia," she said, "But we never talk about my moving to the United States. Never!"

"I thought you would if it were serious," Dylan frowned.

"He has to get back here for another semester yet," Cara said. "This separation isn't quite what I expected when we got together last year!"

There was a surprise towards the end of the evening, because David and Andrew stood up to conduct a small devotional based upon Bible texts that included the phrase 'hide my face' or 'hide your face'.

David read Deuteronomy chapter 31, verse 18, where God plans to punish his people's sin by removing his presence from them: "And I will surely hide My face in that day because of all the evil which they have done, in that they have turned to other gods."

Then Andrew read Psalm 102, verse 2, voicing David's plea for God's assistance: "Do not hide Your face from me in the day of my trouble; Incline Your ear to me; In the day that I call, answer me speedily." David replied by reading the statement of faith expressed in Isaiah Chapter 8, verse 17: "And I will wait on the Lord, Who hides His face from the house of Jacob; And I will hope in Him."

Andrew concluded by reading the promise in Ezekiel chapter 39, verse 29: "And I will not hide My face from them anymore; for I shall have poured out My Spirit on the house of Israel,' says the Lord God."

David then suggested the students acknowledge the gift of the Spirit by removing their masks. Most people were happy to remove their masks by then, if they had not already done so when eating. The fruit juice and laughter flowed freely for the next hour and the first major social event of the semester was declared a success.

After the function finished, Zack and Dylan walked Cara and Stephanie back to the girl's dormitory and said goodnight. Cara noticed that Stephanie gave Dylan a peck on the cheek, but figured it was too soon for her to be kissing Zack, even as a friend. She said, "Goodnight," to her escort in a friendly fashion and thanked him for the lovely evening.

"I hope Kaleb does make it back to Australia soon," Zack said generously. "For your sake Cara."

"Thank you Zack," Cara said. "I'll would be seeing you in class."

"Of course," Zack said. "And I'll help with your Chemistry anytime you need."

Sunday morning, both Cara and Stephanie woke up late and agreed they had both had a surprisingly good time at the Masque Dinner the night before. Then Dylan arrived at reception a few minutes before ten o'clock to see whether Stephanie was ready to go to the Reform Church service.

At the last minute, Cara was shocked to remember that in all the excitement, she had not checked her student mail box on Friday. Urging Dylan and Stephanie to go ahead without her, Cara rushed to the mail sorting area and opened up the little door to her student mail. An air mail letter fell out.

Sometimes Cara's letters and Kaleb's missives crossed over, however, she was pleased to see that this letter was in direct response to her previous letter. Kaleb wrote that he was surprised to hear the police had decided Bradley's death was suspicious, and hoped this would not cause more distress for Stephanie.

Kaleb also said that he was looking into the possibility that he could return to Australia for second semester, as that aligned more correctly with the American academic year. Cara wrote back immediately and said that she would be thrilled if Kaleb managed to return for the second semester of the academic year.

Then she described her new subjects and tried to make them sound entertaining. Finally, she mentioned the Masque Dinner and the way she happened to attend with Zack as her safer options had both deserted her. As an afterthought she mentioned Bede's date with Arthur Mason and the clever way her little sister appeared to be managing the men's activist.

Cara sealed the letter up in an envelope and stuck a stamp she had bought during the week onto it. The post office would not open until the next morning, but the out-of-hours postal slot was easily accessible.

Monday the Agriculture class checked on their seedlings, and marveled at the wonders of plant germination. Then the Agriculture Instructor took the students outside and pointed them at a ploughed field. He told them that he wanted them to dig trenches in which to plant their seedlings out by hand.

Stephanie, whose father ran a market garden, was incensed.

"There are motorized hoes that will do that for you," Stephanie exclaimed.

Cara, whose gardening experience mainly involved lawn mowers and the occasional pot plant, was also surprised. If she was allowed to use a mower to maintain the campus lawns, surely the Agriculture students could use a machine to dig the trenches.

"I want you to know how to do it," the Agriculture Instructor repeated stubbornly. He then showed them how to run a string between two points to establish a straight line along which to dig.

Elisabet shrugged cynically. Her family ran a successful organic vegetable business, down Byron Bay way, and most of the digging was done mechanically. "I think the Instructor wants us to know how it was done in the olden days," she observed.

"Didn't they use oxen to pull plough in the Bible?" Tom said. "Perhaps I should get one of the cows and hitch them up to something."

"I guess he wants to keep us busy," Dylan observed, grabbing a spade. Dylan and Garry set to work and soon had a trench established along one of the lines the Agriculture Instructor indicated.

Cara and Stephanie commenced digging another trench. The sturdy Cara was reasonably comfortable digging, but the slighter Stephanie really struggled. Between them, they were much slower than the guys. Tom, Tess and Elisabet commenced digging the third trench, with Tom digging twice as fast as the two girls.

"March-April is a good time to plant broccoli," The Agriculture Instructor said. "Pumpkins are a good all year crop. Tomatoes, capsicums, eggplants, lettuce, radish, carrot, beetroot and silver-beet, also do well planted in autumn."

"We will come and help you as soon as we have finished this trench," Dylan called out generously.

"Thanks Dyl," Stephanie said. "I'm going to really appreciate that."

"I somehow can't imagine Joelle digging out here," Tom joked. "She might get callouses on her delicate piano fingers."

Tess laughed. "Excavating is not my favourite thing in all the world," she said, "But I guess I can get my hands dirty!"

"Well, digging's a change from assignments at least," Garry observed cheerfully.

Tuesday in Chemistry, the class commenced protein structure and function. During the laboratory they attempted to analyse some meat for Nitrite. The Chemistry Doctor explained that Nitic Oxide was most important in neurotransmission and other biological functions, but because it was very unstable, experiments commonly tested for the related Nitrite and Nitrate compounds. The easiest experiment involved grinding up a small sample of meat and boiling it in distilled water. When the *Sulfa* and *NEDA* reagents were added the nitrite turned a purple colour. The rest of the lesson was spent fiddling around with the spectrophotometer, testing different cultures and solutions.

Wednesday evening, Cara thought that she would go and watch Zack play basketball. It was almost time for the match to begin when she arrived at the gymnasium. She slid onto one of the spectator benches beside Garry and Dylan, who had also come down to the gym to watch the match.

Zack's team were clearly very good at the game. They took control of the ball from the moment play commenced, and passed it to each other so that they outplayed the inferior players on the other team. Zach was an excellent shot when it came to scoring baskets and Cara found herself cheering frequently.

The opposition team, which was being captained by Michael, were clearly trying very hard. Towards the end of the first half, they managed to fight back, intercepting the ball and shooting several baskets. However, when half time was called, Zack's team were still several goals in the lead.

During the second half, it appeared that Michael had assigned himself the task of guarding Zack. While Michael was the younger player, his skills were developing and he managed to effectively deter Zack from scoring several times.

One of the guys from Zack's team, Vincent Wilson, appeared to resent Michael's efforts and performed a couple of fouls against him. This ensued in Michael's team getting awarded penalty shots that resulted in points, and almost brought the scores level.

When the match was finished, Zack turned to Vincent in consternation. "What did you do that for mate?" he exclaimed. "We were winning!"

"Sorry man," Vincent said. "I didn't mean to. I must have got over-enthusiastic or something."

"Well, watch what you are doing," Zack said. "This team has a reputation for being skilled, not rough. That is one reason why we are the best."

"Sure, mate," Vincent said. "At least we won."

"Okay, be more careful next time," Zack said. He then crossed to the benches to join his classmates.

"Good game, man," Dylan said.

"Thanks," Zack said. "I don't know what happened to Vincent though. He is usually a careful player. That's why I selected him for my team this year."

Thursday the Plant Biology class were off into the forest again. This week the Biology Master took them for a drive past the sites of some bush fires from previous years. He explained he had been keeping a journal regarding the regrowth and regeneration of the plant life ever since each fire. He pulled this journal out as they visited each site and added measurements and observations regarding the amount of regrowth.

The Biology Master explained that Australian plant life was unusually fire resistant due to traditional Aboriginal land management practices which included periodic burning. Indeed, some plants were so fire adapted that their seeds required the heat of a fire to trigger germination! Eucalyptus trees were also capable of surviving a fire and growing new branches after the blaze had passed them by.

The afternoon passed in a pleasant fashion as they drove and occasionally hiked between observation sites. Dylan was walking with Stephanie, and Danielle was walking with Garry. This left Cara to walk with the Biology Master. While she had always considered him to be an energetic and endearing character, Cara had never had never really socialized with the lecturer. However, today she began asking him questions regarding the best camping and bird watching sites around Queensland.

"The Brisbane Forest Park, and the Mount Mee State Forest are less than two hours away, and they are great places to find spotted quoll and platypus," the Biology Master said. "The area is also home to the Mount Glorious spiny crayfish, the broad-leaved spotted gum, giant ironwood, and the bobble nut Macadamia."

"It sounds wonderful," Cara agreed.

"If you know where to go, there are several Aboriginal sacred sites, some artefact scatters, bora rings, and dreaming trails," the Biology Master continued. "Steps need to be taken to preserve the wildlife around there because it is so close to Brisbane."

"Yes," Cara murmured.

"The Goomburra Valley is also known for its bird life," the Biology Master suggested. "It's about three-and-a-half hours south."

"That sounds great," Cara said. "Or would be if I had someone to take me."

"Young Dylan has his light jeep now," the Biology Master suggested. "That would seem ideal - although it's not for me to say anything about why you two are not hanging around together at the moment. What would I know? I'm only an old teacher."

"You are not old," Cara felt obliged to say.

The Biology Master laughed. "Older and wiser than you, at any rate," he said. "Young lady."

Friday afternoon the girls met in the cafeteria lounge for Phoebe's official 'hen's party'. Cara had arranged with Damaris to present a selection of biscuits and cakes. They played simple games like pass the parcel, and Phoebe was asked to answer a series of personal questions about Hank. His mother and sister, who had arrived from Western Australia and were staying in the girl's dormitory guest accommodation for the next week, supplied the correct answers.

Phoebe scored eight out of ten for her knowledge of Hank and there was much joking about the marriage having an eighty percent chance of succeeding. Phoebe's Mother brought out an old photograph album and embarrassed her daughter with childhood photographs and memories.

The gifts were semi-practical items such as bikini panties, stockings and petticoats so that Phoebe would be well supplied with underwear in the first few months of marriage. Hank's mother presented Phoebe with a beautiful fluffy dressing gown, which would be warm in winter, if not incredibly sexy. Cara's gag gift for Phoebe were fluffy mini-mouse slippers, but Phoebe expressed herself thrilled with them.

Saturday night the electronic door to girl's dormitory stayed open until eleven pm. The boys had decided to take advantage of this circumstances and screen *The Return of the Jedi* in the men's assembly area. Michael's personal television, which was the largest in the dormitory, and was not programmed to automatically turn off at curfew, had been carried down to the assembly area and connected with a VHS player.

Attendance was by invitation only for female residents. Bede had been invited by Arthur Mason, Cara had been invited by Zach and Stephanie had been invited by Dylan. Of course Damaris was included because of Michael, and Danielle was hanging around with Garry.

Some of the guys had brought bean-bags in from the men's lounge and scattered around the very front of viewing area. Garry was sitting in the front row with Danielle, and Cara led Zach to sit beside them. Dylan sat down on one of the bean-bags and pulled Stephanie onto his lap, where the girl sat docilely.

"Hey, how are you Zack and Cara?" Danielle said by way of greeting. She tossed Cara a cushion: "You might as well be comfortable."

"Thanks," Cara said. She couldn't help feeling somewhat disturbed by the sight of Stephanie balanced on Dylan's knee. As far as she knew, nothing was going on between the two, but it did look intimate, and Cara was surprised to find she felt vaguely jealous.

Arthur turned the lights off and Michael activated the video player. The boys had already fast forwarded through the ads, so that the feature began to play immediately. A hush fell over the room.

Han Solo, Luke Skywalker and Princess Leia began their mad dash across the screen, determined to blow up the evil Empire before the Empire blew them up! All too soon the movie was over and Arthur was turning the lights back on again.

Cara noticed that Danielle was leaning easily against Garry's shoulder, but as the room came back to life, the girl straightened up.

"I will walk you back to the dormitory," Garry suggested considerately and Danielle nodded.

Cara got up to follow. "Are you coming Zack?" she asked.

Zack hung back. "You don't think those two want to be alone do you?" he inquired.

"I really don't know," Cara said. "But you and I don't need to be alone – boyfriend over in America remember?"

"How does that work exactly?" Zack asked cheekily. "Do you send each other cyber kisses?"

"Um what?" Cara was puzzled.

"On the computer – through the internet," Zack said.

"Err no, we write letters," Cara said.

"Snail mail, that can't be much fun," Zack said. "Meet me in the computer lab one period and I will show you how to send an email through the X.400 system on the internet - it is much quicker."

"I don't have an account," Cara objected.

"All students have accounts," Zack said. "Just most of them do not know it. Are you doing Computing second semester?"

"Yeah, it takes the place of Agriculture," Cara said.

"Well you just got to get Kaleb to log in at his university," Zack said.

"The labs not open Sunday. What about Monday? In the morning – around eleven am?"

"Yeah I've got a free then," Cara agreed. "I'll see you."

Sunday after the Inter-denominational praise service, Cara seized the opportunity to talk to Dylan. The others were going to the Reform Church service, but Cara was restless and begged Dylan to go for a walk. He looked doubtful and muttered something about the others joining them later.

"Just a turn around the oval with me," Cara coaxed. "Do you really want more church?"

"Nah," Dylan said. "Okay then Cara, the oval it is!"

They crossed campus and walked over the lawns Cara maintained each week. The oval was right at the back. Maintaining it was a special job and not one of Cara's duties, as there was another student responsible for the sporting grounds.

"You seem to be getting along well with Zack," Dylan remarked.

Cara shrugged. "He is our classmate, and he understands about Kaleb."

"What do you mean?" Dylan asked.

"Zack has promised to show me how to send email to Kaleb," Cara said.

"That's big of him," Dylan remarked somewhat cynically. "Seeing as it is Kaleb standing in the way of you dating him properly."

Cara laughed. "Actually, I got the impression Zack just loves technology."

"Could be - he does do Physics!" Dylan observed.

Cara decided to take the plunge. "I never thought I would be saying this, but I have been missing our friendship Dylan," she said.

"Our friendship - is that so?" Dylan sounded horribly unresponsive. "Well Cara, I spent nearly two years chasing you and had no real girlfriend to show for it until Annie came along."

"I thought I remained your friend," Cara whispered. "Even when you were with Annie."

"You didn't dump me as badly as Annie did," Dylan admitted, "But I don't really want to get back into that position. Being taken for granted really is not cool."

"What is the difference with Stephanie?" Cara asked. "I have it on pretty good authority she is just relying on you because she lost Bradley."

"I know Stephanie needs someone right now," Dylan said. "And I wouldn't take advantage of her vulnerability. But she appreciates everything I do for her. I got the feeling that you never did."

"I did appreciate you," Cara said. "I wouldn't be talking to you now if I hadn't."

"Well you didn't hardly show it," Dylan said. "Not so that anyone would notice."

"Are you romantically interested in Stephanie then?" Cara inquired. Dylan sighed. "To be honest, I don't know what will happen with Steph," he said. "I expect she will eventually get back with Garry. However, if Garry gets seriously interested in Danielle – who knows? Stephanie might be available."

"That sounds suspiciously like a 'yes'," Cara observed.

Dylan shrugged. "Think what you like," he said. "It is not really your business."

They had almost circled the oval by this time. Cara hadn't exactly achieved what she had hoped, but at least she had tried to broach the subject. "I do care," she insisted. "As a friend."

"Perhaps," Dylan acknowledged grudgingly. He glanced at his watch.

"The cafeteria will be opening its doors by now," he said. "Let's go and get lunch. Is the air all clear now?"

Cara nodded, "Sure."

Monday morning Cara met Zack in the computer laboratory during her free period. It was surprising how similar their timetables were, given that he was a senior. However, the subjects all typically slotted into similar time-slots each year.

Following a vague memory of General Computing from her first year, Cara went to sit down at one of the personal computers, but Zack waved her over to one of the special terminals that could access the university mainframe. "We need the Internet," he said.

Cara obediently sat down and Zack indicated the box beside the computer. "That's a modem," he said.

"Umm," Cara murmured.

"Just make sure it's plugged in," Zack said. "You should be pretty right on this machine."

Zack switched the computer on and it began blinking and requesting a user name and password. "Unlike the personal computers where you log straight into the system, you have to identify yourself to the university mainframe," he explained. He consulted a folder next to the computer. "You are Cobrien@SSU.EDU.AU," he said.

"How did you get that?" Cara inquired.

"The university gave it to you." Zack said. Pointing at Cara's name on the list in the folder. "Just type Cobrien in the box. Careful - it is case sensitive."

Cara typed as she was instructed and pushed enter. "Now it wants a password," she complained.

"Your password should be your student number and birthdate

expressed as all numbers," Zack said. "When is your birthday?

"May 27," Cara said.

"Well type your student number, then 0527," Zack said. "The date is American style. There you are, we are in. I will write it down in case you forget. See number 1 on the menu is 'messages'. Type 1 and you will see."

"Hey I got a message," Cara exclaimed.

"That's probably the university administration welcoming you," Zack said. "Now try to send me a message. I am Znestor@SSU.EDU.AU. Put that in the address line."

"I want to message Kaleb," Cara objected impatiently.

"We need him to log on for that," Zack said. "Practice with me, I will get onto the next computer."

"I typed something," Cara said.

"Now push send," Zack instructed. "I got it. Watch for my reply."

"That's amazing," Cara exclaimed as a new message notification began flashing in her inbox. "Please find Kaleb."

"I will if I can," Zack said frowning. "What is his university?"

"Catholic University of America," Cara said.

"Is Kaleb Catholic?" Zack inquired in surprise.

"No," Cara replied. "He just said it was a good place to get a Christian education. What if they are not on this net thing?"

"They will be," Zack said. "The internet went global last year. Besides, the American Universities helped set it up. What is Kaleb's surname?" Zack asked.

"Proctor," Cara replied.

"Well if they are using the same protocol that we are he should be Kproctor@CUA.EDU," Zack guessed.

"I want to try to send a message," Cara exclaimed. "No looking." She typed a brief greeting and hope that they could correspond online more easily than by letter. Then she pushed the button. "It won't go," she said.

"What?" Zack exclaimed.

"I got an error message," Cara said. "Already!"

"Let me see," Zack said. "The Catholic University would not be CUA.EDU.AM. - just CUA.EDU."

"Why ever not?" Cara asked. "I thought I was doing the right thing adding a country abbreviation."

"Because the United States is the base of the internet and they get all the addresses with no extension," Zack explained.

"Okay," Cara said. "My message went this time."

"Kaleb might not log in and see it unless you write to him normal mail and tell him to look," Zack said. "Here, I'll write out the instructions and IT guys his end should be able to get him online."

"Thanks," Cara said. She raced back to her room and scribbled out a letter in the short space left before lunch. She paid for the quickest postage possible and dropped the letter in the post office box. Kaleb would know to check his email soon.

That afternoon in Agriculture, the students tended their seedlings, the majority of which had now germinated, and were beginning to grow into baby plants. Then they continued digging the trenches. By the time the class returned from the Easter break, which was admittedly quite short, the seedlings would be ready to transplant into the ground.

Tuesday afternoon in Chemistry the class moved onto enzymes, which were a type of protein of course. The first experiment involved precipitating casein from milk using an acid. Casein could also be coagulated from milk using the enzyme rennin, so the experiment was repeated using this method.

Then the Chemistry Doctor explained that both of the preceding processes could be used during the manufacture of cheese. The students also used the biuret test (also known as Piotrowski's test) to determine the presence of proteins in foods. When copper sulphate solution encountered substances with several peptide bonds, it turned from blue to purple.

Another experiment involved adding hydrogen peroxide to raw potato to observe the catalase reaction. The catalase would be denatured if the potato had been heated, so it was important the potato was uncooked.

After they had finished the practical experiments, the Chemistry Doctor instructed the students to go to the library straight away and look up the theory, so they did not find their practical reports impossible to write during the holidays.

Wednesday was the day of Phoebe's wedding. There were a few classes in the morning, but the students who were involved in the wedding only attended the most compulsory sessions.

Immediately after lunch, the two bridesmaids, Cara and Debbie began to do their hair and make-up. The university car had been booked to pick them up around two o'clock and take them across to the small church in Northcoast, where Phoebe was waiting nervously. The girls had chosen to dress in a side room of the church hall, so that Hank would not see the bride in her regalia before the wedding.

Phoebe's mother helped the girls into their long dresses, and Stephanie handed the girls bunches of lavender to carry. Bede fussed around adjusting their floral headdresses.

"I can't believe it is my wedding today," Phoebe exclaimed.

"You look absolutely stunning," Cara returned, giving her friend a hug.

"Mum will be pleased she can finally go home," Phoebe said. "Hank and I will be happy to have the house to ourselves too!"

"I'll bet," Debbie said. "Marriage will have other excitements as well."

Phoebe blushed. "We haven't yet, you know," she said. "With less than a year between going out and getting married, we didn't feel the need to rush the wedding night."

"I wasn't judging," Debbie said. "Even though I am going out with a Theology student and all that."

"The church looks beautiful," Phoebe said. "Mum has done such a good job."

"I hear music," Cara remarked.

"Joelle is playing already," Phoebe said. "Some guests must be arriving."

Phoebe's father stuck his head around the corner. "Is my beautiful daughter here?" he asked.

"Yes Dad," Phoebe said. "Is it time?"

"Almost darling, almost," Phoebe's Father said. "Hank is down the front, we are just waiting for the guests to be seated."

This was Stephanie and Bede's cue to leave the dressing room and join their dates inside the church. A few minutes later, Phoebe's Father stretched his arm out to his daughter, who grasped it hesitantly. The bridal party then crossed the church yard and assembled in the foyer.

Joelle commenced playing Pachelbel's *Canon in D*, which Phoebe had chosen as a processional. Cara followed Phoebe sedately down the aisle and took her place opposite one of Hank's cousins who was also the best man. Debbie was next and stood opposite David who was acting as a groomsman.

The beautiful words of the ceremony passed over them, and all too soon Phoebe and Hank were exiting the church to the sweet sound of Handel's *Arrival of the Queen of Sheba*. Then they stood on the steps of the church posing for numerous photographs.

After the formalities, the wedding party and guests sojourned to the church hall, where Damaris had set up a fantastic buffet style meal. This was ideal for a small wedding where the family and friends enjoyed doing a lot of mixing.

Cara was amused to see Michael in the church kitchen helping Damaris. "What would the men's liberationists say if they saw you now?" she teased.

"I'm working," Michael said. "Damaris is being paid to do this, as catering is her own little side business."

"Enterprise is much respected in Michael's family," Damaris said. "I'm glad I fit in that way."

"The food is good too," Michael said. "I'm going to marry this one so I can eat like this every day."

"Oh my," Stephanie exclaimed. "Talk about stealing Phoebe's thunder!"

"Whatever did I do?" Michel looked confused and innocent.

"Just announced your engagement to Damaris," Dylan said. "That is what has stirred the girls up!"

"No, no!" Damaris said soothingly. "Michael merely announced his intention to get engaged to me. We will let you know when it really happens. Some-time after the next holidays for sure."

"We will miss your large television in the boy's dormitory," Garry remarked.

"The wedding wouldn't be for six months or so," Michael said practically. "And I didn't know that my television was all you liked me for Garry!"

"Well, you have been much nicer since you learned to share," Dylan remarked. He had an arm around Stephanie, who was his date for the afternoon.

"Phoebe is going to throw her bouquet now," David announced. "And she and Hank will be leaving soon."

"Try to catch the bouquet Cara," Debbie joked. "You need a boyfriend who is not stuck overseas."

The next day was Maundy Thursday, and those students who had not already left for the Easter break, caught the university bus to Northcoast station. Nortcoast was a nodal point from where they could travel by bus or train to Brisbane and various other parts of Australia.

Cara and Bede caught the train to Brisbane and then flew to Melbourne, where their parents met them at the airport. The family then drove back to Geelong. The only thing Cara regretted was she didn't think she could check her email over the holiday break, and Kaleb wouldn't know which address to use for normal mail.

CHAPTER FOUR: A LOAD OF GARBAGE

Just over a week later, Cara and Bede bid their parents farewell and caught morning flights from Melbourne to Brisbane. At Brisbane airport, they caught up with Stephanie, who had just flown in from Adelaide. The girls all collected their bags and hurried to catch a connecting train to Northcoast.

The train pulled into Northcoast station and the girls climbed out. After a few minutes wait, the university bus appeared, driven by Luke. They threw their overnight bags into the bus, and Luke assisted with the larger cases. A few minutes later, the Greyhound bus arrived from Armidale and Kathy got off. The driver unloaded her luggage and handed it to Luke, who also stowed the cases away in the baggage compartment. Kathy climbed onto the bus and sat down next to Stephanie.

"Hello girls," Kathy said. "Did you enjoy your short break?"

"Yes Kathy," Cara, Bede and Stephanie chorused.

"It did seem extremely short," Stephanie added.

"Easter was early this year, so they gave us less time than usual I think," Kathy said. "Andrew barely had time to visit his parents, and did not come to stay with me at all these holidays."

"Never mind," Cara said. "You will see him all semester."

"Are you looking forward to the second half of the semester?" Kathy asked.

"Yeah, sort of," Cara said. "Our Education assignments will be due, and then there will be exams. Not my favourite things."

"I'm a bit behind on assignments this year," Stephanie said. "Because I spent the time making the bridesmaids dresses instead of studying."

"Bear in mind that behind for you is normal for everyone else," Kathy, who had been Stephanie's roommate the previous year, observed.

Stephanie shrugged, "I prefer not to be under pressure," she said. "However, we are lucky that Plant Biology and Agriculture are mostly completed on a weekly basis. What about you?"

"I love Art," Kathy said. "We are using oil paints this semester." She turned to Cara's little sister. "How about you Bede - Are you looking forward to seeing Arthur again?"

Bede hesitated. "Actually," she admitted. "I'm a little worried about Arthur."

"What about Arthur?" Stephanie inquired.

"You didn't tell me all holidays," Cara objected.

"I don't think he was happy when I did not take him to Phoebe's wedding," Bede said.

"I liked the fact that Phoebe's wedding was just family and close friends," Stephanie said.

Cara nodded. "No outside partners - it was like the old days."

"I have some idea what Arthur is like however," Stephanie said. "He does like things to be about him."

"You seemed to know how to manage him, Bede," Cara remarked. I'm sure it will be fine."

"Cook him some food like Damaris does Michael," Kathy suggested. "I half suspected that's what he was after with you."

Bede laughed. "That might make him too keen."

The bus arrived back at Silver Springs campus and the girls tumbled out. They began organising the transport of luggage to their various rooms.

After dropping her bags in the room, Cara ran to her student mail box. It contained a fat letter from Kaleb, who also assured her he had been connected with his university email system. When the computer room opened on Monday, she would be able to view his successful replies.

Monday breakfast time, Cara noticed a gold ring on Damaris' engagement finger. It was thick and almost as flat as a wedding band. However it was shaped with two grooves which made the ring appear almost like a set of three rings. A diamond was set into each band forming a seemingly random pattern. The diamonds were bezel set and well protected by metal of the band.

"So Michael did propose?" Cara asked.

Damaris laughed. "Yes," she said. "And this ring is solid enough to survive all my work in the cafeteria. I wear gloves a lot, and the low setting will not tear them."

"You are very lucky," Cara said. Despite its less than traditional styling, the gold band contained larger diamonds than most young girls could hope their boyfriends would buy for them.

"Michael's mother wanted a Tiffany style setting," Damaris continued, "But she came to like this one too."

"Well, it's not Michael's mother's ring," Cara observed. Dating someone from a more affluent family did appear to have some drawbacks, including continual input from future in-laws who held the purse strings, but Damaris seemed equipped to handle it.

Classes commenced again and during her free period, Cara struggled through Zack's instructions to sign into her university account and discover Kaleb's replies. Kaleb had even learned how to create an attachment and sent her a cute but pixilated image of a heart that she opened using a simple graphics program.

In the afternoon, the Agriculture class were excited to check their seedlings and find the small plants appeared almost strong enough to survive in the soil outside. The Agriculture Instructor said it was time to transplant the seedlings, so they selected the sturdiest to plant at intervals along the trenches they had dug.

Tuesday the Chemistry students handed in the practical reports they had struggled to complete over the holidays. Cara privately thought they ought to be congratulated for their dedication, but the Chemistry Doctor was too strict to give out such praise. Zack appeared pleased to see her in class and inquired whether Kaleb had managed to connect with email at his university.

Wednesday Cara was beginning to feel settled back at the university. Lunchtime as she sat with her friends, she noticed that Bede was once again sitting with her second year friends, and not Arthur Mason or any of his mates. Cara reflected that might be just as well. Arthur was not the man she would have chosen for her sister. She was not sure exactly who she would have chosen - just not Arthur.

Zack slid into the seat beside Cara. "How are you today?" he inquired.

"Good thanks Zack," Cara replied.

"Are you planning to come and watch basketball this evening?" he asked.

"I don't know," Cara said. "I'll see if I have time after doing research for my Education essay."

Zack turned to Garry: "How are you mate?" he asked.

"Good thank you Zack," Garry replied.

"I was hoping you might reconsider and come back to basketball," Zack said. "I need some steadier guys down there. I've had boys using 'four letter words' to me and disputing perfectly reasonable instructions!"

"That is unusual," Garry said. "Silver Springs University basketball is usually very fair."

"No kidding!" Zack laughed. "Playing well has traditionally been a badge of honour on campus. Now the guys are getting aggressive. It's not just my team, I've had a chat to a few of the other captains."

"I might come down and check it out," Garry said.

"It almost sounds like something I would prefer not to see," Cara murmured.

"It's not too shocking for a lady down there yet," Zack said. "You have to trust me, Cara O'B!"

Cara laughed as she always did when Zack made silly rhymes out of her name. "To tell the truth," she said, "My roommate is not so fond of the gymnasium at the moment."

"Because of Bradley?" Zack inquired, and Cara nodded. "I miss him around the gym too. He would have been someone to share the load with about these guys. It is like the Tony Dantean thing again - except some of these guys have no history of misdemeanors."

"I think Bradley hated having to discipline Tony," Cara murmured.

"As I hate disciplining these guys," Zack agreed. "In fact, I'm trying to mentor them in the hopes it won't require actual discipline."

"Speaking of Tony," Cara said. "Did you ever speak to the police about him having a grievance against Bradley?"

Zack smacked his head. "Oh no, I forgot. I won't be in trouble or anything will I? For obstructing justice?"

"I shouldn't think so," Cara said. "After all we don't really know whether the two matters are related."

"Are the police still investigating?" Zack asked.

"Stephanie hasn't mentioned anything about them closing the case," Cara said.

"I will make the call this afternoon before I forget again," Zack said.

Thursday afternoon, the Plant Biology class had another excursion. This one had a surprising destination - the Art Gallery in Brisbane. Its collection of early colonial paintings demonstrated several phenomena the Biology Master wished to show the students.

The first was the erroneous impressions colonial artists had created of Australian bushlands. They were used to trees with European leaves, and although they could clearly see the difference in Australia plants, their artistic technique could not accommodate the reality of leaves which hung differently. Only Indigenous Australian artists like Namatjira had been able to represent the Australia bush without the misleading overlay of European technique.

Other things the students were required to observe were the changes in the environment as extensive clearing had occurred in the first years of European occupation. A few artists had also collected botanical sketches of the plants species encountered in the early days of settlement. Wildflower painting had been a popular hobby during the Victorian period and some beautiful specimens had been drawn in early sketchbooks.

Friday after lunch, Cara was just donning her coveralls to go and do her mowing before the weekend when there was a soft knock at the door. It was her sister Bede, and she was in tears. Cara abandoned her plans, figuring that she could mow on the weekend.

"Whatever is the matter?" Cara exclaimed, drawing her sister into the room.

"It is Arthur and his mates," Bede said. "They laugh whenever I walk past."

"That doesn't sound so bad," Cara said.

"I'm sure they are laughing at me," Bede said.

"Are you sure you are not imagining it?" Cara asked. "I know in our teens it is common to imagine everyone is talking about us."

Stephanie, who was studying on the other side of the room, looked up from her text books. "I'm sure Bede is over that sort of thing by now," she said. "Are these funny fake laughs?"

""'Yes," Bede sniffed.

"Which boys?" Stephanie asked.

"Arthur, Tony and Vincent," Bede said. "A few boys from my year are copying them too."

"They did that to me once too," Stephanie said. "I take it you haven't made up with Arthur?"

"No," Bede admitted. "He won't say, but I think he is still mad about Phoebe's wedding."

"Phoebe's wedding was invitation only," Cara said. "You couldn't take Arthur without Phoebe's permission."

"I guess he thought we were a regular couple," Bede said. "I don't know."

"You had only been out a handful of times," Stephanie said.

"That's the way I saw it too," Bede agreed.

"But Arthur could have become fond of you," Cara said. "You are pretty - even though you are my sister! And I saw a little of your management technique, which involved a bit of flattery. He probably got the wrong idea about where he stood with you."

"That doesn't make it Bede's fault however," Stephanie pointed out. "Arthur ought to be responsible for his own actions."

"I didn't mean to blame Bede," Cara said. "There is never any excuse for harassment."

"How did you deal with it when it happened to you, Stephanie?" Bede inquired.

"I had a bit of support from the decent guys," Stephanie said. "Guys who did not approve of passive-aggressive persecution tactics."

Cara nodded. "You see us hang around with guys a lot, but the guys in our group are all carefully chosen. They are above practicing any immature chauvinism."

"The guys in my class are a bit immature," Bede said. "That's why I thought Arthur... being a third year... would be better."

"There must be a few nice boys," Stephanie said.

"I don't want to hide behind any guy," Bede stipulated. "I'm not weak."

"I didn't mean anything like that," Stephanie said. "Just that the social system around here is a little male dominated. Having a few guys in your friendship group helps shut the silly boys down. My roommate's boyfriend was great, and it was a while after that I found Garry."

"Why ever did you and Garry break up - was it because you liked Bradley?" Bede asked.

"Remember Garry left university for a semester last year and went to Wollongong University?" Stephanie answered. "He broke up with me because he was worried about his mother's illness and thought he would be away much longer. Bradley was a friend to both of us."

"I liked Bradley," Bede said.

"I think everybody liked Bradley," Stephanie sighed. "That's why his death was such a shock. I miss him every day."

"Strangely, Arthur didn't like Bradley," Bede said. "He said Bradley was all right, but interfered where he wasn't wanted."

"I wonder what that was about?" Cara said. "The basketball committee?"

"I got the impression it was something in the boy's dormitory," Bede said. "Bradley worked as the downstairs cleaner didn't he? He would have seen what went on – wouldn't he?"

"Yeah," Stephanie said. "If you think you know something, and it's not just hearsay - please go to the police. It's no good telling me. And speaking of cleaning, I need to vacuum the women's assembly area before vespers this evening!"

"Okay, I'll see you later," Bede said. "Thank you for the chat."

At the Uniting Church vespers that evening, Cara noted that Bede was seated amongst a group of second year students and well away from the third year boys. The gathering enjoyed the short talk which was delivered by Debbie's boyfriend David. David was always bright and positive in tone and his theological content was well researched.

Everything ran smoothly until after the programme, when Dylan and Zack offered to walk Cara and Stephanie back to the front door of the girls dormitory. As they strolled along chatting idly, the foursome happened to pass Tony Dantean, Arthur Mason and Vincent Wilson, who were loitering near the steps leading up to the women's residence. The boys had not been able to corner Bede that evening, and were looking for someone else to harass.

"Hey Dylan," Arthur Mason called out mockingly. "Are you getting any action from Bradley Parker's widow?"

"What?" Dylan almost exploded.

"Move along," Zack advised, tight lipped. "These are some of the guys I told you were being disruptive in the gymnasium."

Dylan pulled Stephanie closer to him and kept walking. Tony Dantean leered, but he seemed to be leaving the bulk of the dirty work to Arthur.

This was strange, as Tony was typically vocal whenever there was a chance to harass anyone. The bully had been subdued lately, almost as if he were trying to maintain a low profile, but could not quite succeed. The third guy, Vincent seemed somewhat conflicted, although he was following the other youths' example.

"They say that bereaved women can be quite eager in their grief," Arthur muttered suggestively from a safe distance.

"I wonder what it feels like to be a proxy," Tony added in a low but penetrating voice. "I guess it doesn't matter so long as you get some."

Dylan's face was thunderous, and it was only with the greatest of effort that he continued walking. "It is my reputation too," he whispered to Stephanie.

"Shut up guys," Michael said. He was also walking by on his way back to boy's dorm, and noticed the others standing there, looking for trouble. "Don't you have anything better to think about than other people's love lives?"

"Aww - are you joining the weaklings now too, Michael?" Vincent said. "I thought you were one of the men's rights group?"

"What's wrong, Michael?" Arthur jeered. "Too hen-pecked by Damaris to have a bit of a laugh?"

"I'm not hen-pecked - I'm content," Michael said comfortably to his former mates. "Which is more than I can say about you guys. So you didn't score with Bede Arthur, there are plenty more fish in the sea."

"He is right you know, Arthur," Tony Dantean added unexpectedly. "Bede O'Brien isn't worth the fuss, and all you are doing is drawing attention to yourself."

"We don't need to keep our heads down like you," Arthur said somewhat threateningly to Tony.

"Hush," Tony replied. "Whatever made you think I needed to hide?"

"Well – you never know," Arthur said. "There's plenty that could come back to haunt you. You ain't been no angel Tony."

The obnoxious guys appeared to be inclined to argue amongst themselves, and the friends took the opportunity to gain the safety of the girl's dormitory. They stepped into the lighted foyer and the wooden door closed securely behind them. Zack and Dylan immediately turned to their female companions.

"Don't take any notice of them," Zack said. "They are just looking for trouble as usual."

Stephanie was white and shaken. "I know those guys are just nasty," she said. "But don't you think they have a point?"

"What point?" Dylan asked. "Other than their implication I can't get a girl the normal way?" He appeared genuinely puzzled.

"People are beginning to notice that I am spending all my time with you," Stephanie said. "I thought there was no harm in it, but now there is gossip."

"Stephanie please," Dylan begged. He was holding her hands and facing the girl.

"I appreciate everything you have done the past few months," Stephanie said. "But I think we had better both go to the next university function with other people."

"At least promise me you will go with Garry," Dylan begged.

"People would talk about that worse," Stephanie said. "I will find someone nice amongst our friends. You should too Dylan."

Stephanie turned and walked into the restricted area of the girl's dormitory and down the short staircase to the basement. Dylan stood watching her back helplessly. Cara touched his shoulder soothingly.

"Stephanie will work it out," Cara said soothingly. "She always does."

"I could take Stephanie to the next dinner if that helps any," Zack offered sheepishly. "I think she's a nice girl and you are always reminding me that you have a boyfriend in America, Cara O'B."

"You had better ask her yourself Zack," Cara advised. "I don't think Stephanie is in the mood to be matched up by the rest of us."

"I understand," Zack said.

"I will just have to see whether Danielle is seriously interested in Garry or not," Dylan said. "Maybe she'd be happy to go out with me, as I'm her classmate too."

"Stranger things have happened," Cara agreed in a tight voice. "I will say good night to you guys then. Have a good sleep."

She couldn't help notice that neither guy was rushing to ask her out, and both were intensely protective of Stephanie. Then she reminded herself that she had Kaleb. He was way over in America be sure, but he was still officially her boyfriend. Long distance relationships had their frustrations.

Saturday morning at breakfast, Cara noticed that Dylan was chatting to Danielle, and left the table looking pleased with himself. She interpreted that to mean that Danielle and Garry had been 'just friends' after all, and the girl was happy to go to the next university social event with Dylan.

After breakfast, Cara consulted the Adventure Club timetable. The Adventure Club events were additional to the university social calendar, and did not require a date to take along. The other great thing about the Adventure Club was that bus transport was provided and she did not need to worry about whether she could fit into Dylan's light jeep.

It so happened that the Adventure Club were going canoeing at nearby Lake Macdonald that afternoon. Cara crossed the corridor and knocked on the door of the next room, seeking some company. She found that Luke and Tess were already going, as Luke was booked to drive the bus.

Debbie and David had their own plans, but Joelle surprised Cara by suggesting that her boyfriend, Tom, might like the company. The musician placed a call through to boy's dorm using the internal phone, and clearly received a positive response.

"Tom said he would meet you at the bus," Joelle reported back to Cara. "I have to practice the organ for Sunday, so he was going to be alone for the afternoon. He said to thank you for the invite!"

Cara nodded happily. Most of the canoes were built for two, so it was good to be taking a friend along to help with the rowing. "Thanks Joelle," she said. "I'm glad you are cool with it."

Lake Macdonald had started life as a small natural waterway, but the Six Mile Creek Dam had been built in 1965 to enable it to store drinking water. The wall was raised again in 1980 to increase its capacity. The dam was ungated and when the lake exceeded its volume, water flowed down the spillway in a spectacular torrent.

Rowing, fishing and picnicking were allowed at the nearby lake. However, smelly petrol engines, unrestrained dogs, and swimming and were forbidden to maintain the cleanliness of the water. Littering was a serious offence because it could spoil the environment and contaminate the water.

When they arrived at Lake Macdonald, the lake was full due to the autumn rains. However, the spillway was not flowing and the Adventure Club organisers judged it was safe for the canoes, if the paddlers watched out for submerged branches near the edges.

Tom cheerfully hauled out one of the newer canoes which were more comfortable to sit in.

"Thanks for asking me," he said to Cara.

"That's fine," Cara said. "Feel free to hang with us anytime Joelle is busy."

"Oh – I couldn't," Tom said. "She is busy far too often."

"My boyfriend is in America," Cara said. "That leaves me alone a lot too."

"I don't think that is by personal choice is it?" Tom observed.

"No," Cara agreed. "It's simply where he came from. I thought it was so exciting when we got together last year!"

"And now?" Tom queried.

"It's not so much fun while he is away," Cara said. She decided to change the topic, because the conversation was getting a little personal. "It's beautiful out here isn't it?"

"Yes," Tom agreed.

"I love the shape of the lake, with all the inlets and islands," Cara continued.

"Well let's not go too far and get lost," Tom said. "I wouldn't want to get tired arms and get stuck out there."

"I'm sure the bus wouldn't leave us behind," Cara observed. "But it would be embarrassing to be the subject of a search and rescue."

"Speaking of tired arms," Tom said. "What do you think we will do in Agriculture now that the seedlings are planted? They won't need a lot of care."

"Umm, water, fertiliser, pest control?" Cara suggested.

"For three and a half hours every Monday?" Tom exclaimed.

"I don't know," Cara said. "There will have to be something to do while the plants grow. Maybe plant other plants?"

"It will be interesting to see," Tom said. "I'm enjoying the subject as a change, aren't you?"

"Oh yes," Cara said. "Not so much of a change for me, as I have two other practical subjects, but it's good." She held up her hand. "Shush."

"What?" Tom inquired in a low voice.

"Let the canoe float for a while," Cara whispered. "See those birds over there?"

"Do you think they'll come any closer?" Tom asked.

"If they forget we are here they might," Cara whispered. "I've heard this area is great for birds."

"What are they?" Tom inquired. "Do you know?"

"I think they might be wandering whistling ducks," Cara whispered. "See their pinkish brown undersides?"

"How can they wade in the water like that?" Tom asked.

"Long legs I think," Cara observed.

"There's a bird on the lake's edge, in the grass too," Tom whispered.

"I think it's a buff banded rail," Cara said. "But I would need a better view."

"Do you want to move the canoe?" Tom offered.

"No let's stay here," Cara said. "See those funny birds with their tails in the air and beaks in the water? I think they are magpie geese."

"I see the black and white markings," Tom exclaimed. "I also see some ducks and a swan."

"I could float here and watch the birds all day," Cara sighed.

"Feel free," Tom answered. "I don't have any other plans."

It was beautiful and relaxing floating on the lake, but later in the afternoon a cool breeze came up, so Cara and Tom decided to row for the shore.

They met Dylan and Garry on the grass and the boys said, "Hello" to Tom.

"Good to see you out here mate," Dylan said.

"Yeah I like to get out a bit and Joelle is always practicing," Tom said.

"There is always something happening with the Adventure Club," Garry replied. "You are welcome anytime. Maybe you should consider joining up.”

“I might just at that!” Tom said with a grin.

Sunday, Stephanie and Cara attended both the Inter-denominational praise service and then the Reform Church service with Kathy and Andrew. The innocuous company was part of Stephanie’s plan to ensure the gossip about her and Dylan to die down.

Stephanie was something of a veteran at dealing with unpleasant gossip from her first year at Silver Springs University when Jeffrey Mannington had employed the gossip mongers to manipulate the university social situations to his advantage.

Zack slid into the seat beside Cara. “I’m missing hanging with ye, Cara O’B,” he whined.

Cara looked amused, “You can still hang out with us Zack,” she said. “It’s only Dylan we are avoiding.”

Kathy looked surprised. “What’s up with Dylan?”

“Least said, soonest mended,” Stephanie responded shortly. “Dylan has been so kind to me since Bradley’s death that some guys have made inappropriate remarks about our friendship.”

“Which guys?” Andrew inquired.

“Vincent and Arthur,” Cara replied.

“And Tony Dantean?” Kathy asked.

“Not so much Tony this time,” Cara observed. “But a bit. You know what he is like.”

“Whoever spreads slander is a fool,” Andrew said. “Proverbs 10, verse 18.”

“I thought they were jerks,” Zack said. “You should forget them Stephanie.”

“I intend to,” Stephanie said. “But I also mean to make sure they forget me. If I aren't seen anywhere with Dylan, for a while, they can't possibly talk about us."

"Well, Stephanie," Zack said. "I think I can help. Since you said you and Dylan ought to go to the next function with other people – would you like to come to the Autumn Feast with me next weekend?"

"Do you understand I am not looking for a new boyfriend yet?" Stephanie began. "Bradley was only killed last November,"

Zack flushed, but he nodded. "I understand," he said. "But you have got to start going out again sometime."

"Can you imagine what Arthur and Vincent might say about the next guy I go to something with?" Stephanie asked.

"I can only guess," Zack said. "I'm an A grade basketball captain like Bradley was too – that might well come into it. Some of them already have something against me as I'm coaching them on the court. But really they have no right!"

"If you have thought things through then," Stephanie said. "The answer is yes!"

Kathy gave a little cheer.

"That just leaves me to find a date," Cara muttered under her breath, but nobody was listening.

Monday in Agriculture, the Agriculture Instructor announced he was going to teach them how to make mulch so they could enrich the soil for their baby plants. Cara was pleased when Garry offered to help her mix her mulch.

"I thought I would let Danielle and Dylan work together," Garry said.

"For a while there we thought you and Danielle were going to make a couple," Cara said. "You did hang out a lot."

"I found I wasn't ready for a new girlfriend," Garry admitted. "I was almost relieved when Dylan asked Danielle out. This is her last year, so she is looking to get serious."

"I don't want to see Dylan hurt again," Cara muttered stubbornly.

"Perhaps you could tell him that sometime," Garry suggested.

"I tried just before Easter," Cara said. "It didn't work."

"These things happen in their own time," Garry observed. "Anyway, I've asked Bede to the Autumn Feast."

"My sister Bede?" Cara was truly amazed.

"Stephanie told me that Bede was being harassed by those guys Arthur and Vincent too," Garry said. "It might not be appropriate for me to help Stephanie at the moment, but I can do something for Bede."

"At least you and Stephanie are talking again," Cara said. "That's one good thing has come out of it."

"We are talking – discretely," Garry said.

"I maybe ought to warn you though, Bede does like older guys," Cara said. "Sometime, I think nothing would please her better than to steal one of my male friends."

"Better look to Kaleb then," Garry remarked.

"What?" Cara exclaimed.

"I was joking," Garry said. "But seriously, if you two have a sibling rivalry thing going and she likes your boyfriends, then wouldn't be Arthur, me, or even Dylan in her sights – it would be Kaleb."

"Kaleb is not even in Australia," Cara said.

"Are you two still writing regularly?" Garry said.

"Zack showed me how to use email – it's easier," Cara said.

"A bit less romantic in my book," Garry observed. "Easy to delete, hard to fold up in a drawer and read whenever you are missing your girl."

"Oh okay!" Cara laughed. "I know you and Stephanie wrote one summer. I don't need any more details."

Tuesday Cara was eating lunch with Tom and Joelle. Joelle excused herself and hurried away to practice one of the instruments she continually laboured to master. Tom remained at the table eating and chatting to Cara and Elisabet about their Agriculture class.

"Mulching is the first time I've ever been required to make anything go rotten," he joked regarding the compost.

"Yeah," Cara agreed absently. "Tom can I ask you something?" "Sure," Tom said. "As long as it won't hurt Joelle, I would never do that!"

Cara laughed. "No it's nothing suss. It's just – my boyfriend Kaleb is in America and my classmates, whom I thought I could rely on, have other things on their minds."

"I take it you mean Dylan and Garry," Tom observed. "Asking other girls out is sort of understandable, you know."

"I know," Cara sighed. "But who else would be available - you know for the Autumn Feast?"

"Well," Tom said thoughtfully, "There is Joelle's friend Craig, who plays the violin and sings. You wouldn't want to rush him though. He seems reserved around girls, other than Elisabet, whom he is coaching with her music. In fact, some of the guys have been teasing him about being gay."

"Do you think he is gay?" Cara asked. "He is very good looking and artistic."

"In Christian circles, it isn't really something you can discuss," Tom said carefully. "He went out with Joelle once and I believe the date was a success, although it didn't become a relationship. They have been friends ever since."

"Which guys are teasing him?" Cara asked.

"Arthur Mason, Vincent and Tony," Tom said.

"Those guys are so mean, they would tease a guy about being different in any way," Cara observed.

"That's about how I see it too," Tom said. "Craig's a great guy and although he hangs more with Joelle than me, I consider him a friend."

"Could you put in a good word for me?" Cara asked. "I just want someone as a friend. Maybe we could make a foursome with you and Joelle."

"That sounds rather like fun," Tom said. "I will see what Craig says."

"Thanks Tom," Cara said. "I had better get ready for my Chemistry lab now."

Wednesday afternoon was sunny and Cara decided that the lawns could use a good mow. She was enjoying riding up and down the slopes at the rear of the buildings and watching the mower systematically clear strips; and had just pulled level with the rear of the music building when Craig came out, carrying his violin case in his hand. Cara cut the throttle to the mower and drew to a halt. She removed her protective hat so that Craig could recognize her.

"Cara O'Brien?" Craig said, approaching the mower. "Who would believe that was you?"

"Yeah, it's not my prettiest look!" Cara agreed.

Craig laughed nervously. "It looks fine to me. Not your typical female but fine."

"Thanks," Cara said.

"Tom said you wanted to go to the Autumn Feast?" Craig hesitated.

"Yes, just as a friend," Cara said. "Because I have a boyfriend in America."

"Did Tom say anything else?" Craig inquired.

It was Cara's turn to hesitate. "Only that you were being teased by the same guys who are teasing my roommate about being a desperate widow, and laughing at my little sister behind her back," she returned frankly. "Those guys are not worth worrying about."

"I don't worry about them," Craig explained. "I'm completely dedicated to my violin. And the only girls I've gone out with are girls I've got to know in the Music department."

"I've mostly hung out with the guys from my science classes," Cara admitted. "Except Kaleb, and I got to know him in prayer group."

"I'm wondering what we would talk about," Craig began awkwardly.

Cara flinched. "Are you turning me down?"

"Not exactly," Craig said. "I just wondered what you would expect from the evening."

"I remember last year when you performed the solos in *The Messiah*," Cara said. "I thought you were amazingly talented. I'm friends with Joelle and I know how hard she has to practice for every worship she accompanies. I don't have a musical bone in my body, but I can appreciate talent and effort."

Craig blushed. "I will see you Sunday night then!" he said. "I just wasn't prepared for an awkward blind date."

"Nor was I," Cara admitted. "I'm glad you broke the ice."

Craig continued on his way to the boy's dormitory and Cara activated the mower engine once again. She continued mowing her way across the rear section of campus, until all the lawn was neat and clear. Then she rode the mower across to the tool shed. Cara was disgusted to find another black bag of garbage stashed in the hedge near the tool shed. Once again, she threw the garbage into the skip and then continued to stow the mower inside the toolshed, locking it securely behind her.

"The students should know better than that!" Cara muttered under her breath and set off to report to her supervisor.

Down at the student services office, Cara notified the employment programme supervisor that she had twice found garbage dumped in the area to the rear of the tool shed. The work supervisor looked puzzled.

"There are bins in all the dorms," the Work Supervisor exclaimed. "I can't see why the students would dump rubbish at the back of campus."

"Can we make some sort of announcement reminding all students and staff of the correct garbage disposal procedures?" Cara suggested patiently.

"I'll get a notice posted in the campus newsletter and make announcements at assembly," the Work Supervisor said. "This reminds me of something that happened last year – Bradley Parker was complaining about rubbish being left in the boy's laundry. But we got that all cleared up."

"Unless the culprit just shifted to dumping around the grounds instead," Cara suggested.

"I doubt it is related," the Work Supervisor said. "But why would someone not simply put their garbage into the bins provided?"

"Perhaps it is not students," Cara suggested.

"Community persons using campus as a dump do you mean?" the Work Supervisor inquired.

Cara nodded: "A householder exceeding their weekly limit, perhaps."

"You would think the security cameras would record vehicles not registered with the university entering and exiting campus," the Work Supervisor mused. "I will ask around the office."

Cara thanked her supervisor and went up to girl's dormitory to shower before going to tea in the cafeteria. Stephanie was in their room with her head stuck in her books, completing her assignments.

"How did your work go?" Stephanie asked.

"All right," Cara said. "I ran into Craig and we are going to the

Autumn Feast together."

"That sounds good," Stephanie said. "Joelle always said Craig was a great guy."

"Do you know why Joelle never commenced a relationship with Craig?" Cara asked.

"I think because she met Milton," Stephanie said. "And then Tom. Nothing wrong with Craig, although he is artistic and a lot of girls prefer the sporty guys."

"I'm not stealing him from Elisabet - am I?" Cara looked alarmed, remembering that the two appeared to hang out a bit.

"I think Elisabet has a date with Arthur Mason," Stephanie said.

"Arthur?" Cara was surprised.

"Knowing Elisabet." Stephanie explained, "She will insist on Arthur being on his best behavior. With her blonde hair and lovely clothes – she is always being asked out."

"You are currently on your second basketball captain," Cara teased gently. "Not to count Garry, who was a good player too."

"Ha, ha," Stephanie returned. "So I'm a basketball groupie."

"I'm glad you can joke again," Cara mused. "There is something weird though... twice I've found rubbish dumped around the grounds."

"You mean cans and things – like litter?" Stephanie inquired.

"No, this was wrapped and bagged," Cara explained. "Who would do that?"

"Unless the garbage contains something it shouldn't," Stephanie suggested.

"Like what?" Cara inquired.

"Umm empty beer cans, cigarette boxes or *Playboy* magazines," Stephanie said. "They are all contraband on campus, and the tool shed is nearer boy's dorm than here."

"I didn't look inside the bag," Cara said.

"Why not?" Stephanie asked.

"I thought it might be stinky!" Cara exclaimed.

"Yuk. What did you do with it then?" Stephanie inquired.

"Threw it in the large skip, and I would never be able to tell which bag it was now," Cara pronounced.

"Of course not," Stephanie agreed. "Maybe look inside the bag another time, if it keeps happening."

"Did you know Bradley reported the same problem with finding rubbish in the boy's laundry?" Cara asked.

Stephanie shook her head. "Bradley wouldn't have bothered me with something like that. He was pretty relaxed. But he did tell me that the guys sometimes got up to things they shouldn't."

"Do you mean Arthur, Vincent and Tony?" Cara asked.

Stephanie shrugged. "Bradley wouldn't name names, and I didn't assume anything."

CHAPTER FIVE: A BLAST FROM THE PAST

Thursday morning during her free period, Cara dropped by the computer laboratory to check her email and read the latest news from Kaleb. Unfortunately, she was unable to log onto either of the mainframe terminals, because there was a tall, tousle-headed man in a suit fiddling with the computers.

"Hello young Cara," the Computer Technician drawled.

Cara was startled and took a second look. Although the technician was no longer as young in appearance as the current students, he was vaguely familiar. The fellow had filled out around the waist since graduation, but he was not really fat, just a little unfit.

"Jeffrey Mannington!" Cara exclaimed. "Whatever are you doing here?"

"The company I work for in Brisbane has sent me to fulfill their maintenance contract with Silver Springs University," Jeff said. "I will be around here for a few days."

"Oh okay," Cara said. "It's nice to see you again Jeff." The last statement was not particularly true, but sometimes common courtesy required the use of a little white lie. "I must let you get back to work."

Cara hurried to the library where she knew she would find Stephanie. "Guess who is on campus?" she said.

"I dunno," Stephanie said. "Bob Hawke?"

"Not the prime minister silly," Cara giggled.

"Paul Keating then," Stephanie said, naming the controversial federal treasurer.

"No," Cara said. "It's Jeffrey Mannington."

"Oh what's he doing?" Stephanie inquired.

"Fixing the computers," Cara said. "He said he would be around for a few days."

"Good thing we have a Plant Biology Excursion this afternoon then," Stephanie said. "We will be off campus."

"What about lunch in the cafeteria?" Cara exclaimed.

"I will just have to deal with it," Stephanie said.

"Do you want Dylan or Garry to go to the café with us?" Cara inquired.

"No I better deal with this myself," Stephanie said. "No hiding behind any of the guys. You saw where that got me!" She glanced at her watch. "It's time for the cafeteria to open now. Are you coming?"

Sure enough at lunch, Stephanie and Cara had barely settled at a table, when Jeffrey Mannington walked in with his long-time friend Tony Dantean. Tony and Jeffrey conferred for a moment, and then Tony slunk off to sit with Arthur and Vincent. Jeff glanced around the cafeteria and his gaze rested upon Stephanie, who was seated between Cara and Michael. He crossed the cafeteria and addressed Michael, who had been a marginal member of Jeff's group in his student days.

"Hello mate," Jeff said, putting his tray down. "I heard you got engaged."

"Hello Jeff," Michael replied. "Yes, the lovely lady is Damaris who is responsible for most of this food."

"I hope it tastes a little better than in the old days," Jeff remarked.

"I expect it is better with Damaris cooking," Michael said. "I also don't remember you as having much of an appetite."

"Some days I didn't," Jeff replied. "It depended on what was on offer." The computer technician turned casually, as if only just noticing Stephanie.

"Hello Stephanie," Jeff said. "It's been a while."

"Hello Jeff," Stephanie replied with an expressionless tone. "How are you?"

"I am good thank you," Jeff said. "I was sorry to hear about Bradley Parker's death."

"Were you?" Stephanie sighed.

"Of course," Jeff continued. "Such a senseless tragedy."

"I have to agree with you there," Stephanie said.

"How have you been holding up since?" Jeff asked with mock concern.

"The best I can Jeff," Stephanie said. "The best I can."

Jeff put a hand on Stephanie's arm. "If you ever need anything, you know I am only as far away as Brisbane."

"I won't need anything Jeff," Stephanie said, attempting to shrug his arm off, but Jeffrey was persistent.

"I hear there is an Autumn Feast this weekend," Jeff continued. "I will be around if you need some company, while the others are out celebrating."

"I have a date thank you Jeff," Stephanie said.

Jeff looked surprised. "So soon after Bradley's death? It isn't Dylan Perret is it?" He asked. "I heard he was hanging around you like a vulture."

"It is not Dylan," Stephanie said. "And the rest really is not your business."

"I wonder how appropriate it is for you Jeff, practically a staff member, to be coming on to a student," Cara murmured.

Jeff looked innocent. "None of you are children anymore, Cara O'Brien," he said. "And I was also a student here two years ago."

Stephanie rose to her feet. "I have finished my meal," she announced. "Thank you for your kind offer Jeff, but like I said, I am doing as well as I can."

As Stephanie returned her tray to the dishwashing trolley, Kathy and Andrew fell into step beside her.

"Let us walk you back to the girl's dormitory," Kathy whispered discretely. Stephanie nodded.

Cara turned to Jeff: "I have a date for the Autumn Feast too," she announced cheekily. "Thank you for your concern Jeff. I expect Damaris will be outdoing herself with the eats – eh Michael?"

"Oh yes," Michael exclaimed enthusiastically. "All pumpkin pie and scones, and traditional North American Thanksgiving fare." He turned to Jeff enthusiastically. "Say mate, you should find someone your own age and come along too."

Jeff appeared immune to the insult, which Michael had not intended as such anyway. "What a good idea," he exclaimed. "I might just do that!"

"Good luck with that!" Cara said and in turn, made her escape.

In plant Biology that afternoon the class went to visit the orchid association and marvel at the huge range of flower shapes. The president of the association gave them a tour of his greenhouse, and a talk on the special qualities of the orchid flowers.

As was quite often the case, the class returned late from the excursion and had tea alone in the cafeteria. The news had spread that Stephanie's dodgy ex-boyfriend Jeffrey Mannington was on campus, and both Dylan and Garry offered their support.

Stephanie assured the boys she would rather manage on her own during this visit, although she did beg Dylan to check that Zack was still intending to take her to the Autumn Feast.

"If Zack isn't up to the heat, I won't blame him," Stephanie said. "But I would still like to go with him if I can."

"Don't worry," Dylan said. "Zack seemed pretty keen the last time I spoke to him. And the bro-code is unlikely to allow him to let you down."

"We are third years now and no one is afraid of Mannington," Garry observed.

"I sincerely hope not!" Cara reflected.

"You never were afraid," Stephanie said with a faint smile toward Garry. "That was one thing I really appreciated about you."

"I'm not familiar with all the back story," Danielle said. "But Mannington graduated a couple of years ago and has considerably fewer friends on campus than he used to have. I don't think you have to worry."

Friday April 25 was actually ANZAC day off campus, which was a public holiday designed to commemorate the deaths of thousands of allied soldiers at Gallipoli. However, Silver Springs University was indifferent to outside holidays and classes carried on as usual. There was also a strong pacifist philosophy in the Reform Church which forbade even the most respectful commemoration of war.

At tea time Zach burst into the cafeteria looking absolutely furious. "Do you know what that Jeffrey Mannington did?" he exclaimed. "I had the computer programmed to run and print my Physics simulations, when he suddenly shut the system down. Everyone knows that you make an announcement before shutting down, so all the users can back up their work!"

"I'm sorry to hear that," Cara murmured.

"I lost hours of work," Zack continued. "And if I didn't know it would be ridiculous, I would swear he did it on purpose!"

"I hope he didn't," Cara said. "But it sounds a bit like Jeffrey Mannington."

Zack turned to her in surprise. "What do you mean?"

"Jeff is Stephanie's ex-boyfriend," Dylan explained. "He has been known to do some weird things."

"What would he have against me?" Zack inquired.

"Are you still taking Stephanie to the Autumn Feast?" Garry asked.

"Of course," Zack asserted. "I wouldn't give up a date with a fox like Stephanie just because some former boyfriend started hanging around."

"So that might be Jeff's problem with you," Dylan suggested.

"How would he even know Stephanie and I were going together?" Zack demanded. "We haven't exactly publicized it."

"Michael might have access to the seating plan through Damaris," Garry said.

"But Michael is one of the good guys," Zack exclaimed. "He has been ever since last year, when Bradley began to coach him at basketball."

"Michael would just be caught in the middle," Stephanie, who had been sitting quietly, murmured. "Don't blame him, Jeffrey's source of power was always gossip and information. I'm so sorry Zack."

"It's not your fault Stephanie," Zack said. "Don't worry about it. But it makes me wonder what comes next."

"What do you mean?" Cara asked.

"Poor Bradley Parker was hit by a truck," Zack speculated. "Now you are telling me this guy is full of weird malice towards anyone around you." The loss of hours' worth of code had clearly made Zack overwrought and incautious. Stephanie gasped, and all the cheerful chatter around the cafeteria somehow died down to a whimper. Zack felt a presence behind him and swiveled around to face Jeffrey Mannington.

"I can establish my whereabouts for the period of time before Bradley Parker's death, if anyone wants to know," Jeffrey said. "I went to New South Wales on Thursday afternoon to visit my family. A dozen of my relatives can swear that I didn't return to Queensland until Sunday."

"Why did you turn the computer off on me this afternoon Mannington?" Zack demanded. "I lost all my data."

Jeff shrugged. "Just doing my, job Zackary Nestor," he drawled casually. "I'm here to tune up the programming on the mainframe."

"Why didn't you make an announcement over the public address system like the maintenance guys usually do?" Zack demanded.

"I knew that the administration computer had finished backing up, and I wasn't to know that you were doing anything important, was I?" Jeff drawled insolently.

"And why are you eating in the student cafeteria instead of the staff room like the rest of the faculty?" Zack demanded hotly.

Jeff looked innocent once again. "I've got to eat somewhere," he drawled. "Bless me - I somehow forgot to pack my lunch."

A selection of titters ran around the cafeteria. Mostly from first year students who had little idea what the confrontation was about. Jeff crossed the cafeteria to where Arthur and Vincent were sitting, and slid his tray onto the table. He sat down and the throaty sound of masculine laughter crossed the room.

"Sit down please Zack," Stephanie said. "Eat your dinner in peace."

"I can't imagine what you ever saw in the fellow," he muttered.

"Nor can I nowadays," Stephanie admitted. "I was very young back then."

The rest of the afternoon and the evening meal passed without incident. However when Zack inquired whether Stephanie would like him to call at the girl's dormitory to collect her for the Uniting Church vespers, she shook her head.

Stephanie shook her head. "With Jeff on campus, I had better keep a low profile," she said.

Cara had failed to check her student email on Friday and the possibility of letters from Kaleb sitting waiting for her played on her mind. It also occurred to her that if Jeffrey Mannington was working on the mainframe, she might just be able to access the net. So she wandered down to the computer laboratory mid-morning and knocked on the door. Jeffrey was in there, his tousled bent over the computer. He walked over and unlocked the door.

"How can I help you?" Jeff inquired with an air of smug indulgence which made Cara feel about two inches high. However she steeled herself to continue.

"I wondered whether I could check my student email?" Cara stammered. "I'm expecting a letter from my boyfriend."

"Letters from the boyfriend is it?" Jeff was patronising. "Come in then Cara O'Brien."

Cara sat down at the free terminal. She had to wait for it to boot up and load, while all the time Jeffrey was typing away at the other computer. She almost thought he was whistling to himself. "You must be working hard," she murmured to break the awkward silence.

"Yes it's a big job," Jeffrey returned. "How is Stephanie this morning?"

"Stephane is fine," Cara said. "It's really none of your business."

"I knew one of her friends would be along today," Jeff admitted narcissistically. "Stephanie couldn't resist sending a messenger."

"I'm not a messenger," Cara insisted. She was beginning to fell flushed and awkward, which was really strange as she was usually a confident tomboy.

The password request appeared and Cara logged into her account. There was nothing in her in-box, other than an administration announcement that the computers would be undergoing upgrading over the weekend. Yesterday's news really. It was really strange because Kaleb usually sent email every few days, like clockwork. Cara tried refreshing her in-box several times and then signed out, horribly disappointed.

"Found what you were looking for?" Jeffrey almost sounded like he knew that she hadn't.

Cara shook her head and began to beat a hasty retreat. "Nah, but thank you for letting me check."

"You're welcome," Jeffrey said with his nasal drawl. "Have a good day."

Cara entered the cafeteria with a dull expression on her face. She collected her food listlessly and went across to the table to join her friends. Zack noticed her doleful look immediately and asked Cara what was wrong.

"I haven't had any email from Kaleb," Cara confided. "I just went down to the computer lab and checked my email."

"How did you check on a Saturday?" Zack asked.

"Jeffrey Mannington is working on the computers all weekend," Cara explained.

"Hmm," Garry said. "Perhaps you didn't look thoroughly."

"I know how to check my email by now thank you," Cara responded.

"I will come down with you and look again," Zack offered.

"That is nice of you," Cara said, "But I don't want to go near Jeff again. He creeped me out."

"Well if Jeff has the mainframe activated, the other terminals should work too," Zack mused. "The question is, which one can we access?"

"What about the Science department?" Stephanie suggested.

Garry shook his head. "I have the keys, but it's a matter of trust, I would risk my job by letting students in after hours.”

“The library is open till three on Saturday,” Danielle, whose student employment was on the circulation desk and book shelving, contributed suddenly.

“The OPAC is no good,” Zack explained. “We want to access the mainframe, not browse the book catalogue.”

“Not many people know this,” Danielle said. “But there is a terminal for the mainframe down in the archive, next to the microfiche.”

“Really?” Zack looked thrilled. “We might be able to check Cara’s email and I might be able to fix my Physics assignment.”

“I thought you lost it,” Stephanie said.

Zack smirked. “I’m not stupid,” he said. “I activate auto save every ten minutes. I have just got to find the back up.”

“I will show you where this computer is,” Danielle said. “As soon as we have finished eating.”

After lunch Cara, Zack and Danielle crossed campus to the library, where Danielle led them downstairs into the archive area. Here everything was very quiet, as old records were stored in dim light and under temperature control. The ceiling was also so low it almost brushed the top of Zack’s head.

“Are you sure we are allowed down here?” Cara whispered.

Danielle looked amused. “It is available for public research,” she said. “Just not accessed very often. Now to the computer.”

The terminal was located near a small flight of stairs. Danielle removed the plastic cover. She switched it on and entered the library log-in. “You should be able to retrieve your document from here,” she whispered. “My log in has staff privileges, so it will browse your account Zack.”

Zack sat down at the seat and typed a few key strokes. Luckily he was very careful to always give his documents a unique identifying name. The auto save altered that slightly, but was easily identifiable from the date and time.

Zack opened the file and renamed it so he could access it through the correct software. On second thoughts, he pulled a floppy disk out of a rigid case he carried and saved a copy on the portable media.

"You can never be too careful," Zack commented. "Thanks Danielle, you are an angel. I've lost the last ten minutes of work, but it's better than a whole afternoon's worth!"

Cara sat down at the terminal and carelessly typed her log on. She opened her email account and viewed the empty in-box. "See?" she pointed out to Zack.

"Hmm," Zack muttered. He took over the keypad and scrolled down to the storage area for deleted files. Opening that area showed two recent messages from Kaleb. He pushed the button to print and selected the library printer. "There are your email!" he exclaimed.

"Deleted?" Cara exclaimed. "How would that happen?"

"Perhaps you did it by accident," Zack suggested.

"Or perhaps I had some help," Cara suggested darkly. "Could Jeffrey Mannington have done it?"

As if in answer, the terminal darkened before their eyes. Zack pushed the monitor button several times and then shook his head. "Someone shut the mainframe down," he whispered.

"Could he have seen my log in?" Cara inquired.

"He could have, if he was watching that carefully," Zack said. "Danielle's log-in would not have alerted him, but then you used yours. But whoever would watch that carefully?"

"According to Stephanie, Jeffrey was mildly compulsive," Cara whispered. "He might know we are in the library too."

She glanced around the dimly lit and low roofed archive area nervously. "Let's get out of here."

"You pushed print, so your email should be at the front desk," Danielle said. "We can collect it on our way out.

Cara retreated to the girl's dormitory with her email and read them through many times. Kaleb had sent news about his subjects, funny incidents with his family and expressed his hope that he would soon be back in Australia with her. Cara spent the afternoon writing a reply on rose printed paper, as she was unable to access the computer and send email. She stamped it using a spare stamp from her desk and dropped into the after-hours post office slot.

Sunday morning Cara attended the Inter-denominational praise service and then treated herself to an early lunch in the cafeteria. Stephanie had also decided to have lunch early, as in her memory Jeff usually attended the Reform Church, and would be occupied during that time. Unless, of course, he chose to work on the computers all through Sunday.

After lunch, the usual pre-function excitement set in, with girls wasting hours over costumes, hair and make-up. There was no specific dress code for the Autumn Feast, but it did have a fall theme, so Stephanie was putting the finishing touches on a brown cotton skirt patterned with autumn leaves. She was planning to team it with a scoop necked sweater as the evenings were coming in cool.

Cara wasn't sure what Craig liked, and found herself more nervous about the date than she had expected. The theme sounded like the perfect opportunity to dress like a farm girl, so she donned neat brown corduroy jeans and a red and white striped poncho cut out of a piece of woolen material. Under the poncho, Cara sported a white cotton blouse.

Joelle came into their room to do her hair and make-up. The musician was curling her naturally bouncy hair and adding a rustic bow. She was wearing a large checkered flannel shirt as a sort of jacket with a black silky camisole underneath. The outfit was completed by a pair of denim jeans.

Zack, Tom and Craig arrived together to collect their dates and had them paged over the public address system. Stephanie, Joelle and Cara hurried down to the foyer when they heard their names. Joelle greeted Tom with a hug and kiss, Stephanie trustingly extended her hand for Zack to hold, and Cara found herself awkwardly greeting Craig.

"Thank you for picking me up," Cara whispered.

Craig looked a little nervous, but he nodded. "Shall we go across to the cafeteria?" he asked.

"That sounds lovely," Cara replied, taking herself in hand. It was ridiculous that she could be so relaxed talking to all her male class-mates, and suddenly so shy with this artistic young man. "What have you been up to so far this weekend?"

Craig's handsome face lit with infectious enthusiasm. "Well I played the violin for vespers and then again for the Inter-denominational praise service." he said, his love of music written very clearly on his features.

"I noticed you at the praise service," Cara said. "I thought you did very well."

"Thank you," Craig said. "To be honest, I haven't seen you or your roommate around a lot this weekend."

"My roommates' ex-boyfriend is on campus," Cara admitted. "She has been doing a bit of hiding from him."

"Jeffrey Mannington," Craig said. "I remember him from a couple of years back. I've always considered him somewhat self-absorbed and insensitive."

Cara giggled. "My roommate somehow considers Jeff hyper-sensitive," she said. "Stephanie always plays it extra safe around him."

"There might be more than one way of viewing the same person," Craig observed. "Like there is more than one way of interpreting a piece of music."

"How true," Cara agreed. She listened to Craig talk about Music and the Arts. Although he seemed introverted, he was really an interesting person when he opened up. Cara realized she had been missing something by leaving him out of her inner circle of friends. "I like talking to you," she remarked.

"I was just going to say something the same!" Crag said.

They had reached the cafeteria and were seated on one of the outer tables, from where they had a good view of the rest of the café. The tables were decorated with pinecones, pumpkins and candles. Wreathes of autumn leaves hung along the walls, along with sheaves of straw, clearly intended to represent wheat. There was even a special glass jar on each table, where the students on the table could drop small white cards with lists of things for which they were grateful.

The first course consisted of sweet potato scones and traditional pumpkin soup. This was followed by cranberry congealed salad. The salad consisted of fruit in a cranberry jelly, and the students were confused regarding whether the dish was intended to be a sweet or savoury. However, all agreed it was pleasant and different. It was also a relief to the palate of the students who were not pumpkin fans, but had made a heroic effort to eat the pumpkin soup.

The salad was followed by a selection of vegetables, including sautéed beans, glace carrots, baked potatoes and buttered sweetcorn. The main course was a choice of roasted turkey lasagna or vegetarian lasagna. Desert was a choice of pumpkin pie, or traditional apple pie with ice-cream.

"There are a few strange pairings out there tonight," Cara whispered to Craig. Her gaze swept over Garry sitting with her sister Bede, and Elisabet sitting with Arthur Mason, who surely was not her type, but did scrub up well in a suit. Jeffrey Mannington was also sitting with Ms. Louise the Art Instructor, so he must have taken Michael's advice to find himself a date from among the staff.

"Including us," Craig suggested and Cara laughed.

"We are not so strange after all," she said. "I don't get Elisabet and Arthur though – surely she is your friend?"

"Elisabet is a free agent," Craig said. "I don't tell her who to date. I doubt she will take Arthur seriously though… and she rarely grants second dates."

"Have you discussed these things?" Cara asked curiously.

Craig nodded, although the expression on his face was distant. "You should come to the Music department some time when Joelle and I are practicing the classics," he said, changing the subject. "The pieces are much more impressive than what we play for worship."

"Thanks I will," Cara said. She giggled, "Wait till I email Kaleb and tell him that I celebrated Thanksgiving in April! He will think I've gone completely mad."

"It's the right time for the vintage festival in South Australia," Stephanie remarked from where she was sitting with Zack. "That's the South Australian harvest celebration."

"I don't think the Reform Church administration would like to hear you say that," Joelle said. "Because of the wine making associations."

Cara rolled her eyes and exchanged glances with Dylan further down the table. His holiday employment within the grape industry was still a closely guarded secret around the university. She was called back to attention by Craig's gentle hand on her shoulder. "What's going on there?" he whispered.

Jeffrey Mannington had risen from his seat beside Ms. Louise and was approaching their table. "Hello Stephanie," he drawled. "I hope you are having a nice evening."

Stephanie was doing her best to appear indifferent, but was clearly grateful for Zack's casual arm around her shoulder. "Thank you Jeff," she replied. "I hope you are enjoying your date with Ms. Louise."

"I wouldn't call it a date exactly," Jeffrey drawled. "Just two mature friends enjoying each other's company."

"Oh!" Stephanie looked confused. "Whatever you choose to call it."

Jeffrey turned his attention towards Zack. "How's the computing Zackary?" he drawled. "Any more unexpected problems?"

"I didn't notice any issues with the computer before you began upgrading them," Zack returned sullenly.

"Oh surely not," Jeff guffawed. "If everything had been perfect they wouldn't have called me in – would they?"

"I suppose not," Zack admitted. The loss of ten minutes worth of code still rankled with the Physicist, although he had managed to salvage most of that afternoon's work. He rose to his feet and faced Jeff squarely. Jeffrey Mannington was tall, but Zackary Nestor was just slightly taller. "Look I'm eating my dinner now man."

"Have a wonderful evening," Jeff said in a tone that implied the opposite of his words. He turned and slouched his long form back to the table where he had been sitting with Ms. Louise. The Art Instructor appeared to be questioning him curiously as he sat down again, and Jeffrey's body language was dismissive. "Just some students I used to know," he appeared to be saying.

Towards the end of the evening, Larry one of the third year Theology students, rose and read Deuteronomy chapter 26, verses 1-2 aloud:

"And it shall be, when you come into the land which the Lord your God is giving you as an inheritance, and you possess it and dwell in it, that you shall take some of the first of all the produce of the ground… and put it in a basket and go to the place where the Lord your God chooses to make His name abide."

Larry explained that this was the beginning of the harvest festival traditions and asked each of the students at the table to draw a card from the jar in the middle and read out loud what someone was thankful regarding. He then said a brief prayer and told the students to all get back to having fun.

At the end of the evening, Tom and Joelle, Cara and Craig, Stephanie and Zack all walked back to the girl's dormitory as a group. Stephanie and Cara thanked their escorts for the evening, and they left Joelle to kiss Tom goodnight more privately.

Cara was surprised to be approached by the Chemistry Doctor between classes Monday morning.

"Good morning Cara," the Chemistry Doctor said. "I was wondering whether you would have a copy of the practical report you wrote over the holidays."

"Yes," Cara said. "I have the one you marked and gave back to me."

The Chemistry Doctor looked vastly relieved. "I hope the rest of the class are as well organized," he said. "I entered your grades into the university computer, but somehow they seem to have been deleted. I suppose these things can happen during a software upgrade, luckily this class is the only one that seems to have been affected."

"I'll bet," Cara muttered.

The Chemistry Doctor looked at her curiously.

"I will tell the others to bring their assignments back to you," she volunteered.

"Thank you, I would appreciate that," the Chemistry Doctor said. "Have a good day Cara."

He turned and began to trundle his way down to the Science department buildings once again.

"What was that all about?" Stephanie asked curiously.

"Our grades have now gone missing mysteriously," Cara sighed. "Blasted Jeffrey Mannington and the mainframe computer again."

Stephanie looked concerned. "You and Zack seem to have encountered the brunt of the harassment from Jeff," she said. "Perhaps I should leave campus until he is finished."

"It might be an idea," Cara said. "If he can't find you, he may cease bothering your friends."

"I will see if I can stay with Phoebe for a few days," Stephanie announced. "Of course I will still have to attend classes."

That afternoon in Agriculture they checked their seedlings were still surviving out in the ground and continued their mulch production. The Agriculture Instructor said they would be preparing a bed for strawberries, because the berries were the ideal crop to plant in April. The seedlings also required a specially prepared bed of mulch.

The Agriculture Instructor mapped out the space and set the students to turning the soil over, making sure the area was weed free, aerated and fertilised. The Instructor had germinated the strawberry seedlings over the holidays and they were almost of a size to plant. He estimated the seedlings would be ready by the time the students had the bed fully prepared the following week.

After their Agriculture class finished, Stephanie filled out her leave form and placed a call to Phoebe, who sent Hank across to pick her up. Stephanie had packed a small bag and was prepared for a couple of days off campus.

Cara continued across to the cafeteria for tea and settled down alongside Dylan and Garry.

"Did you have a good time at the Autumn Feast?" Cara asked.

"Pretty good," Dylan said. "Danielle is a sweet girl."

"Your sister Bede is quite good company," Garry said. "She knows how to make a guy laugh. How was your evening?"

"Craig is nice," Cara said. "I wish I'd talked to him earlier."

They continued talking in this bland fashion until Jeffrey Mannington entered the cafeteria chattering cheerily with Arthur Mason and Tony Dantean. Although it was not the norm for lecturers to eat in the cafeteria, Jeffrey was accompanied by Ms. Louise. Jeffrey Mannington, Ms. Louise and the boys all sat down at a table the opposite end of the cafeteria to the third year students. Cara had the uncomfortable feeling that they were looking around for someone.

Kathy, who was an Art major, and fond of Ms. Louise in her way, tutted in concern. "I don't want to see Ms. Louise hurt," she whispered.

"In my experience, you can't warn other women about men," Cara whispered back. "Even my sister Bede would not listen when I tried to warn her about Arthur."

"Best to let things be," added Kathy's peaceable Theology student boyfriend, Andrew.

A few minutes later, Ms. Louise approached them however. "Hello Kathy," the Art Instructor said.

"Hello Ms. Louise," Kathy replied. "How are you?"

"Very well thank you," Ms. Louise said. "I can't help noticing that

Stephanie Lowood is not with you tonight."

"No, she is staying with Hank and Phoebe," the words slipped out of Cara's mouth before she could stop them.

"What brings you to the cafeteria Ms. Louise?" Kathy inquired.

Ms. Louise blushed. "Just a friend," she murmured and returned to her seat beside Jeffrey and the boys.

Cara finished her food and returned to the girl's dormitory, where she found the room was very quiet. After an hour, it was time to go to the evening meeting. She hurried down to the women's assembly area and signed in for assembly.

After the proceedings, Cara returned to her room. A while later she was surprised to hear a tap at the door. When she opened it, she found the visitor was the dean in charge of the girls welfare.

"Excuse me Cara," the Dean said. "Is it true that Stephanie is living off-campus and not even with a close relative?"

"Stephanie is staying with Phoebe for a couple of days," Cara said. "She filled out her leave form and had everything approved earlier this evening."

"I'm sorry," the Dean said, "Now this thing has been brought to our attention, I don't think we can allow it. The rules are very clear."

"It is only for a day or two," Cara said. "Stephanie will be attending all her classes."

"She will be missing the dormitory worships," the Dean said. "And the university has a responsibility to ensure both her education and her safety."

Cara argued that Stephanie was safe staying with Phoebe who was a respectable married woman, however, the Dean would not listen and insisted that Stephanie be bought back onto campus. In the end, Cara was able to negotiate calling Stephanie first thing the next morning.

Tuesday Stephanie was brought back onto campus and everything appeared to go quiet. Jeffrey Mannington continued his upgrade of the university computer system and left campus when the task was complete. There were no more incidents, so the group speculated that Stephanie had given him a fright by removing herself from campus and thus out of his reach.

Kathy spoke to Ms. Louise in her Art class on Wednesday and the lecturer appeared to have lost interest in Stephanie's ex-boyfriend.

"Jeffrey Mannington has left campus now hasn't he?" Ms. Louise murmured vaguely when questioned. "Maybe if he had stayed around, something might have happened between us, but he was not a regular member of this faculty."

Kathy concurred politely and returned to her painting. She reported back to her friends later that the lecturer seemed no longer to be 'under the influence' of the manipulative Mannington.

Zack persisted in believing that he was the hero of the piece, for standing up to Jeff, and also accompanying Stephanie to the Autumn Feast. Zack maintained that the moment he stood toe-to-toe with the cowardly man, had proven Jeff was far too weak to take action outside of his domain of computer harassment.

"You may be right," Stephanie agreed with Zack indulgently. "Although I hope he hasn't left any nasty surprises in the system."

"Our regular computing guys would discover them if he had," Zack declared confidently. "And he would risk having his work declared unsatisfactory."

"I expect you are right," Cara agreed. "Jeff seems to be they type that would hate to leave anything that could be used as 'evidence' behind."

Stephanie continued to thank Zack effusively for his support. She even kissed him on the cheek during tea time on Wednesday, which made the Physicist glow with confidence and pride.

"Help me Obi-Wan," Zack misquoted his favoured movie franchise. "You are my only hope!"

Stephanie laughed, because to the girl's thinking, Zack had indeed done a good thing in shielding her socially; but the kiss made Garry frown thoughtfully and declare that it was not really Zack's place to be protecting Stephanie. Stephanie assured Garry that she knew all her friends had been there to support her in their own way, but Garry remained contemplative.

Thursday afternoon, the Biology Master took the class to visit the Brisbane City Botanic Gardens, located on the banks of the Brisbane River. He explained that these gardens were the oldest botanic gardens in Brisbane, and had been planted on the site of original crops grown by the European colonists. Attractions here included the bamboo grove and ornamental ponds. The students were encouraged to observe water species growing in and around the ponds, including the floating leaves of the water-lilies.

The Biology Master explained that the indigenous Macadamia nut tree was planted by Walter Hill in the rainforest area around 1858, and the Dragon trees planted around 1862 had once been milked for their resin. The Forest Red Gum on the river bank were also remarkable because they survived from the era before European settlement. Some of the palm trees had been pushed over by floodwaters in the 1890s and were growing almost side-ways to this day!

Garry had taken to consulting flyers from the University of Wollongong once again and was carrying them around in his shoulder bag. Cara tackled him Thursday evening at tea because she feared that he was contemplating leaving Silver Springs University.

However, Garry explained that by enrolling in summer and winter school units at the University of Wollongong he would be able to graduate a semester early as Applied Science. Graduating early would also allow him to apply for work at places like the Silver Springs Mineral Water factory, the Queensland Railway Yards or some companies around Noosa.

Garry confided to Cara that watching Jeff swagger around campus had triggered some deep resolve in his heart. He was a protective person by nature and had made an effort to support his mother during her illness; now he was frustrated by his role as a poor student, and wanted to enhance his employment options in order to protect the girl he cared about.

Friday evening, Garry had Stephanie called to the foyer to accompany her to vespers. When Cara expressed surprise, and reminded her roommate about the annoying gossip, Stephanie merely laughed. Stephanie said that she believed there were more likely candidates than Garry for the sabotage of Bradley's bike, and the talk would eventually die down. Garry and Stephanie were not holding hands yet, and probably would not be for some time, but their friendship appeared to be back on track.

CHAPTER SIX: THE SHAKING

Saturday morning Damaris visited the room to plan her wedding dress with Stephanie and Bede, who she had asked to sew it. Her wedding to Michael was set for the September holidays, when her flat-mate intended to vacate the house and give Michael and Damaris their privacy. Unlike Phoebe and Hank's wedding, the budget would not be tight, as Damaris was working and Michael's family were wealthy.

"The way I see it," Stephanie began, "There are one or two main dress profiles in fashion. Princess Diana wore a dress that puffed out around her. It was taffeta, which held its shape, had short puffy sleeves and obvious ruffles attached around the neck."

"In some lights it looked cream too," Bede added. "If you don't want to go for dead white."

Damaris opened the magazines and leafed through them. "I know Diana's look is very popular, but I think I am too short for it. I would be lost in all that dress. Besides, it looks like something Michael's mother might pick, bless her heart, but I want my own style."

"Well Phoebe used the Madonna look," Stephanie observed. "Although we could design you a variation."

"I'm too traditional for Madonna I think," Damaris observed.

"Nobody knows what Sara Ferguson will wear when she marries Prince Andrew," Bede said.

The girls paused for a moment. Sarah Ferguson was due to marry Prince Andrew around July that year and her wedding had caught their youthful imaginations. Sarah was a vibrant redhead, feminine and curved and clearly in love with her prince who was not too old to make their youthful hearts flutter.

While the girls of the 1980s had tried hard to rejoice over the marriage of Princess Diana to the Prince of Wales, many had been unable to identify with the couple. The groom, who was almost twenty years older than Australian teens, hardly seemed a romantic figure and it was hard to imagine that the marriage had been a love match.

"There is a celebrity alternative," Stephanie said. "We think you will like this one if you don't want the puffy look."

"It's a bit of a risk because the bride modelling the dress is very tall, but I think it would actually look better on a shorter girl," Bede said.

"Bridgette Nielson is a bit too outstanding in my book, but the design is fantastic," Stephanie said, producing the photograph. "They even say she designed it herself."

"See here is an artist's impression," Bede said, "In this version, the skirt flares out a little more down below. I got the impression Bridgette Nielson's was more of a sheath, this has a slight mermaid effect."

Damaris clapped her hands. "I love it," she exclaimed. "You girls are so clever. The big sleeves made of lace will be just perfect for spring. And I adore the way the yoke is made of lace – it is like a strapless dress and yet it is not."

"What are you going to do about a headdress?" Stephanie inquired. "I don't think we can make anything as beautiful as that." She pointed to the rows of dangling beads sported by Bridget Nielson.

"Now that I have the dress decided, I might let Michael's Mother go crazy buying the veil and accessories," Damaris said. "She will love that and it will make her feel included."

"Clever girl," Bede observed.

"By the way – Stephanie," Damaris said, "Michael said to tell you, he is sorry if anything he said to anyone added to the trouble last weekend. He just thought Jeffrey was just an old friend. He hadn't even known him all that well."

"Jeffrey has a sort of persuasion about him," Stephanie observed. "I have forgiven many people things they did when he was around."

"Thanks," Damaris said. "Michael really didn't mean any harm."

"Have you chosen your flower?" Stephanie inquired. "It would help us to work to a theme."

"Delphiniums or blue orchids," Damaris answered. "Expensive and exotic – which should also please Michael's mother."

"And what colour will the bridesmaids be?" Bede chipped in.

"I'm thinking a deep blue," Damaris replied. "It will provide the most contrast."

"The big shoulders are your special feature," Stephanie mused. "So you won't want to spread them across the bridesmaids. And it' too early in the year for strapless…"

Cara was beginning to get bored by all the wedding talk. It was exciting, but unless Damaris intended to ask her to be a bridesmaid, it didn't seem to involve her. She decided to wander by the Music department, where it would be a good guess she might find Joelle practicing with Craig. In the afternoon, she figured she could throw a few baskets with Zack in the gymnasium.

Sunday morning, Cara attended the Reform Church service with Kathy and Andrew, Stephanie and Garry. David was the speaker and he chose to speak about the fact that the Orthodox churches were celebrating Easter that weekend. He asked how devout Christian groups got so far apart from each other in their beliefs and calculations of dates. It was a rather daring sermon and might have gone down better at the Uniting Church vespers, but David was a very good speaker and carried it off well.

After lunch Cara could not settle to study, despite mid-semester tests looming in the near future. She consulted the Adventure Club timetable and discovered the club would be running a bus down to Little Cove that afternoon. Wishing to be assured of company, she lifted the internal phone and invited Zack to accompany her.

Little Cove was the ideal beach for surfing lessons and offered fantastic waves for experienced long-boarders. Swells ranged from one to three feet in height and the breaks were perfect. The foreshore was smooth and sandy, surrounded by small rocks and lined with trees. Cara and Zack played around using a couple of borrowed boards for a while, and then returned the boards to the bus. The pair retreated to sit upon the sand and admire the view.

Cara found herself watching Dylan and Danielle, and something about the companionable way Dylan was instructing Danielle on the surfboard sent a spasm through her heart. She glanced at Zack, and noticed he too was watching Dylan and Danielle intently.

"I'm sorry you did not get far with Stephanie last week," Cara ventured. "Although you suffered for the date."

"I got a kiss on the cheek," Zack returned brightly. "I really didn't expect anything more. She has a much longer history with Garry."

"Kaleb seems a long way away," Cara whispered. "Sometimes, I get the feeling that I'm just living for my study and my friends."

"I know what you mean," Zack sighed.

"I need something or someone for myself," Cara murmured.

Zack's hand slid across the sand and clasped hers. "Do you want to come for a walk with me, Cara O'B?" he asked.

"Yes please," Cara replied.

The couple stood up and made their way towards the privacy of the trees. Cara's heart was pounding. She had a fair idea what she had just initiated and making out with a new guy was risky and exciting.

Zack located a particularly sturdy trunk and made sure they were screened by undergrowth before pulling Cara into his arms. She shuddered up against him, feeling his lean muscles and reaching her arms up to link her hands behind his neck. As a basketball player he was fit and tall. Zack leant his head towards Cara and began kissing her lips gently, his mouth was hot and Cara responded in kind. His hands were gentle as they began tracing their way up and down her back.

Cara shivered as she realized she was only wearing her bathers. Zack's touch was polite as he made it clear he would not leave the neutral zone of her back without permission. Cara leaned closer and pressed herself against Zack to tempt him. However, as his hand slid slowly along the sensitive skin of her side, she panicked. "Stop," she cried.

Zack froze instantly, although he still held her cradled in his arms. "Stop everything, or just that?" he whispered.

"Stop everything," Cara cried. "This was a mistake. You are not my boyfriend."

"Okay," Zack said. He sounded respectful and didn't even seem angry. "But I could be if you wanted."

"I'm sorry," Cara sobbed, hiding her face in his chest. "I just can't."

"It seemed like it was worth a try," Zack sighed.

"For a moment there it was very nice," Cara admitted.

Zack eased her chin up to face him. "Do you want to know a secret Cara O'B?"

"Alright," Cara whispered.

"I've got a hopeless crush on Danielle," Zack admitted. "I've been in class with her for three years and somehow been friend-zoned. Nerdy, sciency Zack!"

"I'm so sorry," Cara whispered. "You are a nice guy."

"Now your two guy friends come along and suddenly she wants to go out with them," Zack complained. "I reckoned Garry was the greater threat with all his smooth moves from having a serious girlfriend once before, but Dylan is trying his hardest now."

"Garry says that Danielle is looking, because it is her last year at university," Cara said. "Perhaps the timing wasn't right before."

"Perhaps," Zack sounded unconvinced.

"Have you tried asking her?" Cara inquired.

Zack shook his head. "Not recently, and while she is with Dylan – how can I?"

"I'm sorry, I can't help you there," Cara said. "I'm afraid Dylan and I have a history so he wouldn't take a hint from me."

"They look pretty cosy," Zack sighed.

"Appearances can be deceiving, that is what Dylan thought when Danielle was with Garry, but it turned out they were just friends," Cara said.

"Well you and I won't embarrass each other by getting involved then," Zack said.

"You are so right," Cara said. "In a couple months Kaleb will be back on campus and I won't be so lonely."

Her tone was cheerful, but inside Cara felt hollow and empty. What if she couldn't pick things up again with Kaleb after all this time? And she had never desired to move to America for him, so how serious could they be really?

Monday afternoon in Agriculture the students spot checked their seedlings for pests and administered some light control measures. They then dug the mulch through the strawberry patch and planted the small strawberry plants in the ground, making sure the runners were about an inch and a half apart.

The Agriculture Instructor advised the class never to mix tomatoes and strawberries in the same soil, because the two species could suffer from the same viruses. They then covered the area around the little plants with a mixture of straw and pine needles, which the Agriculture Instructor explained was slightly acidic and helped control pests.

Tuesday in Chemistry, the class started the topic of lipids and their role in nutrition. The students observed the film of grease that foods containing lipids left on paper. Their observations were recorded in a table in their workbooks. Then the students attempted to extract lipids from food samples using acetone. It was necessary to wear gloves during this process for safety when handling the solution. They then attempted to observe ion exchange chromatography using a Gradifac system. It was at times like this that Cara was grateful that the more confident Zack had volunteered to be her laboratory partner.

Wednesday during a free period, Cara checked her email and was pleased to find several messages from Kaleb. She opened the first one, read it through, and responded to with a smile on her face. When she opened the second one, however, her expression became a puzzled frown.

Kaleb appeared to be giving her extensive advice regarding dealing with Arthur Mason, Vincent and Tony. Cara read the message through several times. She had not been aware that she had made such a big deal about the antics of the bully boys.

In fact, as Cara read the message through again, she began to gather the impression it was not truly intended for her, as it assumed a fairly personal relationship between the addressee and Arthur Mason, and even referred to several incidents of harassment of which Cara had not been aware.

Cara considered carefully as she wrote a reply. If Kaleb had been using the internet protocol to address Bede and typed a simple error, making Bobrien@SSU.EDU.AU instead of Cobrien@SSU.EDU.AU, the message would have come to her.

Cara wrote a reply informing Kaleb that the message appeared to be more appropriate for her sister Bede than herself. Then she added that while she appreciated Kaleb helping Bede with her problems, she would rather he had been upfront about his correspondence with her sibling.

After working on assignments throughout the afternoon, Cara decided to go down and watch Zack play basketball in the evening. Cara had not been following the competition closely that semester, but she knew from listening to Zack talk that the semi-finals were only a week away.

The match had not begun when Cara arrived at the gymnasium, but the scene was hectic. A number of boys were running around the court practicing their skills, and several unlikely looking guys were even attempting to perform slam-dunks. The pre-game atmosphere was startlingly rough.

Zack walked out onto the court and called out: "Settle down guys, you will tire yourselves. Save some energy for the match."

Most of the boys from Zack's team ceased their frantic activity and walked across to their captain. "Sorry boss," they said. "We got carried away."

"That's all right," Zack said, "But now I need you to focus." A ball bounced across the court and almost hit Zack, who caught it using a deft reflex action. "You too Vincent," Zack said.

Zack had privately told Cara that he was regretting keeping Vincent on his team, but was trying to be as fair as possible. Vincent reluctantly ceased to fidget and joined the team huddle. Zack spent a few moments discussing strategy with his team and then play commenced.

Not very long into the game, it became apparent that Michael's team were playing wildly and without much strategy. However, they appeared very energetic and were often in possession of the ball. They pounded up and down the court, and frequently attempted to shoot baskets, forcing Zack's team to go on the defensive. By half time, Zack's team had scored four hard won goals, and the opposition had five goals.

There was a brief break, during which the players took small sips of water and the two captains tried vainly to counsel their players. The second half commenced with Zack's team looking tired. Michael's team also began to show signs of wear, and with the fatigue, one or two players became careless and performed rough fouls.

The referee called the players on the fouls and awarded Zack's team several free shots. Michael's team players frowned and the culprits swore under their breath, abusing the referee, who grew very red. However, as the words were not clear, they could not be further disciplined.

Zack's team put the free shots to good use and the match closed at six all, which was a draw. The two captains shook hands, before addressing their teams. Michael appeared to be remonstrating with his team, who listened angrily. One or two were heard to mutter things to the effect that they had almost won, so why did their attitude matter?

After the match, Michael approached Zack apologetically. "I'm sorry mate," he exclaimed. "I don't know what got into the guys."

The Referee joined the two captains. "Silver Springs University basketball has always been a clean game," he exclaimed. "You have to control your guys, Michael."

"I feel sympathy for Michael," Zack said. "I am also struggling to make Vincent play fairly."

"I don't know what has gotten into the men," Michael cried. "They don't take instruction during practice - and their energy levels are remarkable – they run rings around me, and I don't feel equal to being their captain."

"You are the captain because you are more highly skilled," Zack assured Michael. "Don't let yourself be intimidated by sheer energy."

The Referee shrugged. "If I was anywhere else, I would say they were 'on something'. But such a thing has never happened at Silver Springs that I have heard of!"

The two captains and the referee concluded their discussion and then Zack approached Cara. "Thanks for coming down to watch," he said. "I'm sorry it was such a miserable match."

Cara was thoughtful. "Is it just the A grade having trouble?" she asked.

Zack shook his head. "The aggression seems to be spreading through all the grades," he said. "It began with a couple of the 'men's righters', but it now involves others. And Michael, who is a 'men's righter', is perfectly fine. In fact, he's always helping me talk to the others."

Thursday afternoon in Plant Biology the class were observing fruit and vegetables. They paid a visit to nearby market gardens and orchards, before retiring to the laboratory to draw a number of samples. They also set up cultures of nitrogen-fixing bacteria from the root nodules of leguminous plants like beans and peanuts to help study the process of symbiosis.

Friday morning, Cara checked her email during a free period and found she had a single reply from Kaleb. In the reply he admitted he had been corresponding with her sister Bede, who had first written to him some months ago.

Once the problems had commenced with Arthur Mason, the

correspondence had become more frequent and Kaleb perceived it as merely counselling Bede. Cara hesitated over her reply.

If Kaleb and Cara were married, Bede and Kaleb would be brother and sister-in-law and such a correspondence would be innocent. However, now she thought things through, there had been a few signs that Bede had fancied Kaleb, maybe even before Cara and Kaleb had got together as a couple.

Garry's words, "Look to Kaleb then", echoed in her head. In the end Cara wrote that she appreciated Kaleb's kindness towards her sister, but she needed to be perfectly sure which O'Brien sister he was returning to Australia to date.

In the afternoon, Cara hauled out the ride-on mower and manicured the lawns that stretched from the rear of campus up to the oval. When she was returning the mower to the tool shed, she noticed one of those black garbage bags left behind once again. She pulled the bag out of the hedge and hauled it into the tool shed, giggling nervously at the ridiculousness of looking at garbage and bracing herself against a foul smell.

Cara tore the bag open. She found she was looking at some small bottles and pill boxes, distributed among a lot of paper waste. "Dianabol", she read. The pills looked like innocent vitamins or perhaps someone's prescription drugs – but so many discarded bottles was weird.

"I had better ask the Chemistry Doctor what 'Dianabol' is," Cara mused. She slipped a small bottle into her pocket. After locking the tool shed, she hurried down to the Chemistry lab, where she found the Chemistry Doctor just about to lock his office and go home for the weekend.

"Could I talk to you for a moment?" Cara asked. The Chemistry Doctor was usually friendly when he was not teaching, so he nodded and turned to face Cara.

"What is it?" The Chemistry Doctor said. "Are you finding assignments difficult?"

"Inside please," Cara murmured.

The Chemistry Doctor looked a little worried. It was not the proper thing for male lecturers to be alone in buildings with female students for fear of accusations of impropriety. However, the serious look on Cara's face prompted him to unlock the office once again. "Come in dear."

Once out of public view, Cara held the bottle up. "What is this?" she inquired.

The Chemistry Doctor took the bottle and read the label. "Dianabol", he mused. "This bottle is empty, but a Chemist could test the residue inside. If it is true to the label it is Metandienone – or 17a-methyl-17b-hydroxy-1,4-androstadien-3-one."

"What is that?" Cara exclaimed.

"It is a compound used as a performance enhancer, as it causes muscle growth, resulting in increased strength and speed," the Chemistry Doctor explained. However, 'Dianabol' can also cause liver damage and high blood pressure."

"Could it cause aggression and mood swings?" Cara inquired.

"I don't know - probably not. Those symptoms would be from the associated testosterone supplement," the Chemistry Doctor mused.

"There were other bottles, but I did not read the labels," Cara said.

"This one is bad enough," the Chemistry Doctor said. "Where did you find it?"

"Someone has been dumping garbage in the bushes at the back of the lawn area," Cara said. "Is Dianabol illegal?"

"That is a grey area," The Chemistry Doctor mused. "Metandienone is not an illicit drug, it is a supplement. It can be used medically. Some sporting organisations are beginning to ban it however."

"Oh dear," Cara murmured.

"It may still come under the *Poisons and Therapeutic Goods Act 1966*, unless it was one of the steroids reclassified last year under the *Drug Misuse and Trafficking Act,*" the Chemistry Doctor mused. "Supplying it on campus where some of our first year students are under eighteen would certainly be some sort of offence."

"I will have to go to the police then," Cara sighed.

"I will come with you if you like," the Chemistry Doctor said. "In fact, I think I ought to, as I have seen the bottle now."

"Do you think they could keep my name out of it?" Cara inquired nervously. "There are rumours that Bradley found similar bags last year – not long before his accident."

"You will have to tell the police that too if they have not been told already," the Chemistry Doctor advised. "Bradley Parker was such a bright young man and his death was such a tragedy."

Cara and the Chemistry Doctor drove to the Northcoast Police Station where they made a full report. The police then visited campus and performed a thorough search of the shrubbery. They said it was a pity that Cara had moved the bag into the tool shed, but they had found some fragments of plastic which showed its original dumping place.

When the matter was reported to the discipline committee, the basketball administration was called into the meeting and the two groups spent many hours in session debating what to do. As a Christian organisation, Silver Springs University prided itself on running drug free and fair sporting competitions.

On the other hand however, as a Christian Institution, Silver Springs University also prided itself upon extending trust toward its students and was reluctant to order compulsory drug testing of athletes. The Silver Springs University basketball tournaments were also internal and hence not subject to any external sporting body.

Some members of the administration were in favour of offering forgiveness to students who voluntarily confessed to having used the substance. Other conscientious members of the administration argued that as there was a health risk involved, the university should ensure all students were tested.

One faculty member suggested notifying parents and letting them discipline their own offspring, but this suggestion proved unpopular as it could create publicity. In the end, it was decided that all young men desiring to compete in the basketball tournament should visit the doctor in Northcoast for a confidential checkup.

Failing to provide a medical certificate meant the students would be ineligible to continue to play basketball. Although this solution was imprecise and addressed general health rather than anabolic steroid use, it was adopted as representing the best fulfillment of the university's various responsibilities to the students.

The debate then moved on as to whether the policy needed to be extended to other university sporting clubs. Zack was exhausted at this point and asked to be excused, so Cara did not hear a report of the details.

Sunday was Mother's Day and after the two special services honouring mothers around the world were finished, a long queue formed for the use of the telephones. In the evening when the call rates dropped, the queue was even longer. Cara had posted a card for her mother earlier that week and she was pleased to hear it had arrived in time.

Monday the new regulations for basketball players were published and

Luke was busy all afternoon ferrying students who wished to participate in the finals to visit the general practitioner in Northcoast. Most students agreed that a health check was not too onerous a requirement, especially as the results remained between the student and the doctor.

Vincent voluntarily reported back to Zack that he was showing high blood pressure. The Doctors had assured him there was every hope discontinuing the steroid use would lead to a return to normal blood pressure over the next few months.

However, Vincent was upset that a product he had been told was a harmless vitamin supplement could have been detrimental to his health in the long term. He gave a moving speech to the boy's assembly which led to several other boys voluntarily removing themselves from the teams until the next semester, when they might be assumed to be 'clean'.

The campus nurse also spoke frankly for a few minutes regarding other possible side effects of steroid use. When she outlined the detrimental effects long term use could have on male fertility, a few boys looked horrified. They all prided themselves on their popularity with the girls, and hoped to have families.

After the nurse and other authority figures had left, a number of boys remained behind in the assembly hall. The ensuing discussion raged for hours. None of the boys who had partaken of the supplement had been told that it was anything more than a vitamin and protein mix, and under the circumstances, most argued that they were innocent.

No one would disclose the name of their supplier, although Tony Dantean received so many dark looks that he left the hall. Several people remarked that his absence from the continued discussion appeared highly suspicious.

Tuesday in Chemistry Cara exchanged a few grateful glances with the Chemistry Doctor, who had helped keep her name out of campus discussion. Given what had happened to Bradley the year before, Cara was grateful not to have to fear retribution from any angry boys. Stephanie also assured her that violence was less likely to occur now that the matter was securely in the hands of the police.

In the evening Cara briefly visited the gymnasium, where Zack was training his team. A player had been borrowed from another team to replace Vincent. Michael and several other captains were also attempting to train revamped teams and the gymnasium was very crowded. It appeared the semi-finals would be happening on schedule, and Silver Springs University would be able to continue to pride itself on running a clean basketball competition.

Wednesday night, Cara and the girls went down to the gymnasium to watch the men's basketball finals. Garry and Dylan had both been conscripted onto teams as substitutes. There had been a debate in boy's dorm as to whether they were eligible, not having played that semester, but the basketball committee ruled they were still members of the league and could both play at the level they had played the previous year.

Stephanie shuddered a little as she stepped into the gymnasium, briefly overcome with memories of Bradley leading his A grade team to victory the last season. Danielle and Cara took her hands, and led the girl to a seat on the benches. This year they were here to watch other boys play.

Zack had done a good job of integrating his new player into the team. They performed well, with an active attack and solid defense, easily overcoming the opposition team. If Michael's team also performed well in the other semi-final on Thursday evening, it appeared they would be opposing each other in the final.

The team Garry had been assigned to did very well, and went through to the B grade final. Garry was only required to go onto the court at the very end, when one of the other players was exhausted. He was briefly active in defense, but later joked that the regular guys on the team had done most of the work.

Dylan sat on the bench, but was not called up as a substitute at all by the C grade team to which he had been assigned. Garry observed this was probably a mistake, because that particular team ended up losing the match and did not qualify for the finals.

After the matches finished, Dylan, Zack and Garry crossed over to the benches and were congratulated by the girls. Now that Cara was in the know, she could tell Zack hesitated wistfully near Danielle, waiting for the girl to finish congratulating Dylan and turn to him.

"Well done Zackie," Danielle finally said, and Zack lit up like a plasma lamp. Cara wondered how she had never noticed before.

"Thank you Danielle," Zack stammered, going bright red. "I was wondering... whether you would like to go to the Basketball Tea with me?"

"I figured I would be going with Dylan and you would be going with Cara," Danielle replied carelessly and Zack's face fell.

"I suppose," Zack muttered. He suddenly looked awkward and nerdy, and nothing at all like a winning basketball captain. Cara could understand how he had become friend-zoned around the more confident Danielle.

"Actually, I'm going with Craig," Cara announced. Craig likely would not know a basketball from a soccer ball, but Cara figured he would still have to eat tea that night, so she could visit the Music department and make it happen. "Zack is available and it will be his big night if his team wins next week!"

Cara pinched Dylan hard on the arm and he looked at her in

astonishment. "What has gotten into you?" the boy whispered. "Are you suddenly jealous or something?"

"Zack is trying to ask Danielle out," Cara whispered.

"Oh so he is," Dylan observed. "But I like Danielle too, so that's tough!"

"How about you settle it like men?" Garry suggested. "If Zack wins the final, he gets Danielle for the Basketball Tea."

"How come nobody is asking me?" Danielle objected. "I don't want to be the subject of some macho bet!"

"Actually everybody IS asking you Danielle!" Stephanie laughed. The only boy currently not asking you out is Garry."

"It's like something from the movies!" Cara exclaimed. "Go for it Danielle – how often do us girls get to be the grand prize around here?"

"Oh okay," Danielle said, finally looking flattered. "Just for the Basketball Tea then."

Cara jumped up and down in excitement. "This is going to be fun," she exclaimed.

"Who do I get if Zack wins?" Dylan grumbled. "I'm back to being good old unwanted Dylan again."

"There is Elisabet," Stephanie suggested. "I think she is still single, and you are much nicer than Arthur Mason."

"Hmm Elisabet," Dylan mused. "She is quite the looker. I might ask her in Agriculture."

Thursday afternoon in the Plant Biology laboratory, the students were checking on some plants they had set up to demonstrate transpiration, and others that had been shaded and rotated to demonstrate the tendency to turn towards the sunlight. They also roamed across campus measuring the circumference of the trunks of trees the Biology Master had been collecting data about for years.

Friday afternoon, Cara wandered into the Music department, where she found Craig practicing. She settled down to listen and waited until he lifted his head from the sheet music. Cara was pleased to notice he was happy to see her, as it would have been very awkward otherwise.

"Hello Cara," Craig said.

"Hello Craig," Cara returned. "That sounded very nice!"

Craig laughed. "As if you know one note from the other!" he joked.

"I might just know that," Cara ventured. "Craig, I told my friends you were taking me to the Basketball Tea."

"Two dates in a row is it?" Craig said. "We must be getting serious!"

"Actually, I was trying to get Zack together with Danielle," Cara confided.

"Intriguing," Craig said. "You must explain how this works."

"Well Danielle was assuming I was going with Zack, so I said, no, I was going with you," Cara elucidated.

"That is as clear as mud then," Craig said. "And who gets together with who if we go out together a third time?"

"I don't know that," Cara laughed. "We will have to wait and find out."

"Okay, so I'm not the most sporting fellow in the world," Craig said, "But I do eat tea. I will take you. When is it?"

"Next Friday night," Cara said.

"Not tonight?" Craig inquired.

"No - next Friday," Cara explained. "They have to play the grand final first."

"Ah, I see how that would be handy," Craig observed. "Otherwise they wouldn't know who to give the little statues to would they?"

"Exactly," Cara agreed.

"On one condition," Craig continued. "Sit down and listen to a bit of music now. It is poor manners only to come in here when you are looking for a date."

"Yeah sure," Cara said. "As long as I have time to mow the lawn later. I have my duties to perform before the weekend."

"Ten minutes at the most," Craig said. "I assure you it will be worth it!"

CHAPTER SEVEN: THE ARREST

Saturday was a lovely sunny day, however Cara was forced to ignore the appeal of the outdoors because she had an Education essay due on Monday. After working hard all day, she went down to the recreation area with Garry and Stephanie and played pool at the tables provided.

Dylan and Zack turned up briefly, but they were so busy teasing each other regarding who would take Danielle to the Basketball Tea, that they were rendered hopeless at pool. Cara sincerely hoped that Zack would play well in the basketball final, because she knew his interest in Danielle was genuine, but Dylan could easily find another girl to pursue.

Sunday morning, Cara attended the Inter-denominational praise service. That day was Pentecost for those churches that observed the liturgical calendar, and Kathy's boyfriend Andrew talked about the inspiration provided by the Holy Spirit.

Cara hoped that she was not being irreverent, as she prayed some of that inspiration would help her with essay. She figured she was about half-way through the words, and on track to hand the paper in on time. By evening she was feeling stale and exhausted, and decided to go down to the lounge to watch some television. When she finished her essay later that night, she went to bed a much lighter heart.

In Agriculture Monday afternoon, the class members were learning to prune. The Agriculture Instructor explained that pruning was essential to promote healthy growth, better flowering and better crops. It was usually done in winter when the plant was dormant, to prepare it for new growth in spring.

Firstly the Agriculture Instructor demonstrated the tools and showed the students how to keep the pruning shears clean and sharp. Then they approached an old apple tree in the orchard. The apple tree had been neglected so that it stopped bearing fruit. However, as apple trees could live for fifty years, it still had some life in it.

The Agriculture Instructor first showed the students how to look for dead and diseased branches. These might be grey or crinkled and lack healthy buds, requiring lopping off immediately to save the rest of the tree. The Instructor explained that apples would form on the terminal buds of branches that were about two years old. He then showed the class how to locate healthy branches and cut them off just before a desirable bud to encourage growth.

Cara glanced ahead to where Dylan was partnered with Danielle, attempting to make as much progress with the girl as possible while Zack was not present. Elisabet, Tess and Tom were working quietly together as usual.

"I thought Dylan was going to ask Elisabet out?" Cara whispered to Garry, who was working alongside her and Stephanie.

Garry frowned, "I can't tell Dylan not to pursue a girl he likes," he began. "And according to the bro-code - Dylan saw her first."

"Danielle and Zack are both fourth years," Stephanie ventured gently. "It is possible Zack saw her first."

"Not within our group," Garry observed. "And that's where the bro-code begins with guys like Dylan and me. What does it matter to you anyway Cara?"

"I have become very fond of Zack," Cara said.

"Go out with him yourself then," Garry advised practically.

Cara held her tongue, not wanting to tell Garry she had already tried that. Officially, she was still with Kaleb and her romantic options were limited.

"I could try talking to Dylan," Stephanie murmured to Cara. "What exactly is it we are trying to achieve?"

"Getting Dylan to play fair in the competition for Danielle," Cara suggested. "So Zack has a reasonable chance."

It was as much as Cara could say without betraying Zack's confidence, but Stephanie nodded wisely. "Alright," she said.

Tuesday was the last Chemistry Laboratory before the practical exam. The class demonstrated the Krebs cycle (which was another name for the citric acid cycle first described by Hans Adolf Krebs) by placing pulverised hamburger Pattie into a test tube along with succinic acid and methylene blue, which would react to the electrons produced during the breakdown of meat and lose its colour.

The Chemistry Doctor appeared keen for the students to distinguish and draw the identifying features of lipids, amino acids, enzymes, nucleic acids, and carbohydrates. He also insisted they understand and describe the pentose phosphate pathway, the citric acid cycle, oxidative phosphorylation and the formation of ATP. Cara left the lab with her head spinning, although she knew they still had a week of lectures and their practical write-up to help her consolidate the material.

Wednesday evening, Stephanie, Cara and Danielle walked down to the gymnasium to watch the men's basketball A grade finals. The gymnasium was lined with extra seats, and the area was full of laughter. The hushed voices of students filled each other in on the latest news regarding the steroid scandal.

Some of the spectators debated whether the disgrace rendered the final matches inauthentic. Other students were more curious than ever, as the scandal had brought the prestige of campus basketball to their attention.

Garry was occupied with his team, so Stephanie and Cara slid into a seat beside Dylan.

"I hope Zack does well," Stephanie whispered and Dylan looked at her curiously.

"What is it to you, Steph?" he asked curiously.

"It is important to Cara," Stephanie answered diplomatically. "And she appears to consider it important to Zack."

"That is double talk for 'you can't say'," Dylan replied cynically.

Stephanie laughed. "You got me!"

"Have you considered Cara might be looking after her own interests here?" Dylan murmured. "Earlier this semester, she told me that she missed our friendship."

"I'm glad to hear it," Stephanie said.

"The friendship she was referring to has always been unequal," Dylan said. "I did everything for Cara, while Cara barely acknowledged me."

"That wasn't quite fair," Stephanie agreed. "But I would expect that if Cara got to the point of asking for the friendship back, she had learned to appreciate you."

"I couldn't be sure," Dylan returned. "Cara is Cara. She thinks she is one of the boys – but she is a girl as well. She ends up bossing her male friends around mercilessly. She is doing it to poor Craig right now."

"Craig is not stupid," Stephanie returned. "I know him, because he is also Joelle's friend."

"I can hear you two," Cara observed. "My ears are getting very red."

"So can I," Danielle added. "Whatever Cara has done in the past, I think you ought to forgive her Dylan – and I don't know what any of that has to do with Zack asking me to the Basketball Tea."

"The match is about to begin," Stephanie said. "Let's watch."

The A grade final was played first. Zack's team faced Michael's team in the spirit of friendly rivalry. Zack's team had historically been superior; but Michael was determined to play a good match. The two captains faced each other for the initial toss. Zack captured the ball and passed it deftly through his team until they scored the first basket.

A cheer ran around the benches, and steroids were forgotten at the display of skill. The spectators leaned forward on their seats. Michael captured the ball and dribbled it around, adroitly avoiding the player Zack had assigned to watch him. Michael passed the ball to a team mate, who returned it to him. Michael faced the basket and scored the second goal of the match.

Control of the ball passed back and forward between the two teams. At half-time, Zack's team was two goals ahead, but that barely mattered compared to the sheer number of baskets scored. At full time, Zack's team was three goals ahead and everyone agreed the game had been well fought.

Zack accepted everyone's congratulations and also slapped Michael on the back. "Well done bro!" he exclaimed. He went outside and took a drink at the taps, and then came inside where he approached Danielle. "Wasn't that a good game?" he inquired.

"Yes Zackie," Danielle said. "You did very well."

"Will you come to the Basketball Tea with me then?" Zack asked.

Danielle glanced at Dylan, who in the face of Zack's win, dared not object. "You won me fair and square," Danielle said.

"Yay! That is my real prize," Zack chortled and sat down between Danielle and Cara.

"Doesn't he remind you of someone?" Dylan muttered.

"Yeah," Stephanie whispered. "Bradley last year."

"Yeah," Dylan said. "The same exuberance and joy at being on top of the world."

"But a few days after his big win, Bradley was dead," Stephanie whispered. "Please don't wish that on Zack."

"I wouldn't," Dylan said. "Even if he has stolen Danielle from me."

Thursday in Plant Biology the Biology Master drove the group to the Mt Coot-tha Botanic Gardens, located at Toowong, in his range rover. These gardens were officially opened to the public around 1976, so they were only about ten years old.

The Mt Coot-tha Botanic Gardens featured a tropical display dome, and an arid garden featuring cacti, which were of special interest on this excursion. After making their required observations, the class strolled around enjoying the beautiful landscaping.

The Biology Master kept himself busy pointing out specific species and particular features of the plants, but the students were out primarily to enjoy the day. A few sly smiles were exchanged between Garry and Stephanie, and Dylan even made an effort to include Cara in his conversations with Danielle.

Friday, Cara handed in her portfolios of lessons and resources for Practice Teaching. This was the main requirement for the semester, as she would be completing three weeks practicum during the mid-year break. She had already applied to a school in the south of Melbourne where she would be able to stay with a cousin while performing her teaching duties.

The evening saw the other basketball finals. The women's A grade was played first, followed by both men's and women's B grade matches on alternate courts. The women's A grade played well, with both Janet and Monica's teams scoring near even number of baskets. Finally, Janet's team drew a goal ahead and were declared the winners at full time.

Garry's B grade team was the next team of interest to play. Garry was sitting patiently on the bench, as it was becoming clear the captain wanted to use his regular players as much as possible. It was a low scoring match, but Garry's team was drawing laboriously ahead.

In the second half of the game, one of the forwards began to look tired and accidentally performed a foul. The captain called Garry up to carry the load instead, and Garry gave a solid performance focused on team work. At full time his team was three baskets ahead.

Garry cooled down and got a drink at the bubblers, before returning to his friends and sliding into the seat between Dylan and Stephanie.

"Good work," commented Danielle from Stephanie's other side, where she was sitting with Zack.

"Yeah congrats mate," Zack added.

Garry shrugged. "It was the whole team's doing," he said modestly.

The C grade match was played next, but attracted far less interest than the A and B grade games. The spectators relaxed and watched lazily. There was the tendency to gossip about the A grade match, but the talkers were shushed politely.

After lunch on Saturday, Dylan invited three friends to go for a drive in the Suzuki LJ. He glanced at Cara when he invited Zack as if to say she ought to notice how generous he was being, because he had no obligation to invite his rival. He even bade Cara to sit in the front passenger seat, and allowed Zack to sit in the back with Danielle.

"Now where shall we go?" Dylan asked.

"Somewhere like Anamoor State Forest," Cara suggested "Where they say you can see platypus if you are quiet."

"I would love to see a platypus in the wild," Danielle exclaimed.

The party all expressed themselves satisfied with the Anamoor forest destination, and Dylan set off. When they arrived, they hiked through the trees to the creek and saw amazing growths of fungi on the logs they passed.

At one point they also discovered a beautiful little waterfall and attractive pool. Finally they came to the rocky little creek, and began a debate regarding where they were most likely to see a platypus. The group decided to sit down on some rocks and wait as quietly as possible.

Cara attempted to lean companionably against Dylan as she once had in the old days, but he pushed her shoulder away gently.

"Kaleb will be back soon, and then things will be just like last year, except with no Annie," Dylan muttered.

"Tell me the Annie story," Danielle said gently. "I don't think I have heard all the details."

Dylan and Cara exchanged glances, silently debating how much detail to share.

"We were a pretty close group," Cara began. "Stephanie and Bradley, Dylan and I. But when Annie joined us last year, she asked Dylan to give up his friendship with me and commit very quickly to her."

"I see," Danielle murmured. "But by the end of the year, Annie was going out with Herman – am I right?"

"Yeah," Cara said. "And Dylan felt burnt."

"I'll bet he did!" Danielle exclaimed. "Well, that explains a lot."

Zack pointed to a shadow along the river bank. "I think that might be a platypus."

"Oh my," Cara exclaimed, almost holding her breath. "Remarkable creatures aren't they?"

The platypus dipped its duck shaped bill and the edge of its furry nose into the water. It then appeared to test the water with one of its webbed feet, before stopping for a moment to scratch its furry body. Then it dived into the water and swam down out of sight. It did not reappear anywhere near them.

"However long can they hold their breath?" Danielle asked.

"I don't know," Cara said. "Maybe he swam away somewhere."

After a while, it became clear that the platypus was not going to emerge. Dylan suggested that they walk back to the car so that he could drive back to Silver Springs University before dark. There was no daylight savings in Queensland, and the sun dropped behind the hills quite early in winter.

On Sunday Phoebe had invited Stephanie back to her house so they could study English together. Although Cara did not do English, she had been included in the invitation and was looking forward to enjoying an afternoon of home cheer. It appeared that studying English was not particularly onerous in this case, as it involved watching some BBC drama productions that Phoebe had somehow managed to acquire on video cassette.

Monday was their last Agriculture lesson and the students checked all the produce they were growing. A few early plants were almost ready to harvest and it was possible they would be taken to the cafeteria for Damaris to prepare very soon.

Then they continued their pruning practice. There was no major assignment for Agriculture, as it was graded on participation. From experience, Cara knew that participation units usually resulted in the entire class being assigned a similar mark, such as a credit.

Dylan appeared to have begun to pay attention to Elisabet, pairing off to work with the blonde, and joking around in an endearing, but not too clownish manner. It looked as though those two were on track for a date to the Basketball Tea, providing Elisabet had not already been asked by someone. This left Danielle to work with Cara, while Stephanie worked with Garry, and Tom worked with Tess.

The next afternoon, their Chemistry laboratory was scheduled to be assessed as a practical exam. Over the years, Cara had learned not to stress too hard about practical examinations. It was usually impossible to achieve a perfect score, but as they also had weekly practical reports, monthly tests and a final theory exam, the practical exam represented only about ten percent of their grade.

Cara worked as hard as she could, sketching the chemical compounds represented by the plastic models and categorising them to the best of her ability. Then she found herself faced with a number of spectroscope and chromatograph print-outs to interpret. She was sincerely grateful for the hours Zack had spent explaining these readings to her.

The last experiment involved mixing 'fake snot' using gelatin, salt and water. Cara found the exercise slightly juvenile, but took the observations that she was required to write quite seriously. At the last moment, she thought to consult the ingredients list on the gelatin packet and discovered that it contained protein, which she would also expect to find in nasal mucus.

Wednesday evening was the Basketball Tea, and all round celebration of the university basketball season. Craig was wearing smart casual, and had his hair neatly cut when he arrived at the girl's dormitory to pick Cara up. She had to admit he looked stunning, even though they were on a 'just good friends' basis.

Garry had given in to Stephanie's pleas not to sit at the winners' table due to her memories of Bradley, so the girl was accompanying Dylan and Elisabet on their date. Dylan looked pleased to have two girls to escort to the function and even bragged about having 'one girl on each arm'.

Craig's face brightened at the sight of Elisabet and Dylan.

"At least we are sitting with someone I know," he whispered. "Elisabet is a nice girl. I would love to see her find someone special."

"It takes two," Cara murmured. "Elisabet dates a lot, but she hardly ever seems serious about anybody."

"Well I used to think that taking a girl to these functions was a waste of time," Craig said. "And I'm afraid I might have hurt her feelings once."

"I never really heard any gossip about you two," Cara mused.

"We both kept it quiet," Craig said. "I'm not much of a dater."

"You could ask her to the next function," Cara suggested.

"That would be next semester, wouldn't it?" Craig mused. "Kaleb will be back, and you won't be needing me anymore." He looked thoughtful.

"Yeah," Cara agreed. She couldn't help noticing Craig had unusually fine features and clear skin for a guy. Perhaps it had been his excessive good looks, as well as his artistic personality that had motivated the bully boys to pick on him.

Just then, Zack rose to announce the A grade girl's results and award the trophy to the winning captain, Janet. He also awarded the 'best and fairest' and 'most improved' trophies. Cara recognized the 'most improved' recipient as Lacey, one of Bede's friends who was rising through the grades and captaining her own team.

Then the winning captain of the girl's competition, Janet, rose and awarded the overall boy's trophy to Zack. Michael received 'best and fairest' and Terrence, a tall boy from Bede's class, was awarded 'most improved'.

Zack sat down beside Danielle to enjoy the rest of his meal. Cara was too far away to see how their date was really going, but both appeared happy. Dylan also looked happy, chatting animatedly to Stephanie and occasionally managing to make the beautiful Elisabet smile.

At the end of the meal, Cara and Craig rose quietly and walked back to girl's dormitory.

"Thank you for asking me out once again," Craig said. "I enjoyed the function more than I expected, and your friends did seem to be getting along well together, which I believe was the point. I wasn't in the mood to linger late though, I hope that was okay."

"It was perfectly fine, Craig," Cara said. "Thank you for escorting me."

Dylan dropped Stephanie and Elisabet back at the dormitory a few minutes later, and Stephanie joined Cara back in their room. The roommate was very quiet and gazed at Bradley's picture for a while. Then she went to sleep with the toy rabbit Bradley had given her, set up on her bedside table looking at her.

Thursday afternoon was their last Plant Biology practical and the Biology Master had set this up as a practical exam. They had to draw and label a number of plants, and count their various parts. They had pictures of unidentified plants to classify according the family, Cara assumed they could not be expected to arrive at the particular species name.

Then the exam began to focus on particular plant samples. Firstly they were shown a sample of moss showing wispy tendrils and asked which stage of its life cycle it had reached. More moss samples were accompanied by questions regarding the content of the capsule and the generations of moss plant visible in each sample.

Then they were then asked to examine a fern plant and describe the nature and function of the brown dots underneath the fronds. They were also asked to identify the heart shaped formation found amongst certain ferns and describe the full lifecycle of a fern plant.

Thirdly they were given a branch of a pine tree and asked to identify its stage of life. Then they were asked to inspect a pine cone and decide whether it contained pollen. If they decided that it did not contain pollen, they were asked to explain what it did contain. This was followed by several more questions regarding the unique reproductive process of the pine tree.

When the students were finished, they went up to the cafeteria to get their tea. They were all relieved the practical exam was over. Cara was glad to have recognized a few of the plants they had been presented with in the practical exam. Stephanie admitted she had been thrown momentarily by the moss, because of all the hundreds of plant families they had studied that semester, she had thought moss were fairly insignificant and had only just managed to scrape up an answer from the depths of her mind.

Dylan and Garry agreed that while the semester had been fun with its constant field trips, the exam had been quite demanding. Danielle expressed surprise that they were all so dedicated to Biology if the incurred practical exams like that every semester!

Friday there were no more classes, because the dedicated study period, also known as 'study vacation' had arrived. Their dormitory room was quiet and littered with books because Stephanie took the study vacation particularly seriously. Cara knew that she too, ought to take this period seriously as she had spent her weekends on outings with the adventure club instead of studying.

The Uniting Church vespers that evening were viewed as a welcome diversion and attracted a full attendance. Zack was sitting with Danielle, clearly attempting to consolidate the progress he had made so far with the girl. Cara slid into a vacant seat on the other side of Dylan, who nodded briefly in acknowledgement of her presence.

Dylan seemed to be in a somber mood. "Bradley has been gone – what – six months now?" he observed.

"Yeah," Cara breathed. "And the investigation into his death is not finished."

"It will be soon," Dylan predicted. "The guys will witness against the culprit, I can feel the tension around the dorm. It has been mounting ever since the steroids were discovered."

"Assuming there was a connection," Cara sighed.

"Two such strange things on campus would hardly have been unrelated," Garry observed.

Stephanie, who was sitting with Garry, shuddered. "How many guys knew anything do you think?"

"Two or three at the most – and they didn't even know that they knew," Dylan observed. "Isolated pieces of information are beginning to fall into place as the boys talk."

"It's still the police's job to put it all together," Stephanie whispered.

"Sure," Dylan agreed.

Saturday afternoon, Cara remembered with a shock that she had not checked the email for messages from Kaleb for a few days. She was momentarily frustrated by the thought that the computer laboratory was closed on the weekend, and then she remembered the terminal in the library archive.

Cara sought out Danielle, who was working in the library. The girl obligingly escorted Cara downstairs and logged her onto the mainframe.

"Thanks," Cara said.

"Anytime, you are welcome," Danielle said. The older girl hovered for a few moments, as if wishing to say something, but upon observing that Cara was absorbed in her correspondence, she left quietly.

Kaleb had sent several email, one message was re-assuring Cara that he was looking forward to seeing her very soon. Cara replied to this message easily, saying how she was looking forward to seeing Kaleb as well. In the next email, Kaleb observed that Cara had not replied for a week. He sincerely hoped that all was well and that it was only study keeping her off-line.

Cara replied, explaining that she had assignments and exams were almost upon her. She was thrilled when a reply popped through almost immediately.

"What time is it where you are?" she typed excitedly. "It's two pm here."

"Almost midnight over here," Kaleb returned. "I was going to log off, when you messaged."

"How exciting," Cara typed. Although the couple had found email a faster form of communication than post, they had never fluked being online at the same time before. There was a small lag between messages, but it was almost like talking.

"A few things have happened," she typed. "Someone has been supplying steroids to some of the basketball players. The police are investigating."

"I half suspected," Kaleb typed with the clarity of distance. "I hope this is the end of the trouble."

"I hope so too," Cara typed. She omitted any mention of her part in the discovery. Email was a written media and the less people who knew the better. "I will see you when you get to Australia, it's only a few weeks now."

Sunday afternoon was devoted to study. Meals were a welcome break, as were the occasional hour of evening television, or joint study session with Zack and Dylan. Although she and Stephanie shared many subjects, Stephanie's study methods were primarily individual and solitary.

Monday lunchtime, the cafeteria was all a-buzz because the police had taken Tony Dantean away for questioning. Vincent and several other students who were bitter regarding their loss of eligibility to play in the basketball final had broken ranks and reported him to the police.

The only person who had witnessed Tony anywhere near Bradley's bike was on the afternoon in question was Arthur Mason, but under the pressure of his peer's indignation, he had also reported everything he knew.

"They say Tony could get two years for supplying the steroids on campus, and up to four years for sabotaging Bradley's bike," Zack reported, sitting down at the table alongside Cara. "Of course, that would be two and four years simultaneously, not six years in total."

Stephanie was looking pale listening to the gossip. "I like to think that even though what Tony did was wrong, he had not meant Bradley to be seriously hurt or injured," she whispered. "Only perhaps distracted from the steroids and worried about his bike."

Tuesday brought Cara's Chemistry theory exam, which she approached in a particularly stressed state. After the exam she felt drained and persuaded Stephanie to accompany her to the campus snack shop for a candy bar. While they were sitting there, Arthur Mason approached. He was accompanied by Michael.

"Arthur would like to speak to you confidentially Stephanie," Michael said. "If that is all right."

Stephanie nodded. "Please sit down Arthur."

Arthur complied. He looked nervous and distraught. "I'm sorry Stephanie," he muttered. "I know I should have spoken up before."

"Thank you for going to the police, Arthur," Stephanie said. "I know it could not have been easy for you. Did you know very much?"

Arthur shook his head. "I knew that Tony was angry regarding his demotion from A grade basketball and blamed Bradley. But other people knew that too."

"What did you know in particular then?" Stephanie asked patiently.

"I knew that Tony had no assignment that afternoon. Most of us had at least one assignment, Tony was a third year then and he was free that afternoon," Arthur began.

"That is circumstantial," Stephanie observed.

"Tony said to me that he would 'slow Bradley down', whatever that meant," Arthur said. "And he went for a walk. I did not know where."

"I see," Stephanie said.

"I did not want to accuse him of something he had not done," Arthur said. "That would be bearing false witness."

"I understand," Stephanie said kindly. "But if someone has committed a crime – then failing to witness would also be false."

"Yeah," Arthur looked sick.

"It's not me that you have to worry about really," Stephanie said. "Bradley's parents require justice. They will never have another son."

"I know," Arthur said. "Once again Stephanie, I'm so sorry."

"Thank you," Stephanie said. "You have been to the police now, I know that took a lot of soul-searching and courage."

"That is very good of you," Arthur said. He looked relieved and allowed Michael to lead him away from the canteen.

Wednesday was a free day, which Cara used to brush up on all her Plant Biology theory. Around mid-morning, an anxious looking Garry called for Stephanie at the girl's dormitory. He was waiting fretfully at the side desk beside the public address system.

"Is Stephanie okay?" Garry asked when he saw Cara, who had heard the summons and ascended the stairs slightly quicker than her roommate.

"I think so," Cara said. "Last night was something of a turning point for her. She hadn't had so many reminders for a while, but she seems to be up and about okay this morning."

Stephanie arrived just then, and Garry turned to Stephanie: "Do you really want to study or would you rather go for a walk?"

Stephanie brightened. "I would like to go for a walk to Bradley's grave if that is alright," she said.

"That is fine," Garry said. "If I can take you?"

Stephanie nodded, and Garry turned to Cara. "Do you want to come?"

"No, you two go alone," Cara said. It would be the first time since the funeral that Garry and Stephanie had visited Bradley's grave together, which must represent some sort of turning point.

Thursday was their Plant Biology theory exam, and both Cara and Stephanie were relieved when it was over. Plant Biology was Cara's last exam, except for Education, which would be the following week.

Friday lunchtime, Cara was sitting with Andrew and Kathy, Stephanie and Garry in the cafeteria, when Larry approached their group.

"I need to talk to Stephanie," Larry said plonking himself down on the seat. "I'm also very sorry".

Cara knew that Larry was a theology student, and one of the gentlest persons she had ever met. She could not imagine what he had to apologise regarding.

"What for?" Stephanie asked.

"I knew that Tony was extremely frightened when the news of Bradley's death arrived," Larry continued. "I comforted him for several hours that night."

Stephanie looked serious, remembering that fateful evening. "I'm sure you meant well Larry," she said.

"All of us guys were shocked, and in grief I didn't think anything more about it," Larry continued. "It was only recently, with the discovery of the steroids that I began to think about the about the words Tony used."

"Like what?" Cara asked curiously.

"Tony muttered he 'only wanted Bradley to forget the bottles'," Larry said. "I thought it was something personal between the two of them and let it go."

"Instead it was a confession of sorts," Stephanie said. "I imagine you were as shocked as the rest that night, Larry."

"I was," Larry admitted.

"Easy to doubt your memory," Cara suggested.

Larry nodded. "I was concerned with everybody's grief and shock," he said. "Including my own – Bradley was a friend."

"I take it you have been to the police now," Stephanie said.

Larry nodded. "I had to."

"Even your testimony doesn't make the case open and shut," Stephanie murmured. "The police still have to tie Tony to the actual bike."

"I'm sure they will find a way," Larry said.

"From what you say, Tony never intended Bradley to get killed,"

Stephanie said. "Which does relieve my mind a little. However, if he were truly repentant, he ought to have gone to the police himself and faced the consequences."

Larry shuddered. "I assume he hoped he would get away unpunished," he said. "But imagine living your life with that hanging over your head."

"Unthinkable," Stephanie said. "Much better to have faced the consequences. Although, while he may not have intended Bradley's death — there is still the matter of the steroid dealing."

"That makes his behaviour seem much more serious," Larry said. "Long term, it could have affected a lot of people's health."

"That's not my issue," Stephanie said. "My concern is the loss of my nearest and dearest, I have to put the rest aside."

"I appreciate your point of view, however, some of the guys affected by the steroid scandal were my dormitory mates," Larry said. "So I wonder whether if I had said anything sooner – someone might have been spared the experience."

Saturday things came to a head between Zack and Danielle. The pair had been hanging out as friends ever since the basketball tea, but Zack was becoming concerned he might be 'friend-zoned' once again with the senior girl. He mumbled something about 'caring for her deeply' and Danielle looked surprised.

"You and I have been friends for years Zackie," Danielle replied.

"But I don't want to be JUST FRIENDS," Zack exclaimed, going as red as a beetroot. "I never have!"

"How come you could never tell me this when we were alone?" Danielle exclaimed in mortification. "We have known each other for nearly four years now!"

"I get shy around girls," Zack said. "Not so much with Cara, because she is not so girly, but especially so with the girls I like."

"Why are you telling me now?" Danielle inquired.

"Well we are both graduating at the end of the year, and we could lose contact," Zack labored valiantly to express himself. "I couldn't bear for that to happen."

"We wouldn't lose contact," Danielle said. "But as to our becoming an item – I will have to think about it."

"All right," Zack relaxed into silence. It was all he could hope for at this stage.

On Sunday after lunch, Cara decided to go for a swim in the university pool, which was warmed by solar pipes. It was a nice sunny day, around 20 degrees Celsius (68 degrees Fahrenheit), which was warm for June in Queensland.

Cara knew that she really ought to swim with a buddy, so she invited Dylan to meet her down by the pool. When she arrived, she discovered that Dylan had invited Zack, and Zack had invited Danielle. In turn, Danielle had invited a few of the fourth year girls.

"This is quite the party," Cara remarked surveying the group.

"Yes," Dylan remarked.

Cara could see that he was noticing how comfortable Zack and Danielle appeared together with their contemporaries. Although Danielle appeared reluctant to admit it, she and Zack had the potential to be an excellent couple.

"I will race you to the end of the pool and back," Dylan suggested and took off swimming.

Cara braced herself against the side of the pool and straightened out into a long glide, before cleaving the water with strong clean strokes. Dylan was a robust swimmer and occasional surfer, but she almost caught up to him.

"No fair," she cried when they both reached the finish line. "You started early."

Dylan paused, treading water and looking thoughtful. "Have you heard from Kaleb lately?" He asked.

Cara nodded. "Yes," she said. "We are both very busy with study and exams."

"Is he still planning to come back for second semester?" Dylan inquired.

"Yes," Cara said.

"It's easy to forget people when they aren't here," Dylan mused.

"Oh yes," Cara agreed. "Too easy."

She felt like there was something significant she ought to be saying to Dylan, but could not find the right words, so she simply splashed him. Dylan laughed and splashed her playfully back. It was the most relaxed they had been together for almost a year.

Monday Cara visited the lecturers' offices and collected her assignments from the boxes outside their doors. She collected some of Stephane's assignments too, and her roommate became slightly misty-eyed because apparently collecting her assignments had been one of Bradley's endearing habits.

Tuesday Stephanie sat her English exam and Cara spent the afternoon mowing the lawns at the rear of the buildings. She did not know who would mow during the long holidays while she was away, probably a caretaker.

Wednesday was the Education exam, which was also Cara's last exam for the semester. Cara and all her friends, with the exception of Phoebe and

Kathy who both had History on Thursday, were now finished their exams.

In the afternoon, Cara visited the computer laboratory and made one final check for email messages from Kaleb. She also sent him a farewell email. Communication would be much slower over the break, but she hoped to see him again in person as soon as the second semester commenced.

Thursday Cara and Bede, who had also finished exams, caught the university bus to Northcoast. They then caught the train to Brisbane and the aeroplane to Melbourne where their parents were waiting to pick them up. Both girls intended to have a lovely holiday before practice teaching at their chosen schools. Worries such as the arrest of Tony Dantean and the steroid scandal were far from their minds.

CHAPTER EIGHT: SECOND SERVICE

As Cara rode the university bus back to Silver Springs from Northcoast station at the beginning of August, her heart was thumping because she would be seeing her boyfriend Kaleb again very soon. Kathy and Andrew, who had arrived at Northcoast on the bus from Kathy's parent house in Armidale, were busy chatting to her sister Bede, while Cara was lost in a dream.

"Eh what?" Cara asked, suddenly realizing that Kathy had actually been trying to talk to her.

"I asked whether your practice teaching went well," Kathy repeated.

"Oh yeah," Cara said. "With a bunch of grizzling students, and laboratory full of equipment and dangerous chemicals – what can go wrong?"

"Everything - by the sounds!" Kathy exclaimed.

Bede laughed. "It sounds a bit like Home Ec, with kids and stoves and knives all in one room," she exclaimed.

"You have to be safety conscious," Cara observed. "And strict, but I got through."

"I think I had more fun in Art," Kathy observed. "Although I always have to battle against the student's perception that the period is a bludge."

"Same in cooking," Bede exclaimed.

Cara noticed that Kathy was attempting to shove her hand across her face. "What is that?" she exclaimed, looking at the unusual ring on her friend's right hand. It was mostly flat and yet the top was shaped like two hands meeting in a heart shape below a crown.

"It's a Claddagh," Kathy explained. "Andrew gave it to me because as a poor Theology student, he cannot afford to marry me just yet."

"It is interesting," Bede remarked. "Is it a friendship ring?"

"It is a fidelity ring," Andrew explained. "The two hands are joined in friendship, the heart represents love, and the crown represents faith or loyalty. Some say the symbols also represent the Trinity."

"I see," observed Cara, "It's very unique."

Kathy's boyfriend Andrew was clever with symbols and was often quoting Bible verses that were amazingly apt for their everyday lives. It was almost to be expected that he had found a ring which held its own sermon. However, the ring was made from real gold and Kathy seemed very happy.

"Thank you," Kathy said. "In the olden days, it was used as either a betrothal or wedding ring."

"How long have you two been together now?" Bede inquired. "Is it a year yet?"

"Ten months," Andrew replied.

That was a shorter period of time than Cara and Kaleb had been going out, Cara noted with a shock. Although six months of Cara and Kaleb's relationship had only been correspondence, which was not particularly satisfying for two passionate young people. And Kaleb had corresponded with Bede, which didn't count because Bede was her sister – or did it? A little cold hand of alarm clutched Cara's heart.

They arrived on campus and Luke dropped the girls off at their dormitory first. Luke and Andrew helped carry the bags inside and the amusing warning, "Man in the dorm," was published over the public address system before they were allowed to enter.

After the boys left, Cara found herself alone in her room because Stephanie had not yet returned. Deciding that unpacking alone was boring, she knocked on the adjacent single room and was ushered into Kathy's presence.

A little mischief entered into Cara and she said: "I hope you and Andrew have found other ways of expressing your commitment to each other besides the ring!"

Cara was greeted by a brilliant blush from Kathy. 'Who would have thought?' she mused. Despite being a Theology student, Andrew was clearly no prude!

"You two have actually done it?" Cara exclaimed, thinking of all the sleep overs Kathy and Andrew had at each other's parent's houses each holidays.

"I'm not saying anything," Kathy replied with her face as red as a beetroot. "One of my fears in going out with a trainee minister used to be that there would be no affection. I'm happy to find that is not a problem with Andrew."

"What is it like?" Cara inquired.

"All I can say is that you need to wait for the right person," Kathy said. "I am so glad I never went very far with my first two boyfriends - everything with Andrew has been just perfect."

"Tell me more," Cara cried. "Was it at your parent's house or his?"

"Neither," Kathy said. "We have too much respect to do that! We just made out a bit... discretely of course."

"So where?" Cara persisted.

"If you must know, miss nosy, I was practice teaching in Byron Bay because I have cousins there," Kathy explained. "Andrew came up to visit, and because there was no room in the house, he booked into a caravan park. It was so lovely to have so much privacy on the weekend."

"Perhaps when you graduate at the end of the year, you could get your own place," Cara suggested. "Or even marry Andrew."

"It depends where I get work," Kathy said. "We discussed a few of those options."

"But you are not quite engaged?" Cara inquired.

"We are engaged to be engaged," Kathy said.

"I never heard of such a thing!" Cara exclaimed, although in the back of her mind she thought she might have. Couples struggled to find different ways to describe their levels of commitment to each other. "Tell me more."

Kathy shook her head. "I really can't," she said. "It is too embarrassing and you are full of naughty assumptions, Cara O'Brien."

Cara returned to her room and began to pull a few items out of her suitcase and hang in her wardrobe. At last she heard her name called over the public address system. After a quick glance in the mirror to make sure her hair was in place, she hurried downstairs. Kaleb was waiting for her in the foyer and her heart thumped when she saw him there. He was so tall, so slim, so dark and so handsome!

Cara approached him with hands outstretched. "Hello there," she cried.

Kaleb took both of her hands and looked Cara up and down. "It has been so long!"

"Ah yes," Cara said. "Shall we – er, go for a walk?"

"Good idea," Kaleb exclaimed.

The couple walked out of the foyer of the girls' dormitory and into the relative privacy of the university grounds. Cara noticed they were holding hands loosely.

"What are your plans, now you are back?" Cara asked.

"Just to study really," Kaleb said. "My timetable is a mess! I'm ahead some units and behind others. I also did a stint of preaching practice at an all-black church in America which was signed off by my university and the experience will be accepted here."

"That's good," Cara said. "How long do you think you can stay?"

"I think I can swing from August this year, till June next year," Kaleb said.

"What about Christmas?" Cara inquired.

"I'm not sure," Kaleb said. "Is there any possibility your parents might have me?"

"They might, but it wouldn't be pretty," Cara chortled. "My mother calls you 'that black boy'."

Kaleb laughed. "I am black," he agreed. "It is something to be proud of over in America."

"We don't talk that way in Australia – or if we do it isn't considered polite," Cara said.

"I do have another option," Kaleb said. "I have been talking to the university about the possibility of my doing ministry with Indigenous Australians and seeing how they respond to me."

"Over Christmas?" Cara exclaimed.

"It is as good a time as any," Kaleb suggested.

"Yeah," Cara murmured. She must have forgotten how focused Kaleb was on his goals in the ministry, and how everything was an opportunity with him. He really wasn't very relaxed.

"While you have been away, I have been going on Adventure Club outings," she confided. "The bus transport was provided and I didn't require a date."

"Now I'm back," Kaleb said, "I am hoping to resurrect the prayer group, Andrew tells me they have not been meeting without me."

"Of course," Cara said. "But surely not when it clashes with Adventure Club outings!"

"Are you still in the choir?" Kaleb inquired. Choir performance had been an interest they had shared the previous year.

"No," Cara said. "All that was fun for a semester. However, I have had a heavy subject load with three late afternoons. I even dropped basketball."

"I'm sorry to hear that," Kaleb said. Cara wasn't sure whether he was referring to the choir or the basketball. Being tall and light on his feet, Kaleb was usually in demand amongst the basketball teams himself. It was another of the things they had in common when they met.

"I think we have both changed a bit," Cara said.

"I haven't exactly changed," Kaleb said. "But I do feel a strong need to focus on the future."

"Okay," Cara said. "Do you want to keep dating me?"

"Of course I do," Kaleb said. "Do you?"

"Oh yes," Cara exclaimed. She hadn't waited a whole six months for nothing! Kaleb walked her back to girl's dorm and gave her a small kiss outside the front door.

On Monday, classes commenced again and Cara easily lost herself in the whirl. She did not share any classes with Kaleb, as he was classed as a second year and shared some of his classes with Bede. However, she looked around for him at lunch in the cafeteria, and found he had saved a seat for her next to Kathy and Andrew.

"Hello," Cara said.

"Hey there," Kaleb replied cheerfully.

"How was your morning?" Cara inquired. "I missed you at breakfast."

"Yes, I had to rush for a seven thirty lecture," Kaleb said. "Sorry about that."

"Do you and Andrew share any classes?" Cara inquired curiously.

"Ah yes," Andrew replied. "Would you believe this boy is ahead in his Greek and Hebrew?"

"Really?" Cara exclaimed.

"Yes," Kaleb said. "Those were subjects I knew were required by both institutions, so I prioritised."

"Nice," Cara said.

"While I remember," Kaleb said bashfully. "I have this for you." He pulled out a colourful woven band about twenty centimeters long, with thin strands at either end. "It is a native American friendship band."

"I didn't know we were exchanging gifts," Cara said in surprise. "But thank you. It will make a very nice bookmark."

Cara slipped the band into her jeans pocket, and noticed that Kathy was giving her a strange look. "Are you all right Kathy?"

"Yes, it's nothing," Kathy said. "Aren't you going to give Kaleb a kiss in exchange for his gift?"

"Of course!" Cara exclaimed and lifted her face to give Kaleb a quick peck. They were in a crowded cafeteria and all that. Public demonstration of affection could get a couple into trouble.

After lunch, Cara had her first Information Processing class. This unit had now replaced Agriculture as her chosen house requirement. The student numbers in the unit were limited because there were only about a dozen personal computers. The Biology majors, including Stephanie, Garry, and Dylan, had chosen computing.

Danielle, who used computers in her work in the library, had also signed up. Several Theology students, including Andrew, David and Larry had chosen computing in the hopes that being able to use an office computer would complement their sermon writing and record keeping processes. As it was an open subject, their girlfriends, Kathy, Debbie and Anita had also signed up to keep them company.

The first class covered the theory of information, why record keeping is important and how computers help people manage information. Some of this information seemed very basic, but it was also tied together with mathematical theory and information law. Towards the end of the class, the students got to turn the computers on, and practice the basics such as formatting their own disks and saving files.

The Chemistry unit that Cara was completing this semester was a new unit entitled 'Environmental Chemistry', which covered the cycles of important elements, such as phosphorus, hydrogen, oxygen and metals on the planet. It also covered methods of testing soil, water and air for pollutants. Like Biochemistry the semester before, this unit was also interdisciplinary, containing aspects of geology, geography and ecology.

The first experiments were designed to confirm their knowledge of the water cycle. Melting ice, boiling water and collecting condensation as it cooled seemed almost too simple for their level, but Cara wrote down the required observations and answered the questions seriously.

Then the Chemistry Doctor explained that due to the difficulty of demonstrating the nitrogen cycle, they would perform a simulation called the 'Nitrogen Game''. This game required the students to label a number of stations around the room as points in the nitrogen cycle, for example, atmospheric nitrogen; proteins in plants or animals, ammonia in wastes, or nitrates in soil and water.

Each student started at a different point and rolled a dice to determine where they would move next. They kept a record of their journey and would compare it later in discussion. The game showed the variety of paths a nitrogen atom could follow through the cycle and the endless nature of the cycling. Zack found it most amusing whenever he was turned into urea and excreted; and Dylan was entertained that they got to 'play a game' during a third year subject.

Cara began talking to Garry, as they had both entered into the soil as organic matter. Cara had been a nitrogen atom in a plant leaf that had dropped, and Garry had been a small animal that had died. They were waiting for bacteria and fungi to break them down, and had to throw the correct number to acquire a method of release from the soil back into the cycle.

Garry had not completed a practice teaching placement over the mid-year break, but had gone straight into an intensive winter school at the University of Wollongong. The unit he had completed had been entitled 'Laboratory Procedures' and had a strong focus on occupational health and safety.

Cara was about to ask Garry more about his aims in combining these subjects with his current studies, when she rolled a release into ground water. Garry's next dice roll indicated that he was picked up by a plant and they parted company.

The final hour of the laboratory was occupied in setting up a terrarium designed to simulate a cyclic chemical environment. It contained earth mixed with potting mix to provide some extra nutrition and a reservoir of water. Several hardy plants were planted and the lid was sealed. The glass case was then placed in a position where it would receive adequate sunlight, but not be overheated.

The terrarium was not to be opened all semester. The idea was for the water to evaporate in the sunlight and condense against the glass, causing rain as in nature. The plants ought to absorb sunlight and nutrients to grow. They should also cycle carbon-di-oxide and oxygen during photosynthesis and respiration. Eventually the terrarium might run low on nutrients, but it ought to be self-sustaining for a period.

Wednesday afternoon, Stephanie and Bede were working on the bridesmaids dresses for Damaris' wedding. They had decided on a design with a simple cap sleeve, which provided the right contrast to Damaris' wedding dress with its exaggerated sleeves, but did not leave the shoulders bare. The dark blue dresses were semi-fitted, with unimpeded lines flowing down from the scooped necklines to a little above the knee, where fluted panels were joined into the seams to match Damaris' mermaid profile.

"The dresses are lovely!" Cara exclaimed when she saw the pattern. "Who is Damaris having as her bridesmaids?"

"Her cousin and Michael's sister," Stephanie answered. "No one from the university because she only did a one year course here after all."

"The girls have already been measured for their dresses," Bede announced. "Michael's sister visited from Brisbane yesterday and brought Damaris' cousin with her."

"You were busy in Chemistry," Stephanie explained. "And they didn't stay very long, but went back to Damaris' place."

"I can't believe the wedding is so soon," Cara murmured.

"Just over six weeks," Stephanie reported.

"Luckily Stephanie and I are fast dressmakers," Bede said.

"Plenty of time with two of us on the job," Stephanie said. "And the wedding dress is nearly finished!"

Bede stretched out her arm and Cara caught sight of a gaily coloured band tied around her sister's wrist. "Why have you got my bookmark around your wrist?" she cried.

Bede looked puzzled. "I haven't," she said. "Kaleb gave this to me."

"Yours is still tucked into your Biology textbook," Stephanie said. "I thought you simply weren't wearing it because you aren't into girly stuff."

"What?" Cara exclaimed.

"They are friendship bands," Stephanie explained.

"I asked Kaleb to bring them back from America," Bede said. "Because I just love Native American handcrafts."

"Oh I see," Cara said. A few things began to fall into place, including Kathy's strange look when she called the band a book mark, and Kaleb's unusual bashfulness. "So I should be wearing it?"

"Yeah," Bede said. "Get Kaleb to tie it on for you."

In Biology that semester the class was doing Zoology. This involved a more in-depth study of the animal kingdom than they had done in previous years. They were starting with all the characteristics and features of birds. Cara was mildly disappointed the Biology Master said they would not be spending hours 'bird watching' and that they could observe the local species in their own time if they wished.

During the laboratory the class investigated the properties of eggs, using hen's eggs purchased from the supermarket. They also analysed an abandoned nest the Biology Master had discovered on the ground one day when he was out walking. The star of the lesson was the pet budgerigar the Biology Master had brought into the laboratory from home.

Friday morning when she was getting dressed, Cara noticed the Indian friendship band sticking out of her Biology text. She shrugged and picked it up, knotting it casually around her wrist. Kaleb smiled when he saw her wearing the bracelet.

"I am glad you are finally wearing this," he said, giving her wrist a friendly touch.

Cara blushed. "I honestly didn't know what it was when you gave it to me," she said. "And some days when I'm gardening or doing Biology I would get it dirty. Like yesterday – I was actually handling bird droppings."

"They are machine washable you know," Kaleb said. "And one day I could get you something – er, better."

Cara laughed, ignoring the hint. She wasn't used to romantic gestures and she was not sure that she was ready to get serious with Kaleb just yet.

"I was thinking this afternoon, we could go and sign up for the choir again," Kaleb suggested.

Cara shook her head. "This afternoon I have to mow the lawns."

"I could sign us both up," Kaleb suggested.

Cara shook her head. "I loved hanging with Kathy and Andrew last time we were in choir, but I feel like I have done that already."

"We would get to go on trips together," Kaleb explained patiently. "If I sign up and you don't, I will be going without you."

"We would go on trips together if you joined the Adventure Club instead," Cara countered. "Lots of people find God in nature and I don't think I want to do the full-on Theology student's girlfriend thing again."

"What are you saying?" Kaleb inquired.

"I might need you to do the Science boyfriend thing for a change," she said.

"Fair enough," Kaleb said. "What does that involve?"

"Bird watching, whale spotting, camping and lots of other fun things," Cara exclaimed. "Next weekend the Adventure Club have chartered a boat for a three hour whale watching cruise just off Noosa, and I was hoping we could go together."

"That does sound like fun," Kaleb admitted. "I have to get to class now – shall we talk about it lunch time?"

By lunch time, however, Kaleb had talked to David and joined the worship committee. This activity represented excellent experience for Theology students, as it included facilitating the services in cooperation with the university chaplains. Some of the Theology student's girl friends were also involved and they performed tasks such as running the overhead projector and displaying the song lyrics.

The worship committee had a rotating roster. Unfortunately, it also required a serious commitment of time, and on the weeks that Kaleb would be involved with worship, he would be very busy.

"I am glad you are involved," Cara exclaimed. "The experience will look great on your resume."

Cara knew that the most successful of the ministerial students were the ones that gathered a lot of experience, but she was mildly disappointed he clearly did not share her interest in the environment.

Kaleb went off with David to attend his first worship committee meeting and Cara went off to mow the lawns. At tea that evening, Kaleb chose to sit talking to Larry as the other couples slunk away for their Friday evening kisses.

Even Debbie and David said, "Goodbye," politely and suggested that they meet up again in an hours' time at the Uniting Church vespers. When Kaleb and Larry finally finished chatting, Cara asked to be escorted back to the foyer of girl's dormitory.

Kaleb gave her a chaste kiss on the cheek and Cara climbed the few steps down to her room, wondering whether the relationship was really what she had expected it would be upon his return.

Saturday at breakfast, Kaleb announced that he had called a meeting of the prayer group for that afternoon.

"You will be there, won't you?" he asked Cara anxiously.

"Yes, of course," Cara replied.

"I'm going to have to spend the morning preparing," Kaleb said. "Plus, because I'm ahead in Greek, I'm in Andrew's class and it is very demanding."

Cara sighed. "I guess I will study too," she said, although she had hoped for a little shared recreational activity.

The prayer meeting Kaleb was organising commenced shortly after lunch in the cafeteria lounge. David and Debbie, Andrew and Kathy, Anita and Larry were in attendance, as well as a couple of second year Theology students called Mathew and Christopher that Kaleb had recruited.

As Cara slid into the seat beside her boyfriend, she was surprised to see Bede enter the café lounge.

"I thought I would take a small break from sewing," the younger O'Brien sister whispered. "You didn't mind Kaleb inviting me, did you?"

"Of course not," Cara returned. "It's only a prayer meeting!"

Kaleb commenced by thanking everyone for attending and asking for prayer requests. Most of the students volunteered requests such as inspiration for their studies, and Debbie's elder sister was pregnant with a second baby, so Debbie wanted to pray for a healthy pregnancy.

When it was Kaleb's turn, he suggested they pray for peace between the Iran and Iraq regions, and also that the United States government be restrained from use of its new defense programme, also known as 'star wars'.

Andrew suggested several events from earlier in the year, including the victims of the Chernobyl accident, and the families of the crew of the space shuttle *Challenger*, who must still be grieving. Larry also suggested they pray about the sudden downpour that had fallen in NSW earlier that week, overloading many drainage systems.

After the prayer meeting, Cara waited around for Kaleb to invite her on a stroll, as it was still early for a Saturday. Kathy and Andrew had diplomatically offered to walk Bede back to the dorms, leaving Cara and Kaleb alone.

Kaleb finished gathering up the Bibles and papers he had provided for the meeting and turned to Cara. "I have to take these back to the boy's dorm."

"The campus snack bar is still open for another hour," Cara ventured.

"I will meet you over there in a few minutes then," Kaleb replied. "It really would be boring for you to walk these back to men's assembly area with me."

"Okay," Cara said. She felt in her pocket to make sure she was carrying a little money, probably just enough for a Milk Way bar; and strolled towards the snack bar, which really was placed ridiculously close to the cafeteria anyway.

Stephanie and Garry were sitting in the snack bar at a personal computer terminal someone had the smart idea of setting up for game playing.

"Don't tell me you guys still haven't beaten *King's Quest*," Cara exclaimed.

"I have," Garry explained, "Now I am showing Stephanie the way through, and she likes hunting for secret areas."

"You two are so lucky you are both nerds!" Cara muttered.

"I get the impression something is wrong," Garry observed.

"Yeah," Cara said. "This year with Kaleb seems different than last year. We don't want to join the same extra-curricular activities."

"Last year choir counted for your Community Involvement subject, which was mighty convenient,' Stephanie observed.

"Hmm," Cara mused. "I hadn't thought of that. It did seem that I gave up less to accompany Kaleb to his Bible stuff last year."

"Here comes Kaleb now," Stephanie whispered.

"Hey dude," Garry greeted. "How's everything going?"

"Hello Garry, hello Stephanie," Kaleb said. "It sure is great to be back.

I've joined the worship committee and should be heavily involved in organising weekend services."

"That sounds very rewarding," Stephanie reflected diplomatically.

"It should be," Kaleb, said sliding an arm around Cara's shoulders. "The only problem is that my little bird here, wants to go on boat trips and all sorts of exciting things, which I won't be able to join."

An hour later, the snack bar closed and Kaleb walked Cara back to the girl's dormitory. She steered him away from the front entrance towards the rear door which led directly onto the basement. This door was open as well as the others, but the area was shrouded by trees.

Cara pulled Kaleb behind one of the trees and slid her arms up around his neck to link her hands behind his neck.

"Ah of course," Kaleb said. He bent his head and gave her a quick kiss on the mouth. Cara pulled him closer and returned the kiss with fervor.

"Um Cara," Kaleb said, pulling his head back. "I've got to ask you something."

"Sure," Cara said.

"I'm going to do my best to stay in Australia, but if my church should call me home, I might have to serve in America," Kaleb said. "If I do, are you coming with me?"

"I don't know," Cara said.

"What do you mean – you don't know?" Kaleb demanded.

"You have never asked me before," Cara said. "I need time to think about it."

"Either you love me and would come to America with me, or you don't and wouldn't," Kaleb said. "I understand it could be a difficult decision, but I need to know now, before we get more serious."

"I love you, but I love Australia too," Cara said uncomfortably.

"That's what I thought," Kaleb sighed. "In all the months we have been corresponding, you never once mentioned coming to the United States if I could not get back to Australia."

"However would I do that?" Cara exclaimed.

"I don't want to get ahead of myself," Kaleb said. "But two words — fiancé visa."

"Oh!" Cara said. "My parents would hate that!"

"I know," Kaleb said. "Bede told me."

"I just want to have fun with my boyfriend, for whom I waited a whole six months," Cara cried.

"I understand that," Kaleb said patiently. "But I need to know if we have a future."

"I will tell you tomorrow," Cara promised.

"Alright, I will pick you up for the services," Kaleb said.

Sunday morning, Cara grabbed a quick breakfast and then spent her time making sure her hair and outfit were neat for the services. Stephanie appeared to sense something was wrong.

"Are you okay?" Stephanie inquired. "You got in before me last night."

"Not really," Cara sniffed. "Kaleb won't kiss me properly!"

"What do you mean?" Stephanie asked.

"Do I have to draw you a roadmap?" Cara snapped.

"Yes, actually," Stephanie said. "Do you mean mouth, neck, shoulder or chest?"

"Mouth of course," Cara said. "I've never really gone much further — have you?"

Stephanie blushed. "Bradley and I were serious you know," she said. "We kissed and cuddled."

"Yeah, you still wear his ring," Cara observed. "Has Garry ever asked you to take it off?"

"No, and I don't think he ever will," Stephanie said. Of recent times, however, she had transferred the double heart signet ring Bradley had given her back onto her right hand instead of her left. "It's not like I can go off and be unfaithful with Bradley."

"Of course not," Cara affirmed. "Kaleb has asked me the big 'going to America' question – he wants his answer soon."

"I guess he wants to know," Stephanie observed practically.

"Duh!" Cara exclaimed. "He never wanted to know before."

"Perhaps he always wanted to know, but never asked," Stephanie suggested.

"I don't know, I thought last year we were happy," Cara mused.

"Last year you were freshly in love," Stephanie concluded. "Things change over time."

The girls heard Cara's name being called over the public address system. "That's me now," Cara said. "Wish me luck."

Cara descended to the foyer and placed her hand in Kaleb's. Together they looped around the front of the girl's dormitory to the women's assembly area, where the Inter-denominational praise service was being held. Cara was content to sit quietly, as she had not yet made up her mind what she was going to say to Kaleb when they had their talk.

She glanced around, recognizing everything that was so familiar, from Zack's blonde Polish head and beside him, Danielle's shorter brunette profile, to the candles on the altar. Her dear friends Kathy and Andrew, sat with Tom and Joelle; and further down the pew, Garry sat with Stephanie. Phoebe and Hank were both on campus for the services and would likely join their friends in the cafeteria for lunch.

David and Debbie, Larry and Anita were all very close. Some distance away, Craig was seated with Elisabet, but she had not heard anything about how things were going for those two. Perhaps they were a couple, perhaps they were still bound by their mutual reserve into being 'just friends'.

Silver Springs University and Silver Springs friends were currently Cara's world. However, she knew that things changed. They would all graduate eventually and perhaps find employment in different parts of Australia. Phoebe was already married, and Damaris and Michael would be married in September. Kathy would graduate at the end of this year, and Garry was hastening his graduation with summer and winter classes.

It seemed that Cara was the only person not moving toward her future. And yet, she had thought she was working on her future by completing her degree. She tried to think of herself moving to America, to enjoy the adventure of travel and make a life with Kaleb, whom she loved. Somehow, she could not get the picture.

Cara's eyes rested on Dylan, sitting alone amongst his best friends, who were all partnered. She suddenly knew that whatever she did, wherever she went, she could not leave Dylan. Dear, Silly Dylan! Dylan who had courted her until she had convinced him to give up and move onto other girls. Dylan who had once seemed so immature, but had become serious, supporting Stephanie in her grief, gaining holiday employment and buying himself the light jeep. Dylan who was only just beginning to talk to her naturally again.

The Inter-denominational praise service had concluded and Kaleb placed his hand under Cara's elbow, guiding her out of the women's assembly area and into the campus meeting hall. Kaleb liked to attend both services and was leading her straight into the Reform Church worship.

Cara, busy with her internal revelation, meekly followed. They sat down next to Kathy and Andrew.

After the Reform Church service, Kaleb led the way into the cafeteria. The lunch conversation was very pleasant and included Phoebe and Hank who were visiting, but Cara allowed it to wash over her. Eventually, Kathy noticed.

"You are quiet today Cara," Kathy observed.

"I'm thinking," Cara said.

"That's not like you," Phoebe observed. "I don't mean that in a nasty way."

"I know what you mean," Cara said.

Kaleb and Andrew were absorbed in a conversation about cars with Hank. Hank had all sorts of interesting blokey things to say because of his work in the mechanical workshop. It was still Andrew's dream to purchase a small vehicle for himself and Kathy, and free them from reliance public transport during the holidays.

Eventually Hank and Phoebe said, "Goodbye," and Kaleb turned to Cara.

"Shall we go for a walk?" Kaleb inquired.

Cara nodded. "I'm ready," she declared.

They placed their trays on the dishwashing trolley and left the cafeteria. The murmur of lazy weekend diners faded away behind them, and Cara turned towards the oval, which was close but would be deserted at this time. She waited till they stopped and sat down on a wooden bench designed for the occasional spectator. She could have given Kaleb her answer earlier, but being seated seemed more civilized somehow.

"I'm sorry," Cara said. "I don't think I could move back to America with you."

Kaleb sighed. "I guessed as much," he said.

"Why didn't you ask earlier?" Cara asked. "I really thought you might be happy in Australia."

"I might be at that," Kaleb said. "But it's not a sure thing. I would like to have both options available."

"I see," Cara murmured. She decided to be completely honest. "To tell the truth, there is someone else."

"Dylan," Kaleb murmured.

Cara was surprised. "How did you know?" she cried.

"The way he doesn't talk to you anymore," Kaleb said. "We used to all be friends and now he prowls like a lone lion."

"Nothing happened with him while you were away," Cara was able to say honestly.

"I doubt he would allow it," Kaleb said. "You are going to have to work hard to get his friendship back."

"Yeah," Cara sighed.

"If that is the situation with you," Kaleb said, "Would you mind if I asked Bede out?"

"Bede?" Cara echoed.

"You know – your little sister," Kaleb said. "If you are already looking at Dylan, you cannot be angry if I move on as well."

"I don't care what you do," Cara said casually. "I mean I do care, but only in a good way."

"So can I ask Bede?" Kaleb persisted.

"It's a bit weird, but sure," Cara said.

This time, when they said "Goodbye", Cara and Kaleb merely shook hands. It was the end of an era, the death of her first real romance, and rather sad in its way.

The gossips had a juicy tip-bit to talk about all the next week, because on Sunday the tenth of August 1986, Kaleb Proctor left the cafeteria at lunch time holding hands with Cara O'Brien. The same Kaleb Proctor entered the cafeteria again at tea time holding hands with Bede O'Brien. Except for those few students who could never remember the difference between the two O'Brien sisters anyway, this was material enough for a great scandal!

CHAPTER NINE: WHALE WATCHING

Cara really did not mind Bede going out with Kaleb, but she thought it might be best to concentrate on her own activities for a while, and keep a low profile for the next few days, so she did not come to the attention of the gossips. This was more like one of Stephanie's typical coping strategies than Cara's, which were usually more full-on, but it seemed appropriate for the situation.

Monday in Computing, they were set up with a program which acted as an individual typing tutor. Each student was required to practice during class and in their own time as well. It was essential that they achieve a typing speed of ten words per minute to continue the course. This was far less than the secretarial students were required to achieve, which was more like seventy words per minute, on a manual typewriter as well as a computer. Cara quite enjoyed the mindless little typing drills, they were almost like a relaxation exercise.

Chemistry was somewhat more challenging on Tuesday. Their lecture had been on atmospheric chemistry, and some of the most important chemical reactions in the different layers of the atmosphere had been discussed. The laboratory exercises focused more on photochemical processes, which were reactions triggered when a compound absorbed sunlight.

Certain molecules could absorb photons from ultra violet light and become 'excited'. This could lead to colour change or heat production. The Chemistry Doctor demonstrated the process by placing samples of luminous compounds in a carefully enclosed box which prevented the students from looking directly at the ultra violet light source and receiving eye damage. As an additional precaution, they were all wearing safety glasses.

One photochemical reaction important to all life on earth was photosynthesis. The students extracted chlorophyll by crushing green spinach and observed its spectrum under the chromatograph. Other photochemical reactions were unfortunately involved in the formation of harmful smog. The students were given a case study to read and a chart showing the sources of air pollution. The exercise required them to generate formulae for all the sources of photochemical smog mentioned in the case study.

Finally the class checked the progress of their terrarium, noting that the plants appeared to have taken root and survived. Condensation on the glass walls of the case showed that the water cycle was progressing satisfactorily. The Chemistry Doctor challenged the group to name some differences between the terrarium system and the earth.

Cara suggested the system was smaller than earth and had more limited nutrients, Garry observed there were no animals and Zack began to speculate whether the potting mix they had used might have introduced any microbes into the system. This discussion ran overtime, and the class barely managed to snatch some left-overs as the cafeteria was closing its doors.

"If this keeps going, we might have to get the Chemistry Doctor to ring the cafeteria like the Biology Master does for us," Garry said.

"Sounds good," Zack said. He did not do Biology, but his Physics laboratory regularly ran overtime, as the students struggled with the various meters and machines. As a consequence he had survived on some very meager evening meals.

Cara had been promising herself she would not do anything outrageous to get Dylan's attention, but he was giving a good impression of being the only person on campus not to have heard the gossip about Kaleb and Bede. Finally she could not resist dropping a hint.

"Are you guys going on the whale cruise on Saturday?" Cara inquired casually.

"We wouldn't miss it for the world," Garry said. "It sounds so romantic, I'm definitely taking Stephanie."

"I've asked Danielle," Zack said.

"I don't have anyone to take," Dylan muttered.

"Adventure Club outings don't require a date," Cara announced bravely. "I'm going solo."

"Whatever happened to Kaleb?" Dylan inquired.

Zack gave a snort. "Haven't you heard man? Kaleb is going out with the other O'Brien. He did a sister switcheroo!"

"Kinky," Garry observed. "I'm sorry Cara."

"Don't be," Cara said. "I'm perfectly okay."

"How did it come about?" Dylan asked curiously. "Who dropped who?"

"It was mutual," Cara said. "I couldn't see myself moving to America."

"And Bede can?" Zack inquired. "I wouldn't have thought it of her, being such a home-maker and everything."

"Apparently she can," Cara replied.

"Your parents are going to hate that!" Garry observed.

"That's the hilarious part," Cara said with a guffaw. "They were so set against me going, and now they are losing their baby."

"I guess I can go on the whale cruise on my own," Dylan remarked glumly. "I have been doing enough of that lately."

Cara noticed that Dylan deliberately did not invite her to be his date.

She could have rationalized that he was being cautious after her break-up, but more likely he was still being wary as he had been ever since Annie. However, at least he would be on the boat.

Wednesday morning flew by as Cara and Stephanie both had classes. After lunch Stephanie said she had something to tell Cara back in their room. She scrabbled through the papers in the top drawer of her bedside table and produced a printed sheet. "Bede asked me to help her with this."

Cara took the paper and glanced at it. "The Man-Made Fiber Producers Association design competition," she read. "I don't see any reason why you two shouldn't have a go at this."

"Look at the prize," Stephanie said.

"One year's internship across various fashion houses," Cara read. "Includes airfares, accommodation and modest expense allowance. Joint entries are permitted but only one entrant can claim the internship."

"In Washington," Stephanie pointed out. "AMERICA!"

"I see," Cara mused. "Well you are a brilliant seamstress and Bede has been making great progress with her designs… You two could be in with a chance."

"You don't mind?" Stephanie exclaimed.

Cara shook her head. "No, Bede can do as she likes!"

"I thought we might do a tribute to Chester Weinberg," Stephanie said. "He was a brilliant designer, but he died last year from a mysterious illness. Some people say it was AIDS."

AIDS was a new and frightening infectious disease. It could be transmitted through contact with blood and other bodily fluids and there was no known cure.

"Hmm very seventies," Cara said, viewing several pictures. "That should suit you – I'm not sure what style Bede is developing."

"At the moment, Bede is into everything American Indian," Stephanie said. "But I'm sure we can find a way of mixing the two. The main criterion is that we use man-made fibers."

"American Indian," Cara said looking down at her wrist, "I guess I should take this friendship bracelet off and turn it back into a bookmark."

"Under the circumstances, I would do that," Stephanie advised. "I still don't get why you aren't more upset by Bede's behaviour."

"It's because I'm in love with Dylan," Cara murmured.

Stephanie laughed scornfully. "No you are not! Dylan has offered himself to you on a plate hundreds of times and you never took him."

"But he was always there," Cara complained. "And now he is not, I want him. Doesn't that make a kind of sense?"

"Good luck convincing Dylan that!" Stephanie exclaimed.

"I won't try to move too fast," Cara said.

Thursday afternoon in Zoology, the Biology Master drove the class to Mapleton Falls. It was about three quarters of an hour's drive south of Silver Springs and formed part of the Blackall Ranges. Mapleton Falls was also home to the Australian peregrine falcon, the wompoo fruit-dove, the Cascade tree frog and the endangered giant barred frog, as well as many species of reptiles.

The Biology Master explained that the Mapleton falls were composed of rich volcanic soil, which had been worn down by water over the centuries. The rich soil supported subtropical rainforest plants, which in turn sheltered many birds and animals. In the rainy season, the falls cascaded spectacularly due to the extra water. However, they flowed picturesquely even in winter.

The walk to Mapleton Falls lookout where Pencil Creek plunged off the cliff into the valley took fifteen minutes instead of the proscribed five, because they stopped to listen to bird calls and observe other signs of wildlife occupation along the way. When they reached the falls, the students were rewarded by the sight of the Australian peregrine falcon flying high above the cascade.

Then the Biology Master wanted to hunt for frogs along the causeway. Frogs were easier to spot in summer than winter, but they caught a brief glimpse of a tree frog. They were unable to spot a giant barred frog, and the Biology Master expressed himself concerned because he had not been able to document one since 1982. He explained that the clearing of land upstream and decreased water quality had reduced populations in several key streams.

After that, the group went for a walk along the Wompoo circuit, and listen to the doves give their distinctive three syllable 'wook-a-woo' call. As always, the Biology Master was a terrific bundle of energy as he strode along the 1.3 kilometer track and only paused when he found something he wanted to observe.

Cara divided her social time evenly between Danielle and Dylan during the trip. She did not want to appear too eager or needy. Normally in her tom-boyish enthusiasm, she did not have time for self-consciousness, but she was wary of remarks that even her best friends might make regarding her being on the rebound.

Friday afternoon after mowing the lawn, Cara was mildly bored and decided to drop by the Music department to see how Craig was doing. Not stopping to go back to the girl's dormitory to shower, she brushed down her overalls and took off her shoes, leaving them beside the door. Craig was writing something on manuscript paper when Cara entered. He looked up after a minute.

"Hello Cara," Craig said. "I hope you are not looking for a date again."

"No," Cara said. "Just bored. I think I'll give the dating thing a miss for a while."

"I heard what happened between your boyfriend and your sister," Craig remarked. "That sort of thing is why I stay out of the university relationship scene."

"Yeah," Cara said. "It's no big deal really. If she hadn't been my sister, I might have been mad."

"Weird logic," Craig said. "Some people would be extra mad because she was your sister."

Cara shrugged. "Staying with Kaleb would have required an effort I didn't want to make. I thought you and Elisabet might have been going out by now?"

"Elisabet is a sweet girl and we are good friends," Craig said. "But somehow – neither of us is the effort making type either."

"I would make an effort for the right guy," Cara declared.

"I see," Craig said. "Well, I'm too wrapped up in what I'm doing right now to be bothered."

"What is it you are doing?" Cara inquired curiously.

"Writing my own symphony," Craig said. "It's a major project and very ambitious."

"Let me see," Cara said.

Craig lifted up his manuscript paper and Cara could see several other closely scripted sheets underneath it.

"Oh wow," She exclaimed. "Has it been performed?"

"Some Music department friends have helped me play it through – but not publically yet," Craig said.

"I think you are amazing," Cara said. "But I better go and get out of these dirty clothes before tea."

"I'll see you another time then," Craig said. "Feel free to say hello anytime."

That evening when Cara heard Stephanie's name called over the public address system for vespers, she decided to go down to the foyer with her roommate. As she had hoped, both Dylan and Garry were waiting in the foyer and they fell into step together comfortably as a group. She even managed to make a joke or two that helped Dylan laugh.

Saturday after lunch, the members of the Adventure Club and their selected guests all lined up beside the university bus, waiting for Luke and the chaperones to arrive. When Luke unlocked the bus, the students all scrambled inside to select their seats.

Stephanie sat down with Garry, and Cara selected the seat immediately across the aisle from the couple. She slid across into the window seat and watched the bus door closely. Dylan climbed into the bus, and appeared to hesitate. Cara deliberately caught his eye and smiled.

"Is this seat saved for me?" Dylan asked, indicating the seat next to her.

"Sure," Cara said. "Anything for a friend!"

"Thanks," Dylan said shortly.

"I hope we see whales today," Cara said.

"I believe there is a good chance," Dylan said. "They swim from the colder waters to the tropical waters, and go right past the coast at this time of year."

The bus turned a corner and Cara was thrown against Dylan. "Sorry," she whispered, trying to straighten herself.

"It's okay," Dylan said, steadying her shoulder with his arm. "Try to relax."

The bus pulled into the car park at Noosa Harbour and the students climbed out. Two magnificent catamarans were moored at the wharf. Luke locked the bus and sent the Director of Student Services, who was chaperoning the trip, to enquire which boat was theirs.

Their assigned catamaran was a large white streamlined vessel, with a body that rested between two hulls, and appeared to be hovering on the water. It had a large cabin, with rows of seats which had been bolted securely to the floor. Windows on either side allowed the students to look almost directly into the water, where any dolphins or whales would be easily visible. A few adventurous students raced to the rea of the deck where the seats were not fully sheltered by the cover.

Cara turned to Dylan: "It's too tame for me inside – would you come and sit out the back where we can feel the wind?"

Dylan laughed. "Okay," he said. "Stephanie and Garry will probably spend the cruise wrapped up in themselves and barely notice the whales anyway."

"Come on then Dylan," Cara said tugging his arm impatiently, "There are only a very few seats left outside."

Soon cries of excitement were rising from the cabin as a school of porpoises came into sight.

"Oh my," Cara cried. "I wish the deck was at the front!" She leaned out over the water, "I think I can see them now!"

"Careful," Dylan exclaimed, and automatically placed an arm across her back to steady her, and prevent her from falling over the side. Cara giggled, she seemed to have found a good way to get Dylan to hang onto her.

"Look," Cara said, pointing into the water.

Dylan steadied himself against the rail with his other arm and peered over Cara's shoulder. "They certainly are cool!" he exclaimed.

"There are little ones with their mothers," Cara exclaimed.

"Yeah," Dylan agreed. "Fantastic!"

"Say Dyls," Cara ventured from the comfortable circle of his arm, "The Computer Tea is coming up next Saturday."

"So it is," Dylan said. "Dating again, that's all the university seems to be about sometimes! I don't know how we are expected to get an education."

"I know," Cara said plaintively. "And all our friends except us are hooked up."

"Don't look at me that way Cara," Dylan objected. "I can't resist your sad eyes."

"Well – take me to it then," Cara wheedled.

"I've always got the impression you found anybody other than me more exciting," Dylan frowned. "Where is Mr. Music?"

"Craig is busy writing a symphony," Cara explained. "He is pretty cool in his own way – but I need someone with whom I have more in common."

"Like what?" Dylan inquired.

"Sporty, adventurous, and nature loving," Cara began. "With a good sense of humour."

"Going to America with Kaleb would have been an adventure for you," Dylan suggested stubbornly.

"Too far, and no fun without my friends," Cara replied. "One friend in particular…."

"You have always treated me as part of the furniture," Dylan muttered. "And I mean that quite literally!"

"I need furniture," Cara murmured. "It's very handy stuff."

"Say again?" Dylan demanded.

"I need you Dylan," Cara whispered, with her eyes fixed persuasively upon his face.

"If you are messing with me Cara," Dylan exclaimed, "I warn you that my heart won't take it."

"I wouldn't do that," Cara promised.

"I will rig the Computer Tea with you," Dylan said. "But nothing more, I'll need to take things slowly to make sure you are for real this time."

"I understand," Cara said jubilantly, having maneuvered Dylan into the position she wanted. "Look over there – that creature is much larger than the porpoises."

"I think it's a humpback whale," Dylan whispered into her hair. "Really?" Cara asked. "Impressive isn't it?"

"Yeah," Dylan agreed.

Cara noticed that although they only had one date arranged, and had agreed to take things slowly, Dylan's arms felt very comfortable around her. Their warmth was familiar and realistically permanent.

Sunday morning, all the students who had been on the cruise wanted to sleep late. Consequently they gave the early praise service a miss. Dylan and Garry collected Cara and Stephanie for the subsequent Reform Church service, and then they went to the cafeteria for a lazy lunch.

After lunch, Cara announced that she had to study for Education, because she had a test coming up as well as an early essay topic. She looked at Dylan expectantly: "Would you like to meet in the library?" she asked.

"Sure," Dylan said. "I need to study for the Ed test too." He was attempting to sound casual, but Garry gave him a curious look.

"Anything going on between you two?" Garry asked.

"The usual," Dylan shrugged. "Nothing you need to worry about."

"If that means what I think it means," Garry said, "You had better not hurt my friend again, Cara."

"I wouldn't dream of it," Cara exclaimed indignantly.

Stephanie laughed. "Simmer down you two. Dylan and Cara are a big people now, they can make decisions for themselves."

Cara giggled and made her escape, going back to the dormitory to collect her books. At the last minute, she slid the Computer Tea questionnaire into the back of her Education folder. Dylan was waiting near the library door and looked somewhat self-conscious for a young man who presumably only had study on his mind.

"I thought we would find a table at the back of the stacks where it is pretty quiet," he said.

"Good idea," Cara agreed. The rear stacks would do very well, as few students were keen enough to study on a Sunday, and the couple would have some privacy.

Dylan led the way to a table and put his books down. The Computer Tea questionnaire dropped out of his education text and he picked it up.

"Do you want to do this right away?" he suggested.

"Yeah," Cara said. "Then we can get to real study!"

The pair slid into seats side by side and placed their questionnaires on the table. Generally, couples who wanted to attend the Computer Tea together filled out identical questionnaires, and the computer, which was really only able to match data, would rate them as 'compatible'.

The first question required them to identify a favourite sport. Both Cara and Dylan had played university basketball, but had too heavy a laboratory load to currently commit to a competition team. They quietly debated whether to select basketball or swimming. In the end, Cara ticked basketball and Dylan followed suit.

The next questions dealt with height and weight. Cara was tall for a girl and Dylan was two inches taller, so both were a good average. However,

Dylan suggested they add a little height just for a joke and they both put down five foot eleven inches. Then the pair turned to questions such as identifying their favourite lecturer.

"None of the Science lecturers are ever an option," Cara murmured.

"Too few Science students," Dylan observed.

"Well who do we have to choose from?" Dylan said. "Neither of us has ever had the History Professor, and the Theology Lecturer is the one that teaches ancient languages, which Education students almost never do!"

"We did compulsory English units in first year," Cara said doubtfully.

"Did you particularly enjoy them?" Dylan snorted.

"Not really, but don't tell Stephanie," Cara giggled.

"So we won't choose the English Professor then," Dylan said.

"The Computing Lecturer," Cara said. "How did he make it on the list?"

"Hmm, Computing is occasionally fun," Dylan said. "Tick!"

There were one or two more questions, things like their ideal Saturday night and a self-assessment of their personalities. Cara and Dylan completed these with much mirth, choosing comical answers that matched neither of them.

When they were finished, Dylan folded the forms and promised to drop them in the box in the cafeteria first thing tea time. "We should be put together on the basis of those forms," he said.

"Well, it has worked for every other couple," Cara mused. "Previous years."

"Couple?" Dylan reflected quizzically.

Cara blushed. "Do you think it's a bit too soon?"

"I would like to actually go out before we make any assumptions," Dylan suggested.

Monday afternoon, Cara had progressed using the typing tutor so that she was no longer typing nonsense combinations, but small words and using all her fingers. She was averaging about six words per minute and would soon be able to attempt the review test to establish her speed.

Dylan slid into the seat in front of the computer next to Cara. He made a comical face and began to practice his own typing.

"How's it going?" Cara whispered.

"Not bad," Dylan said. "My big old fingers are like a bunch of bananas, but otherwise I'm getting the hang of it."

"Shush," Stephanie whispered. "The Computing Lecturer is watching."

"Our favourite lecturer," Dylan murmured and Cara laughed. The other students looked puzzled. Very few of them had apparently selected the Computing Lecturer as their favourite on their Computer Tea form.

Tuesday afternoon in Chemistry, the students set up some longer term experiments. They labelled three glass jars and filled them with a mixture of river water and distilled water. Jar one was the control, to which nothing was added. Jar two received half a spoon of powdered fertilizer, while jar three received half a teaspoon of dishwashing detergent.

The jar tops were sealed with cheesecloth and the jars were placed on a sunny window sill. They would be observed for the next two weeks to model the effect nitrate and phosphate pollution had on lakes. The 'polluted' jars would likely turn green from algal growth quicker than the control jar. The students would then test the oxygen content of the liquid at weekly intervals using a Clark Electrode Probe.

The class also noted and observed the colour and strength of several plastic bags, before shutting the control bags away in a dark cupboard and pegging the experimental bags onto the planter outside the classroom window, where they would be exposed to the elements.

The last experiment they set up involved marigold pot plants. The students mixed water and vinegar to mimic acid rain. They then watered the control plant with normal water, and sprayed acidic water on the experimental plants. The effect on the plants would be observed over a few weeks.

After the experiments were set up, the Chemistry Doctor asked the students to begin their write-ups explaining the chemical reactions behind each environmental process being observed. He also asked the students to research information about the Severinghaus Electrode for the following week.

Wednesday Cara asked Bede to sew her a denim skirt that was a bit shorter than her usual knee length, because she wanted to show a little leg around Dylan. Cara confided to her sister that she was very excited about their first date.

"I've always know," Bede observed. "At home it was 'Dylan this' and 'Dylan that', even though you swore you didn't see him as a boyfriend!"

"Kaleb and I never got very physical, if it is any comfort to you," Cara ventured.

"I know," Bede said smugly. "We have surpassed you already."

Cara had thought she was cool with this conversation, but she found her hands curled in to fists involuntarily. She deliberately uncured them. "Too much information Bede," she cautioned.

"Sorry," Bede murmured. She was busy measuring and had not noticed Cara's fingers. "A short skirt only takes a couple of hours, especially as denim gets machine hemmed."

"Thanks then," Cara said. "I appreciate it."

Bede laughed. "It's a bit different to see you worrying about your appearance sister."

On Thursday the Biology Master took the class to the Queensland Museum on the South Bank. There they spent the entire day viewing the fantastic biodiversity collections.

Most of the specimens in the museum were sourced from Queensland's land and aquatic habitats. However, there were also specimens collected from nearby Indo-Pacific regions and a smaller number of foreign species acquired from zoos and other museums.

The students collected worksheets from the education desk at the museum and browsed through the display rooms filling out the questionnaires. The Biology Master pointed the class in the direction of a number of animal skeletons and added his excited commentary regarding the variations in structure.

Around one o'clock the Biology Master suggested the class take a break for lunch, and they all ate their sandwiches on the lawns outside the museum. Garry and Dylan went for a quick walk to the canteen, while Danielle, Stephanie and Cara sat beside the planters talking to the Biology Master. When the boys returned, they had purchased cans of soft drink which they handed around the group.

After lunch, the class began its tour of the museum once again, this time visiting the marine rooms full of specimens of coral, sea sponges, sea urchins and sea stars collected from nearby beaches and reefs. There were also long tables of shells, and the remains of worms and other unique animals.

Finally it was time to climb back into the land rover and drive back to Silver Springs. The group arrived just in time for the end of the evening meal in the cafeteria.

Friday morning Cara had classes, and in the afternoon she mowed the lawn. Riding the mower around the lawn proved a great time to dream, and Cara was amazed to find she was full of butterflies regarding her up-coming date with Dylan for the Computer Tea. Entering a relationship with a long time male friend like Dylan felt very serious. If it did not work out, Cara would lose Dylan's friendship for sure this time. However, it also felt right.

After tea, Dylan invited Cara for a sunset walk. They strolled down to the suspension bridge as both the walks known as 'girls' way' and 'boys' way' were surrounded by trees and would soon become too dark for safety. When they reached the suspension bridge, they sat down on the grass looking across the water and Dylan slid an arm around Cara.

"Imagine us doing this," Dylan whispered.

"I don't have to imagine it, we are here," Cara replied. "I like being with the group, but I also like being alone with you!"

"Yeah me too," Dylan said.

"So tomorrow will be the start of something," Cara murmured. "Why not tonight?" Dylan's arm was warm around her, but she noticed he had not make any move to kiss her as yet.

Dylan shrugged. "I just want to take you to the Uniting Church vespers tonight. Tomorrow will be our first official date."

There was no point arguing with that. "Okay," Cara murmured.

"You have a cute profile," Dylan said, tracing his finger across Cara's forehead and down her nose. He finished by giving her nose a gentle pinch. Cara was glad Dylan was becoming his comical and teasing self once more. Still no kiss however – perhaps Dylan wasn't the romantic type – but all guys liked to have fun didn't they?

"It must be time to get back to vespers," she whispered.

Bede delivered the completed mini-skirt to the room Saturday morning. Cara topped the mini-skirt with a white fitted t-shirt with lace insets that she had not worn much before, to create a more feminine look than usual.

"You look very pretty," Stephanie observed.

As per her usual, Stephanie had been experimenting. She had chosen a stretch knit in aqua, which was currently very fashionable. The dress had a low waist, below which a full skirt swung. The fitted bodice narrowed down on one shoulder, but sported a drape and large bow on the other.

The girls heard their names called over the public address system and grabbed their cardigans in case the evening was cold. They then descended the stairs, where Dylan was waiting for Cara, and Garry was waiting for Stephanie. The walk across to the cafeteria was short and they collected their table numbers at the door.

However, there was an unexpected problem. Stephanie and Garry had matching table numbers, but Cara and Dylan did not. It was unheard of because couples had been successfully 'rigging' their Computer Tea dates for years. Dylan turned to Cara.

"Did you er – change anything?" he asked.

Cara shook her head. "No! Did you?"

"No," Dylan said. "Well we had better see who we have got instead of each other."

The pair approached Cara's assigned table, and saw Vincent sitting opposite her assigned seat. Vincent seemed pleased to see them.

"Hello Vincent," Cara said. "I guess you put down that you liked basketball?"

"Oh of course!" Vincent said.

Cara began to laugh. Vincent must also have chosen some other options that they had put down as a joke.

"Is there a problem?" Vincent asked. He caught hold Cara's wrist. "Please don't refuse to sit with me, or I won't have a date."

"It can't be that bad, surely?" Cara said. She looked helplessly at Dylan, hoping that he would assert himself and lay claim to her company.

"Since the steroid drama, I have lost a lot of friends," Vincent explained. "Some guys don't believe I didn't know the steroids were dangerous. Other guys think I should not have reported Tony for supplying them."

"I'll see you later, then Dyls," Cara said, taking pity on the boy.

"Okay," Dylan said. He turned and began to look for the table to which he had been allotted. Cara watched him leave with a sinking heart. Every fiber of her being wanted to call him back.

Restraining herself, Cara turned to Vincent. "I'm sorry if people have been mean to you since the steroid scandal," she said. "I must say I'm a little surprised, however. We are Christians here at Silver Springs, and we believe in forgiveness."

"Not when it has affected someone we know personally, it seems," Vincent mused philosophically.

"I guess that is harder," Cara said. "Also because Christians aim to do the right thing, we are not always generous about other people's disgrace."

"Yeah," Vincent agreed.

"Wasn't there something similar happening in Jesus day?" Cara suggested. "The Pharisees had all their rules – but Jesus spent his time with the poor, sick and other rejects of society."

"True," Vincent said. "It doesn't help me around campus though."

"I'll speak to Zack," Cara said. "I still have physics with him, although he hangs with us less, now he is going out with Danielle."

"I would appreciate that," Vincent said. "Technically, I'm allowed to play basketball again this semester, having paid for my sins by dropping out of the finals last semester, but I know the teams don't feel the same about me anymore."

"You know by next year, this could all be forgotten," Cara said. "Maybe not for Tony, he will receive some legal penalty, but for the victims of his scam."

"Oh I hope so," Vincent said. "Thanks for saying that."

The cafeteria staff and Hospitality students delivered the entree of broccoli and potato croquettes with a cheesy dipping sauce. The pea and ham soup was also delivered with a plate of small party pies. Cara looked at them in surprise.

"You can dip them in the soup if you want," Damaris, who was helping serve, explained. "It is Aussie street food."

"Oh wow, I've never had anything like it," Cara said.

"The pie floaters are popular late on cold winter's nights I believe," Damaris said.

"Pie good, soup good," Vincent said. "Together, yum!"

"You see – a hit with the blokes," Damaris exclaimed. She moved along to serve the next table.

"I wonder what the main course will be?" Cara mused. In addition to the food, the décor was downtown and slightly rough, with the Music students taking turns to rise up and pretend to be street buskers.

"I dunno," Vincent said, "But this is good so far!"

When the main course was served, it turned out to be a choice between fish, beef or vegetarian patties in baguette buns with coriander and sweet chili sauce. Cara took the opportunity to question Damaris why the computer had not placed her with Dylan.

The Chef looked surprised and a little shamefaced. "Err," she said. "I'm sorry, where there are a number of similar forms, the computer can't decide on its own. I had always heard you say Dylan was not the man for you!"

"Things change," Cara whispered. "We haven't announced it, but we do intend to be together."

"I'm sorry," Damaris said. "But Vin's a good guy really – he used to be popular before the steroid scandal."

"I know," Cara said. "Tony dragged a lot of people down with him. So who did you put Dylan with?"

"One of the second years," Damaris said. "The A grade basketball captain Janet, I think."

"Oh," Cara's eyes were big. "I hope he doesn't like her too much!"

"Well, she definitely wouldn't have given Vin the time of day the way things are at the moment," Damaris whispered. "Michael tells me about these things."

Cara sighed. "The sporting crowd guys don't change much, they just find different things to pick on."

"Look you have done a good thing sticking with Vin tonight," Damaris said. "You just got to get your own man back as soon as possible!"

The rest of the evening ran smoothly, with desert turning out to be a selection of iced and cream filled donuts. A few of the girls squealed in horror at the calories they contained, but most were tempted to eat one or two anyway. Damaris said that her team had great fun perfecting the donut dough and decorating each donut individually.

After the Computer Tea finished, Vincent walked Cara back to the girl's dormitory. She looked around for Dylan, but only caught a brief glimpse of him dropping Janet off at the girl's dorm too. At least he did not appear to be kissing the girl goodnight!

CHAPTER TEN: THE GEOLOGY CHALLENGE

The next morning Cara found her roommate regarding her quizzically.

"You haven't ditched Dylan already have you?" Stephanie inquired.

Cara laughed. "No," she said. "Of course not."

"Well then, whatever happened at the Computer Tea?" the roommate asked.

"The computer stuffed up and matched me with Vincent," Cara sighed. "I was going to swap with whoever Dylan was assigned, but Vincent begged me to stay with him. Apparently he has been having a hard time socially."

Stephanie looked puzzled. "How so?"

"The basketball set won't let him back into their inner circle, as far as I can gather," Cara explained.

Stephanie laughed. "Some of the best and the worst of the guys play basketball," she said.

"Exactly," Cara agreed.

"So you stayed with Vincent out of the goodness of your heart?" Stephanie observed. "You better watch out, because you are beginning to sound like me!"

Cara shrugged. "It was only an evening," she said. "I expect things will get back on track with Dylan soon."

"Dylan and Janet were sitting near us," Stephanie said. "They appeared to be having a nice time."

"Hum," Cara said. "I'm glad Dylan had a good time." The girl was struggling with a mixture of feelings. Of course she was pleased that Dylan had enjoyed his evening, but she was also disappointed that they had not had their first official date. Moreover, if she were honest, she was a little jealous. Janet, who was an A grade girls' basketball captain, sounded too much like a rival. Annie had appealed to Dylan last year because she was sporty and confident.

Cara was barely dressed and ready by the time her name was called over the public address system. She took one final look in the mirror before going up the stairs to the foyer. She had not been able to resist wearing her mini-skirt again, but today she had it teamed with a black top. Black pantyhose outlined her legs, and the flat soled shoes set the outfit off perfectly.

When Cara saw Dylan waiting by the reception desk, she wanted to hug and kiss him. Instead she gave him a friendly punch.

"What was that for?" Dylan exclaimed.

"I heard you had a good time without me," Cara said.

"No point having a miserable time," Dylan said. "Not only would that have wasted my evening, it would have been rude to Janet."

"I bet you were pleased to find she was your date," Cara cried.

"I was rather," Dylan said provocatively. "I'm surprised she is still single."

"Now you are trying to make me jealous," Cara asserted.

Dylan looked perfectly innocent. "Going with our computer assigned dates was your idea," he retorted. "How am I trying make you jealous?"

Cara ignored the taunt. "You know perfectly well what I mean," she said.

"Well are you jealous, or were you simply relieved to see Vincent waiting for you instead of me?" Dylan inquired.

"Of course I'm not jealous," Cara said huffily. She found she was not as good at expressing her feelings as she had always believed. "I just feel some natural loss when my man has a good time without me."

"Okay," Dylan fell into step beside her. "What do you want to do about it?"

Cara wanted Dylan to grab her and perform a public demonstration of affection so that everyone on campus knew that they were together, but she didn't dare say that. Especially as he hadn't even kissed her in private yet.

"Nothing," she said lamely. "We will have other opportunities, I guess."

"How about you forget everything and come for a drive in the Suzuki jeep with me after lunch?" Dylan said. "Just you and me, exploring the national forest."

Cara relaxed. "That sounds great," she said. "We can look for native birds and animals."

Dylan and Cara crossed campus to the meeting hall and sat together in the Reform Church service. After that they went to the cafeteria for lunch and sat with their friends Debbie and David, laughing and chatting.

The pair politely refused all invitations to afternoon activities and began to walk down University Drive towards the student car park after lunch, when they were hailed by Stephanie and Garry. Dylan felt obliged to invite these two best friends on the afternoon outing and they had a great time, but still had not had their official 'first date'. It was frustrating!

Monday afternoon, Cara achieved her ten words a minute in the typing tutor. This meant that she could move onto some of the other tasks using the word processor, such as producing correspondence. There were also fun activities including making greeting cards and posters using a combination of templates and clip art.

"I see you two have made up," Tom said, sliding into the seat next to Dylan.

"We've always been cool," Dylan observed wryly.

"I thought – last Saturday night – I saw you with Janet and Cara with Vincent," Tom murmured in confusion.

"That was the silly computer's fault," Cara explained.

"Well Joelle, Anita and I have had a debate," Tom admitted. "The girls think you two are finally a couple, and I'm more conservative, I say just good friends."

"More like the couple end of the spectrum," Dylan said.

"Yeah, we realised we were meant for each other," Cara said. "But there is still a bit of talk about Kaleb and Bede, and we don't want to stir things up again."

"I get it," Tom said. "So should I say anything to the girls?"

"Yes," Cara said. "We would like our friends to know."

Tom returned to his original seat beside Joelle, and Cara and Dylan exchanged glances. One set of friends had worked them out, but there were many more to go.

Tuesday in Chemistry, Zack began telling his fellow students that the Physics Lecturer was planning a trip down to Brisbane on Friday night to attend a 'Creation versus Evolution debate' run by The University of Queensland.

"The Physics department is really small," Zack explained, "And even if we only book the mini-bus, we can fit a few more, so the Physics Lecturer suggested that we invite the Chemistry students as well. So how about it?"

"It sounds like fun in a nerdy sort of way," Cara said.

"I would be bringing Stephanie," Garry said. "She does Biology."

"Any chance of grabbing a meal out while we are out there?" Dylan who always had a healthy appetite, asked.

"I don't know," Zack said. "We are leaving here after the University tea time and the Physic Lecturer is amazingly ignorant about things like food."

"Maybe stop for supper after the debate," Garry suggested. "Even the Physics Lecturer must have heard of McDonalds."

"Do you think it is possible the Physics Lecturer could sign late forms for us girls?" Cara said. "If we are not back by ten thirty, we could get into trouble."

"I expect so," Zack said. "Fill out your late forms and I will give them to him. Between the debate and travel, we could be pretty late."

"Thanks," Cara said.

The class had been researching carbon did oxide and oxygen sensors in the library. They were also due to set up homemade filters designed to capture particulate pollution from various locations around the campus. The Chemistry Doctor admitted that the particular technology required was still in development. This meant that their practical work was pushing the current boundaries of ecological science.

They also made observations regarding the conditions of their ongoing experiments. The plants in the terrarium were growing, although Cara observed they looked a little thin, possibly due to limited nutrient availability. The plastic bags were showing a few signs of wear, but plastic could take months or even years to biodegrade. The plants that had received the acid spray looked a little stunted, compared to the control plants. All the experiment would be continuing until the outcomes were more documentable.

Wednesday morning Cara had several theory tests, as they were almost a month into the semester. She had a test for Education and some theory for Practice Teaching. Moreover, the Biology Master was keen to check their learning in Zoology. It was always stressful when several lecturers picked the same day to administer their assessments, and she walked into the cafeteria lunchtime relieved and light headed.

"How did you go?" Dylan asked.

"All right, I think," Cara replied. She hadn't seen much of Dylan over the last twenty-four hours, as she had skipped combined assembly and convocation to revise for her tests. Sitting still and studying was foreign to Cara's nature, but she could force herself at times.

"That's good," Dylan replied. "I think I did okay too." Dylan wasn't much better at sitting down to study than Cara was, but he did what was necessary. And he had not been distracted by beginning the semester with a break-up.

"I'm glad it is over," Stephanie said, and Garry nodded.

The Biology class were the only ones who had three tests that day, the rest of the third year students merely had Education and Practice Teaching tests. However, most students felt that two tests on the one day were pressure enough.

Thursday's Zoology laboratory was held on campus. Cara and Stephanie, who both adored cats, were thrilled to find they had a cat as a subject of observation. One experiment was to discover whether cats could be right or left pawed in a similar fashion to human hand preferences.

They patiently dangled string and toys in front of the cat and recorded the number of times the cat reached for them with each paw. They also threw cat pellets and other treats to the animal to observe its reaction.

The Biology Master instructed the class to set up a goldfish tank in the laboratory. Once the fish was settled in, the students observed its breathing rate by visual inspection of gill movement. When they placed fish food in the water, the fish also exhibited 'excited' behavior, swimming at an increased pace and orienting towards the flakes.

The boys were sent outside to catch a cricket without harming it, so they could experiment by exposing the creature to a range of temperatures. When warm, the cricket chirped faster than when it was cool. The rest of the laboratory was taken up viewing microscope slides of worms and internal cross-sections of other small invertebrates.

Friday evening after eating their tea in the cafeteria, Stephanie and Garry, Cara and Dylan, Zack and Danielle met the rest of the Physics students around at the university mini-bus parking station. The Biology Master had joined the Physics Lecturer as one of the chaperones, and Cara found she was really looking forward to the outing.

It took the university mini-bus around fifty minutes to reach Brisbane and then it had to cross the city until it arrived at The University of Queensland. Luke dropped his passengers off in front of the main entrance and drove away in search of suitable parking.

The Physics Lecturer turned to the students and waved a bunch of vouchers in their faces.

"Stick with me," the Physics Lecturer said. "I have all our tickets."

"Do you know where to go?" the Biology Master inquired.

"This way I think," the Physics Lecturer suggested.

They followed a series of posters that announced a visiting Professor of Geology would be debating with Creationist representatives that evening. The arrows which led towards one of the major lecture theatres on campus.

The party from Silver Springs University filed in and sat in their assigned seats. All around them students from The University of Queensland and interested members of the community were filling the other seats. Cara allowed Dylan to take her hand.

"It's much bigger than Silver Springs University," Cara whispered.

Garry nodded. "So is Wollongong University," he murmured. "That is how they can offer so many more subjects."

The Geology Professor rose to speak first. He proved to be an entertaining speaker, confidently outlining a history of the planet Earth which included matter breaking off from Mars and shedding a fragment which also became the Moon. He was using geological time frames with numbers that were almost incomprehensible to Cara's mind. She couldn't imagine times periods that long.

"He is not citing references," Stephanie observed.

"I assume this is from his own research," the Biology Master suggested.

"Still, I would like to know if other geologists, physicists or astronomers agreed with him," Stephanie said. "I've never heard of Earth breaking off from Mars."

"I know what you mean," the Physics Lecturer said. His eyes were shining with enthusiasm. "He hasn't gone right back to the 'Big Bang'."

The Geology Professor then began describing conditions on earth and mentioning developments in the animal kingdom. He spoke of primates (or monkeys) beginning to walk and learning to use tools. He then skimmed lightly over time until till the present day.

"I assume there is fossil evidence for this," Cara suggested.

The Biology Master nodded. "Some," he admitted. "Every science sees things slightly differently however."

The Geology Professor then began to criticise Creationists. He pointed back to a series of calculations done by Archbishop Usher and ridiculed Christians for accepting these as fact. He laughed about the story of the flood and Noah taking two of every animal onto the ark. Two germs, and two sharks even!

"Surely our beliefs aren't that rigid?" Cara whispered. "When I was a child, I asked Grandma O'Brien whether the whales went onto the ark, and she said maybe they swam alongside the boat. And she was a strict Christian!"

"Yeah, there are a lot of explanations the Geology Professor is disregarding," the Physics Lecturer murmured.

A representative of the Creation Science Foundation rose to answer the Geology Professor's arguments. "Evolution is 'just a theory'," the Bishop began. "Not 'fact' as The Geology Professor claims".

The group from Silver Springs University nodded in satisfaction. Under the scientific method, all ideas were theories, until tested and supported by evidence. Most remained theories even when supported by a reasonable body of evidence. Evolution and Creationism were really on a similar footing. One was a story recorded in an anthropological document and the other was a theory developed by Charles Darwin. Both were ways of explaining the world.

However, the debate went downhill from that point. The Geology Professor shouted abuse at the Creationist and even dared him to risk electric shock because 'electricity was just a theory'. The audience laughed, but the Physics Lecturer shook his head.

"Very unprofessional of him," the Physics Lecturer moaned. "And he is representing academia too!"

The Bishop then insisted on painting all Evolutionists as Nineteenth Century Darwinists who had not progressed in their thinking during the last hundred years of research. Moreover, he made things worse by denying parts of Biology, including natural selection, which were actually demonstrable in nature today.

"He is making Christians sound dumb," Cara whispered.

The Biology Master nodded. "Yes, unfortunately," he whispered.

Even though they were Christians and Creationists, and even though The Geology Professor was sometimes over the top, Cara and Dylan found themselves liking him. He was funny and he referred to science which they were studying.

The representative of Creationism made little attempt to base his arguments on research and refused to meet the Geology Professor half-way on points of solid scholarship. However, they shuddered when the Geology Professor then began to ridicule the Creationist's academic qualifications. Even though his degrees might be in Theology, and didn't qualify him to speak on scientific grounds, it was unlikely they were phony degrees purchased from a print shop!

The debate ended and everyone clapped wildly. The majority of the attendees were students of the secular university and subsequently fans of the Geology Professor. The group from Silver Springs University were probably one of the few educated Christian groups present, and their viewpoint was unique. They quietly made their way out of the lecture theatre and towards the edge of campus.

"Young Luke said he would meet us at the side gate around ten fifteen if possible," the Physics Lecturer said.

"It's ten past ten now," the Biology Master said. "You better all hurry."

After the group climbed back onto the university mini-bus, Zack asked the Physics Lecturer if they could go somewhere for a snack. The Physics Lecturer, who was busily presenting the students with an informal review of the debate, happily agreed. The Biology Master asked Luke what might still be open past ten o'clock and the driver suggested McDonald's.

"It's on Gympie Road at Aspley and quite on our way back to Silver Springs," Luke assured the two professors.

"Take us there at once," ordered the Physics Lecturer, and the Biology Master agreed. They were heartily glad that there was something better than a service station to which they could take the students.

The bus pulled up at McDonalds and the students piled out. Inside was cosy and warm, somewhat like a 1950s' diner. Dylan approached the counter, and ordered thick shakes and cheeseburgers for himself and Cara. The students led active life-styles and could afford the calories.

Zack and Danielle slid into the booth opposite Cara. "What did you think?" Zack asked.

"Well it was my first real debate," Cara said. "But I thought they both sounded silly. Unfortunately the Creationist ended up sounding sillier."

"So you would say the Geology Professor won then?" Danielle suggested.

Dylan returned to the table with their order. "Nobody really won," he said. "They didn't even address each other's arguments."

"I reckon we could do better at Silver Springs University!" Cara said. "We at least have Christian scientists who understand their science." She glanced pointedly at the Physics Lecturer and Biology Master, who were settled into a booth talking animatedly together.

"The Chemistry Doctor might have a bit to say too," Dylan remarked thoughtfully.

"It is an interesting idea," Danielle agreed.

The students finished their snacks and chatted about various things. There was a general consensus that a Creation versus Evolution debate back at Silver Springs University sounded like a good idea. The Biology Master suggested that the Zoology class lead the defence for the Evolution side, while the Physics Lecturer volunteered to organize the defence for the Creation argument.

They climbed back onto the bus in a cheerful mood. Dylan led Cara to a seat somewhat isolated right down the back where they could cuddle up in the dark as the bus drove along. As he slid his arm around her shoulders he leaned close to her ear:

"You looked pretty tonight," he whispered.

"Thank you," Cara said blushing. Although she was never going to turn into a fashionista like her sister, Cara had worn her most fashionable high-waisted jeans that showed off her bottom to advantage. Over this she had a comfy windcheater to protect herself from the cool of the evening. The cherry pink was very feminine, and set off her light brown hair and rosy cheeks.

The bus pulled to a halt on Silver Springs campus, directly in front of the girl's dormitory and Luke waited to see that the girl's had accessed the residence safely, before driving across campus to drop off the boys. The bus was often parked at the back of boy's dormitory when not in use, although its usual staging point was the rear of girl's dorm.

Saturday morning, the normally energetic students slept in and arrived at breakfast late. News of the previous evening's debate had somehow travelled around campus, and a group of Theology students were lingering at Cara and Stephanie's favourite table discussing the event. Of course, as Theology students, they were all biased towards the Creationist argument.

"I heard the Geology Professor was losing so badly that he got frustrated and swore at the Bishop," David reported.

Cara frowned. It was too early in the day for this sort of thing. Stephanie remained quiet. Kathy, who was sitting with her boyfriend Andrew, gave them an apologetic smile.

"I believe the Professor was quite obnoxious," Larry added. "I even heard the Bishop might be going to sue him."

"What are you guys talking about?" Dylan and Garry approached the table, and sat down.

"The Creation versus Evolution debate last night," David said. "Luke told us all about it."

"I'm not sure he heard quite the same debate that we did," Garry suggested diplomatically.

"Oh – did you guys go to it?" David looked intensely interested.

"Our classes did – the Physics and Biology Lecturers organised our trip," Dylan admitted. "That would be how Luke heard bits of the debate. But he was off with the bus a lot of the time."

"So what else happened?" Andrew looked more open-minded than some of his colleagues.

"Well," Garry hesitated, "Most of the time – the opponents were at cross purposes. Each presented their ideas – but they didn't really try to convince the audience. It degenerated into a hissing match quickly."

"I think our origins is an emotional matter," Andrew observed. "People who believe in Creation believe very strongly, and so do people who believe in Evolution."

"The operative word there is 'believe'," Dylan observed. "Both sides 'believe'. Neither side really used a lot of science or fact. The Geology Professor began to – but then he did not bother – and it was an insult to the audience. We thought that as Christian scholars, we ought to be able to do better…"

"Better than the Bishop?" David looked fascinated.

"Well – I suppose he was under pressure – and I don't know what sort of information he had about his opponent to help him prepare," Garry explained.

"That's true," Larry admitted. "So in your opinion – who won?"

"I didn't think anybody actually won," Dylan said.

"The audience all left believing exactly what they had believed in the first place," Garry concluded. "Unfortunately, because it was the University of Queensland, support for the Evolution side was very high."

The Theology students nodded. Garry's statement confirmed their beliefs about secular institutions.

"Still it was very good of them to host the debate," Andrew observed thoughtfully. He offered to carry Kathy's tray across to the dishwasher, and the couple left the room. David and Larry both mentioned some major Bible assignment that was a big deal for the third year Theology students, and left with their girlfriends.

Cara turned to Zack, who had joined them with his girlfriend Danielle. Most people had finished breakfast and the cafeteria was now quiet. It was the ideal moment to bring up a more sensitive matter.

"Changing the subject somewhat," she said. "Vincent was talking to me at the Computer Tea. It seems he is having a hard time."

"I think I know what you are going to ask," Zack sighed. "His loss of standing among the basketball crowd."

Cara nodded. "It seems a pity now everything is over," she murmured.

"Cara you need to understand that Vincent was demonstrating aggressive behavior for some months," Zack explained. "Finally we found the steroids were to blame. However, the guys remember him making fouls, swearing and abusing them."

"Surely they can forgive him?" Cara asked. "It is a Christian competition after all."

"All the more reason to expect sporting behavior from the competitors," Zack asserted.

"I truly believe Vincent is repentant," Cara said. "It seems wrong somehow to continue holding grudges against him."

"Vincent doesn't even remember that behavior clearly to apologise properly," Zack said. "I've included him back into the competition at B grade level, but it will take time."

"I guess that is all anyone can do," Cara agreed. "Thank you Zack."

Sunday was the last day in August and the morning dawned clear and sunny. Cara reflected that back in her hometown of Geelong, it would be cold and rainy. The tropical climate of south-east Queensland certainly had its advantages. Dylan collected her early for the Inter-denominational praise service, and then the morning was so beautiful that Cara begged him to take her for a drive instead of attending the following Reform Church service.

They purloined some fruit and drinks from the cafeteria in case they did not make it back in time to have lunch on campus, and stowed them all safely in an Esky cooler-box.

"Should we invite Stephanie and Garry?" Dylan inquired.

Cara shook her head. "They will have gone into the Reform Church service by now," she said. "And I must admit, I have been missing being able to talk to Stephanie recently. I can't believe that my room-mate is among the last to accept our relationship."

"She just knows you too well," Dylan snorted. He led the way to the student car park and opened the passenger side door of his jeep. "Jump in my darling."

Cara pretended to throw something at him, but she obediently clambered into the vehicle. "My sister knows me way better, and she said that she knew it had always been you for me!"

"Well then she knew you better than you knew yourself," Dylan returned. "I must say it explains what she did."

"Yeah!" Cara agreed. "But I still want Steph and Garry cool with us - and soon."

"It will happen," Dylan said. "Garry is half way there already. Stephanie is over-cautious when it comes to relationships. She was slow to accept Garry the first time, then slow to accept Bradley and even slower still to get back with Garry."

"I can't say I blame her now you mention Bradley," Cara said. Her eyes filled with tears at the memory of Bradley. He had been tall and good looking, as well as kind and friendly; and consequently his death had been a great shock to the whole group.

"Where shall we go?" Dylan said.

"Do you remember the day the Adventure Club went to Lake MacDonald?" Cara said. "I saw a few birds that day. I think we would see more if we sat still and watched for a few hours."

"I hope that is code for making out?" Dylan asked hopefully.

"Not exactly," Cara blushed. "I would really like to spot a few birds."

"I keep a bird and animal diary in the Jeep," Dylan said comically. "Just in case the girl I'm with doesn't want to make out."

"Very funny," Cara said. "You're not really like that."

"Nah, there's only ever been you, then Annie and now you again," Dylan admitted. He drove down University Drive, and after a few twists and turns, entered Lake MacDonald Road. Pulling up at the lakeside, he parked in one of the designated parking areas before unloading the car of a modest picnic rug and their lunch provisions.

"We will have to walk the rest of the way," Dylan announced.

Cara fell into step beside Dylan as they strolled through the bush in search of the perfect spot. They wanted somewhere that appeared safe to sit, free from ants and other crawlies. They also wanted some bushes to screen them from the lake, because the best bird sightings were made when the birds did not know they were being watched. Screening from the other direction would also be handy if things got romantic between them.

They finally found a suitable spot and Dylan spread out the picnic blanket. Cara settled down to watch the lake closely for birds, the sun was warm and the plants around them were tangy with natural scents. She poured a little juice and sipped it from a plastic cup, as the walking had made her thirsty.

"Look over there on the lake," she began. "It's not a duck – it's a great crested grebe."

"That tiny bird at the edge of the lake is about to step out onto a lily pad," Dylan breathed. "Amazing it actually supports him!"

"I think it's a jacana," Cara said, leafing through the ages of their *Australian Bird Book*.

"Stay quiet and more will come," Dylan ordered.

"Next time, you can pitch a small tent for me," Cara whispered.

"That sounds like a plan," Dylan said. "In fact in the future, someone might even build a little bird watching hide right here."

"Do you think so?" Cara asked.

"Yeah maybe, you never know," Dylan said lazily.

Dylan enjoyed watching birds every bit as much as Cara did, but he was also alone with the girl of his dreams. He placed his hand on her knee. Cara was too busy watching the birds on the lake to object, so after a few moments, Dylan slid his hand a little higher.

This time Cara noticed and considered objecting, but decided Dylan was only touching her thigh, and she was safely encased in her jeans. She let his hand remain, and because he was truly a gentleman under his clownish exterior, Dylan did not try to push things any further. Cara was pleased.

CHAPTER ELEVEN: CHRISTIAN SCIENTISTS ARISE

Monday was the first day in September. The days were getting warmer, as it was technically spring. Dylan and Cara agreed that it was a pity to be stuck inside on such a nice day, and agreed to go for a swim. As soon as computing was out, each raced for their respective dormitory to get changed into their bathers. They met back at the pool for an afternoon swim before tea.

The temperature was around twenty-six degrees Celsius, and Cara dived straight into the water from the deep end. Then she swam briskly up and down the length of the pool. Thus energized, she began to float and enjoy herself.

Dylan climbed into the pool more sedately and performed a couple of laps at a steady pace. "Which one of us won the last time we raced?" he asked as he glided into her vicinity.

"I can't remember," Cara said. "It's been a while."

"I think it was me," Dylan replied provocatively. That was mildly unfair, because Dylan was the stronger swimmer, even enjoying the occasional surf.

"Perhaps you cheated," Cara murmured lazily. "I don't want to race today."

"Alright," Dylan said. "Let's just muck around."

Dylan caught Cara to dunk her and suddenly they were laughing, churning up the water together. Luckily they had drifted down to the shallow end and Cara escaped him easily.

She squealed and pretended to be frightened, and Dylan pursued her, catching her and pinning her gently against the pool wall. Cara was giggling. Once she would have condemned Dylan for his uncouthness, now she suddenly found the horseplay very exciting.

Dylan stopped with his hands on Cara's shoulders and she briefly thought he was going to kiss her, but his laughter died and his expression became serious. "I could not take you breaking my heart again you know," he whispered.

"I wouldn't do that," Cara said. "Trust me, we have always been friends."

"I'm not just your rebound bloke you know," Dylan said.

"Of course not," Cara shook her head. She was searching for the right words. "Dyls, I'm not good at explaining my feelings… but you are incredibly important to me."

Dylan let Cara go and she slipped against the tiles, almost banging her head. Luckily he caught Cara again and steadied her. He held her to him as if she were something precious.

"I'm sorry," he said. "I didn't mean that to happen."

"It's okay," Cara said, although it wasn't really, as she was slightly shaken.

"I know I used to be a comedian," Dylan whispered, "But I really will look after you in the future."

"I know," Cara agreed. "I liked the clown you and the serious you - whenever you let him through. I just wasn't so happy about the bitter fellow you became after Annie broke your heart though."

"Nor was I," Dylan said. "So Cara we are agreed, if we do this it - is to be long term?"

"Oh yes," Cara's heart was beating hard. Her legs were tangled with Dylan's in the water and although the cool liquid was taking the heat out of their contact, she knew they were no longer just good friends.

Dylan pulled Cara closer and kissed her neatly on the mouth. His kiss was firm and assured, and much more demanding than Kaleb's had ever been. It was the kiss of a best friend, a passionate lover, and a long term partner. Cara submitted happily, knowing these were kisses that could make her content for the rest of her life, as God had always intended for a man and a woman.

A few minutes later, Dylan let her go, and Cara became aware of other students joining them in the pool area. The few brief moments of privacy had been very precious, as the kiss had served to cement their relationship and point the way forward to a future together.

"It's not long till tea," Dylan said. "It's amazing how time flies."

"Let's finish our laps and then go up to the cafeteria," Cara suggested. She had brought a large towel and change of clothes down to the pool area with her.

Tuesday in Chemistry, the lecturer reported that he had been talking to the Biology Master and Physics Professor. All three lecturers had agreed that Silver Springs University could host a better Creation versus Evolution debate than the one they had attended at the University of Queensland. It might not be quite so widely publicised and attended, but could still be opened to all the students and the local community.

"The Physics Professor has booked the campus meeting hall for Saturday evening, the thirteenth of September, which gives us about eleven days to prepare," the Chemistry Doctor said.

Dylan and Garry nodded. "That sounds good!"

"It will require a bit of research," the Chemistry Doctor warned. "Zack – if you agree – you will be the leader of the pro-creation team. The

Physics Professor and myself will give you as much help as we can."

"Cool," Zack said.

"Garry, you will be the leader of the pro-evolution team, under the guidance of the Biology Master," the Chemistry Doctor announced. "I'm sorry, this will be in addition to your regular assignments if you agree to do it."

"It's cool," Zack said. "I'm a fourth year and something like this will look good on my graduation script as campus leadership."

"Same for us, although we are only third years," Dylan said. "I assume I'm on Garry's team?"

"You and Cara will have to choose," the Chemistry Doctor said. "Please try to bear in mind that the Physics class is quite small too – so Zack might need one of you."

"We will sort it out," Dylan said, with a glance at Cara. "How would you feel about being on opposite teams Cara?"

"It could be a laugh," Cara said. "I feel my strength is more in the field of Biology – so I will definitely go with Garry and Stephanie."

"That puts me with Zack and the Physics crew," Dylan said.

"I will make sure the announcement reaches the campus newsletter then," the Chemistry Doctor said. "Now I need your full concentration on today's laboratory. Remember that measuring pollution is a relatively new – but vitally important field."

The rest of the afternoon was spent checking the plastic bags they had planted in the garden for signs of deterioration, testing the water in the experimental jars exposed to sunlight, and observing the marigold plants that had been sprayed with acid rain. A quick circuit around campus showed that the makeshift filters which had been placed near the main road were collecting more dust and discoloration, than those in sheltered places around campus.

Wednesday afternoon, as Cara was sitting in the library struggling to write up her Chemistry practical report, Dylan and Zack were reading an article on thermodynamic evidences for Creation, and conversing in mysterious whispers. Cara resolutely ignored the boys, she would be having a meeting with Stephanie, Garry and anyone else who was joining their side of the debate later.

Thursday the Zoology class went on an excursion to the nearby Queensland Reptile and Fauna Park, managed by Bob and Lyn Irwin. The park had been open since around 1970, and doubled in size in the early 1980s. Bob Irwin was a leading expert in the study of reptiles and amphibians, and his wife Lyn was active in animal rehabilitation. Dylan had actually met her once or twice the previous year, when he had joined a wildlife rescue group for his community involvement project.

The Biology Master was a great admirer of Bob Irwin, and their son Steve, who was involved in the government run East-Coast Crocodile Management Program. Captured crocodiles were being brought back to the Reptile Park and a new 'Crocodile Environmental Park' was under construction to house the huge creatures.

Cara shuddered as they viewed the magnificent creatures in their enclosures. The saltwater crocodile might be considered endangered, but they were certainly large enough and dangerous enough. Their jaws would easily bite through an arm or leg, but luckily they preferred to take their prey unawares, so the alert keepers moved around the area in relative safety.

On the return to Silver Springs, the couples sitting in the back of the Landover were tired and relaxed. Stephanie was leaning against Garry, while Danielle sat up the front with the Biology Master. Dylan kept his mouth hovering near her neck and Cara felt the light brush of his lips.

"Did you just nuzzle my ear?" she whispered.

"And what if I did?" Dylan returned, neither admitting nor denying the gesture.

"I dunno," Cara whispered back. "I don't mind."

"What do you want to do tomorrow?" Dylan whispered.

"I have to do my Education essay," Cara said. "Then perhaps a swim. I volunteered to present my topic earlier than usual this semester."

"Better than having everything due later in the year," Dylan observed.

"That's what Stephanie says," Cara giggled. "I don't see it quite the same."

This time when Dylan nibbled gently on her ear. It was unmistakable.

"I'm a crocodile," he whispered.

"Steady on there!" Cara exclaimed. "I might need my ear."

"What if I don't want to?" Dylan murmured.

"You won't have any girlfriend left for another day!" Cara laughed.

"Now you put it that way," Dylan said. "Of course."

Friday after classes finished for the day, Cara spent some time mowing the lawns. After she had finished, she was unusually hot and sweaty, and stained with green smears of grass. As she passed the Music department, she heard the tinkle of piano keys. She peeked in the door and noticed Joelle was practicing with Craig.

"That sounds good, guys," Cara called when the musicians came to a break between pieces.

Craig looked pleased. "It is an item for vespers," he said.

"Lovely," Cara concluded.

Joelle glanced at her watch and looked startled. "Is that the time?" she exclaimed. "I promised Anita and Larry that I would be available to run through tonight's songs."

Joelle gathered up her manuscripts and hurried out of the room. As Joelle left, Elisabet entered, carrying a sheaf of music books of her own. Cara waited until the third year settled down on one of the practice instruments before commenting.

"I didn't know that you played, so beautifully Elisabet," Cara exclaimed.

Elisabet blushed. "I don't play to the standard required for a Music major," she admitted defensively. "But Craig has encouraged me to continue training in my own time. I take private lessons like."

"Good on you," Cara said. "It's nice to see someone learning something new."

Cara really did feel hot and sticky, so she continued on her way to girls' dorm to have a shower ahead of the hordes of girls who would be 'making themselves more beautiful' for the weekend social events. Dylan called her down for tea soon after she was changed, and they crossed over to the cafeteria.

Around six o'clock, subscriber trunk dialing cut in and the price of making long distance calls was reduced. There were queues to use the telephone each evening, but this weekend, the congestion was much greater because the first Sunday in September was Father's Day in Australia. All the students were making sure that they placed at least one call home that weekend. Many had also posted cards and were checking to see whether the mail had arrived in time.

Saturday morning, Cara and Stephanie, together with Garry and a couple of second years, met the Biology Master to begin planning their defense of Evolution. A quick survey of the material showed that the theory accepted by modern scientists differed significantly from that outlined by

Charles Darwin in his *Origin of Species* and later volume, *The Descent of Man*.

Darwin's first observations had been circumstantial, and it could be said he had been perfectly correct in his descriptions. It was the fact that he had connected all the creatures into a sort of family tree that was so controversial. Then adding man, and treating humans as mere animals, had all sorts of racist and social implications as well as scientific.

"Can you believe that Charles Darwin was actually a Christian?" The Biology Master exclaimed. "He reported his first set of findings in perfect innocence – totally unaware of the shocking impact they would have on our Christian beliefs."

"There are clearly patterns in the animal kingdom," Stephanie observed. "Those remain, and they can be one of our arguments. The creatures can be organized into a hierarchy as well, from single celled organisms, through the invertebrates to the vertebrates."

"The Creationists can shoot that argument down with the intelligent design argument," Garry objected.

Stephanie shrugged. "Let them!" she said. "It is our job to make a passable argument for Evolution, not to actually prove it. We are Christians after all."

"Then there is the fossil record and what it implies about the age of the earth," the Biology Master added. "And carbon dating and what it implies – although the Physics Professor is sure to have Zack point out the assumptions that C14 measurement relies upon."

"Natural Selection is demonstrated in the breeding of pet varieties," Stephanie asserted.

"Add to that the genetic similarity of humans and chimpanzees," the Biology Master concluded. "And those will be our main arguments."

"They will probably hit us with the arguments of the incredibly low probability of life occurring spontaneously, and the tendency towards entropy or chaos, however you like to look at it," Garry observed.

"That doesn't matter," the Biology Master said. "Once again, we don't have to win – we just have to make a credible presentation and show the world that Christian scientists are not all as ignorant as that Geology Professor claimed."

Saturday afternoon Cara was glad to escape their room, as Stephanie had begged off any more planning, due to having double booked herself with sewing. Damaris' wedding dress was tacked together and ready for a secretive fitting before the final stitching. Damaris' cousin and Michael's sister were also arriving in the afternoon to try their bridesmaid's dresses on for size. Stephanie and Bede were dropping fragments of fabric all around the room and spreading patterns out across the bed. It was nowhere near as messy as when the girls had been cutting the dresses out, but it still was quite hectic.

Sunday morning at breakfast, Cara giggled when she saw Zack and Danielle. "We have some great arguments prepared for you," she said mysteriously.

It was true, Garry had sat down with some text books after the group discussion and worked out an excellent description of the theory of evolution as accepted by modern scientists. He had added a couple of stipulations to account for the fact that they were Christian scientists, but the science remained basically the same, and proved that there had been developments in understanding since Charles Darwin.

Zack grinned in return. "I think we have some good arguments prepared for you too!" he said.

"I can't wait until the debate," Stephanie said. "It's going to be such fun!"

"Should we be comparing notes?" Garry asked.

Dylan shook his head solemnly. "No, let it be a surprise and test of our adaptability," he said. "I'm sure the Geology Professor and the Bishop did not compare notes beforehand."

"But they weren't friends," Stephanie pointed out logically.

"And don't look like they ever will be," Zack laughed.

Cara found keeping secrets from Zack and Danielle easier than keeping their research from her own boyfriend. She kept having to stifle giggles during the Inter-denominational praise service and subsequent Reform Church service. Andrew and Kathy were sitting nearby, and the devout Andrew gave her several stern looks. Unfortunately, this only amused Cara more.

The problem was solved in the afternoon by the necessity of other study. After completing her essay, Cara had to design a tutorial handout and speech to go with it. When Stephanie had finished her paper, she went to Bede's room to continue working on the wedding and bridesmaid's dresses. Cara was left alone to work in the quiet dormitory room.

Monday morning, Cara and Stephanie presented their Education topic to their tutorial group. Cara flattered herself that the information they had presented had been very informative, and the discussion Stephanie had facilitated had been quite animated. Together they ended up with a mark of 8/10.

With the Education presentation out of the way, Cara was cheerful at lunch and in the mood to enjoy computing in the afternoon. Data entry errors could cause the program to come to a halt, but generally, fiddling around with the new technology was interesting and typing a satisfying change from hand writing.

Tuesday morning classes went well. In the afternoon, they had their Chemistry laboratory. The Chemistry Doctor checked briefly that the plans for the Creation/Evolution debate were progressing well, and then ordered the students to concentrate upon that day's laboratory.

"We are going to have some fun today," the Chemistry Doctor declared, leading the students towards a large aquarium. "Funnily enough I discovered that some of the best water tests available on the market were sold in pet shops, and designed for testing aquarium water.

The boys were checking the components in the pool water testing kit and exclaiming in satisfaction. Garry especially, who planned to take more technical subjects through Wollongong University, was fascinated.

 "What I am going to get you to do is set up the aquarium and then test the effects of pollutants and impurities without any fish present," The Chemistry Doctor instructed, and Stephanie looked relieved that no fish would be hurt.

"I'm sure a demonstration of suffering fish would be graphic," Garry observed. "But it happens enough in nature… we don't have to cause it in here."

"Like when?" Stephanie, who had a kind heart, looked disturbed.

"Whenever there is an oil spill for starters," Dylan observed. "We hear about those in the news, and didn't we discuss the effect on birds and fish earlier in the semester?"

"You are quite right Dylan," the Chemistry Doctor agreed. "Can anyone think of another example?"

"When chemical pollution from factories is washed into the river by heavy rain or flooding," Garry suggested.

"Correct once again," the Chemistry Doctor said. "In the second half of the semester, your research projects will cover the environmental impact of a specific power plant, factory or mine. I want you to be thinking ahead and researching a topic."

"Ooh," the students groaned.

The Chemistry Doctor looked stern. "Finish the Creation/Evolution debate first," he suggested. "I will get you to nominate your topics the week after that! Now – in an environment such as the aquarium – what would be the main sources of pollution?"

"The fish excreting," Dylan remarked with amusement.

"Food going bad," Garry suggested. "I have heard it is important not to overfeed fish."

"People doing things in the room," Stephanie suggested. "Like spraying fly spray."

"What about the water we add to the tank in the first place?" Cara asked. "If that is not clean enough… the fish will be in trouble from the beginning."

"All good answers," the Chemistry Doctor looked pleased.

The class spent the afternoon in happy experimentation. They tested the acidity of the water, using both test strips and the laboratory ph meter, remembering that many fish species prefer water that is 'neutral', or around 7 on the ph scale. The presence of carbon and magnesium in the water could make it 'hard', and this factor could also be tested using a reagent. The final test measured the salinity of the water, which would vary between salt-water and fresh-water environments.

Wednesday afternoon, Cara was sitting in the library with Zack, Dylan and Garry. They had to look up all the explanations for their laboratory findings, and provide chemical formula to describe the water chemistry. All four had their heads deep in their textbooks, when they were approached by Lacey, who occasionally wrote articles for the campus newsletter.

"Could I interview you about the Creation versus Evolution debate?" Lacey asked eagerly.

"Sure, why not," Zack said casually.

Lacey turned to Zack. "I hear that you are going to be quite the hero, defending our beliefs against the evils of Evolution," she began. "Is that correct?"

"It's err, one way of putting it," Zack replied. "I am the leader of the Creation team, if that is what you are asking."

"What arguments are you going to use?" Lacey demanded.
Zack looked cunning. "I can't possibly reveal that in front of members of the opposition," he remarked.

"Fair enough," Lacey said. She turned to face Garry. "Aren't you afraid that you will have to go before the Discipline Committee if you promote Evolution on campus?

"What?" Gary exclaimed. "Say that again."

"Aren't you afraid you will be in trouble if you promote Evolution on campus? Lacey repeated.

"That is what I thought you said," Garry looked astounded. "No! I wouldn't expect to be sent before the Discipline Committee for participating in an approved campus activity. Three professors have been in charge of organizing the event!"

"But you are promoting belief in Evolution," Lacey insisted.

"In the interests of promoting a balanced Christian point of view, I have agreed to review the scientific evidence for Evolution," Garry said. "As you said, Zack is promoting Creation - and he would look silly with no one to debate against."

"So you are not an 'Evolutionist'?" Lacey inquired.

"Well, I don't want to undercut my own position on the night," Garry said. "But I don't think it would be right to call me an Evolutionist. I'm as much a Christian scientist as Zack here."

Zack nodded. "Yes, he is," he confirmed.

Lacey looked slightly disappointed. "I think I have all the information I need now," she murmured, and began to retreat.

Dylan hooted. "I was expecting her to begin on me next," he said.

Stephanie looked thoughtful. "Lacey might have a point," she admitted. "This is a very conservative campus. Garry will be facing almost as hostile an audience as the Bishop faced at the University of Queensland."

Thursday the Biology class visited the Lyell Deer farm at Mount Sampson. The sanctuary had been established around 1984 with a herd of 20 deer purchased from a farmer, and the property involved some land unsuitable for crop farming, including 10 acres of uncleared bush, which was protected because it was considered a rare ecological region.

Stephanie was especially excited to visit the deer farm and interact with the animals. The Biology Master viewed Stephanie's excitement with indulgent humour, and handed the students a worksheet that directed them to consider issues surrounding the husbandry of introduced animals in Australia, the development of feral populations and the effect upon native Australian wildlife.

"He doesn't just take us out for fun you know," Dylan whispered in Cara's ear.

"Aww," Cara moaned, her face displaying mock dismay. "I always thought he did."

On Friday Garry called a final meeting of the pro-evolution team. He handed out cards that he had painstakingly typed up on the computer, outlining the various arguments.

Each team member had to select an argument or two, and be prepared to present the information. Moreover, if the material on their card appeared likely to counter the argument presented by a pro-creation team member, they were to stand and deliver their contents at the most opportune time.

Stephanie had asked each team member to bring a couple of outfits along to the meeting so she could check what they were planning to wear. The girl believed in studying diligently, but in a contradictory way, she was also a fashionista who believed passionately in the power of dressing for success.

Garry was going to wear his church suit, because that was standard for a male who wanted respect on campus. Cara had wanted to wear jeans and be her usual comfortable self, but Stephanie had persuaded her to team a pair of black dress pants with a neat cross-over jacket borrowed from Bede. This outfit suited the recent trend towards 'power suits' for women. Stephanie's own blue suit featured shoulder pads, with an added epaulette extending from the top of the point where the sleeve joined the body.

As Saturday evening approached, Cara became more nervous. It was one thing to get caught up in the excitement of attending a debate, but quite another to perform in a debate in front of several hundred people herself. Dylan and she were on opposite teams, so while he gave her hugs, she had to rely on her own team members for real support.

At last the moment came, and the two teams climbed up onto the stage in the campus meeting hall. Looking out at the sea of faces, Cara developed a new appreciation of the challenges that faced the Theology students as they trained to become ministers. And they weren't all naturally outgoing in the first place - Kathy's boyfriend Andrew was the prime example of a quiet sweet guy who had developed his public speaking skills regardless of temperament.

CHAPTER TWELVE: CREATION VERSUS EVOLUTION

One of the Theology lecturers had been asked to open the debate with a prayer for guidance and blessing. Cara felt a short respite as the prayer washed over her. Then the Physics Professor rose and testified regarding how they had attended the debate between the Bishop and the Geology Professor at the University of Queensland.

"With all respect for the Bishop, who so bravely faced the Geology Professor," the Physics Lecturer said, "We felt that our excellent group of Christian scholars, here at Silver Springs University might be able to offer a more coherent response to the issue."

The audience clapped cautiously, as sometimes making a noise was not acceptable in the campus meeting hall. However, the debate was not a church service, so after a few seconds, the clapping hands became more confident.

The Chemistry Doctor rose and introduced the teams. "You will recognize your fellow students and colleagues," he said. "Zackary Nestor has kindly agreed to lead the pro-creation side of the argument, while Garrick Morton has agreed to represent the Evolutionist argument for this evening."

Once again, there was cautious clapping, a little cheering and a smatter of booing.

Garry rose to his feet. "Man has always questioned where he came from," he began. "You will perhaps say this is unnecessary because we have the Biblical explanation."

A number of Theology students nodded in agreement.

"However," Garry continued, "God gave us our minds, with which to think, our eyes with which to see the environment and our hands with which we can touch our surroundings. It was natural, that over time, that new explanations would arise."

A few people clapped. Garry had done a good job of preparing the predominantly Christian audience to listen to him.

"The Greek philosopher Aristotle, who lived from around 384 B.C. to 322 B.C proposed a 'ladder of life', where simple organisms might gradually change into more elaborate forms," he continued.

There were a few hisses, but Garry held up his hand. "Please listen," he begged. "Around 1809, the French zoologist Jean-Baptiste Lamarck suggested a theory of development based on the evolution of new traits in response to the environment. According to Lamarck, the neck of the giraffe stretched as it reached for food. This was a theory based on the 'use and disuse' of abilities, leading to 'acquired characteristics'."

Several people laughed, and Garry paused to let them.

"In 1798," he continued, "'An Essay on the Principle of Population' was published by Thomas Robert Malthus. This was a rather frightening book that predicted the world would soon be overpopulated. It did however, have a strong influence on Charles Darwin and Alfred Russel Wallace, who were both influential in proposing the theories of Evolution and 'Natural Selection' as we have come to know them today."

"There have been a few changes over the years, but the basic principle involved is Darwin's assertion that the fittest plants and animals survive to reproduce and create the next generation," Garry continued. "Natural Selection is a term used to describe the environmental influence that removes the unfit from the population."

The audience shuffled it's feet uncomfortably.

"Another tenant of Evolutionary theory is that elements combine naturally to form compounds," Garry then ventured into deep science. "Some organic molecules may have formed more complex molecules called 'polymers'. These may have eventually evolved to form cells that developed into living organisms, and the simple organisms may have evolved over time to form complex organisms and even man!"

A smatter of boos and hisses erupted from the audience. Garry ignored them and gestured politely to Zack.

"Thank you for listening to me," he said to the audience. "It is your turn now, Zack."

Zack rose to his feet with a grin. "Well, before I start questioning our friend Garry here about the probability of his theory… I would like to tell you about Creation."

A few people cheered and the audience began clapping.

Zack gestured for silence. "In Genesis, it tells us that God made the earth in seven days. I am reading from the New King James version: 'In the beginning God created the heavens and the earth. The earth was without form, and void; and darkness was on the face of the deep. And the Spirit of God was hovering over the face of the waters. Then God said, 'Let there be light'; and there was light. And God saw the light, that it was good; and God divided the light from the darkness. God called the light Day, and the darkness He called Night. So the evening and the morning were the first day'."

"I'm going to skip ahead a bit," Zack announced. "Then God said, 'Let there be a firmament in the midst of the waters, and let it divide the waters from the waters.' So the evening and the morning were the second day…Then God said, 'Let the waters under the heavens be gathered together into one place, and let the dry land appear'; and it was so…"

People in the audience were nodding happily, especially the numerous Theology students in attendance. "That is right," someone muttered.

"Then God said, 'Let the earth bring forth grass, the herb that yields seed, and the fruit tree that yields fruit according to its kind, whose seed is in itself, on the earth'; and it was so," Zack read. "So the evening and the morning were the third day. Then God said, 'Let there be lights in the firmament of the heavens to divide the day from the night… and it was so…. Then God said, 'Let the waters abound with an abundance of living creatures, and let birds fly above the earth across the face of the firmament of the heavens'. So God created great sea creatures… and every winged bird…"

Zack took a deep breath: "Then God said, 'Let the earth bring forth the living creature according to its kind: cattle and creeping thing and beast of the earth, each according to its kind'; and it was so."

"Finally, He made man," Zack announced. "Then God said, 'Let Us make man in Our image, according to Our likeness… Then God saw everything that He had made, and indeed it was very good. So the evening and the morning were the sixth day."

Stephanie rose to her feet: "Reading the people a story they like!" she said. "Isn't that kind of cheating Zack?"

A few people tittered. Most people prepared to listen to the counter good naturedly.

"I don't think so," Zack responded. "The Bible is what Christians base their beliefs upon."

"Some people would say that is an anthropomorphic account and not a scientific document," Stephanie suggested gently.

"It may well be," Zack admitted. "And yet Genesis could be both anthropomorphically and scientifically true!"

Several rounds of applause greeted this statement.

"Isn't it true that some Christians are beginning to downplay the literal six days of Creation to make the story more acceptable to science?" Stephanie asked. "That idea makes me sad."

"It is true that some Anglican Bishops are moderating the miracles in the Bible, to make it 'easier to believe'," Zack admitted. "But I am not."

"I am glad to hear it," Stephanie said. "On the other hand – if your account is true – why can we find scientific explanations for natural phenomena?"

"Well, we only need to look at the Gospels for examples of multiple accounts of the same event," Zack said, and some Theology students nodded. "Taking an example from science – light is both a wave and a particle. This is an enigma and yet it is accepted by science."

The audience did not really want science from Zack. He was correct, but he had lost them somewhat. Stephanie sat down satisfied. Zack was feeling the heat, so he also sat down.

Felipe, who was one of the second year Physics majors, took the stand and turned the argument back towards Garry. "Garry, why don't you tell us more about Charles Darwin? Wasn't he the fellow that said we descended from monkeys?"

Laughter flittered around the campus meeting hall. The idea of men descending from Chimpanzees was comical if you had grown up believing otherwise. There were many other facets to Evolutionary theory, but Evolution could be painted as a fanciful tale if the monkey-to-man aspect was over-emphasized.

Garry stood up to present his next segment. "The works of Charles Darwin were influential because they introduced the idea of classifying organisms on the basis of their genealogy. Carl Linneaus had previously classified organisms and divided them into groups according to similarities and differences. After his voyage around the Galapagos Islands, Darwin, was honestly convinced that the similarities between organisms indicated their descent from a common ancestor, and therefore a 'degree of relatedness'. It is undeniable that some significant and notable patterns can be demonstrated in nature."

"I'm not going to be so dim as to try to deny the patterns in nature," Felipe said with a grin. "I wonder however, Garry, whether you are able to tell us what Linneus was looking for when he established his classification system?"

"Linneus was actually the son of a minister, and a devout Christian, you may be interested to learn," Garry said with a sigh. "He was looking for evidence of the Creator."

"Intelligent Design in other words?" Felipe whooped. "And he found it?"

"Yeah!" Garry allowed his opponent to savour the victory, before going on. "Dariwn's observations were backed up to a certain extent by the works of Gregor Mendel, who was actually an Augustinian Monk. He deduced that our hereditary material (known as genes or chromosomes) occurs in pairs and is passed on to the next generation, usually one half from each parent. Mendel's work on peas has formed the basis of much modern genetics."

"Mendel sounds like a smart guy, but there is a difference between growing a few peas and creating millions of different species of plant and animal," Dylan said assertively, rising to his feet.

Felipe took the opportunity to sit down.

"Oh certainly," Garry agreed. "But genetics can also be seen in the breeding of pet varieties. All dogs were once the same and now there are poodles and great danes! In the case of pet animals, man has acted as a natural selector and bred each dog for their different traits."

"Interesting," Dylan said. "Garry I just wonder - how did the original animal come into being? Do you have a theory about that?"

Garry started looking tense. "In the 1950s, a scientist by the name of Sidney Fox managed to develop polymers under laboratory conditions that were thought to resemble those of primitive earth. These proteinoids were able to catalyze reactions. It is thought that something similar may have brought about life on earth."

"Created a single cell, that grew into an animal you mean?" Dylan inquired. "What is the probability of that do you know?"

"I'm sure you are about to tell me," Garry said with an air of resignation.

"Scientists have calculated the probability of life occurring spontaneously at 1 in 10 to the power of 40,000," Dylan said. "That is a number so unlikely I cannot even imagine it!"

"Well, I'm not limited by the power of your imagination," Garry said smartly. "Recent articles on the number of proteinoids in the sea, according to the huge volume of water make the odds sound much better."

"Even so, the proteinoids have got to be there in the first place," Dylan asserted.

"Fox managed to get them to develop in a lab," Garry replied. "And what equation did you use to get that number? Drakes' equation – which was actually designed to calculate whether there might be life on another planet?"

Dylan had the grace to blush. "Some of the factors in Drake's equation were too difficult for me – so I just looked it up!"

Garry sat down. "That's a pretty intense bullet I managed to dodge," he whispered.

Zack stood up again. "I would like to introduce a new argument," he said. "According to the Second law of Thermodynamics, the usable energy in any closed system will decrease over time, and the entropy will increase. To those of you who do not study science – I will explain that entropy is randomness – something like chaos. So without God – everything would be likely to fall apart."

"Now Evolutionists argue that more complex organisms develop out of less complex organisms," Zack continued. "That would seem the opposite to what the Second Law of Thermodynamics stipulates."

Cara rose to her feet. "That argument makes a number of assumptions," she said. "Including an equation between the complexity of organisms and amounts of energy."

"All arguments make assumptions," Zack replied. "That doesn't make them wrong! What else do you have Cara?"

"I would like to talk about the fossil record," Cara said, becoming a little flustered. "There are many sedimentary layers, which would imply the earth is much older than the six thousand years often cited by Christians."

"That six thousand year figure was calculated by Bishop Usher, and I can't find it in the Bible," Zack said. "So I don't feel obliged to defend it. Instead, I will quote Job chapter 36, verse 26: 'Behold, God is great, and we do not know Him; Nor can the number of His years be discovered'."

The audience, who had begun to look bored by some of the high science, were pleased to hear a Bible text cited so aptly. A few people clapped. A few others, who had grown up with the theory that the earth was about 6-10,000 years old, began to look concerned.

"But the dates Geologists calculate – they are so large - I cannot even conceive of them," Zack continued.

"The ages Geologists calculate do assume a reasonably steady rate of sedimentation," Cara admitted. "That can be disrupted by things like flood and earthquake."

At the word flood, the audience leaned forward. Cara was on the

Evolution team, but they wondered whether she was going to mention fossil proof of the great flood? Such a concept was exceedingly dear to the hearts of some.

However, she continued: "To be honest, only God can conceive of such massive time spans. Psalm 90, verse 4: 'For a thousand years in Your sight are like yesterday when it is past, and like a watch in the night'.

"I hope that you are not going to promote the theory that the six days of Creation are really six thousand years," Zack scoffed.

"I wouldn't make such a silly one-to-one correspondence," Cara replied loftily. "All I am saying is that only God can understand such things. Job chapter 38, verse 4: 'Where were you when I laid the foundations of the earth? Tell Me, if you have understanding'."

The audience clapped. They appreciated Bible texts being well quoted, no matter which side was doing the quoting.

"While we are on the subject of the fossil record," Zack continued, "You will have to admit that no skeleton that is half-way between species has been found yet."

"There have been a few anomalies," Cara objected.

"There have also been fakes," Zack asserted loudly.

The audience clapped heartily at this, and Cara waited politely to regain their attention.

"The Piltdown man was indeed a fake," Cara admitted. "Although it puzzles scientists to this day."

The audience clapped. They liked Cara's ability to admit when her side got things wrong.

"However, many of the Indonesian specimens appear authentic," Cara ventured. "I would find it difficult to deny the existence of the Java man, also known as *Homo errectus* or the Neanderthal."

"I thought the Neanderthal was also debunked as a myth," Zack laughed.

"Scientists keep rearranging their beliefs, and unfortunately many fossils have been tampered with," Cara admitted. "Professional jealousy – and someone wanting to prove or disprove Evolution or problems with the carbon dating system."

Zack nodded with false sympathy. "I can see how that would happen," he said.

"Before the remains that are labelled 'homo' and assumed to share their genus with modern man, scientists place another series of fossils," Cara continued. "Mostly found in Africa and known as Australopithecus. Australopithecus is quite disturbing because it has a small braincase."

"It is not half man, half monkey though is it?" Zack sounded reasonably confident.

"No, it is not considered the 'common ancestor' of man and monkey," Cara admitted. "The 'common ancestor' has never been found."

"Aha," Zack sounded triumphant.

"It is tempting for us as Christians to ignore these fossils or explain them away as mistakes," Cara said. "After all – many are fragmented when they are dug up. I'm a Christian too, although I stand over on the Evolution side. I say there are many things that we do not understand or know… Deuteronomy chapter 29, verse 29: 'The secret things belong to the Lord our God, but those things which are revealed belong to us and to our children forever, that we may do all the words of this law'."

The Chemistry Doctor rose to his feet. "I am going to suggest that we take a break now," he said. "I think you will all agree that our students have done well in presenting arguments from both sides."

"Is it finished?" a few voices called from the audience. "Who won?"

"The debate section is finished," the Physics Professor announced, rising to his feet and joining the Chemistry Doctor. "As Christians, we aren't so much into talk of winning and losing. We hope that you will all take away food for thought that will help you discuss this topic more intelligibly with anyone who questions you in the future."

A few people clapped and the Theology students nodded in satisfaction. Answering people's questions in the future would be a good witness.

"We think Zack won," the murmur ran through the audience. "He had the best points!"

"The programme isn't quite finished," the Physics Professor continued. "For those of you who wish to return after the break, we will be having a prayerful discussion of the Big Bang Theory. This discussion will be quite technical and isn't for mere entertainment. I suggest that if you are not truly interested, you go on about your usual Saturday night leisure activities."

He then invited the Theology Lecturer to close the debate with a prayer that all would ponder upon what they had heard.

The audience filed out of the campus meeting hall slowly, and the two teams climbed down from the stage in relief.

"You did well!" the Chemistry Doctor exclaimed. "Very well indeed."

"I thought you guys were going to get a bit more technical," Garry complained. "What about God as activation energy and The Big Bang Theory as a confirmation rather than contradiction of Creation?"

The Physics Doctor sighed deeply. "We decided that the campus crowd probably could not take the mixture of theories and it was best to keep our Creation account – traditional. Those things will come up at the later discussion."

"Do you expect many people to return for the later discussion?" Stephanie asked.

"Many of the visiting families will want to go home," the Chemistry Doctor admitted. "And a lot of students will conclude that they have seen the exciting part of the evening already. We might get a few very earnest Theology students."

The Physics Professor sighed. "We once tried to offer a science subject especially for Theology students – but it didn't attract enough enrolments."

"I think I will give the second half a miss," Stephanie said. "I have a lot of sewing to do. It's only a week until Damaris' wedding and the dresses need all the finishing touches."

"I think I would like to wind down and relax," Cara said. "I'm not as interested in the Physics and Chemistry side of things as some of you."

She looked hopefully at Dylan, but he shook his head: "I will walk you back to the dorm," he said, "But I want to come back for the rest."

"I'm curious too," Garry said. "I can talk science any day, but the Theology students don't join us very often."

Garry looped his arm around Stephanie's shoulder and began to guide her towards the stairs. Dylan and Cara followed, while Zack attempted to convince Danielle that as she had not taken part in the debate as a team member, she ought to accompany him to the discussion.

Sunday morning at breakfast, David and Larry approached Zack and congratulated him on "winning" the debate. Their girlfriends, Debbie and Anita sat down with the girls and added their praises more subtly.

"I know your arguments were in-line with our beliefs," Larry said, "But I thought you did a good job."

"Didn't you hear the Physics Professor?" Zack retorted in amusement. "There were no winners and losers."

"I don't mind," Garry said. "Our team did its bit."

"You were good too," David added generously. "Just a little too technical at times. All those names and terms."

"Thanks, I tried to keep that to a minimum," Garry observed slightly ironically.

Larry turned to Cara, "I loved your Bible quotes," he said. "I didn't expect quotes from both sides!"

"I thought it was a good touch," Cara said, and Larry nodded.

David glanced at his watch, "We have to hurry to get to the Inter-denominational praise service," he said. "Come on Debbie, Come on Larry and Anita."

"Congratulations again Zack," Larry said as he left. "Good work Dylan."

Zack turned apologetically to Garry and Stephanie. "I'm sorry, there is likely to be more of that."

"Like I said," Garry echoed. "I really don't mind. The real win was the number of Theology students we managed to attract to the after-discussion."

"What was that like?" Cara asked curiously.

"Well to be honest, I was glad the lecturers were conducting that one," Garry admitted. "It was highly technical."

"It was nice to just participate," Dylan agreed.

"I was surprised to find out that the Big Bang Theory had actually been around since 1927," Andrew observed. He had just arrived at the table with his girlfriend Kathy, who enjoyed the occasional sleep-in on a Sunday morning. "And it was developed by a Catholic priest who was also an astronomer."

"Most people think that because the Big Bang is a scientific theory – it threatens the Creation story," Zack added. "I find it very complimentary actually."

"If you start with no stars, atoms, form, or structure in other words - a 'singularity'," Garry said. "It absolutely confirms Genesis chapter 1, verse 2: 'Now the earth was formless and empty.' NIV."

"I like the old King James Version," Dylan said. "It is an even better match – 'And the earth was without form, and void'."

"The initial inflation of the universe took less than a second," Zack said, "Which seems to confirm 'Then God said' and it was so!"

"If you go through the order in which scientists suggest things happened, ignoring their figures about hundreds, billions or thousands of years – you do find a similar order to that of the creation story in Genesis. Heat with no stars, then light, atmosphere, waters…" Andrew began.

"You might be pushing it there," Dylan observed. "It does depend on the particular theorist and the account."

"Oh of course," Andrew agreed.

"What I like, is that scientists admit, they cannot account for the cause of the Big Bang," Zack said. "That leaves us free to put God back into the equation."

"I especially like that!" Andrew agreed. "I think we could talk about this for hours… and a lot of people believe there is only one account of creation in the Bible. The one found in Genesis. There are at least three. Genesis chapters 1-6, which people know very well. Job chapter 38 and Isaiah chapters 40-48. Of course, the Isaiah account is a bit scattered. I like chapter 45 the best myself."

"There are some isolated bits in the Psalms too," added Stephanie, who loved the Psalms for their poetry.

"Yes," Andrew rose to his feet and kissed Kathy on the cheek. "If I hurry, I can still make it to the praise service. I will call for you at the dorm between services, my dear."

"Okay," Kathy said. She was clearly glad of the extra time to eat and make herself pretty before the Reform Church service.

Stephanie and Garry rose to their feet. "As people are looking edgeways at us for having presented the Evolution argument last night, I think we had better attend both services," Stephanie said. "Coming Cara?'

"Yeah sure," Cara had finished her cereal and was ready.

"I'm a good Creationist, but I suppose I will come too," Dylan joked, standing to follow his classmates.

Sunday afternoon and all Monday, the students were busy with assignments. The mid-semester break was due to begin on Friday, and a number of lecturers had declared an arbitrary deadline of Wednesday afternoon for all assignments from the first half of the semester.

The only exceptions to this were Stephanie and Bede, both of whom were occupied by 'secret wedding business'. Michael, who was the groom, was also occupied with wedding business, and had to pack all his belongings and move them across to Damaris' rental by the end of the half semester.

The Biology class all had a chuckle when two second year Theology students, Mathew and Christopher, approached them Monday at lunch and inquired whether their lectures were full of tension, seeing they 'appeared to disagree so much'!

"We are actually the best of friends," Dylan said with a laugh. "You do know that the debate was just make-believe don't you?"

"Whatever do you mean?" Mathew asked, looking puzzled.
"Garry isn't really an Evolutionist," Dylan explained. "He just had to talk like that for the night."

"That's a relief," Christopher observed quite seriously. "I was a bit worried about him there."

"Trust me, I'm a Christian and a scientist," Garry replied. "Evolution is just something I have had to study."

Mathew looked puzzled. "Why did you have to study it?" he asked.

"To understand the wickedness of the world," Dylan quipped impishly.

Mathew and Christopher took him seriously though. "That is good," they said. "Just so long as you don't get led astray."

"Seriously," Garry said. "Evolution is in the textbooks and on the curriculum, so Christians cannot afford to appear ignorant."

"Of course not," Mathew agreed.

"This other member of the 'Evolution team' here, is actually my girlfriend," Dylan said, referring to Cara, whom the boys had been inclined to ignore, because she was female, and they were very traditional.

"Ah yes," Mathew said. "You quoted some Bible texts."

"Yeah, I did," Cara said, and subsided. She had her five minutes of glory.

Mathew and Christopher moved on about their business, and the science students exchanged amused glances.

"We shouldn't be mean," Stephanie declared. "Some of the Theology students are very nice guys really!"

"But you prefer me, don't you?" Garry joked.

"Of course," Stephanie agreed. "You are practical."

"Am I practical?" Dylan teased, turning to Cara.

"I dunno," Cara said. "Not always – but I prefer you too - if that is what you are really asking."

Tuesday was the final Chemistry laboratory for the half semester. It turned out to be a theoretical session, where they read through the World Health Organisation publications regarding air pollution. The 1958 paper recognised the 'adverse' health effects of air pollution, although it unfortunately assumed these effects were limited to respiratory tract irritations.

Subsequent reports considered the effects on plants and animals, as well as documenting standards. These reports didn't list all the pollutants or suggest how the 'permissible levels' ought to be determined. By the mid-1960s however, the documents contained suggestions regarding filtering emissions and controlling traffic.

"If all this was known twenty years ago?" Garry just had to ask, "Why was so little done?"

"Greed, consumerism and convenience," the Chemistry Doctor suggested.

"Faith in nature to cure itself too, I would suggest," Zack added optimistically.

"But according to this information – systematic monitoring only commenced THIS YEAR," Dylan exclaimed. "And at a few stations!"

"I expect it actually isn't easy to measure something like air," Cara observed, thinking back to some of their more frustrating laboratory experiences.

"These people seem to know how to do it!" Garry was adamant.

"There is a significant gap between 1972 and now," Dylan said, attempting to leaf through the articles.

"To be fair," the Chemistry Doctor suggested, "Some of the latest efforts might not be published."

"I thought scientists liked to get their findings out these as soon as they were confirmed," Dylan said, reflecting on the scientific method, which included the directive to 'publish'.

"I'm going to work in this field," Garry said, his eyes shining with determination. "Maybe not my first job – that might be just for money and experience – but soon after that!"

"I will support you in that," Cara said. "Although I think I want to work with animals and birds."

"And I will be supporting you in that," Dylan added gallantly. "Animals and birds need clean air!"

"Indeed they do," Cara agreed.

Wednesday, a lot of assignments were due. Everyone was panicking and rushing, even the studious Stephanie, who worried until the last sheet was stapled and the paper actually dropped into the submission slot.

Thursday, the Biology Master had replaced the regular laboratory session with a practical test. This had the advantage of being completed in the one session, and the disadvantage of being every bit as stressful on the nerves as the regular practical exam. In fact, Dylan and Garry joked that they would not need a 'prac exam' after that test.

Friday, classes were finished by lunch time. Dylan and Garry spent the afternoon helping Michael move his things into Damaris' rental accommodation, and then the group caught the bus to Brisbane, where Damaris' and Michael were getting married. The location was convenient for Michael's family, because Michael's older sister lived there.

Cara and Dylan, Stephanie and Garry, Bede and Kaleb had booked into a youth hostel overnight. The youth hostel was cheap, costing the students around $10 each for bunks in a dormitory room.

The dormitory was unisex, so there was some risk that they would be in trouble if someone reported them, however, Dylan declared that common sense ought to reign, and anyone who thought that any couple got up to mischief, while sharing with two other couples and a pair of random backpackers, was quite crazy.

Saturday morning dawned beautifully fine, and the students packed their light bags and checked out of the youth hostel. They then began making their way towards the historic Albert Street Uniting Church, which was incongruently becoming hemmed in by city skyscrapers.

The guest list was mostly comprised of Michael's family and friends, however, Stephanie and Bede were especially keen to see the dresses they had sewn being worn down the aisle. Arriving at the church, they sneaked into the back. This allowed them to avoid the main crush of Michael's intimidating family, and also get the first view of the bride when she arrived.

Michael was standing up the front with his father and brothers, looking pale and nervous. As Damaris arrived, the organ began to play. Stephanie and Bede peered desperately along the aisle to get a view of the bridal dress. The satin had a lovely sheen and the edges showed a crisp finish.

The bride's youthful shoulders were emphasized by the feature sleeves, and the seamstresses nodded. They had given the sleeves just the right amount of bouffant, so they were feminine and pretty, but not too exaggerated. The beaded lace and appliqués were complimented by the beautiful tiara and cathedral length veil Michael's mother had bought for Damaris.

Stephanie and Bede exchanged happy glances. "The overall effect is great," Stephanie whispered.

"Every stitch was perfect," Bede whispered in satisfaction.

"Damaris and Michael will be very happy," Dylan added, "That's what really matters."

The girls gave him warning looks and moved on to analyzing the bridesmaids' dresses.

"I think the blue was a good choice," Stephanie whispered. "Especially for a church of this size."

"I thought it was a little formal," Bede whispered, "But it does work – and the orchids are magnificent."

"It must have cost a fortune to decorate the church," Stephanie whispered. "With all those flowers."

After the ceremony, the students attended the reception, before heading straight to the airport. Stephanie and Garry were going to spend the holiday in Wollongong, while Kaleb and Dylan were accompanying Bede and Cara back to Melbourne to meet the girl's parents.

It was ironic that the senior O'Brien's had once feared Kaleb might take Cara back to the United States, but it was now confirmed that he would be taking their youngest child, Bede, overseas. Bede was the parent's favourite daughter and they had always allowed her to do whatever she wished.

CHAPTER THIRTEEN: A COUPLE OF COMPETITIONS

The week and a half in Geelong simply flew by. The house seemed crowded with the two male visitors, but the O'Brien parents were clearly struggling to come to terms with the new developments in their daughter's lives. Several unenlightened locals had suggested that Kaleb, despite his neat appearance, might belong to an African gang, and this concerned Cara, even though she had broken up with him.

Cara was concerned for Bede too, noticing the way people looked at her sister and the African-American young man, as they strolled along hand-in-hand. If Kaleb went ahead with his plan to minister to an all-Black church in the United States, then Bede would be the one to find herself the odd one out.

Overall, the visit was a necessary exercise in relationship building, but represented something of a bit too much of a good thing. Only Grandma O'Brien seemed genuinely thrilled, as she sensed great-grand children were not too far off in the future. Besides, the old woman had experienced the move from Ireland to Australia, and acknowledged that there was a lot more to identity than the colour of one's skin and country of residence.

Upon the return to Silver Springs, classes commenced again. Monday morning was full of greetings; and accounts of holiday activities were whispered in the transitional moments between lectures. Many people were curious as to what it had been like to take her ex-boyfriend home, as well as her current boyfriend. Cara was well over all that, and while there had been an odd moment or two, she primarily wished her sister well.

During the afternoon computing tutorial, the students mastered spread sheet use and constructed a simple database. While these activities reminded Cara of an introductory computing subject the class had completed in their first year, there were differences. Some of the computers were new, and the operating systems were migrating from inbuilt BASIC to DOS or in the case of the Apple, Mac OS.

The rest of the semester, their assignment required demonstrating proficiency at the computers for personal use. Cara had chosen to focus on the spreadsheet, because she could see it would be handy for all sorts of lists, budgets and reports. Some of the other students were focusing on the publishing packages, generating resumes, newsletters and posters.

Tuesday, the students were due to commence their major projects. Cara had chosen to study the environmental impact of the Mount Isa mines. Copper, lead, zinc and silver were all mined near Mount Isa, and a lot of the metals were also refined nearby.

Mining had the potential to create a great deal of waste and pollution, however, the mines were so important to the economy that they had received special dispensation, with lenient environmental standards being applied. The smelter plants released sulfur dioxide in close proximity to the city of Mount Isa; and furthermore the mines were thought to be the highest atmospheric emitters of Sulphur dioxide, lead and other metals in Australia.

Lead could be detected in the soil and even the blood of children whose families lived close. Cara felt that her work was very topical, as the previous year, Professor Graeme Jameson of the University of Newcastle had been commissioned to improve the design of flotation columns used as zinc concentrate cleaners.

Wednesday, Bede and Stephanie were keen to get working on their entry into the Man Made Fibers Design Competition. Cara tried to escape, but they conscripted her to act as the model. While she stood there being draped and measured, as well as overhearing the girl's technical conversation, Cara became interested despite herself.

"I know that you love the sixties and seventies," Bede was saying to Stephanie. "And the designer we have chosen to honour is famous for his smooth lines – but I think we still ought to create designs that would sell in the 1980s."

"True," Stephanie agreed reluctantly, dreams of boho glamour going out the window. "And it is mostly your entry."

"A peplum is a smooth line," Bede suggested. "Why not have a jacket with a peplum?"

"Add a large button at the waist and a shawl collar," Stephanie observed. "That would be very flowing."

"And a short four gore skirt," Bede added.

"That could be our office-wear option," Stephanie observed.

"I fancy a shirt-dress in a large red and black plaid," Bede mused. "With perhaps a crossover back, and two back tails that are longer than the front."

"No waist," Stephanie suggested, "Just large buttons down the front and an optional belt."

"Do you think that could count as our plus size offering?" Bede inquired.

"It has a touch of plus size glamour about it," Stephanie agreed. "And yet, I can see it worn over leggings for the smaller sizes."

Bede twitched some sample swatches of faux fur and imitation leather. "I would like to do some work with these," she said. "All the luxury of fur and leather, but no need to hurt any animals because it is synthetic."

"The trouble is," Stephanie observed seriously. "Fur and leather appear so dramatic, people rarely have opportunity to wear them. I'm thinking, maybe a tailored coat – with straight lines, not fitted. The body of the coat would be in a wool-like blend, to tone it down and the trimmings could be faux fur."

"What trimmings were you thinking?" Bede asked curiously. "Fur collars have been somewhat overdone."

"Agreed," Stephanie said. "But epaulets are in… and cuffs… depending how luxe you wanted the coat to look."

"What about imitation Buckskin pants and skirts?" Bede suggested. "We run the risk of looking a little ethnic – but it looks very comfortable. Also Chester Weinberg was fond of fringing the edges, which would go well with a buckskin theme. In fact, I think we are almost channeling him there!"

Stephanie and Bede had a few more decisions to make, but they were satisfied for the afternoon. They made their sketches, closed their books and set Cara free. She wandered downstairs, where she found Dylan had arrived at reception and was just about to call for her.

"I've been wondering where you got to since lunch," he said. "I was hoping you would like to come for a drive?"

"Yeah, sure," Cara said. "Should we ask Garry?"

"We haven't been alone for over a week, what with your family, your sister and your ex," Dylan complained. "Why would we ask Garry along?"

"Stephanie is busy sewing," Cara murmured. "Garry could be lonely."

"Garry is a big boy," Dylan said impatiently. "He will look after himself. Hop in!"

"Okay," Cara complied. "Where are we going?"

"The State Forest or Glasshouse Mountain," Dylan said. "Your choice.”

“Glasshouse Mountain,” Cara said. In the back of her mind, the memory of Bradley’s delight in the mountain area remained. She pushed the sadness away. Even Stephanie hadn’t mentioned Bradley for a while, and Dylan wanted a romantic afternoon.

Thursday afternoon, the Biology Master took the students to Noosa National Park. They parked the Land Rover and commenced walking through the bush on one of the walking trails. Their ultimate destination was Hells Gate, where they would be doing some turtle spotting.

However, on their way through the park, there was a chance of seeing koalas, a short-nosed bandicoot, common ringtail possum, or brushtail possum. The birdlife included: the eastern ground parrot, glossy black cockatoo, eastern yellow robin, rufous fantail, satin bowerbird and crimson rosella.

The Biology Master instructed the students to walk quietly and keep their eyes open. If they were very lucky, once they reached the headland they might also catch a glimpse of dolphins playing, or even see a migrating humpback whale.

The walk was very pleasant, and when they reached the headland, they settled down to watch patiently. The edge of the cliff was dangerous, so the viewing point was slightly back, but the view of the ocean and ten metre plunge into the ravine was spectacular. There were a few turtles swimming in the ocean below, but they were a long way away and visibility was disappointing.

The Biology Master suggested that the students walk back along the coastal track, where they passed a goanna sunning itself, and a small colony of wild turkeys. The blue water of Alexandria Bay sparkled in the sun, and the sand was a beautiful clean colour.

The Biology Master warned the students to be prepared to close their eyes if they encountered naked swimmers, because the beach was so secluded, it was sometimes treated as a 'clothing optional' site by the locals.

The students were slightly disappointed there were not more turtles walking on the beach, but the Biology Master explained that the nesting season began in October and lasted until March. About January, the baby turtles hatched in the sand and made a survival dash for the sea.

"There is talk of building a new tourist and research facility nearby," The Biology Master confided in excitement. "I believe a site around Mooloolaba is being considered."

The students looked excited.

"Unfortunately, you will have graduated before it opens," The Biology Master added.

"Still, it's a great idea," Garry said.

"There is a lot of work to do in conservation too," The Biology Master remarked. "Discarded plastic bags are especially dangerous to the turtles, because if they eat a bag, they will not be able to digest it. Their digestive systems get blocked, which usually proves fatal."

"Which turtles nest here?" Dylan inquired curiously.

"The main species that nest along the Sunshine Coast beaches are the Loggerhead turtle and the Green turtle," the Biology Master said, peering carefully up and down the shoreline. "Aha, I think we found an early one!"

The Biology Master was pointing to a slight mound in the sand. The area around it had been carefully smoothed down by the mother turtles' flippers to make it appear as though nothing of significance was buried under the surface. However, a few feet away, the tell-tale pattern of the turtle flippers led from the mound back into the sea.

"It is like a tyre track," Dylan laughed. "I could have sworn a bike had been through here."

"Not deep enough," Garry observed.

The girls were gazing at the small circle in delight. "Incredible," Cara breathed.

"I won't disturb the nest to show you the eggs," the Biology Master said. "Because I don't want to put the baby turtles at any risk. Enough get discovered and eaten anyway. It is a cruel world!"

The class continued their hike through the sand more carefully after that, mindful that precious things could be underfoot at any step. Then they rejoined the hiking trail through the bush back to the Land Rover, returning to campus late for tea as was often the case after a practical.

The majority of the third year girls rarely worried about the upcoming campus social events, because they were secure in the knowledge that they would go with their boyfriends. However, Friday after tea, Elisabet knocked on their dormitory room door, looking for some girl-talk about the coming Greek Feast on Sunday night.

"How is the music?" Cara asked.

Elisabet flushed a little. "It is coming along well," she said. "I had played before coming to university – I just wasn't as terrifyingly advanced as the Music majors."

"And instead of giving up – you decided to keep going?" Stephanie exclaimed. "I think that is great."

"Thanks!" Elisabet looked pleased. "Craig encouraged me. He is a great mentor. I was wondering whether we could have a chat Steph?"

"Sure," Stephanie said. "You don't mind Cara do you – we can trust her?"

Elisabet was one of the few girls who was still single. At first, Cara had assumed it was because Elisabet was reserved, but then she had realized that Elisabet was not lacking in self-confidence. In fact, the other girl was pretty and dressed well. She had no lack of invitations from the boys, and apparently was just fussy.

"Well," Elisabet began, "Hypothetically speaking… what would you do if you had been asked to the Greek Feast by Tom, say?"

"Tom?" Cara exclaimed. "I didn't know he and Joelle had broken up!"

"They have been having problems," Stephanie mused. "Joelle doesn't pay Tom much attention."

"She is always busy with practices and worships," Cara agreed. "But problems – and broken up – those could be different things."

"Tom is a nice guy and a friend," Stephanie mused. "And he is in our English class… but as we are not sure they are broken up – it is a difficult question."

"I think I would steer clear," Cara said. "You don't want to be blamed for their breakup."

"On the other hand, refusing Tom wouldn't force him to stay with Joelle," Stephanie said.

"That is right," Cara said. "But it would keep Elisabet's reputation safe."

"You are right," Stephanie agreed. "It is Elisabet's decision though."

"Well, say Felipe had asked me as well?" Elisabet mused.

"Oh – that is easy," Stephanie said. "Felipe has no complications."

"I think you are lucky to have two invites," Cara concluded. "And Felipe might be a year below us – but he is mature because of the persecution he suffered before escaping South America."

"He is smart," Stephanie said. "You don't get to be a Physics major for no reason."

"So you girls would take Felipe then?" Elisabet reflected.

"Given the timing and the circumstances, yes," Cara said.

"What sort of guy are you looking for?" Stephanie asked curiously.

"No one seems to have suited your taste yet."

"Oh – I don't know," Elisabet said. "Blonde and surfy – a bit like Dylan – but more serious, confident and committed – maybe even a Theology student."

"Most of the Theology students are taken," Stephanie mused. "They tend to commit early."

"Felipe is not blonde," Cara said. "He is serious and committed however. Perhaps when he has been in Australia longer he will learn to surf."

Elisabet laughed. "It's only for one date!" she said. "Thanks girls."

"Single dates can lead to more," Stephanie observed.

"I like to take things slow," Elisabet said. "Anyway, I will tell Felipe at worship."

"When will you tell Tom?" Stephanie asked, suddenly serious.

"Hypothetically – if I don't mean to say 'yes' – do I really have to go and embarrass him with a 'no'?" Elisabet prevaricated.

"It might help," Cara said. "If you still had a class together that would be ideal – but it's the weekend already."

"Maybe you will bump into him at a meal," Stephanie suggested. "I think I know what you are thinking… don't draw attention or the harm might be done anyway."

Just then, Cara and Stephanie's names were called over the public address system. Dylan and Garry would be waiting for them at reception. The girls hurried downstairs and joined their boyfriends for the Uniting Church vespers.

Saturday morning at breakfast, Damaris was in charge of the cafeteria. Cara and Stephanie took the opportunity to ask her how she was enjoying married life. Damaris replied that everything was wonderful. Michael and she had gone on a Whitsunday Cruise as their honeymoon, and Michael was settling into her rental accommodation very happily.

Several nearby Theology students were joking about experiencing life as Jesus knew it at the Greek Feast Sunday night.

Damaris looked indulgent. "It is a Modern Greek night, not an Ancient Greek night," she whispered. "I don't have the heart to correct them!"

"Let them have their fun," Stephanie agreed.

"So we might get a little Zorba and plate smashing?" Cara inquired.

Damaris wrinkled her nose. "Greek music certainly," she said. "But I must insist you refrain from throwing any plates around."

After Dylan and Cara had finished their breakfast, they approached the seating plan for the Greek Feast. Dylan put their names down on the seating plan next to Stephanie and Garry. Andrew and Kathy added their names on the same table; and Andrew, seeing Joelle and Tom passing through the cafeteria called out, invited the couple to sit nearby.

"Hey Tom," the Theology student cried. "What are you guys doing about the Greek Feast?"

It was Joelle who answered: "I thought we might give it a miss," she said. "I have a lot of practice to do for the Alumni weekend, which is the weekend after. The Music Master has invited me to his house for the afternoon to discuss the music."

"That is alright for you, but it would be mighty dull for me, my dear," Tom objected.

"You can sit with us, Tom," Kathy suggested, and Andrew put Tom's name down on the seating plan.

"There it's sorted!" Andrew said.

"Okay," Joelle said and went about her way as if she really did not care. "I'm due over at the Music department already!"

"Thanks Andrew," Tom said.

Elisabet paused beside the seating chart briefly. "I'm going with Felipe," she remarked casually before entering her name and that of her date, on the same table, but at the opposite end of the group.

"Have fun," Tom said casually, and strolled away in the direction of boys' dorm.

Cara and Stephanie exchanged glances. "I don't know what that was all about," Cara whispered. "But Joelle is so risking losing Tom."

"She has been warned," Kathy said, somehow overhearing the undertone. "But Tom can't be expected to miss everything just because it suits Joelle. He won't come to any harm with us."

"I guess it is something they need to sort out," Stephanie murmured.

"We can't force people to be stay together, and we certainly can't force people to be happy," Kathy said. She viewed Stephanie sternly. It wasn't that Stephanie was horribly prone to interfering in other people's business, but the girl could be a bit of a do-gooder.

The students all left the cafeteria and went about their day. Stephanie and Bede were working hard on their Man Made Fiber designs as the contest entry was due soon. As Cara worked on her assignments, she heard the girls arguing softly about an evening entry.

Stephanie wanted to continue the smooth lines of their previous designs, but Bede had suggested a full skirt for the evening dress, to take into account the current fashions which were very bouffant. Stephanie had insisted on a fitted bodice, and at the last moment, the girls decided to make the gown a one shoulder affair, with a large bow on the seam. Then they began arguing gently about what colour to make the sample gown.

Sunday morning, Cara and Dylan attended both the Inter-denominational praise service and the Reform Church service. After lunch, they spent some time in the library working on their research projects. While Cara was working on the Mount Isa mines, Dylan had chosen to study the Gladstone Aluminum smelter. This was a relatively new smelter as it had been officially opened in 1982. Unlike older industrial sites, which had grown up close to the target resource, the Boyne Island smelter had undergone extensive planning. It was Dylan's task to determine whether the installation actually any safer for the environment than older ad hoc industrial plants.

Sunday evening, the students all gathered in the cafeteria for the Greek Feast. October was the month in which the Greeks celebrated their 'National Anniversary' or 'No Day". This was the day on which they had refused to surrender to the Italians during the Second World War.

The celebration began with Greek spiced and twice cooked potatoes. These potatoes were boiled and then roasted, with the marinade making them delicious. A Greek salad with traditional olives, baby spinach and feta cheese was also placed upon the table. The meat option was lamb skewers.

When the serving platters began to look empty, the Hospitality students brought out more dishes, including a couscous and meatball dish, with mixed bean salad. A side dish of hummus with pita bread for dipping proved very popular for both vegetarians and meat eaters.

The crowning glory of the feast was a spinach and ricotta pie baked in a flaky pastry. After the savoury course was consumed, they were served a selection of almond butter biscuits and other authentic tasting Greek sweets.

"Elisabet and Felipe appear to be having a good time," Cara whispered to Dylan.

"Felipe is a good guy," Dylan said. "I got to know him a bit when we were planning the Creation defense."

"Wouldn't it be nice if they got together?" Cara whispered.

"I suppose," Dylan said. "Elisabet is pure arts and Felipe is all science however. That doesn't leave them a lot in common…." His attention wandered in typical Dylan fashion. "I see old Tom's coping alright with being here alone."

"Forget other people," Cara said suddenly. "Let's concentrate upon ourselves." She didn't want to gossip about Tom in to his male friends if he had not said anything to them. "How long have we been going out now?"

"Give or take a day or two – seven weeks," Dylan said. "We should be planning something special for next weekend. That will be our anniversary."

"Congratulations!" Stephanie and Garry, who had overheard the conversation in one of those brief moments when the dating couple were not solely focused upon themselves.

"Thanks," Dylan said.

"Well, it is the Alumni weekend," Cara admitted. "We aren't really involved in that. Except I did volunteer for weekend duty."

"So did I," Dylan laughed. "And that was without even consulting you!"

The cafeteria and other essential services did not run themselves on the weekends, and all students were expected to donate one day's effort to keep things going. The Alumni weekend meant little to the current students, so it was a popular pick for weekend duty. This time however, Cara had a thought.

"What if someone we know comes back to visit?" Cara asked.

"We could ask Damaris to put us on serving instead of burying us down the back," Dylan suggested. "But mostly, people wait until their five or ten year anniversary to return for a visit."

"And after our duties are finished – we will have a little celebration of our own," Dylan suggested.

"That sounds good," Cara agreed.

The Greek night came to an end and Dylan walked Cara across to girls' dorm. They stopped in the shadow of a tree several meters away from the front door for a good night kiss, deftly ignoring the dozens of other regular couples doing the same thing.

Monday after tea, Dylan and Cara were lying in a quiet spot on one of Cara's nicely mown lawns, taking advantage of the warm evening to make-out. October had to be one of the nicest months, dry and balmy, until the rains started. The only drawback was the high fire danger in the bush.

Dylan and Cara weren't in any danger of igniting the literal sort of fire, but things were getting heated. They were quite happy with what God had given them in the relationship sense. As they paused for air, Cara heard another couple approach and sit down on the grass the other side of the small shrubbery.

Dylan covered Cara's mouth gently with his hand and signaled to her not to speak, leaving the other couple remained completely unaware of their presence. The female companion spoke. It was Joelle.

"I have something to tell you," Joelle said. "I think it is good, but I don't know how you will take it."

"Not more practice," Tom sighed.

"Maybe," Joelle said, "But that's not it."

"I hardly see you as it is," Tom's tone was complaining.

"The Music Master entered me into a scholarship plan that sponsors a number of young Australian musicians to go and perform at Christmas concerts around the UK," Joelle said. "I would be away almost the entire Christmas break."

"Are these Christian concerts?" Tom inquired.

"Some," Joelle admitted. "It is more of a classical programme though… and performances at places like Albert Hall can make a musician's reputation."

"Who else would be going?" Tom asked.

"Craig might be," Joelle said. "I haven't heard whether he got in or not. No one else from Silver Springs is even near qualified."

"No Larry – no worship committee?" Tom sounded relieved.

"Of course not," Joelle said. "Why would you mention Larry?"

"You were keen on him for a while last year," Tom observed.

"With respect, because I know he is going to be a minister and everything," Joelle said, "Larry was rather cowardly last year – he could have let me know where I stood much earlier and saved me some pain."

"I thought so too," Tom said. "That's why I get concerned when you spend so much time practicing for worships with him."

"Anita comes along," Joelle objected. "We are never alone."

"Anita was in the picture last year too," Tom said. "Larry didn't technically or physically two-time anyone… but it wasn't the action of a true friend."

"I am aware of that," Joelle said with a sigh. "Is that all that worries you about my practices?"

"Well I miss you of course," Tom said with a laugh. "But you getting too involved with one of the Theology students is my main fear. You would be wonderfully suited to be a minister's wife."

"It's you I'm going out with," Joelle murmured. "So how do you feel about Christmas?"

"I'm vastly relieved that was the reason for your preoccupation," Tom said. "And we might have visited each other late in the break – but the festive season is really a family matter. It's your parents you need to ask."

"They are keen for me to go to the UK," Joelle admitted. "I should be back by mid-January, then we will celebrate Australia Day as a late Christmas."

"That is okay by me so long as I am invited," Tom said.

There was the sound of some kissing, and then the other couple got to their feet and left.

Dylan released his hand from over Cara's mouth when Tom and Joelle were a safe distance away, and both began to giggle.

"I didn't mean for us to eavesdrop," Dylan said.

"I think Tom is very understanding towards Joelle," Cara said.

"It probably won't be the last drama for them," Dylan said. "I know you girls like to help each other out, but like I was saying at the Greek Feast – it's best to stay out of it. You had no way of knowing what was really going on."

Tuesday, Stephanie and Bede showed Cara their final designs for the Man-Made Fiber competition. After much arguing about being traditional or creative, following smooth lines or being 1980s, the two girls had settled on a two piece ensemble for their bridal entry. It featured a fitted bodice with paneling.

The panels were covered in nylon lace, and each was shaped along the lower edge and flared out below the waist to create a jacket-like effect. The boat-shaped neckline was cut so wide on the shoulder, as to be almost off-the-shoulder. A tiny cap sleeve had been added, and hand-made satin flowers had been appliqued all the way around the neck.

The separate skirt was fitted at the top, but also featured panels that flared out around the ankles. The dress was not ground length, but allowed for the glimpse of a nylon lace legging, which the girls had added as their lingerie entry. They had shaped a matching turban out of satin and lace to add an exotic touch, and a tulle veil could be attached to the back of the turban if the wearer desired.

"After all the final touches are complete, the outfits will be submitted to the competition," Stephanie said.

"Do you have to post the actual dresses across to the United States?" Cara asked.

"No!" Bede looked horrified. "That would cost a fortune and I would never get them back."

"We submit sketches, so the drawings have to be very good," Stephanie said. "And photographs also – to prove that the designs are practicable and can be made up. Even close-ups of the final details to show the workmanship."

"If we were to win, they might ask to see the originals," Bede said. "I would take them across with me. Although, maybe not the wedding dress – because I've promised that to Stephanie. It was cut to fit her."

"It's not ground length," Stephanie blushed. "I could use it as a graduation dress…"

"Or Garry could propose," Cara teased. "That is why he is trying to graduate early isn't it?"

"Among other things I guess," Stephanie said. "Garry's life has been complicated by his mother's illness."

"She's in remission now isn't she?" Bede asked anxiously.

"Yeah," Stephanie said. "But with something like that – you don't know… the only thing we do really know is that if she needs him again – he and I won't be breaking up over it."

"I'm glad your entry is almost complete," Cara said. "Now I have to go to the library and do more research for my Chemistry project. Stephanie, you are lucky you have too full a timetable to be forced to do Chemistry."

"Oh I would have loved to do Chemistry," Stephanie said, somewhat maddeningly. Of course, that was Stephanie all over – her insatiable academic curiosity would have had her enrolled in every subject the university offered if the lecturers had allowed.

Cara groaned and went off to the library to join Dylan, Garry and Zack, who were all waiting for her. The Chemistry Doctor did not actually come up to the library to check that his class was faithfully researching, but if he had, he would have been well satisfied by their diligence.

The news that Joelle had a sponsored performance tour in the United Kingdom spread quickly through the group. Dylan and Cara waited until Joelle told them herself on Wednesday to add their congratulations.

Craig was sitting between Elisabet at lunch. It was unlike him to linger over his food, but Cara had noticed the dedicated musician had been becoming more sociable of recent times. He congratulated Joelle sincerely and admitted that he had missed out on the sponsorship programme.

"I guess they couldn't take us both, or they specifically wanted a pianist," Craig said. "I have been giving some time to composition instead of practice, so Joelle may have outshone me in her practical skill."

"I think your violin is wonderful," Cara breathed.

Dylan nodded. "I'm always impressed when you do an item mate," he said.

Cara thought that Elisabet looked a bit misty eyed. Of course, she could not tell whether the girl envied Joelle's relationship with Tom, who had some of the surfy good looks Elisabet admired; or whether she simply envied Joelle winning a Music competition. Elisabet was quiet, but she also seemed ambitious.

Stephanie was deep in conversation with Joelle, "so how long will you be away?" she was asking.

"I leave a few days after exams finish here," Joelle admitted. "The concerts are scheduled for their Advent season, although they are not all Christian. Some are purely classical and one is connected to a secular pantomime."

"Will you be away over New Years?" Garry inquired.

"I think they are allowing us New Years for recreation and sight-seeing," Joelle said. "Then there are a series of concerts from Epiphany until mid-January. After that, I will be free to come home."

"It is convenient that the entire tour occurs during our long break," Cara observed.

"Oh indeed!" Joelle replied. "I find it strange, that they take so little time off for Christmas – although they do enjoy organizing concerts and services for that period."

"I think it is all the snow," Tom remarked. "Who would want their long holidays to be frozen over?"

"Someone who likes snow-skiing I expect," Cara suggested. "But I expect you are right. Kaleb always told me the American holidays were different than ours too."

"I think I like what we have," Dylan mused. "Sun and heat and everything Australian!"

CHAPTER 14: A MATTER OF JUSTICE

The weather broke the Thursday before Alumni weekend, and the rain began to pour down. Even the Biology Master agreed that it was not a good day for an excursion, and set the students to performing tasks that could be completed in the laboratory. This included inspecting skeletons, viewing a documentary on marsupials; and then researching the metabolism of the koala, which was restricted to eating certain species of gum leaves, and uniquely adapted to digest a substance that was almost poisonous.

Friday afternoon, Cara struggled to get her mowing done despite the wet. Visitors had been arriving all afternoon, and past graduates were occupying all the guest rooms on campus. Many more would seek lodgings in the motels and caravan parks of the nearby settlements of Northcoast and Eumundi. There was a rumour that Melanie and Jonathon, who had graduated at the end of Cara and Stephanie's first year, were returning to enjoy the Alumni celebrations.

Melanie had been a student dean; and a friend and mentor to Stephanie. The more independent Cara had not required mentoring to the same extent, but she remembered Melanie as a nice girl. If anything, too nice, because her boyfriend had also been friends with Stephanie's ex - Jeffrey Mannington, and Melanie had been unable to see through the bully boy's behavior.

"It will be so much fun to see Melanie again," Stephanie said as they were dressing for vespers that evening.

"Aren't you worried that Jeffrey Mannington might come along too?" Cara asked her roommate.

Stephanie shrugged. "Jonathon and Melanie have been married almost two years now, and have a baby," she said. "I don't think they see much of Jeff anymore."

"Do you think they have heard about Tony?" Cara asked.

"I expect they were as shocked as anyone," Stephanie replied. "We all knew Tony could be a bit mean – but no one expected he would be charged with steroid trafficking and sabotaging Bradley's bike."

Their hair and make-up done, the girls went downstairs to meet their boyfriends. Vespers were especially crowded that evening and they had a struggle to find an available pew. The majority of the visitors were five or ten years older than the current students, and some even looked old enough to be their parents' generation.

"I'm glad I have weekend duty," Cara whispered. "Then Dylan and I have some anniversary plans. I'm not sure what they are yet – but Dylan will have worked something out."

"I have study to do," Stephanie whispered. "I've fallen a bit behind schedule helping Bede with the design competition. And then Garry and I thought we would swim in the university pool. We figured the visitors would have little interest in doing that!"

"Yeah – they have their meetings," Cara conceded. "The pool area is probably pretty safe."

The group was leaving the women's assembly area when Stephanie spied her old friends, Melanie and Jonathon. "They are here!" she exclaimed in delight and began to wave.

"You haven't forgotten tomorrow have you?" Dylan asked Cara, casting a humorous look around the crowd. "With all this excitement to be had?"

"Doing something with you will be just perfect," Cara exclaimed. She stood on tiptoe to kiss him. Dylan was only of average height, but that was still a pleasant centimeter taller than her.

Garry faithfully accompanied Stephanie across to her reunion with Melanie and Jonathon, while Dylan walked Cara back to the reception area of girl's dormitory. Later Stephanie reported that Melanie and Jonathon were on campus for the weekend with friends from previous years, whom the current students had never met.

The next morning, Cara and Dylan arrived at the cafeteria early. Damaris assigned them to the server, where they ladled out portions of food for the current and visiting students. Towards the end of the assigned meal time, they were allowed to leave their stations to have a small meal of their own.

Cara grimaced. "I think I prefer dishwashing – at least I get to eat first and then begin duty."

"Dishwashing runs late," Dylan said. "We don't want that!"

After their breakfast duty was complete, Cara and Dylan joined Stephanie and Garry for a swim. As Garry had predicted, the pool area was relatively quiet, quieter even than the library, where the previous students kept trundling by for a look-see.

Stephanie had brought some of her books down to the pool area, and began to read while the boys enjoyed an extended swim. Cara sighed and picked up a book too. She kept up to date with her science subjects because they were demanding and pressing, however, there were always Education readings to catch up on, and sometimes, she was just plain bored by the compulsory subjects.

All too soon, it was time to go back and serve lunch. The afternoon passed in a similar manner and then Dylan and Cara performed their duties serving the evening meal. After the meal finished, Dylan turned to Cara with a grin.

"Damaris was most sympathetic and agreed to pack a picnic for us," he explained.

"Nice," Cara murmured. It certainly was an improvement over taking what was left of the last serving tray for themselves. "Where are we going?"

"I thought we would drive over to Noosa and watch the moonrise on the beach," Dylan said. He glanced at his watch. "We will have to move quickly if we want to though."

"Of course," Cara said.

She stopped by the dormitory to sign out and grab a light cardigan. Then she followed Dylan to the Light Jeep. They drove out to the beach and ate their picnic tea listening to the soft sound of the waves, and watched the purpling of the sky and twinkling of the stars, as the moon rose over the ocean.

The couple lingered on the sand for several hours, however, they still had to return Cara to the dormitory by ten-thirty, when the electronic doors automatically locked. The curfew got a bit frustrating as the students became older and more independent.

Sunday the Reform Church service had been moved to the gymnasium, because it had a larger seating capacity than the campus meeting hall. The afternoon was full of meetings designed to occupy the visiting Alumni, but of little relevance to the current students.

The cafeteria was crowded at meal times, and meals ran late due to the extra diners. Luckily, however, Dylan and Cara had finished their day of weekend duty and the next day was being covered by another set of volunteers. Somewhere between Sunday night and Monday morning, most of the visitors left. The resident students were mostly relieved to have the campus back to normal, and even grateful their regular classes resumed.

Everything was getting back to normal, when they were intercepted at lunch by Phoebe and her husband Hank. No longer being residential students, both Phoebe and Hank had to pay for their meals at the cafeteria.

"Are you studying again?" Cara asked lightly.

Hank shook his head. "No," he said. "I have been invited to do my Instructor's ticket down at the airfield, but I'm not quite ready. It is a matter of a few more flight hours… and a little money. Houses and weddings cost a lot you know."

Cara laughed. She had always liked the practical, mature Hank, although she had never once considered dating him herself.

Hank turned to Stephanie with a look of concern on his face. "I have to go to Brisbane for the rest of the week," he said. "Tony Dantean's case has gone to court and I am called as a witness because I serviced his bike the day before."

Stephanie nodded. "Bradley's father is giving the victim impact statement," she said. "It was better him than me. I have been able to find another boyfriend – but the Parkers will never have another son. They will also never have grandchildren unless they adopt mine." Her eyes filled with tears.

"Every effort has been made to keep the students out of this, I believe," Hank said. "Stephanie and Kathy were among the last to see Bradley – but the time he left campus is more clearly corroborated by the entry he made in the leave book."

"The good old leave system," Cara murmured. "Finally useful for something."

"Cara, I believe you found the discarded bottles, but the police must have found enough evidence on their own raid not to need your testimony," Hank surmised.

Cara nodded. "I made a statement, but even in that the Chemistry Doctor protected me as much as he could."

"A few of the boys, including Arthur Mason and Vincent, have made statements that will be used for evidence," Hank continued. "But no one is being charged with 'obstruction of justice' or 'withholding evidence'. They all knew so little, that no one is considered a collaborator."

"I know," Stephanie said. "Some of the boys have apologised and explained to me. Even those who took the steroids were ignorant of the fact they were consuming a banned substance."

Cara nodded. "The whole scheme represented a monstrous abuse of campus naivety."

"I will let you know as little or as much as you prefer," Hank said. "About what happens in Brisbane?"

"I wouldn't mind knowing how Tony got corrupted," Stephanie said. "He may have been a bully, but he had a Christian background the same as the rest of us. I'm not much interested in the other details."

"Not even the outcome?" Hank asked in surprise.

Stephanie's eyes were hooded. "I expect there will be a punishment of some sort. It won't bring Bradley back."

"It is about justice," Hank said.

"As Christians we are all about forgiveness," Stephanie said faintly. "Nothing that is done to either the truck driver, who lost control of his vehicle, or Tony, who interfered with the bike, will bring Bradley back. EVER."

"It's about rehabilitation too," Hank said.

"How so?" Cara inquired.

"They have education and work programmes in prison," Hank observed.

"We had education and work programmes here," Stephanie said listlessly. She stood up and hugged Hank. "Thank you so much for doing this. For being the one to go down and witness about Bradley. For proving he was not careless and didn't contribute to his own death."

Public displays of affection between people who were not courting couples were somewhat infrequent on campus. Stephanie's gesture drew the gaze of the other students. Phoebe, who had been hovering at a discrete distance, hurriedly stepped forward and placed her stamp of approval on the gesture by hugging Hank and Stephanie both at once.

"It helps to know that your blessing goes with me," Hank said. "Some people think I shouldn't be witnessing at all. Didn't the Apostle Paul say Christians should not go to court?'

"That was against each other," Cara said. "This is upholding the law of the land. Even when it is broken by accident or ignorance. Romans chapter 13, verse 1: 'Let every soul be subject to the governing authorities. For… the authorities that exist are appointed by God'."

"My other concern is that Phoebe will be alone while I am away. I'm not taking the car, and she just got her license, so she will be able to drive herself on and off campus," Hank said. "But she will be lonely. And if anybody thinks to take their resentment out against her… I just couldn't bear it."

"We will look after Phoebe," Stephanie promised. "Either she could stay in the dorms with us – or we could spend a couple of nights at your house."

Hank looked pleased. "I will leave you girls to work out the details than," he said. "Come Phoebe – if you have finished class for the day, we have much to do at home before tomorrow."

When Phoebe arrived at class on Tuesday she confirmed that Hank had left for Brisbane. He would be staying with someone he had met through work, which would allow him to get to the court whenever required.

Stephanie appeared calm enough at first, but in the afternoon, she asked whether she could join the Chemistry class in the library.

"You usually prefer to study alone," Cara objected.

"Not today," Stephanie admitted. "I would prefer the company. I will be quiet and do my own research while you are doing yours."

"The Chemistry Doctor said we had to work in the library," Dylan observed. "He didn't say we had to be alone."

That settled it. Stephanie slid into the seat alongside Garry. "What are you doing?"

There was a quiet murmur as Garry spent a few minutes explaining his research. He had chosen the Tarong coal fired power station in Queensland, which was a relatively new power station, opened in 1984. The station featured new technology designed to reduce emissions. It was early days yet, but Garry was making an attempt to assess its emissions compared to an older coal fire plant, such as Vales Point in New South Wales.

Tuesday night worship was combined worship, where both the males and females met in the women's assembly area. Stephanie remained calm while the boys were with them, but after worship, she began to stress about the trial.

One of her coping mechanisms had always been study. Cara watched in bemusement as Stephanie opened her thickest text books and settled down to read them late into the night. Yawning, she turned her back on the little reading lamp so she could sleep. When she woke up the next morning, Cara observed that there were dark lines under Stephanie's eyes, because she had studied but not rested.

"That does it!" Cara exclaimed. "We will stay with Phoebe tonight. The televisions won't be programmed to turn off at ten o'clock, ruining any movie," Cara said. "And we could even have the boys over. Phoebe is a married woman, so she could chaperone us!"

Stephanie laughed a little at the idea of Phoebe as chaperone. "Staying with Phoebe sounds like fun then," she admitted.

So that afternoon, Cara and Stephanie signed the leave form at the reception of girl's dorm. Then they jumped in the car with Phoebe, along with their small overnight bags, and drove back to her place. They spent the afternoon happily experimenting in the kitchen, making spaghetti bolognaise for tea and caramel coated pop-corn for later. Dylan and Garry arrived around five o'clock as guests for the meal. The boys stayed until just after eleven o'clock in the evening, and then reluctantly returned to campus.

"Take care," Dylan whispered into Cara's hair as he left. "And don't let Stephanie stress too much. She does carry a lot of baggage."

"I think we are all worried about the court case," Cara whispered.

"For sure," Dylan said. "There is even some unrest in the boys' dormitory."

"Really?" Cara muttered.

"Yeah," Dylan said. "Some guys are frightened they might be called to witness, even though at this stage it looks as though they won't. Most cannot believe that something like this would happen to someone they knew!"

"It is difficult," Cara murmured.

"Garry and I have talked, and we honestly don't know what the best outcome would be," Dylan confided. "Punishing Tony won't bring Bradley back…. And it might not even redeem Tony."

"Our concern is losing Bradley," Cara said. "We keep forgetting that Tony also put a number of other guys health at risk with the steroids."

"True," Dylan said. He kissed Cara good night and left.

After they boys had left, Phoebe turned to the girls with a conspiratorial look on her face. "The late night television line-up is a little weak. Shall we watch a video?"

"What do you have?" Cara looked interested, and Stephanie, who adored movies because they 'told stories' just like books, also looked keen.

"Hank bought me *Beverly Hills Cop* for my birthday," Phoebe said. "It is action and comedy rolled together, starring Eddie Murphy."

"That is sure to keep us from worrying!" Cara exclaimed.

The girls settled down to watch the movie, and Cara noticed that Stephanie fell asleep on the couch before it was half-way though.

"Never mind," Phoebe whispered. "It is a video – she can easily see the ending another time."

"She was exhausted," Cara observed.

"Don't you worry she gets too emotional?" Phoebe whispered. "We all cared about Bradley. I even went out with him before Stephanie did."

"I don't know," Cara said. "Stephanie's grief seems natural. And she doesn't mean to underrate the sorrow that you feel. I think it's just - now you have married Hank – we tend to forget about your relationship with Bradley."

"Hmm," Phoebe said. "Well I hope this week sees the end of it. Justice is one thing, but dredging all the grief up again is another."

"It's not ideal," Cara agreed, and settled back down to watch the movie.

The next day, the Zoology class had an excursion to the Lone Pine Koala sanctuary. As they drove along the Bruce Highway, the Biology Master explained that the Lone Pine Koala Sanctuary opened in 1927 to shelter koalas, who were at that time being hunted for their fur. Over the years, the sanctuary had also become a haven for many other Australian native animals.

The students entered at the main gate, passing the gift shop and cafeteria. Then they viewed the cockatoos, bats and birds; before strolling to the furthermost end where the platypus were housed. After viewing the platypus, they walked back into the central area to view the koalas, turtles and Tasmanian devils.

Across the other side, they spent quite some time in the free range patting and feeding area. Then they came back past the wombats, cassowary's, amphibians and reptiles, along a side path that led towards a barn full of more domesticated animal breeds. In the afternoon, just before they left to make the trip home, the colourful lorikeets all assembled to be handfed.

Friday afternoon, Hank returned to Silver Springs. He and Phoebe attended the Uniting Church vespers, and then the group retreated into the recreation area, where one of the lounges was available for mixed groups. Andrew and Kathy followed them and sat down quietly.

"Tell us how the court case went," Garry asked. "Then perhaps we can let it go."

Hank and Phoebe, who had already discussed the matter privately, exchanged glances. "Tony received two years for 'possession of a prescription drug without a prescription'," Hank began. "On the issues of drug trafficking – the case became very technical – as apparently the law hasn't defined steroids as narcotics yet."

Cara nodded, and she glanced at Stephanie, who had always said she did not want to know all the details.

"I'm okay," Stephanie said in response to Cara's unspoken enquiry. "Go ahead Hank."

"Regarding the charges of supplying a substance, the law got all caught up on the amount," Hank continued. "Tony claimed that he had never handled anything like five kilograms, which is where the supply becomes classed as commercial."

"Another technicality was that he didn't appear to be making a profit from supplying the steroids. It was more of a self-importance thing – to help his team mates and other campus athletes perform at their best."

"So he got away with that?" Cara exclaimed. "It doesn't seem right!"

"I didn't follow it all," Hank said. "I believe the concerns around those offenses led to the maximum penalty being given for possession."

"I see," Phoebe sounded serious. "Now what about Bradley's bike?"

"Regarding Bradley's bike," Hank continued. "Tony was charged with 'Endangering the safe use of a vehicle'. Under section 467 of the criminal code act, the maximum penalty for this is life imprisonment."

Hank stopped and looked at Stephanie. "I know you didn't wish that upon him."

"No," Stephanie's eyes were wide. "That would have been two lives lost – over what was partially or essentially an accident."

"Endangering is a charge which hinges upon intent," Hank said. "There was no evidence that Tony had intended Bradley to get hurt. Tony himself broke down and cried. He admitted putting the water in Bradley's fuel tank, but said he had never in his wildest imagination, thought that anyone would be injured."

Stephanie began to sob. "I told you so," she said. "Even Tony wouldn't want Bradley hurt."

"It was a prank," Hank continued. "A nasty one. He wanted to see Bradley inconvenienced. Possibly angry. Unable to leave the car park. At the most – cost him a call out fee for a mechanic."

"Yeah," Cara said. "And campus pranks are so common that we don't ever stop to think they can hurt anyone… you know the birthday short-sheeting of the bed… and hiding something for the fun of seeing our friend hunting for it… that sort of thing."

"Tony meant a little more harm than that," Phoebe observed. "It wasn't simply a birthday prank."

"Oh of course," Cara subsided.

"The court believed that Tony had never meant to cause Bradley serious injury," Hank said. "So that charge was dropped and replaced with the regulatory offence of 'Unauthorised damage to property'. This carries a penalty of a $500 fine, which Tony was ordered to pay."

"It almost seems too little," Phoebe breathed.

"That is what I thought at the time," Hank said. "However, because someone was injured in the consequence of Tony's actions, the court was also able to order Tony to pay compensation to Bradley's family."

"Ah good," Stephanie murmured.

"Bradley's father was allowed to speak again and he said that no amount of money would compensate him for the loss of his son," Hank continued. "The Judge tried to get him to accept an amount covering at least the funeral and travel to attend the court case…"

Stephanie shook her head. "They have lost everything Bradley could have done for them in old age, but his family wouldn't see it in financial terms. "

"Bradley's father would not accept anything," Hank said. "Mr. Parker insisted that he would bury his own son – and his main concern was that Tony reformed. He was allowed to ask for mandatory counselling, regular studies with the prison chaplain and a number of hours of community service for Tony in lieu of compensation."

"I hope it works," Cara muttered.

"I believe the judge accepted his request," Hank said. "Although I lost track of which suggestions became binding."

"When I left Brisbane, Bradley's family and Tony's family, who had been strictly segregated during the court proceedings, were tentatively planning to go out for a meal together," Hank reported. "Tony's family had to admit Bradley's father was exceedingly generous."

"Bradley had a generous spirit just like his father," Stephanie said. The girl appeared committed to having a lengthy cry, but overall, relieved that the matter was over.

"Mr. Dantean even said Mr. Parker had managed to secure concessions for their son that they – as the perpetrator's family - had not hoped to achieve," Hank explained. "Mr. Parker in turn declared that one boy had been lost, but he saw no need for two to be lost."

"One final thing Hank," Stephanie begged. "If anyone ever tells you who the truck driver was, or what was wrong with his truck that it couldn't stop that night, I don't want to know."

"I personally think it was a matter of the wrong place and wrong time," Hank said. "I won't be pursuing that information myself either."

"I know it's a cliché," Cara said, "And I risk sounding like a Theology girlfriend once again, but do you think we could close this discussion with prayer?"

"That's a good idea," Andrew said. "Would you like me to lead the prayer?"

"Yes, thank you Andrew," Hank said. "I've seen and heard enough of the dark side of life over the last week. I would love to hand my worries over to God."

The students bowed their heads, and each one in their turn, confided their pain and worry to the Lord. Andrew closed the prayer session with some fine sounding words of faith and trust, and everybody had to admit they felt a little better.

CHAPTER 15: MODERN DAY MESSAGES

Dylan enjoyed an early morning surf, and Saturday he had gone out at dawn with a bunch of male friends. Cara was eating a lazy breakfast in the cafeteria when he arrived, slightly damp and full of life.

"You should have come," Dylan remarked, reaching for the jam.

"You guys only had so much room in the car," Cara said.

"We can always take another car," Tom said with a grin.

"I know you guys like to go on your own," Stephanie said. "Even Garry doesn't always go with you."

"Garry isn't exactly a beach babe," Dylan scoffed.

"Whatever you mean by that!" Cara exclaimed.

"It takes a real surfy to want to get wet this early in the morning, even in humid October," Stephanie observed.

"I think it does," Mathew agreed. He was the only Theology student among the bunch, but he was as keen as any of the guys.

"So what are we doing for the rest of the day?" Garry asked, changing the subject.

"Assignments," the boys groaned.

"We might play a little pool in the evening," Tom suggested. "Just to keep you girls company."

Cara also had assignments to do as well. After saying goodbye to Dylan at breakfast, she heaved a heavy sigh and got her books out. There was only a month left before exams, so all the readings were due in the next couple of weeks. The Chemistry Doctor also wanted their research project handed in, so that only left a fortnight to complete her research.

Zoology write-ups were due each week, and although the excursions were fun, the Biology Master always found tedious and complicated questions to ask about the creatures they had seen. Sometime around midday, it began to rain, so staying inside and studying became more appealing anyway.

Sunday Cara attended the Inter-denominational praise service, and then the Reform Church Service. As the pressure to complete studies escalated, so the temptation to skip church services increased. However, the Theology students from their own year, David, Luke, Andrew and Larry were now regular speakers at the service. It was awkward telling a friend, or the girlfriend of a friend, that she had missed their sermon.

The afternoon was once again taken up by study, although Dylan and Cara met in the library to complete their Zoology together. In the evening, Damaris had invited them to visit her house and see how she and Michael were getting along. They joked about the tea being left-overs from the cafeteria, but Damaris did wonderful things, so that the food was even better after its repurposing and second heating.

"I just love casseroles," Cara sighed, finally putting her fork down. "When we are married, we will eat casseroles all the time."

"Is that so?" Dylan replied dangerously, and Cara found herself becoming unaccustomedly flushed.

All the girls hoped that their boyfriends would one day propose, although there were the occasional puzzling boyfriends that never did; and the random boyfriend who dumped their long-term girlfriend just to propose soon after to another girl. However, it was every girl's worst fear that she might start the marriage talk before her boyfriend was ready, and chase him away altogether.

"I didn't mean right away," Cara stammered, but it was alright, Dylan was grinning.

"Got to get fed somehow," he said. "Now I know what I am in for… lots of left-overs. If they are as good as Damaris' I will be okay."

"You could learn to cook yourself," Stephanie said sharply, although she was very into traditional role divisions between herself and Garry.

"I'm good enough for a camp cook," Dylan said. "But one does get tired of toast and eggs."

"Certainly," Damaris agreed.

Monday was another rainy day, and a busy one. Initially the computing class had seemed very relaxed, almost like a free afternoon to muck around on a computer, but the Computing Lecturer was expecting results before the end of semester.

In addition to their projects, there were a number of tricky tasks and print-outs that demonstrated their mastery of the software. And when computers decided to be helpful, they were very helpful. However, when the machines decided to be stubborn, like corrupting a perfectly good file because something had gone wrong during saving, they were very frustrating. Cara was glad that she had kept several sets of backup on separate disks.

Tuesday when Cara was preparing to work on her Chemistry project, Elisabet and Stephanie were studying together in the room. The girls had a number of novels, poetry books and plays spread out around them.

"I sometimes think you have too much fun doing an English major," Cara commented. "Reading stories!"

"There is more to studying Language and Literature than that!" Stephanie returned hotly.

"Relax - I think she is joking," Elisabet giggled.

"It's a joke that gets old," the usually pacific Stephanie sniffed. "It's like that time I was standing in line, and the Education Professor implied to one of the other students that I got my grades without effort. I wish I really was that sport of genius!"

"It's okay Steph," Cara said. "I know you work hard. And if anyone forgets the fact – it's because you usually work ahead."

"Thanks," Stephanie was easily soothed.

"I'll see you at tea, or when I get back, whichever happens first," Cara said. "Have fun Elisabet."

"Work hard Cara," Elisabet advised in a friendly fashion.

Cara left the girls to their impromptu tutorial in the room and crossed to the library, where she was due to meet Dylan, Garry and Zack. By now they were used to the Chemistry Doctor failing to check up on them. They expected the limits of trust in would be tested when the lecturer began to mark their projects.

Wednesday, Stephanie and Elisabet were still cloistered in the room together. Apparently they had a joint presentation to do by the end of the week. Cara knew that Stephanie and Elisabet had shared their English classes since first year, but social factors had generally limited their acquaintance.

Stephanie was on a tight budget that had inspired her to develop her talent in sewing. Elisabet, on the other hand, had beautiful clothes purchased with the proceeds from her family's successful business. Stephanie was inclined to hide under a layer of protective shyness, while Elisabet was inclined towards assured reserve. It was good to see the girls' mutual interests finally overcome these barriers and blossoming into friendship.

Thursday the Zoology class were lucky to have a fine day, although past experience had taught them the Biology Master would take them out in the elements if he was so determined. They visited Lake Weyba, where some 45 acres of Eumarella Shores was in the process of being declared a "Nature Refuge". The lake offered some unique habitats, including mangroves, wetlands, fish and oyster habitats, and Melaleuca and Eucalyptus trees that provided havens for birds.

"Some of the birds here migrate all the way to China and Japan," The Biology Master observed. "We have had an agreement with Japan since 1974 to protect the 'East Asian - Australasian Flyway'."

"What does the agreement do?" Garry asked.

"It prevents the sale of 'foreign birds' and promotes the sharing of research information," the Biology Master replied. "And prohibits the taking of eggs, except by Indigenous hunters and gatherers."

The Biology Master then explained that the name 'Weyba' was derived from the aboriginal word 'waiam' which means 'flying squirrel' or 'stingray'. The land originally belonged to the Gubbi Gubbi language group, who considered parts of the area sacred.

After the arrival of Europeans, much of the land was used for farming and market gardening. Relations with the Gubbi Gubbi became hostile, when the Indigenous people speared livestock in return for the loss of their traditional hunting area.

This led to a massacre in the area appropriately named "Murdering Creek". Cara and Stephanie shuddered at the tale, while they were happy to live in Australia, they wished that the settlement process had been more harmonious and less violent.

"Around ten butterfly species, forty four bird species, eight mammal species, five reptile species, one frog and one toad species have been identified here," the Biology Master said, handing out lists complete with scientific names. "There are also three hundred bird species and including a number that are endangered, marine species include shark and ray species that utilise the lake as a nursery, along with mud crabs, sand crabs, mullet and prawns."

"The creek eventually flows into Noosa Sound," the Biology Master continued. "Where fish species include bream, estuary cod, mangrove jack, trevally, flathead and whiting."

The students spent an interesting afternoon hiking around the edges of the lake, marking off bird and animals species they managed to identify. Occasionally they were not sure which species they had spied, and when the Biology Master was not close enough to provide a better identification, they had to mark down a guess.

Friday night, Andrew Grosvy was the speaker for the Uniting Church vespers. He commenced by observing the date and asking whether anyone realised what day it was. One or two students raised their hands and tentatively suggested it might be Halloween.

Andrew nodded. "Excellent," he said. "It is Halloween tonight…. But before you get too distracted by visions of witches with black cloaks, black cats and pumpkins – I wonder whether anyone can tell me what else it is today?"

An Evangelical student raised their hand. "Reformation Day!"

"So it is!" Andrew said. "What a remarkable coincidence."

Andrew went on to describe the earnest monk, Martin Luther, nailing his arguments to the church door the evening before the medieval 'All Saints Day', when he knew there would be a maximal church attendance. This simple attempt to communicate with his fellow scholars had a ripple effect that spread throughout Europe.

"The different denominations have interpreted the terms of the Reformation differently," Andrew concluded. "However, Martin Luther's main point was that everyone should read their Bible."

Saturday at breakfast, Stephanie had a recollection that 'All Saints Day' had traditionally been a day for remembering the recently deceased, and asked her friends to visit Bradley's grave with her. The rain had cleared up and the day was looking fine and pleasant for a walk.

"It's been nearly a year now, hasn't it Steph?" Garry asked softly.

Stephanie nodded. "In about a weeks time, it will be one year since Bradley died," she observed.

"I'm happy to come with you," Kathy said. "What will we do about flowers?"

"We might be able to gather some wildflowers on our way down there without harming the environment," Dylan said.

"That is certainly a possibility if we take the bush walk instead of University Drive," Garry suggested.

"Are you sure you all want to come?" Stephanie asked.

"Bradley was a friend," Cara asserted solidly.

None of the friendship group had significant other plans, so they all agreed to accompany Stephanie on a pilgrimage to Bradley's grave. As they walked along the bush walk, they plucked a few wild flowers, and some greenery, so that by the time they reached the cemetery, they had a modest arrangement to leave on Bradley's grave. Bradley had been a down-to-earth, natural type of guy, so he would have liked natural brush.

After the trip to the cemetery, the group wandered back up University Drive, where the walking was much easier. The clouds were gathering, and they were glad to reach the comfort of the cafeteria before any rain drops fell.

Sunday at lunch, Cara and Dylan were relaxing after having attended the Reform Church service, where there had been no mention of 'All Saints Day' which the Reform Church did not celebrate. The couple were sitting with Kathy and Andrew, Stephanie and Garry, when David approached with his girlfriend Debbie, and slid into a seat beside Andrew.

"I enjoyed your message on Friday night," the Theology Student remarked conversationally to Andrew.

"Thank you," Andrew said. "It's always nice to get a bit of peer feedback."

"What you said about manmade tradition in the Middle Ages, reminded me of what Jesus had to deal with in the form of the pharisaical tradition," David observed.

"Now you put it that way, you have a point," Andrew said.

"Do you think that every few hundred years, we get overburdened with our manmade philosophies and require a good clean up?" David proposed.

"It is an interesting idea," Andrew said. "There is a clear pattern in the Bible where Israel kept wandering from God's truth and required a recall. However, I'm not sure we can always expect a major figure like a reformer to appear and perform the cleansing for us."

"A reformer is often not accepted in his own time," David said thoughtfully.

"And we are all understandably cautious about people making claims to be religious leaders in modern times," Andrew said. "In the light of Jesus warning about false prophets in Mathew 7:15."

"False prophets aren't confined to modern times," David murmured soberly. "And the Lord said to me, 'I have not sent them, commanded them, nor spoken to them; they prophesy to you a false vision, divination, a worthless thing, and the deceit of their heart'. Jeremiah chapter 14, verses 13 and 14."

"It's a worry," Andrew agreed. "However, there must be some form of revelation for more recent times."

"Perhaps each of us is responsible for our own return to the Biblical truth," David suggested.

"In the final reckoning, I expect that is true," Andrew said. "But we need some support and guidance."

"That is what ministers are for," David pronounced. The two Theology students appeared satisfied having successfully negotiated a tricky circle that ended up in justifying their prospective jobs.

Larry had been sitting nearby listening avidly. "If you were to suggest someone as a nineteenth or twentieth century reformer – who would you nominate?" he interjected.

"Um," Andrew looked confused. "If I'm allowed to go back a little further – Charles Wesley."

"Charles Wesley does fulfill the criteria of a call to returning to the Biblical basics, and he is already accepted as the founder of the Methodist movement," David agreed.

"I think you might be playing it a little safe," Larry retorted provocatively. "What about Aimee Semple McPherson?"

"You would be more familiar with her because of your work experience placements with Charismatic Churches," Andrew returned. "Why don't you tell us about her Larry?"

"Aimee was born in 1890 in Canada," Larry said. "Her family background exposed her to a mixture of Salvation Army and Methodist theology. She became famous as a revival tent speaker and interpreter of tongues. She finally settled and her followers built a large church in Los

Angeles, from where they believed they could witness to the world."

"It is an interesting suggestion," Andrew said.

"I think it is significant that Aimee was an interpreter of tongues," David said thoughtfully. "The Apostle Paul said that an interpreter must be present during any episode of tongues. 1 Corinthians chapter 14, verse 28: 'But if there is no interpreter, let him keep silent in church, and let him speak to himself and to God'."

"Wasn't Aimee also associated with faith healing?" Garry inquired practically.

Larry nodded, "Jesus and the apostles also performed healings."

"The Catholic Church requires at least one 'miracle' in order to name a saint," Dylan said thoughtfully. "But things like public healings make me skeptical."

"What I do like about Aimee Semple McPherson," Garry put in, "Was that I've heard she started her career by advocating Creationism – at a time when the Theory of Evolution was just being introduced to the American public school curriculum."

Andrew nodded. "That was admirable," he agreed.

"Our current criteria – that Andrew and I just crafted between us – was of someone who preached a call to the Biblical basics," David reminded his companions. "So far, it has been established that Aimee Semple McPherson attracted a lot of people to the revival, and established a church. I believe that may have resulted in the Assemblies of God?"

David glanced inquiringly towards Larry, who nodded.

"But we are not sure Aimee exactly advocated a return to the basics," Andrew concluded.

Larry nodded. "Some people feel that her association with Hollywood in her later years reduced her credibility," he admitted.

"It is a fascinating topic," Garry said. "Let me know how you go with your research if you pursue this any further guys. However, I have to go and do my assignments."

"Me too," Cara and Stephanie said.

Monday many of the students had classes in the morning and the afternoon, so it was tea time before the group resumed conversation regarding modern religious leaders who might be considered reformers.

"I take it you, David and Larry chose to discuss the Nineteenth Century because it was easier than attempting to quantify the Twentieth Century," Stephanie began, a slight frown creasing her brow.

"Exactly," Andrew said. "It seemed generally safer."

"Wasn't the Nineteenth Century in general known as a time of spiritual revival?" Debbie asked.

"Spiritual and spiritualist," Stephanie added. "That's what makes me worried."

"When the nations around Israel worshiped idols – did that make our God - an idol?" David asked.

"Of course not," Stephanie laughed. "But where there is smoke, there is fire. The Fox sisters were mediums, Arthur Edward Waite was a spiritualist and designer of tarot cards, and Joseph Smith was a metal diviner as well as founder of Mormanism. Moreover, they all lived around the same time, give or take a few years."

"What about Mary Baker Eddy – the founder of Christian Science?" Garry suggested. "I did some research overnight. Christian Science also represents a positive Christian response to the theory of Evolution. I like some of their pamphlets and books."

"Some people called her a prophet," Dylan observed. "I'm not sure on what grounds."

"Mary Baker Eddy also had a lot of friends who were spiritualists, even if she rejected their ideas eventually," Andrew observed. "They also say she had a temper and got into fights – if you are using the 'fruits' test of character. Matthew chapter 7, verse 20."

Stephanie shuddered. "We all lose our temper occasionally – please don't judge anyone by that!"

"Of course, no one is perfect Stephanie," Larry added comfortingly. But I think the point is – Christian Science did more than merely attempt to reconcile Christianity and science. Garry probably needs to do a little more research on that one."

"Garry will as soon as he has finished doing his real science," Garry returned smartly. "You can rest assured of that Larry."

Tuesday was the last afternoon assigned to their Chemistry projects before they were due to be handed up. Once again, Cara met Zack, Dylan and Garry in the science area of the library and the group set up on a large table. Cara politely asked Zack how his project was going.

Zack, said that he was researching Uranium mining, which was one of the most controversial topics available. His object of study was the recently de-commissioned Mary Kathleen Mine operated by Rio Tinto. This had been a huge open cut mine and the site was currently under rehabilitation.

When the Chemistry class arrived at the cafeteria that afternoon, Andrew, Larry, David and their girlfriends were waiting for them, along with Garry's girlfriend Stephanie. The Theology students appeared to be eager to resume their debate regarding modern religious leaders.

"How was the 'real science Garry'?" Andrew asked with a grin.

"Very scientific," Garry replied, also with a grin. "Have you come up with any more candidates?"

"David believes he has," Andrew admitted. "But he wouldn't tell us before you arrived."

"It's nice to be considered important," Dylan returned.

"Go ahead," Cara said. "Who did you come up with David?"

"William Miller!" David suggested. "He seemed to be at the root of much of the revival movement in the Nineteenth Century."

"Interesting idea," Larry said. "I would have to read up on what he preached - apart from his attempt to predict the second coming."

"I've read a couple of quotes or journal entries that made William Miller sound like a very spiritual sort of person," Andrew said. "Spiritual in terms of enjoying a personal religious experience, I mean."

"Wouldn't the fact that he got the date for Christ's return wrong automatically rule him out?" Cara inquired.

Andrew shook his head. "We were talking about reformers," he murmured. "Persons who preached a return to the basics, not necessarily prophets who could predict the future. If he was sent to call people back in to relationship with God, a small mistake in the details might be irrelevant."

"Jonah preached the fall of Nineveh, and then when the people repented, God changed his mind," David observed. "The embarrassment of his failed prediction was a cross that Jonah had to learn to bear!"

"What about Miller's early association with the Masons?" Stephanie asked.

"Well the Masons were originally a trade guild," Garry observed. "I don't know when or how they became an alternative to religion."

"Perhaps it is as simple as Christians being advised not to belong to trade unions," Dylan suggested. "Wouldn't their so-called 'secrets' have been mathematics, geometry and other building techniques?"

"The Masons may have been associated with the Templars at one time," Andrew said. "Although there is not a lot of evidence."

"Another interesting point," Larry said. "I'm going to have to look into William Miller and the outcome of his message. A number of groups did grow out of the tent crusade."

His meal finished, Garry picked up his tray and carried it across to the dishwasher compartment. Stephanie and the others followed, as there was not long gap until the commencement of combined worship. The programme was being conducted by Kaleb that evening, with several younger Theology students, Mathew and Christopher assisting with the prayers.

Wednesday lunch time, Cara had a question for the Theology Students. Most of the students at Silver Springs University came from protestant backgrounds, and she had to admit, there was a strong Presbyterian influence on her own thought.

"Do we discount Mother Mary Mackillop and Sister Teresa because they worked within the Catholic Church?" Cara said.

"Controversial," Andrew mused. "Controversial indeed - young Cara! I believe there is some talk of making Mary Mackillop a saint. She established schools and did a lot of charity work."

"Mother Teresa also does a lot of wonderful charity work," David agreed. "But I think we are now beginning to mistake works for message."

"What do you mean?" Stephanie asked.

"True reform points people back to God," David observed. "It may result in the establishment of a denomination, and it may involve humanitarian work, but neither is not its primary purpose."

"But thank you for introducing the point into our discussion," Larry said. "Your challenge will help keep us honest!"

Thursday afternoon, Zack invited Cara and Dylan, Stephanie and Garry to watch the men's basketball semi-finals; and Danielle joined them on the spectator bench. They were all a little late because of their Zoology laboratory, but all enjoyed watching the match very much.

"Zack's team have been doing very well," Danielle observed. "You wouldn't know he had any trouble last semester."

"I do not know how he has the time!" Cara exclaimed. "The role of Captain must be very demanding."

"He think it is worth his time," Danielle explained.

"I don't see Vincent anywhere," Cara said, glancing around.

"Zack tried to help Vincent," Danielle said, "But he sort of dropped out of the basketball scene. A few of the guys that were banned from the finals last semester also found it hard to get back onto teams."

"I thought the ban wasn't permanent," Cara said.

"It wasn't," Danielle admitted, "But the stigma remained. Perhaps the guys will have forgotten by next year."

"I see Michael is still playing, despite been an outdoor married student," Stephanie observed and waved encouragingly.

Zack's team was well disciplined and functioned like a well geared machine. Their offence was excellent, and their defense adequate. The opposing team, captained by Michael, was just that little less skillful, and Zack's team steadily outscored them. By half time, they were two baskets ahead; and by full time, despite the best efforts of the opposition, Zack's team were five baskets ahead. They were declared the winners and the two captains shook hands.

"Being a married man hasn't improved your game," Zack laughed.

"I have done my best," Michael joked. "I must admit I have had a few distractions! It has also been harder to motivate the guys this semester."

"Unfortunately, that is true of some for mine too," Zack agreed.

"Perhaps one of the other teams will give you a better match," Michael suggested.

"I hope so," Zack agreed. All the teams had been affected by the steroid scandal and were only beginning to regain their level of comradery. They would play each other next and then whichever won the other semi-final would be his opponents for the grand final match.

Both captains then approached the spectator bench to receive congratulations and felicitations from their friends.

Friday afternoon, Cara was enjoying lunch with her classmates when David arrived with fellow Theology students Andrew and Larry. He had a beatific smile upon his face, and was waving an envelope that he had found in the student mail box.

"Guess what guys?" David cried. "I have been granted a scholarship from the Reform Church."

"Congratulations," Stephanie said.

"Fantastic!" Cara added. "What does the scholarship do?"

"It will pay my tuition fees for next year," David said. "That means that if I have a summer job, I can use the money for something else."

"That is wonderful news," Andrew said. "And with all your work in campus leadership, I cannot think of anyone who deserves it more. Unless it be Larry…"

"Larry applied for a small grant from the Charismatic Churches," David said. "I don't know whether has got it."

"There are grants for different purposes," Larry explained. "Some simply cover text books, others may cover an experience placement… and a few help with university fees, because the government does not help Theology students."

Larry did not specify what sort of grant he had applied for, so the friends assumed that he had not heard whether he had been successful in obtaining one yet.

"I know what I would do with my money once my tuition fees were paid," Andrew mused.

"If you are thinking what I am thinking," David said. "A vehicle?"

"Yeah!" Andrew said. "It would give you independence as a student and be essential for the ministry."

"I wouldn't want to spend too much," David said carefully.

"Perhaps Hank could do something up for you?" Cara suggested, referring to the fact that Phoebe's husband was a mechanic.

"That's a thought," David said. "Although, I wouldn't want an old bomb."

"I'm sure Hank would guide you towards something serviceable," Stephanie said.

"Do you think this will put you in a position to marry Debbie?" Andrew asked, in acknowledgement of how long the wait was before Theology students could afford to support a wife.

"Maybe we could get engaged," David said thoughtfully. "Not married. My fees are paid, but I have to live on campus to take advantage of that."

"Getting engaged would be nice," Debbie murmured modestly.

"Well whatever you decide to do, it is good news," Cara agreed. "I wish you two all the best."

CHAPTER SIXTEEN: OFF, OFF AND AWAY

The weekend flew by with its usual assortment of religious meetings, assignments and leisure activities. The Adventure Club had organized its annual picnic for Saturday afternoon, in conjunction with a local equestrian school.

Cara had never ridden a horse before, so she was thrilled to take a short turn, along with a number of other students who were beginners at the sport. She mounted a placid pony, and with Dylan at her side on another horse, carefully padded along the recommended route to the picnic area, where the horse handlers helped her dismount.

A simple lunch of cold chicken and salad had been provided; along with a vegetarian alternative for non-meat eaters. Cara relaxed, sipping a mixture of blackcurrant juice and lemonade. Desert consisted of fruit ice-blocks extracted from a huge cooler-box packed with ice. The day was humid, but luckily not rainy, so a good time was had by all Adventure Club members and their guests.

After lunch had been eaten, some lucky students got to ride horses back to the stables, while others followed more sedately on foot. Cara and Dylan were walking, because they had not been able to be bothered pushing their way to the front of the queue to ride a horse on the return journey. They had both enjoyed their rides, but were not prepared to sacrifice the peace of the beautiful afternoon with competitive behavior.

The only drawback was that they spotted a snake or two sunning themselves in the warm afternoon along the side of the bushwalk. Generally, snakes were harmless if one did not disturb them, but coming upon one unexpectedly did inject a strong dose of adrenaline into the system!

Sunday after attending the church services, Zack, Cara, Dylan and Garry organized a cooperative study session in the library to complete their chemistry projects. Danielle and Stephanie came along to keep their boyfriends company and quietly worked on their zoology write ups.

Monday was a long day with the computer laboratory running all afternoon. The students were tempted to try to steal a little computing time to spend on their most pressing assignments, but the Computing Lecturer seemed to have become less relaxed and more vigilant this end of the semester.

Tuesday, the Chemistry assignments had to be handed in, and each student had to present a summary of their findings to the rest of the class. Some time was then spent on discussion, which was pretty interesting, as the students were all genuinely interested in the environmental impact of each other's focus industries.

The Chemistry Doctor also took a turn, presenting some of his own research on petroleum pollution in storm water, the main sources in local industry and its effects on some of the lakes. The students were amazed to learn the importance of intact drains, safe fuel storage and clean workshop floors in preserving the local environment. Even the smallest business appeared to be able to play a part in the safe disposal of waste.

Then they performed a final check on the ongoing experiments including the terrarium, the condition of plastic bags they had exposed to the elements, and the amateur pollution detectors that had been set up around campus.

Wednesday, Cara was invited by several girls she had played basketball with the previous year to watch the women's basketball finals. It was a great match with both teams being energetic in attack and defense. Happily, Cara's friends won the match and were congratulated heartily.

The girls asked Cara whether she missed playing, since she had dropped basketball for her afternoon classes. Cara had to admit she did miss the sport a little, but she had been doing so many other things, including hiking, swimming, and commencing a relationship with Dylan, that she hardly noticed.

Thursday was the men's basketball final. The double standard that applied to most campus sports meant that this event attracted far more spectators than the women's basketball. Benches were brought out from storage, and the gymnasium was turned into a minor stadium for the event.

Zack had invited Dylan and Cara, Stephanie and Garry, Kathy and Andrew along especially to watch. As their zoology laboratory was notorious for running late, Danielle slipped out early and headed up to the gymnasium in order to catch the beginning of the game and save seats for her classmates. The Biology Master frowned when he noticed her leave, and then relented and sent the others on after her, saying they could finish up next lesson.

When the friends arrived at the gymnasium, the teams were stretching and warming up. The other semi-final had been a hard fought battle, and the team Zack now faced were capable of giving them some competition. The referee called everyone to order and the teams assembled on the court. The two captains faced each other for the initial ball toss.

Zack managed to touch the ball first and sent it spinning towards his vice-captain. The opposing team sprung into defense and the vice-captain was forced to pass without attempting a goal, however, Zack's team managed to retain possession of the ball.

Zack's team were marginally stronger players. They controlled the ball a little over sixty percent of the time, and while scoring was fierce and the score relatively close, each goal was hard fought. By half-time they were a mere one goal ahead. During the second half, a number of goals were scored and the spectators, cheered frequently.

The opposition captured the ball after the goal and attempted to monopolise it, however, Zack's defenders managed to prevent them scoring again. Zack caught the ball on a full toss from one of his team members and sunk a final basket just before the whistle. This meant Zack's team finished the game two goals ahead, and the victory was conclusive.

Zack shook hands with the opposing captain, and accepted congratulations from all the players. Then he crossed to the spectator's bench to claim his winner's kiss from Danielle.

"Does this remind you of anything?" Cara whispered to Stephanie. She knew she ought to be cautious of reminding Stephanie of anything to do with Bradley, but she was pretty sure her roommate's mind had gone there already. To speak of it would merely be a relief.

"Yeah," Stephanie's voice was choked with tears. "I hope that it works out better for them than it did for us."

"Oh – I'm sure," Cara whispered.

Garry had a protective arm around Stephanie's shoulders. "Let's walk back to the dormitory," he said.

"I will see you back there later," Cara said.

Cara and Dylan remained behind in the gymnasium to watch the B and C grade finals. Dylan had once played C grade, so he still had an interest in the outcome. Besides, it was a gala night and all the action was in the auditorium.

Friday morning, Cara woke up mildly tired from the night before. Someone had suggested they drop by the canteen for celebratory cans of soft drink, and the sugar had kept her awake in the night. Stephanie also appeared somewhat under the weather. The girl was sitting at her desk, combing her hair and gazing aimlessly into the mirror on the bedroom wall.

"It's been a year since Bradley's death," Stephanie whispered.

"I know," Cara said. "You aren't going to freak out or anything are you?"

"No," Stephanie said. "I've got Garry now. But doesn't that make it worse? I'm forgetting Bradley."

"I'm pretty sure Bradley would want you to be happy," Cara asserted. "Didn't he step aside for you to go out with Garry the first time? And then he was a real gentleman about waiting for his chance with you."

"Yeah I know," Stephanie said. "But it's like he doesn't exist anymore."

"He doesn't," Cara said. "But that does not mean he didn't." She giggled self-consciously because she had created something of a tongue-twister.

"I guess," Stephanie said. "Well I better get to breakfast and classes!"

"I'm right behind you – although I don't feel like it," Cara said.

Saturday morning at breakfast, Cara and Dylan knew that something was up when Garry invited Stephanie for a walk down to the suspension bridge. She glared fiercely at Dylan when he naively suggested Cara and he accompany them.

"We have our own plans for the morning," she hissed.

"Do we?" Dylan looked surprised. "But of course, my dear."

Garry and Stephanie left, and Dylan helped himself to a second plate of cereal. "What was that all about?" he asked.

"I thought that Garry and Stephanie would like to be alone together," Cara explained.

"They are a couple, they are always going off alone together," Dylan observed, quite happy to be where he was.

A couple of hours later, it began to rain, driving most of the courting couples inside. Garry and Stephanie joined Cara and Dylan in the recreation area, where they were enjoying a casual game of pool. Stephanie looked glum, and Garry did not look much better.

"Cheer up guys," Dylan advised. "The rain won't last forever."

"It's not that," Stephanie said. "You might as well know. Everybody knows everybody else's' business around here anyway."

"Oh?" Cara exclaimed. This wasn't sounding good.

"I proposed," Garry said. "I thought it might cheer Stephanie up."

"That's not the right reason to propose," Cara said.

"I meant all the other stuff too," Garry said.

"And I turned him down – because to be honest – I'm afraid of losing another fiancé," Stephanie said.

"I think your timing might have been a little off," Dylan observed.

"Sure," Garry replied. "It was either the perfect timing or the worst. I couldn't know which."

"Forget it please Garry," Stephanie said. "Ask me again next year."

"Like when?" Garry asked.

"Well – Easter might be nice," Cara suggested. "Phoebe's wedding was very romantic."

"Girls!" Dylan snorted.

"It's about getting my confidence back," Stephanie said. "And believing that plans we make for the future will be permanent."

"Remember I'm aiming for a June graduation," Garry warned.

"Another perfect time to propose," Cara suggested.

"I'm sure Garry is finding you very helpful Cara," Dylan interjected wryly.

"I don't mind," Garry observed amiably. "It's not every day one gets insight into the female point of view on these things."

"I am thinking of doing it on Valentine's Day," Dylan said. "If I ever work out when Valentine's Day is!"

"It is February 14," Stephanie suggested helpfully.

"Notice I didn't say which year, Cara O'B," Dylan joked.

"Oh away with you," Cara said amiably. "I doubt you will ever propose."

"Ye of little faith," Dylan jeered. "I'm hurt."

"Well just don't stuff it up like I did," Garry warned. "Give me a cue; I want to take a turn." As Garry leaned over to play pool, a small box made showed a square outline in the pocket of his jeans.

"You even had a ring," Cara exclaimed.

"It is my Granny's garnet she gave me just to propose with," Garry said. He pulled the box out and opened it up. A solid gold ring with a row of three heavily-set reddish brown garnets appeared.

"Try it on, Stephanie," Cara urged.

"I have," Stephanie said modestly. "It looks very pretty, but I don't want to be tempted."

By Sunday, the atmosphere in the group appeared to have returned to normal. Garry appeared to have understood and accepted Stephanie's reasons for turning down his proposal. Of course, in Cara's opinion, Garry was a very understanding sort of guy. Stephanie seemed to be cheering up as well.

Monday all the practical work for Computing had to be handed up in a portfolio. The students spent the laboratory session creating print-outs and other forms of evidence that they had completed their assigned tasks. These evidences were attached to their reviews of the chosen focus software packages. At tea, everyone was relieved that one more subject was basically complete.

Tuesday was their last Chemistry laboratory for the semester. The Chemistry Master had set up a number of investigations as a practical test, to be completed in the laboratory within a specified period of time. Cara found this nerve wracking, the only positive being that the test was handed in at the end of the afternoon, and left no practical write-up for the students to complete.

Wednesday evening was the Basketball Tea. Zack and Danielle, Michael and Damaris were seated at the table of honour with the other A grade players. Amongst the presentations, Terence received 'most improved' and Zack's vice-captain was presented with 'best and fairest', despite his modest protestations. Two of the second year girls, Lacy and Moira received the awards for the women's competition.

Cara and Dylan, Garry and Stephanie, were seated further away this semester, on a table for non-players. They were happy to just enjoy the event and eat a little junk food. Further down the table, Cara noticed that Elisabet and Felipe were sitting together, however, when she gently teased Elisabet about going on a second date with Felipe, the reserved girl merely murmured that they were 'just good friends'.

Cara laughed and retorted that so were most couples on campus. Elisabet then blushed and deigned to admit that perhaps Felipe was a little keen on her.

Thursday Cara completed the Zoology Practical Exam, which was almost as stressful as the Chemistry Practical exam. Biology being Cara's major, she was just a little more accustomed to practical tests for the subject, but the Biology Master always managed to bring some samples out of the storeroom that were very hard to identify.

Friday was the first day of 'study vacation'. While this was a period of serious preparation for their exams, Cara appreciated the freedom from classes and disruptions. During this period, she was able to set her own routine. Sharing several subjects with her boyfriend also meant that she and Dylan could study together, quiz each other and generally support each other.

Monday afternoon, Cara had her Education exam. This had been her least favourite subject, but was a good one to get out of the way as her first examination. This was followed by Computing on Tuesday morning. The Zoology exam was held on Wednesday afternoon and then Cara had one blessed day of relief before she sat her hardest exam of all, Chemistry.

Saturday was blissfully study free for Cara, Dylan and Garry. All exams involving graduates had been scheduled early, so Zack, Danielle and Kathy were celebrating their freedom. Stephanie still had English to go, and the Theology students were also very stressed because their most feared subjects, Greek and Hebrew had been placed late in the examination timetable.

Sunday was the last day of November and the first day of Advent. A special candlelight evening tea and worship had been organized despite the examination season. The mood was restful and peaceful, as all the students took time out to recall Israel's eager wait for the promised Messiah. At the end of the evening prayers, the first candle on the Advent wreath was lit and some special verses recited.

Cara thoughtfully held off packing her things until Stephanie had finished her English exam, and then both girls set to with goodwill. Graduate placements began to be announced and all final year students were keeping their ears open for their names being called over the public address system.

Kathy, who was graduating from Primary Teaching, had applied for work in South East Queensland, in the hopes of still being able to see Andrew regularly. However, when her placement came through, it was Dalby in the hinterland, almost three hours away.

Michael gained work in business in Brisbane, which sparked earnest discussions between him and Damaris about whether the distance was commutable, or whether Damaris would apply for work in Brisbane also. With her Hospitality qualification and work experience, Damaris was confident of getting employment.

Arthur Mason was pleased to be granted a business position in Sydney, and bragged in a manner that reminded the students Arthur had once been one of the mean guys. Zack and Danielle, who had applied to be together, were both going to a school in Perth. It represented a long journey, but worked for the couple as one of the few available double placements.

"The school will be lucky to have you," Cara declared, while giving the couple her congratulations.

"Your turn will come next year," Danielle said, giving Cara an unexpected hug.

"I have no idea where Dylan will want us to go," Cara said. "I know he loves Newcastle, but the other day I caught him looking at New Zealand on the map. He said we could have an overseas holiday and be paid for it, if we took work elsewhere."

"It does sound pleasant," Zack agreed. "Both Danielle and I are looking forward to our great Western Australian adventure, and they say the coast is very beautiful too."

"I have been looking at real estate," Danielle said with a blush. "It appears more affordable in the west."

"Of course, we would have to get married to buy a house together," Zack said. "So we will probably accept being billeted somewhere until we are ready."

That really only left the matter of roommates for the next year to be decided. As seniors, the fourth year students were all entitled to single rooms. However, their final year also represented their last chance to share a room. It was a perplexing decision because both options had a certain appeal.

"It has been fun rooming together," Cara said to Stephanie as they packed their things for storage over the long break. "However, I think I will claim my single room for next year."

"Elisabet and I have been talking," Stephanie said, "And we have decided that as we share a major, we would like to share a room."

"I'm glad you will have someone," Cara said. "Do you know what any of the others are doing?"

"I think Joelle has claimed her single room," Stephanie said. "Maybe Tess too. Anita is rooming with Debbie… and to be honest, we are getting to be a small group."

"We will have to hang out with Bede's class a lot more," Cara observed. "My baby sister!"

"Your baby sister who grew up and stole your boyfriend," Stephanie joked.

"Oh yes," Cara said. "How could I forget? Luckily – I had a better bloke on hand."

"You really do love Dylan don't you?" Stephanie inquired.

"Yes – I do," Cara said. "We are so suited, and we have so much in common. I cannot believe I made him wait so long!"

Cara attended the graduation ceremony on Sunday. As some of the students graduating were her very own classmates, who had completed shorter courses, the festivities seemed more personal than on previous years. Then after congratulating the graduands, and eating their final meal on campus, Cara and Dylan dropped Stephanie and Garry off at Northcoast, where the couple planned to catch a train to Wollongong and visit Garry's family.

Finally, Cara and Dylan hauled their own bags into the Suzuki Light Jeep, and Dylan secured the luggage so it would not bounce around and hit the back of their heads if they came to a sudden halt. Then he turned the key in the ignition and warmed the engine gently.

"Are you ready for a road trip, Cara O'B?" Dylan asked with a grin.

Cara slid her hand onto his knee. "I will go anywhere with you," she answered. "No drive would be too far or too long."

"That's sure lucky," Dylan observed. "Because it is about ten hours to Newcastle, and we will need to take several rest breaks. Never mind, the way we are going the views are spectacular… and I've got the tent in the back in case we need to stop at a caravan park."

"Where did you have in mind?" Cara asked curiously.

"Glenn Innes, Armidale, Tamworth, anywhere that takes our fancy!" Dylan said. "The entire north New South Wales countryside awaits your pleasure."

"Now hope does not disappoint, because the love of God has been poured out in our hearts by the Holy Spirit who was given to us."

Romans 5:5

(New King James Version)

ABOUT THE AUTHOR

Cecelia spent some years volunteering as a counsellor. She hopes that sharing her insights (in fictional form) can help empower modern youth. Life is all about being true to yourself – and maintaining your deepest beliefs.

Cecelia is also the author of:

Special Pictures to Talk About (ISBN: 978-0-646-97235-0), which developed out of her work on language delay and speech development in Kindergartens.

Silver Springtime (ISBN-13: 978-0-6481160-1-1), the first of a series of period romances following the developmental struggles of a group of teenagers attending a Christian university in the 1980s.

All for Love: on the Charity Dating Show (ISBN: 978-0-6481160-2-8), the first of a reality television spin-off romance series.

Mystic Evermore (ISBN: 978-0-6481160-0-4), the first of the vampire series "Nevermore Parables".

Saints and Sinners (ISBN: 978-0-6481160-4-2), the second of the vampire series "Nevermore Parables".

Faith and Love (ISBN: 978-0-6481160-3-5), the second "Silver Springs University" Christian college romance story.

Autumn Secrets (ISBN: 978-0-6481160-5-9) the third of the vampire series "Nevermore Parables".